From interior designer to author, Linn B. Halton, who also writes under the pen name of Lucy Coleman, is the best-selling author of more than a dozen novels and is excited to be writing for both HarperImpulse (HarperCollins) and Aria Fiction (Head of Zeus); she's represented by Sara Keane of the Keane Kataria Literary Agency.

Linn won the 2013 UK Festival of Romance: Innovation in Romantic Fiction award and her novels have been short-listed in the UK's Festival of Romance and the eFestival of Words Book Awards.

Living in Coed Duon in the Welsh Valleys with her 'rock', Lawrence, and gorgeous Bengal cat Ziggy, she freely admits she's an eternal romantic.

Linn is a member of the Romantic Novelists' Association and writes feel-good, uplifting novels about life, love and relationships.

@LinnBHalton
www.facebook.com/LinnBHaltonAuthor
linnbhalton.co.uk

Also by Linn B. Halton

Christmas at Bay Tree Cottage
The Secrets of Villa Rosso
A Cottage in the Country
Falling: The Complete Angels Among Us Series

A Greek Affair

Linn B. Halton

A division of HarperCollins*Publishers*
www.harpercollins.co.uk

Harper*Impulse* an imprint of
HarperCollins*Publishers*
The News Building
1 London Bridge Street
London SE1 9GF

www.harpercollins.co.uk

This paperback edition 2019

First published in Great Britain in ebook format by
HarperCollins*Publishers* 2019

A catalogue record for this book
is available from the British Library

ISBN: 9780008324476

This novel is entirely a work of fiction.
The names, characters and incidents portrayed in it are the work of the author's imagination. Any resemblance to actual persons, living or dead, events or localities is entirely coincidental.

Typeset in Birka by Palimpsest Book Production Ltd,
Falkirk, Stirlingshire

Printed and bound by CPI Group (UK) Ltd,
Croydon, CR0 4YY

For Billy, Lily, Joe and Maddie – twinkle, twinkle little stars!
You inspire every single moment of every single day.
Love you always and forever x

Prologue

'Antonio, we're back,' I call out, kicking the door shut with the heel of my boot.

Juggling Rosie on one side and groceries on the other, I drop the carrier bags down with a soft clunk on the worktop, then deposit the little one on the floor. I hope that sound of glass on tin doesn't mean there's an imminent chance of a wine puddle. Yanking the bottle out to check, I see that it's still intact. Phew! I could have fallen at the first hurdle as wine is a key component in my little plan.

Tonight, I'm planning on having a romantic evening with my husband. I'm going to insist that we watch a film together and relax a little, once Rosie is asleep. Assuming she settles before I come back down to find him snoring on the sofa, like so many nights recently. But then he's out as much as he's in these days due to *work pressures*. I worry that he's running himself into the ground and I hate that he steadfastly refuses to talk to me about it.

I look down at little Rosie, levering herself up on the vegetable rack so she can grab hold of a carrot.

'Yum, Rosie. Carrots are good for you.' I make an

encouraging face and she stuffs the end into her mouth, then grimaces. It's hard not to laugh.

I sweep her up into my arms, settling her back on my hip and head off to see what Antonio is doing. He said he was working from home today but he's very quiet.

'Let's go find Daddy, shall we?' Rosie looks up at me and grins.

'Dada,' she replies, waving her carrot. If only I could get her to actually *eat* one, I'd be delighted.

Walking into the upstairs office something doesn't look quite right and I stop to gaze around. Why has Antonio been tidying up when he said he was going to be busy? He gave me a grateful hug when I said I'd take Rosie off to do the shopping to give him some peace and quiet.

His laptop isn't on the desk and his work diary isn't there, either. Nor his briefcase. Ah, I expect he's been called into work. I just assumed he was still here and that his car was in the garage.

'Daddy's gone to work, Rosie.' Little eyes look up at me and she frowns. But as I continue to scan the room a cold feeling starts to wrap itself around my core.

Rosie wobbles but I clasp her to me as I rush into the bedroom, pulling open the wardrobe door adjacent to the bed. I gasp and stand back, unable to comprehend the hangers now stripped bare, some lying in a tangled heap at the bottom.

I snuggle my arm around Rosie's shoulders, giving her a reassuring squeeze as my feet carry us back into the office. Placing her down on the floor I slam the door shut and begin frantically pulling out the drawers of Antonio's desk.

It's clear some things are missing as the top drawer is half empty. When I pull out the bottom drawer, though, it's stuffed full of letters. All I can see is red ink staring back at me as if it's become the new black. I grab a handful and stare down at them for a moment in sheer disbelief before throwing them on the desk.

Overdue ... final demand ... debt collection agency ... notice of enforcement ... County Court Judgement. Looking down at the open drawer, there must be over fifty similar letters and I collapse down in a heap onto the chair. My head is spinning and my hands are trembling.

Tears fill my eyes as I look across at Rosie playing, blissfully unaware that our world has just come crashing down around us. My pocket begins to vibrate and I pull out my phone, hoping it's Antonio. Maybe this isn't what it seems, at all ... but then I see it's Mum calling. I switch it off and sit back, tears silently falling in a torrent down my face. I'm too numb to take it all in. None of this makes any sense to me and I simply don't know what to do, or where to turn next.

Wake Me Up, I Must Be Dreaming

'Here to present tonight's very special award is our reigning travel ambassador, the inimitable and charismatic Caroline Blakely. Please join me in giving a very warm welcome to a ground-breaking journalist who has become an icon of our daytime TV screens.'

There's a wild round of applause as Caroline begins the walk across the stage to the podium. Looking extremely elegant in a long, slinky black dress that hugs every perfect little curve, she delivers her trademark wave. She lingers until the applause gradually begins to subside; I'm transfixed and can't take my eyes off her. I never dreamt I would ever see her in the flesh.

'Thank you, ladies and gentlemen, for such a wonderfully warm welcome to the annual Traveller Abroad industry gala evening. I'm absolutely delighted to be here tonight to present this year's Top Travel Blog award. But it's also a celebration of a group of truly inspiring people who have set the internet alight. With their wonderful posts about destinations both home and abroad, their social media following and interactions are a lesson in how to capture the attention of your target audience. They have helped boost not only the domestic travel industry, but have been instrumental in raising the profile of many small businesses who constantly struggle to gain visibility.'

There's a pause while Caroline delicately prises open the envelope, no doubt being very careful not to ruin those beautifully manicured nails of hers. I slide my own, home-manicure job beneath the table, letting my hands rest out of sight on my lap.

Stealing a glance at each of the other eight nominees seated around the table, I wonder who the lucky winner will be. Of course, this is in between trying to make a convincing job of looking like I belong here and am taking it in my stride. My fellow bloggers all appear amazingly calm and professional on the surface. They are all in with a real chance of winning, so I can only hazard a guess at how difficult it must be to maintain your composure when you are so close to victory.

The pressure is mounting with each second that passes and, like the true pros they are, each of them does an admirable job of displaying that well-practised smile. The one that says it's all about the nomination and not the actual winning part. Which it isn't, of course, unless you are like me – the wild card. I'm simply delighted, and a little shocked if I'm being honest, to be here rubbing shoulders with the best. I suspect my blog hits will double in figures tomorrow off the back of this one evening alone.

So, while the dress was an unexpected expense, it will hopefully pay for itself several times over. More visibility means more hotels will be clamouring to be featured and, in turn, more advertisers will want to partner-up. Maybe living the dream isn't such a distant prospect, after all. I want to give up the day job and become a full-time travel blogger. But I know that's a big ask and that's why I'm giving it everything I have – every spare minute of my time.

To put things into perspective, I'm the newbie and it was only fifteen months ago that I decided to expand my website to blog about my travels. As a freelance photographer, it made sense to add my own holiday snaps and as more and more visitors asked about the locations I featured, I began posting useful information about each destination. And it's grown from there; well, I suppose exploded is a more accurate description. I was lucky enough to bump into the iconic pop star, Harry Martin, on one of my first trips abroad. I cheekily asked if I could interview him about his stay at the prestigious Altar Bar resort in Cannes. To my complete and utter shock, he agreed; right place, right time, I suppose. I obviously caught him in the right mood. The interview went viral and suddenly my website was well and truly on the radar, plucked from obscurity and being shared all over social media.

But this is an extremely prestigious award and for the winner it will mean a flurry of very lucrative sponsorship deals – big money. Everyone with something to sell wants to advertise on the hottest blogs and the winner will be on fire! Trying not to be at all biased, as she also happens to be my best friend, I genuinely believe that Sally's name will be on the card inside that envelope again this year. She's been there since the start of this blogging phenomenon and I'm still only on the fringes of the mutually-supportive, travel-blogger network. But I've seen enough to know the award has been the subject of an almost unbelievable amount of speculation on Twitter and Instagram since the nominations were announced ten days ago. It is *the* trophy every travel blogger dreams of winning. And that's why the tension now is almost tangible.

'And the winner of this year's Top Travel Blog award is...'

I reflect upon the stark reality that if I was at home now I'd probably be working on Rosie's papier-mâché project. I mean, expecting a nine-year-old to model an entire island is a tall order. It's also a lengthy process, as it has to dry in stages. The deadline is looming—

'...The Sun Seeker's Guide to a Happy Holiday.'

I join in with the clapping and then I tune back in; my stomach suddenly feels like a yo–yo as all eyes are on me. It hurtles to the floor at speed and then zips back up again, making me gasp.

'Go! Move those feet lady, you only flippin' won!'

Sally Martin, my blogger friend and constant inspiration, gives me a shove and suddenly my feet seem to take on a life of their own. They propel me forward in the direction of the stage, while the room around me becomes a blur. *Focus, Leah, fainting is not an option, so pull yourself together.* As I approach the steps I lift my dress slightly, for fear of tripping over in my ludicrously high heels while I make the ascent. If I'd thought for one single moment that there was even the slightest chance I could win, then I would most certainly have worn flats.

Each second seems agonizingly long, until finally I'm standing next to the celebrated host herself, thinking now is not the time to have a fangirl moment. Caroline hands me the award and I take it with both hands, hoping no one can see that I'm trembling from head to toe.

Turning and finding myself staring back at the assembled audience, I clutch the sizeable, cut-glass crystal award to my body. I don't want to drop it and look totally inept. Cameras flash and I almost pinch myself. Is this real, or have I slipped into a warm, fuzzy dream from which I'll wake up to find it's just me and the waiting staff as they clear the tables? I'm so tired from working such long hours to make ends meet, that anything is possible these days.

An expectant hush falls over the room. My mouth is so dry that I have no idea whether I'm capable of forcing out anything at all, let alone something suitable enough for such a grand occasion. Caroline gives me an encouraging smile. She is the queen of daytime TV and it obviously takes a lot of skill to make everything look so easy, but I clear my throat as people are looking at me expectantly.

Placing the award down on the podium in front of me releases my hands to nervously smooth down my gown. It's a pale silver-grey, the silky, floor-length fabric inset with lace panels. With a deep V at the back and a fishtail detail that gives a very modest little flair, I'm aware that it rather flatteringly accentuates my recently-acquired, enhanced rear profile.

'Um ... I ... as you can tell I really wasn't expecting to be standing up here tonight, so I will admit that I'm both thrilled and honoured—'

There's another little ripple of applause, which thankfully gives me a few more seconds to compose myself; but this is going to be the shortest acceptance speech on record.

'I feel truly blessed to accept this wonderful award on behalf of my daughter, Rosie, and myself. We have been so very grateful for the support we have received from the travel blogging community and the amazing visitors who keep coming back to read our posts. To have our work acknowledged by people we so greatly admire is the icing on the cake. All I can say is a heartfelt thank you, as this means so very much to us.'

Caroline can see that I'm too overwhelmed to continue and she leans in as we air kiss. It's like an elegant dance move, or a disaster if you get it wrong. As soon as it's over, I beat a hasty retreat back to the nominees' table before my nerves cause me to collapse in a heap on the floor.

'A very worthy winner, indeed,' Caroline's words ring in my ears, even above the tumultuous applause.

I place the award on the table while everyone is listening to the final speech and manoeuvre my phone out of my evening bag and into my lap so I can text Mum.

Take a deep breath, Mum. I'm holding the trophy!!! The Sun Seeker only bloody won! Your daughter and granddaughter did it! Beyond thrilled, won't sink in ... will see u later. Lx

Okay, the grammar police would have a field day and maybe, just maybe, there are a few too many exclamation marks in there, but woo-hoo! Something unbelievably wonderful has happened and I'm struggling to take it all in.

Tonight, though, I feel like a million dollars for one simple reason: this is validation – and it does feel like it's been a long haul. All those late nights spent online after putting Rosie to bed, often extending way into the early hours of the morning, have finally paid off.

With my previously almost non-existent rear stuck to my typing stool as if someone had superglued it there, every hour of sacrifice has been worth it and I'm feeling vindicated. Of course, the fact that it also helped me create a little junk in the trunk is a bonus. I'm no longer that painfully thin, straight up and straight down sort of girl I had become for a while. Stress is a fat-buster, in tandem with destroying just about everything else in your life. Blogging helped me to blot all of that out. But I digress, because what tonight means is that my gamble paid off. I wasn't just reaching for an impossible dream, as so many people very kindly took the time to warn me.

I brush off thoughts of the handful of online haters who left mean comments on my lovingly-penned posts. And the spammers who left drivel that had to be deleted, wasting some of my precious online time each night; comments that looked like someone's cat had been sitting on the keyboard and refused to budge.

But the best bit of all? When my daughter, Rosie, wakes

up tomorrow morning and I tell her what has happened, I get to see that little face of hers light up with pride! It isn't just my blog, but *our* blog, because we are a team of two, and now it's official – we're up there with the best.

Back to Reality

'Mum, it's so heavy! Where are we going to put it?' Rosie's eyes are like saucers, she's so excited and I know it's going to be difficult to get her to focus on breakfast.

'The clock is ticking, Rosie, you need to eat that cereal and head up to the bathroom to clean those teeth. Yes, it's quite something, isn't it? And *What's in Rosie's Suitcase?* is an important part of the website – high five me, girl.'

Our hands collide in mid-air as Mum walks into the kitchen.

'Are my girls celebrating? I'm so proud of you both. How did you feel wearing that gorgeous dress, Leah? It was right for the occasion, wasn't it?'

I tried on so many dresses to find something smart enough to wear, but when you are restricted to the budget rails there's only one place to go if you want something special and that's to the Next clearance sale. When I first saw the Lipsy tag hanging from the dress I half-closed my eyes as I turned it over to reveal the price. At fifty per cent off it was affordable, just, but even without trying it on I knew it was going to be perfect.

'Yes, Mum, I felt like I was dressed for a red-carpet event.'

She smiles, easing herself down into the chair opposite me with a cup of tea in her hand. Mum stayed overnight to look after Rosie, and Dad is picking her up later this morning.

'Well, it was an awards ceremony. And you should have let us pay for it, Leah. You've been working so hard now for such a long time and you deserve this win. I thought you said Sally was the number one favourite, though?'

I sigh. Sally was overjoyed for me, last night. But we all work hard, because with blogging everything is so transient. People click, scan and click away. Your content must grab and engage the reader at first glance and the visuals need to be strong to justify them lingering long enough to read the whole article. And then add you, hopefully, to their favourites or, even better, subscribe so that they receive your posts via email.

'I can only assume it's because of my photographic background that my graphics look so professional. Sally says she's envious of how quickly I pull them together and I always thought she was just being kind.'

Mum shakes her head while I move the trophy out of arm's reach of Rosie, so she'll go back to eating her breakfast.

'You underestimate yourself sometimes, Leah. I don't know anyone else who works as hard as you do. You don't just have two jobs, you have two very intensive jobs. You can't manage on five hours' sleep each night forever, honey.'

'I'm done, Mum.' Rosie pipes up, pushing back on her chair. 'I'll be ready in five. Promise.'

She's such a good girl and a blessing.

'Don't forget your homework, Rosie,' I call out, but she's running up the stairs two at a time and the noise will, no doubt, drown out my words. 'I know, Mum. But photography takes me away from home and the website is something that I can work around the school runs. You and Dad can't keep dropping everything to come over and babysit every time I'm away. It's difficult being a one-parent family and I want to be here for Rosie all the time. This is our future and this award might tip the scales and increase my income enough to cover all the bills. This could be it, Mum.'

She's already clearing the dishes from the table, unable to sit still for more than a few minutes. I guess the apple doesn't fall far from the tree; it's no wonder I'm a workaholic. But I'm working to maintain a reasonable standard of living for Rosie and for me. Besides, every trip to review a hotel or feature a resort is a free holiday. It's quality time for us both and having a job that's also a lot of fun would be a blessing. Unless you find yourself having to fit everything into weekends, days off and working late into the night to get the reviews and posts written up, as I've had to do. Which pretty much sums up my life, now. I yawn, unable to disguise the tiredness that never seems to leave me these days.

'There. Look at you! The last thing you needed was another late night. Why don't you let us collect Rosie from school and have her for a mid-week sleepover? I'll make sure she does her homework. You can invite a friend around, relax for a couple of hours and maybe get an early night for a change.'

Having one's mother constantly worrying about one's lack of any sort of a social life can be rather demoralising at times.

'Mum, we're happy as we are. Having Rosie makes everything I've been through worthwhile. I don't need a man in my life to make me feel complete, really I don't.'

Mum turns away from loading the dishwasher to look across at me. I know it's hard for her, too.

'But what about Rosie, Leah?'

'We had the conversation several years ago and she never refers to it. Rosie has accepted that her father isn't coming back and she knows how much she's loved by the people she does have around her. Her teacher says she's one of the most well-adjusted kids she's ever met. Checking that she isn't having any problems is the first thing I ask at every parents' evening I attend.'

'That's because she's bubbly, like you. The glass is always half-full and if you both continue through life with that ethos, then you won't come to any real harm. But the day will come when Rosie will want to spread her wings. What happens when it's time to let go a little, as she wants to spend more and more time with her friends? It's a natural progression. If an opportunity to find love comes along, Leah, don't look in the other direction. Think about it, that's all I'm saying.'

As we grab coats and don our shoes, it's a quick hug all round before we head out.

'Thanks, Mum. You are a star and thank Dad for being the taxi service, yet again.'

'That's what we're here for, honey. And was that a *yes* to the sleepover?'

Rosie's eyes light up.

'A sleepover with Grandma and Granddad, tonight?'

I roll my eyes. 'Guess it's a *yes*, Mum,' I mutter, as I steer Rosie out of the door. We're already eight minutes late and it's going to be impossible to get a parking space anywhere near the school. Oh well, I guess winning a prestigious award doesn't make you that special, after all!

~

Sally and I are lying at opposite ends of the sofa, a glass of white Grenache in our hands as we toast each other.

'I really was rooting for you, Sally. I feel awful because you are one of the blogging icons.'

She shakes her head, mid-sip.

'I won it the very first year and just sporting that nominee badge again for the next twelve months will boost my income nicely. I've already had two very lucrative new clients jump on board since the announcement ten days ago. Besides, you and Rosie have taken it up a notch. I love her little feature, advising kids on what to pack and reviewing games, gadgets and items that will slot nicely into that case of hers. She's become quite the intrepid little traveller since you began blogging.'

It's true; we've been on over a dozen fully-paid trips abroad already, and five within the UK.

'It was her idea, actually and although I do proofread her posts, it's entirely her own work. We talk through what she wants to say but I don't interfere, I simply steer. She loves the freebies and testing things out is fun. But last night came as a total shock and you're right, the offers have already started to roll in. This could finally allow me to give up the freelance photography work.'

'You are a deserving winner, Leah, and you should be proud of what you've achieved. If I was going to lose to anyone, I'm delighted that it's you because it's about time life gave you a break.'

I turn down the corners of my mouth in mock self-pity. 'I agree. This abandoned mother, parenting her only child, is in dire need of a lucky break.'

She raises her eyebrows. 'No, that came out all wrong and you know it. What I mean is that you must stop feeling guilty for walking away with the award, lady. And anyone who works as hard as you do, deserves to reap their rewards. You've paid your dues, it wasn't a lucky break at all. Now this is your time to shine.'

It's been seven long years, and although those years have been a nightmare, I kept pushing forward.

'You're right, of course. I'm tired and I have to head up to North Wales tomorrow to take some shots of a trout farm for a magazine feature.'

Sally gives me a sympathetic look.

'But that's a three-and-a-half-hour trip from the Forest of Dean. Up and back in a day?'

I nod. 'Yep. The photos will probably only take an hour.

I'll drop Rosie off at school and head straight up there. Mum and Dad will collect her in the afternoon and wait here until I get back.'

'I don't know how you do it, Leah. Fingers crossed those advertising and sponsorship deals come in thick and fast. What's the daily hit rate, now?'

'It eclipsed fifteen thousand unique hits for the first time, yesterday.'

She looks me in the eye.

'You need to put up your advertising rates in line with your new status as the winner of such a prestigious award.'

Cradling the glass in my hands, I admit that's not something I'd considered. But Sally is right and that alone could make all the difference. And, yes, there is a little thrill that courses through my veins hearing someone else refer to me as a *winner*.

'Anyway, what did you think of the outfit? I didn't look too dressy, did I? Posh frocks aren't really my thing.'

'It was perfect – you looked the business. And that's quite an ass ... et you have going on there now, girl. It suits you; the gaunt look wasn't really your style.'

I smile. We both agree on that score.

'Yep. I finally fill out a dress from the front to the back, again. My problem now is that if I'm going to be sitting down in front of the laptop every day from here on in, how am I going to maintain it and not pile on the pounds?'

'When you've cracked that one,' Sally says, jiggling her growing jelly-belly, 'let me know.'

A New Routine

The problem with being the sole breadwinner is that you can't afford to take any risks, whatsoever. There is no safety net. Running this little, two-bed stone cottage in the middle of the Forest of Dean is a modest enough outlay by a lot of people's standards. However, I do appreciate the fact that we are still luckier than many, because I'm a survivor and Rosie is, too. We have learnt to live quite happily within our means. Yes, I'd love the big house with half an acre and two cars sitting on the drive. Who wouldn't? But the cottage is pretty, and we're surrounded by stunning views and forest walks.

To the front of the property is a road which leads on down to a cul-de-sac. We don't get passing traffic, only neighbours coming and going. While our rear garden is small, it backs onto a swathe of forestry commission land. We have all the benefits of some beautiful, old trees with none of the worry of having to maintain them.

We don't want for anything and I figure that teaching Rosie to live on a budget is a good discipline. It's something that has become second nature to her and she's used to making choices and accepting that she can't simply ask and have.

I was holidaying in Italy when Antonio Castelli first crossed my path; his dark hair and wide smile was the first thing that attracted me to him. When I returned three months later to meet his parents, Guido and Zita, we had already fallen madly in love – the sort of madness that empties your head of everything else – and life became a waiting game. It was agony being parted and I lived for our evening chats via Skype and the constant stream of texts we exchanged daily. I slept with my phone under my pillow and I know Antonio did the same.

Then we had the agonising decision of where we would settle after the wedding. I felt awful for his family when, after careful consideration, we decided to make the UK our home. Mum and Dad were relieved, but knowing that Antonio's family were so far away was a little cloud on our new horizon. And the paperwork to make it happen was the next nightmare on our journey.

Little did I know that less than three years later it would all be over, leaving me clutching little Rosie to ease the pain in my heart. But now that's all firmly in the past and I'm extremely proud of my confident little nine-year-old, who is probably a little bit wiser than her years because of what we've been through. I was determined to conquer whatever obstacles life placed in front of us because nothing is going to rob us of the happiness we deserve.

I scan down the emails in my inbox and a smile breaks out on my face. One of the emails is a link to the press release issued by the Traveller Abroad publicity team and there it is – a photo, front and centre, *the* Caroline Blakely handing little old me the trophy.

When I rang the photographic agency to break the news that I was drastically cutting back on my hours, they were shocked, but for me it's a step forward. Next on the to-do list is a total re-design of the website, taking out anything related to my photographic work. Then I need to maximise advertising space, add a rolling banner so that I can accommodate a number of premium rate advertisers instead of just the one, and review my schedule of charges.

I reach out for my coffee mug, only to find it empty.

'Now that's another thing you need to tackle, Leah,' I admonish myself.

If I'm going to be sitting here working very long days, and nights, in order to develop The Sun Seeker's Guide to a Happy Holiday into one of the best blogs out there, I need to stop comfort eating. It's a habit I've developed to get me through those long evenings with only the glow of the computer screen to keep me company. I'm the first to admit that I often find myself reaching out for a biscuit, or four, and after a string of cups of very strong coffee I tell myself it's wine o'clock. Okay, so I only have the one glass but it's a large one, as I convince myself I deserve a reward for working such long hours.

All that stops *now* – no cheating. Also, no biscuits, or cake, or chocolate. One coffee to get me going in the morning and then I'm on the water and herbal teas.

A wicked grin creeps over my face. But think of the

upside! No more dashing around the house before breakfast getting suited and booted, spending half an hour on hair and make-up. I can throw on a jumper over my PJs and leave early enough to get that prized parking space right next to the school gates. The only space nestled between the end of the zig-zag lines and the start of the double yellows. The one everyone covets so they can watch their little darlings walk the three strides up to the member of staff on duty who ushers them inside.

I glance across at the sparkly crystal award sitting in pride of place in the middle of the bookshelf. Sally was right: I deserve this and I'm going to make it work.

~

'Mum, are you really going to be around all the time now?'

'Mostly. Why?'

'I'll still spend time with Grandma and Granddad, won't I?'

Rosie is sitting opposite me at the kitchen table, her little face crinkled up into a frown.

'Of course you will. You can still have sleepovers whenever you want and we can pop over after school at any time for a visit.'

I can see she's putting this together and I know there's a question coming.

'When someone dies, where do they go?'

Ah. I suspect someone at school has lost a grandparent and the kids have been talking.

'Well, your soul goes to another place. Some people call that heaven. But usually people only die after they have had a long and happy life and they leave behind lots of wonderful memories.'

Now she's toying with the chips on the plate in front of her, aimlessly pushing them around.

'But what if you don't want them to go?'

I walk around the table and kneel down next to her, easing the fork out of her hand.

'When we truly love someone, they remain in here.' I place my hand over my heart. Rosie's eyes follow my every move. 'They are always with us. Grandma and Granddad are fine, darling. There's nothing at all to worry about.'

She hangs her head.

'I don't want anyone to die, Mum. I like things the way they are.'

I wrap my arms around her, planting a kiss on the top of her head and then smoothing back her long, dark brown hair away from her face.

'Life is all about change, Rosie, and mostly that's a good thing. The only thing that's changing for us right now is that we're going to have a new routine. Life won't feel quite so rushed and I'll be here whenever you need me. That's a good thing, isn't it?'

At last, the smile is back on that pretty little face of hers.

'Yes, Mum. I like it when we can have dinner together and watch TV before bed.'

It's always the small things that children miss when life gets hectic. There have been too many nights when I've missed dinner entirely, barely arriving back in time to put her to bed. It hasn't been fair on Mum and Dad, and it hasn't been fair on Rosie.

'Well, I like that too and if you've finished here let's quickly clear this away and curl up on the sofa, together.'

Her smile broadens enthusiastically and I find myself taking in every little detail. My little girl is growing up so very quickly and I wonder, fleetingly, how different life would have been for her if Antonio hadn't left us. But he did, and I'll never forgive him for that.

I'm in the News

It's the start of week two of the new regime and I've made two new discoveries, already. Firstly, that living in PJs isn't quite me and the postman was beginning to wonder what was going on. One morning when I also happened to be having a particularly bad hair day, he asked me if I was feeling any better! The other discovery is that sitting in the same position for hours on end isn't good for you. Even if you can avoid the snacks and sugary drinks, your body starts to rebel. I've invested in some track suits and after being caught lusting over a fitness tracker, Mum and Dad turned up at the weekend with two neatly wrapped little parcels. Mine was a Vivofit with a gorgeous red strap and Rosie's present was a watch.

'Just a little congratulatory gift,' Dad said, as we opened the boxes.

I couldn't protest, but it did bring a tear to my eye as we had a group hug.

Suddenly, my mobile kicks into life and I see that it's Sally.

'Morning. I've just retweeted you and shared your latest post,' I inform her.

'Thanks, I'm running behind this morning. I'll be online shortly to reciprocate. I've only just had time to glance at the free paper. Did you know there's an article about you?'

I gulp. 'No. What, in Saturday's paper?'

'Yes. It's a nice little article, actually. Well done, you! Anyway, must make a start but I have that Monday morning feeling. Maybe I need a little sugar fix.'

'Well, I've just done my first walk of the day and am about to make a chamomile tea.'

Sally groans. 'Okay. Point taken. It's mind over matter and I'll have a cup of tea instead. You're beginning to sound like a health nut, but I do hope some of it rubs off on me. I need to get back to the gym, that's for sure. Catch you later.'

I rummage around in the sitting room for the paper and when I can't find it, I ring Mum.

'Only me. Do you have a copy of the local paper? I can't find ours and Sally says there's something in there about the award.' I can't keep the incredulity out of my voice.

'Oh, that will be Keith. Dad said he bumped into him in the supermarket. He's one of their reporters and Dad told him all about your success. Roger?' Mum calls out to Dad and I wince, as she hasn't pulled the phone away from her mouth. 'Leah's on the phone. She says Roger did an article on her – what fun!'

Fun?

'Um ... Mum, can you find it for me? What exactly did Dad say?'

'Only how proud we were that you'd won an award. He's found the paper. Oh, my!'

It's a positive exclamation but a chill runs down my back.

'Gosh, there's even a photo of you. How wonderful! Roger, ask next door if they'll let us have their copy. I'm going to frame this one and we need a copy for Leah to show Rosie.'

I feel like a bystander.

'Don't worry, Mum, I'll go online to read it. Must go.'

'Don't forget you're both here for dinner on Wednesday night. I'm making spaghetti bolognaise.'

'Wouldn't miss it for anything.'

My phone is already nestled between my shoulder and my chin, as I Google the paper's website.

It's probably a quarter of a page in total judging by the length of it and the headline is *Leah Castelli Brings Home a Top Travel Award*. I breathe out a small sigh of relief. Clearly this is based on the press release circulated by the *Traveller Abroad* publicity people and not merely the gushy words of a proud father. It's all good publicity, just rather unexpected.

It's time to head out for my second walk of the day and when I leave the house my head is buzzing. I up the pace a little, gradually calming down, and my thoughts return to the latest changes I'm making to the website. Then inspiration strikes and I come up with a way of cramming in more sponsored ads by including them in posts. I want the website itself to look informative, rather than to be covered with adverts and this solution would solve that problem.

Walking might be healthy but it's also uninterrupted thinking and planning time.

~

At gym club, I watch enthralled as Rosie executes a perfect back-flip. She lands with apparent ease and both feet planted firmly on the ground. Throwing up her arms, she arches her back and maintains a dignified pose. Her face is beaming.

'Good work, Rosie. Nicely done.' Miriam Peterson's approval is enough to make Rosie's cheeks glow.

That was certainly a shining example of a perfect landing but every time I watch her perform my stomach does its own involuntary flip.

Miriam waves out to me and heads across the mats in my direction. Even so, her eyes are everywhere and she doesn't miss a thing.

'Liesel, relax those shoulders!' Her voice booms out across the studio floor.

'I hear congratulations are in order,' Miriam says, with a gush. 'I read the article and that's quite something.'

I can feel my cheeks reddening, as this has caught me off–guard.

'Yes, it was a bit of a surprise, though.'

'Ah, well, it's nice to have an interesting hobby and all those free holidays. I'm envious!'

I try not to frown.

'It's a bit more than a hobby,' I add, but my voice begins to trail off.

'A hobby with benefits,' Miriam laughs, totally missing the point.

'It is very hard work, actually.'

Why am I feeling so defensive? Miriam doesn't understand any more about my industry, than I do about hers.

'Nice, though. Guess you'll be flying here, there and everywhere, now.' It's dismissive and her tone is beginning to irritate me.

'I only blog about places I'm happy to endorse one hundred per cent. Being a critic isn't always easy but it's gratifying when a client invites me back after making improvements.'

Even her smile is now annoying me; it's patronising.

'You get a second trip? Amazing. And all those freebies for you and Rosie to test. I bet you never have to buy anything holiday-related.'

I give up.

'Rarely,' I concede, deciding it's simply better to agree and change the subject. 'That was a perfect back-flip Rosie performed there.'

'If she worked harder, she'd make the team.' Miriam's gaze doesn't falter and I can see she feels I don't push Rosie hard enough. But Rosie is happy attending two classes a week and taking part in demonstrations; the fact that she isn't interested in competing is entirely her own decision.

And that's where Miriam and I differ so greatly. You can't force someone into doing something and I'm not going to put pressure on Rosie for simply wanting to take part for the sheer fun of it. Much to the annoyance of the sometimes scary Miriam Peterson.

The Word is Spreading

I modelled my approach to evaluating a holiday venue on *the* iconic hotel inspector, Yolanda Jackson. I figured from the outset that whilst I didn't have the scathing tone and quick-to-anger attitude I've witnessed her dishing out so often on her TV programme, I do admire her integrity. And the way she is simply trying to help owners to raise their standards so that visitors get value for money. That's essential if they want to stay in business.

Today's post contains several parcels addressed to Rosie, and I always leave her to open them herself. Aside from that, now I'm back from my walk it's time to hit the emails.

With Easter only ten days away we already have a day trip to a theme park and a visit to a children's petting zoo in the diary. It looks like our next trip abroad isn't until the summer half-term holiday, at the end of May. So even if the UK turns out to be wet and windy, which is often the case for bank holidays, hopefully we'll be basking in sunshine.

Surely it can't get any better that that?

~

'Rosie, can you see who's at the door please? I'll be there in a second.'

I press 'send' on the email I've just finished and a little frisson of excitement makes my stomach do a dip.

'Mum, it's Naomi and Callie.'

There's a lot of laughter coming from the hallway as they all barrel into the kitchen.

'Well, this is a nice surprise, neighbour. Shall I pop the kettle on?'

Naomi shakes her head, still laughing at whatever the girls found funny, as she walks over to give me a hug.

'No, sadly we can't stay. We're on a mission.' She looks across at Callie, her eleven-year-old daughter.

'I'm doing a walk for charity, Leah. Will you sponsor me? It's five miles and I've been training, so I know I can do it.'

'Ah, that's great, Callie. When is it?'

'Saturday morning.'

She hands me the form and I take it, grabbing a pen. It's for childhood cancer and who wouldn't want to give to that cause?

'That's very kind, Leah. Every little bit helps.'

'My pleasure and way to go, Callie – that's awesome. Well done, you!'

'Can I give some money too?' Rosie pipes up. We all turn to look at her.

Naomi flashes me a glance and I nod.

'Of course, Rosie. You can spend your savings on anything you want and I can't think of a more deserving cause.'

As Callie and Rosie lean over the form on the table, Naomi gives me a look of 'ahh!'

'Sorry I've been absent lately, I had meant to pop down now I'm around a little more.' I do feel guilty and I miss our interaction since Callie moved to the senior school last September. Her school is the other side of town and it's not possible to do both trips and car share anymore.

'I understand, Leah. Besides, judging from the papers, you've been very busy. First the local and now the national papers.'

'What?' It comes out like a pistol crack. Why am I always the last to know about these things?

'I saw it in the *Daily News*, this morning. It was a big spread about the travel industry and some sort of awards ceremony. I didn't know your blog was so popular. I mean, I knew you had a website for your photography business, but I had no idea! And is that your award?'

She looks over to the bookshelf and I nod, thinking maybe I should move it somewhere slightly less noticeable. But I work from the kitchen table and it's the hub of the cottage.

'Yes. It was unexpected news but very welcome. I'll be focusing on that in future and the *Rosie's Suitcase* feature is a big part of it.'

Rosie's smile extends from ear to ear, as Callie gives her a gentle nudge.

'You're practically famous,' she grins. Rosie blushes.

'Can I give Callie one of those sun protector sprays? They're brilliant, Mum, they don't feel gluey on your skin.'

I laugh and Naomi joins in.

'Of course. How about one of the inflatable cool bags, too? They're next to your wardrobe in the black bag.'

The girls head off upstairs and even though there's a two-year age gap between them, I ponder on the fact that only a couple of inches in height separates them. In terms of maturity, Rosie is ahead of her years. Should I be sad about that?

'Thanks for your donation, and Rosie's. We have a lot to be proud of with our girls, don't we? I'd heard on the grapevine that you were working from home full-time now, but didn't want to barge in and break up your working day. That must be a real relief, though,' Naomi says.

'It is, to be honest. You were brilliant with the car sharing. And Mum and Dad have lived their lives around my schedule but now, finally, I can ease the pressure on them. The award has made all the difference but, ironically, I didn't give winning a moment's thought because I was nominated alongside the best bloggers I know.'

I indicate for Naomi to take a seat while we wait for the girls to return.

'Rosie will, no doubt, ask Callie for feedback on the freebies for her next review. She's turning into a right little journalist.'

Naomi's eyes widen. 'She's an old head on young shoulders, that's for sure. Anyway, share the rest of your news – what trips do you have coming up?'

I try to contain my excitement.

'Well, today I've been offered a chance to be flown out

to a cruise ship for forty-eight hours. And a family-run hotel in Athens are keen for me to feature them and are offering Rosie and me a five-day stay during half term.'

Naomi's jaw drops.

'Don't say anything when the girls get back as I haven't told Rosie about Athens yet and for the cruise I'll have to go on my own as it's in term time.'

'Wow! Now I understand why you've been working yourself into the ground. You've made it happen, Leah, and no one deserves it more.' Callie looks suitably impressed. It gives me a warm glow for a moment and then I stop to think about her words.

Am I being a tad oversensitive here, or does everyone around me feel that I'm a bit of a sad, and therefore deserving, case?

'I guess, but maybe it's my turn for a little boost from the universe.' I mean, everyone is due a little good luck every so often, aren't they?

'Well, when you're constantly sending out good karma, you gotta eventually get some back!'

Is Naomi right? Or is the residue of my anger and resentment still festering in the pit of my stomach, waiting to be unleashed? Sometimes I feel like there are two of me, the good Leah and the bad Leah. The bad one wants to scream, but the good one won't let it. *That's negative, Leah, and it's not a road you want to travel down.*

'Let's see what the girls have discovered, shall we?'

All Aboard

Short notice about the cruise is good – tomorrow, the fifteenth of May, is departure day. With my working life so busy and the workload mounting after a hectic Easter holiday period, it doesn't give me any time to fuss. Just enough time, in fact, to sort things out at home and pack a medium-sized suitcase. Rosie does her own packing for her stay at Mum's and decides that she's going to take a few of her 'test' items with her. One is a disposable toiletries pack with more things in it than we have in our bathroom cabinet.

When I drop her off I get a wonderful hug, until Scruffy – the dog who lives next door to Mum and Dad – sneaks under the fence and bowls into the garden.

'Scruffy! You came to see me!' Then Rosie is off playing and I'm already forgotten.

Mum, as usual, is a little anxious but trying not to show it.

'Just remind me again what the itinerary is for this wonderful little trip of yours?'

I sigh. I'm a grown woman and still she worries.

'In the morning, I'm catching the 7.25 a.m. flight to Nice from Gatwick airport; then a shuttle bus will take me to Port Hercule, Monaco. Now stop worrying!'

I roll my eyes and she laughs.

'Me? Worry? Never! Just take care of yourself and ... well ... have fun, anyway.'

She wasn't going to say the *have fun* part, but one look at my face stopped her before she could begin reeling off the warnings.

Her hug tells me she won't rest until she sees me again in three days' time.

~

Nestling back in my airplane seat, I'm thinking first class would have been a nice touch. And I'm rather dismayed to find out that food and drink is no longer included in the price of the ticket. It's only just over a two-hour flight to Nice airport but the time difference means you lose another hour on top of that.

It's fast approaching one o'clock by the time the shuttle pulls into the vast car park at the port. I text Mum to confirm I've arrived safely and that everything is fine. A quick glance out the window confirms that it's a bit of a walk with the luggage along Quai Rainier III. It stretches out rather magnificently, hovering above the deep blue waters of the Mediterranean Sea. The guy sitting next to me on the bus has been quite chatty on the journey and I learn that he's joining the ship for the remainder of the cruise. The next two stops are in Italy – Portovenere and Portoferraio – then it sails on to Corsica, ending the tour in St Tropez.

'I'm only here for forty-eight hours to review the latest addition to *Sun, Sea & Tide's* fleet. I gather it's only six months old, although I'm not sure how many trips she's already made,' I tell him.

'Interesting, so you've done this before then,' he remarks, as we wait for the other passengers to alight. We're sitting in the back row where we have a lot more room. It's a bench seat for four people in total but he, too, is travelling alone and we both instinctively headed towards the rear of the bus. I still don't know his name and I feel a little awkward now, suddenly asking.

'Well, I haven't, actually. This is my first experience of being on a cruise ship. It's rather exciting. And you?'

'My umpteenth trip,' he replies with an engaging smile. 'It's an easy way to relax. You have the option of doing very little and simply enjoying everything on offer, or taking part in excursions and seeing the sights. I work in finance with long hours and lots of back to back meetings, so for me it's about switching off from everything and enjoying some fresh air. Home for me is in Leeds, how about you?'

I nod, acknowledging it's a full itinerary without the hassle of making all those arrangements.

'The Forest of Dean in Gloucestershire.'

I wonder why he's travelling alone. A cruise must be much more fun if you have someone with you to share the adventure.

'Ah, a place I've yet to visit. I think it's safe to make our way to the front. I'm Harrison Buchanan, by the way.'

He offers his hand and we shake, then begin to make our way along the narrow aisle between the seats.

'I'm Leah Castelli.'

'Is that an Italian surname?'

I swallow hard. This is a question I'm going to have to get used to answering from people who don't know me and my history. 'Yes. I met my husband when I was on holiday but we're separated now. I still use my married name because I have a young daughter.'

I can see he's embarrassed. 'I'm so sorry, Leah, I didn't mean to pry. Here, let me grab that case for you.'

He quickly lifts my case out of the trailer behind the shuttle and extracts the handle for me, before manhandling his own, rather large, suitcase.

As we follow the snake of people along the quay, taking time to admire the azure blue water that surrounds us, it's obvious Harrison is a seasoned traveller. Maybe he's even done this particular route before, as he seems to know his way around. I'm rather grateful I can simply follow his lead. My eyes are darting everywhere; I'm taking in as much of the detail as I can and suitable phrases are already jumping into my head in preparation for writing my article.

The lavish display of the lifestyle of the rich and famous is reflected in the sparkling white boats moored up, almost as far as the eye can see. This is how the other half live. As we walk towards the ship it seems to loom up like a huge, white mountain and it feels decadent. The sheer scale is breathtaking and as it gleams, with the beautiful blues of the sky and the sea as a backdrop, it almost looks unreal. Like some clever computer graphic that is so perfect it tricks the eye and the scene suddenly comes alive.

We are quickly welcomed aboard the *Vista Blue* by the cruise director and some other members of the crew. While we're waiting for our cabins to be made ready we're shown into a large room where there's a buffet all laid out in readiness. Waiters circulate with glasses of wine, cocktails and soft drinks. I simply follow on behind Harrison and after we fill our plates he indicates towards a large table in the centre of the room. We exchange quick 'hellos' with the two couples already seated. He's good at engaging people in conversation and it's helping to alleviate my nerves as I settle myself down next to him.

As more couples join our table, everyone seems eager to share where they are from and their previous experiences onboard cruise ships. There is a real buzz in the air. Half an hour later our names are called and we are split into small groups. Just before we go off in different directions to be escorted to our cabins, Harrison turns to me.

'Do you have any plans for after you're settled in? We don't sail until eleven tonight and it seems a pity not to spend at least a couple of hours sightseeing. What do you think?'

I wasn't expecting that and I'm not sure if I should take him up on the offer.

'I'd love to, but I ought to start work. It's a huge ship and I want my report to cover as much as possible.'

He looks disappointed. 'Okay. But as an experienced sea dog I know my way around a ship and I'd be happy to do the tour with you. This is actually my second trip on the *Vista Blue*, so I know the shortcuts.'

It's tempting but I'm not sure I feel totally comfortable attaching myself to a stranger.

'Nothing too strenuous,' he continues. 'We'll catch a taxi into Monte Carlo, walk a part of the F1 circuit and then head off in the direction of the casino. You can't possibly write a review without selling the benefits of a few hours in port now, can you?'

I find myself laughing at him. 'Okay. I'll trust that you'll get us back in plenty of time before the ship sails. Or I'll be in big trouble.'

'I'm very trustworthy.' He winks at me as we part ways.

At least our cabins don't appear to be anywhere near each other and I fleetingly wonder if I'll be glad of that fact.

'I'll meet you back here in an hour,' Harrison calls over his shoulder. 'Wear comfortable shoes, it's quite a walk.'

'This way,' our stewardess calls and I quicken my pace to catch up with the little group to which I've been assigned.

A Floating Mirage

Life doesn't get any more surreal than this, I reflect. The stewardess looking after my suite is aware that I'm a travel blogger, which takes me by surprise. If the welcome she gives me is the same welcome she gives to all her passengers, then I'm very impressed. She also hands me a folder with lots of information about the ship itself, which I assume is to help inform my article.

As for the suite itself, well, it's way beyond any expectations I had. Obviously, everything is new but the marble-lined bathroom has what the stewardess referred to as a rainforest shower experience and a separate bath. It also has low level lighting for nighttime use. The walk-in storage space for my clothes is more than adequate for quite a long stay, but then it is a double suite. Everything feels sumptuous – in shades of cream, keeping it light and bright, but with vivid splashes of lime green and rich purples to give it a contemporary feel.

An even bigger surprise is the balcony, with floor to ceiling glass doors, which I wasn't expecting. It's a generous size at probably around ninety square feet. Totally unbelievable! I feel spoilt, as if this is all too good to be true.

I'm conscious that time is slipping away and I don't even bother to investigate the minibar, or try out the impressively-sized TV. I glance longingly at the crisp, white bed linens with the furry purple throw and cushions. I feel like collapsing down onto it and drifting off into a peaceful sleep, but instead I spritz my face with some cold water and apply a little lip gloss.

The route back down to the Observation Bar to meet Harrison isn't quite as straightforward as I thought it would be and I'm a few minutes late.

'I thought you'd stood me up,' he calls out, walking towards me.

My face must reflect the panic that starts to rise in my stomach, then he begins laughing.

'Sorry, I'm teasing and it's confession time. I do have a vested interest in making sure your report covers all bases. When I said I work in finance, I do: for the parent company which owns the entire fleet of cruise ships. For me it's a cheap break away, I'm afraid. It's a hard life, isn't it?' He grins at me and he has no idea how glad I am to hear that in one way, although maybe not the other.

'Did you know I was coming?' I ask, relieved that at least he's not looking for an onboard romance. But also a little puzzled as to why he didn't say something earlier on.

He stops laughing and gives me a frown.

'No, of course, not.' He sounds a little offended. 'I started speaking to you because I was simply being friendly. When you travel alone you learn to make an effort and I find that people are generally very receptive. But when you told me why you were here I thought you, too, might appreciate a little company. I'm guessing that you don't often travel without a companion, to be so suspicious of my motives?'

Am I being just a tad paranoid here?

'Rarely. My companion is usually my nine-year-old daughter. It's just that my report will need to be totally independent and I can't be influenced in any way. I mean, everything I've seen so far is top quality but I'm also here to discover any potential downside to what's on offer.'

He strokes his chin, his eyes filled with laughter once again.

'You think I'm trying to influence you? I'm afraid I'm not that clever; my skills lie with getting the numbers to work. I've always wanted to walk the F1 circuit; just the bit from the start of the tunnel up through and around the infamous Grand Hotel hairpin bend. With that in mind, I put together a little sightseeing programme to while away a few hours before I head back to the ship for dinner. It involves some walking and a bit of jumping in and out of taxis. Seriously, there is no catch and sitting next to you on the shuttle bus was a total fluke, I promise. I'm a nice guy, really. Recently divorced, no kids and a big mortgage so I can't do anything to jeopardise my income. I'd be silly to try to meddle, now, wouldn't I?'

My eyes scan his face and, in fairness, he has an innocent look about him. He is very attractive with his light-brown hair and those murky-grey eyes. I'm guessing he's maybe ten years older than me, so early forties. *Relax, Leah, because this is what you do for a living now and you can hitch a ride here with someone who already has a little tour put together. What possible harm can it do?*

~

We walk back along the quayside to the terminal, where there's a taxi waiting for us. Harrison gives the driver some directions and settles back in his seat.

'Prep for the race starts about six weeks before the day, so they are already nearly a month into it,' he informs me.

It isn't long before the driver pulls over to park up and Harrison points to the start/finish line. Today the traffic is free flowing, but busy. It's hard to believe that in two weeks' time it will turn from a normal, busy road into a starting grid. Harrison taps the partition and asks the driver to wait nearby for us, giving him a *thank you* nod. Maybe inspired by his position on the grid, the guy then rams the car into gear and pulls away from the kerb a little too fast for my liking. Aside from some marks on the road where the cars line up, there isn't very much to see, but Harrison seems satisfied.

'Now we're heading off to the tunnel. It will probably take us a couple, maybe three hours with coffee stops, before we jump in a taxi to take us back to the ship. Are you happy?'

I'm already snapping away, taking as many photos as I can in the hope that at least a couple of them will be useable.

'Perfect. The coffee is on me and let me know what the

taxis cost and I'll split it with you, it's the least I can do.'

He grimaces. 'I'm a man who has learnt the hard way that it doesn't pay to argue with a woman.' He defers to my request and I can see he isn't really happy but then, this isn't a date. I know he works for the company but it is always a comfort to have someone to chat to when you are on your own, and it's still a generous offer.

It's clear that while everything is functioning normally, preparations for the race are well underway. There is a hive of activity going on with staging and scaffolding being set up at various points on our journey.

Getting back in the taxi, it's only another short ride before Harrison taps on the partition again and we pull up in a layby. Proceeding on foot, the trek through the tunnel is great fun and it turns out to be surprisingly ordinary and very narrow, so there isn't much to see. However, as we walk along on the right-hand side we catch views out over the sea, a constant reminder of our stunning location. Looking down onto the hypnotically blue ocean there are some craggy rocks and a seagull stands surveying the scene. Simply knowing F1 cars will be whizzing through this section again soon is a little thrill.

'I can't believe racing cars drive through here,' I exclaim.

'I think their speed drops down to around thirty miles per hour as it's so tight. There is a long list of cars that have hit into the walls on the bend, or in the tunnel itself. Overtaking isn't an issue because it's impossible; keeping your wits about you and getting a good steering lock on is what this part of the race is all about.'

I guess he's a big fan. I do watch the highlights as I have a passing interest, but only because I think Lewis Hamilton is so charismatic that he's well worth watching.

As we climb higher and higher the views are unbelievable. It's steep, tight and must be very difficult to navigate given the length of the cars. My calf muscles are screaming already and I struggle to keep up.

Because it's so tiring on the legs we stop twice for coffee. The highlight for me is the Place du Casino, a lavish public square in Monaco's most famous of neighbourhoods. Also on the square is the Monte Carlo Opera House. Two stunning buildings in a perfect setting, as the square features an impressive fountain and a terrace with jaw dropping views of the coastline.

This leads us on to the Jardin Exotique, which is in the more modern section of Monaco and borders on the older, historic centre. Perched on a steep cliff it, too, looks out across the dazzlingly beautiful sea vista. Lush vegetation and a climate that doesn't have wildly diverse extremes means that the hillside conditions are perfect for tropical plants and succulents. The craggy mountainside is covered with a plethora of species from Africa, Latin America, Cape Town and even Mexico.

Being away from the roads the air is sweet and clear; only the slight breeze gives a little relief from the balmy heat. Breathing in the warmth and the tang from the sea, it's intermingled with little whiffs of fragrances given off by the blooms on some of the luscious and more exotic plants. I can see that Harrison is equally impressed.

'If I was wealthy, I'd probably be fawning over the rather expensive shops we've walked past on our way here. But I've seen everything I need to give my readers a tiny glimpse into the delights on offer and I'm thrilled about that. I'm so glad you talked me into doing this today,' I admit.

Harrison is not only a good companion, but he's knowledgeable. I feel like I have a tour guide accompanying me. I'm surprised how quickly the afternoon passes before it's time to flag down another taxi and return to the ship.

We arrive back at the quayside shortly before half past five, after a very enjoyable few hours. My notepad is full of jottings and I have taken probably thirty, or even forty, photographs.

When we part, I thank Harrison and shake his hand. He's interesting and I'm really enjoying his company but it's disappointing that I'm not feeling any chemistry between us. Even though he is a head-turner. But then I haven't really looked at a man since Antonio left. I assumed that was because getting my life back onto an even keel required all my focus. But what if I'm never going to feel that flush of excitement over someone again? What if it wasn't just my pride that was shattered when Antonio left? What if there's something permanently damaged inside of me? Maybe I'm just not worthy of having someone's love because I can't seem to hold onto it.

'Ah, is this my dismissal?'

'No, more of an apology,' I admit. 'I will still need to be taking notes and photographs to record the details ready for my write-up. It's too easy to forget this isn't just a holiday for me. So, it won't be the usual relaxing dinner and leisurely browse around the ship, I'm afraid. I don't think it's fair that I inflict that on you.' *And I don't want to mislead you in any way*, my conscience is urging me to add, but I instantly dismiss that thought.

A part of me is hoping he'll brush it off and suggest we meet up anyway, just for the company, but he doesn't. Suddenly I find myself feeling the teensiest bit disappointed.

Don't Judge a Book by its Cover

After a long Skype session with Rosie and an hour on social media, I can't wait to hit the shower.

I am excited and in a good mood, but it is rather lonely. I'm used to sharing pretty much everything with Rosie and it feels odd to be away from home for a few days without her. She would have loved this entire experience, but school is more important and she'll thank me for honouring that principle when she's older. I hope.

It's rather daunting now that I'm ready as there are seven very different styles of restaurant onboard. Leafing through the details in the handbook I decide to opt for the chic, Parisian fine dining located on deck ten, aft. Aft? Well, it might take a little while for me to get my bearings, that's for sure.

I head out to the elevator and it's easy enough to find the right deck. As I'm not sure where exactly the restaurant is located, I'm going to tag along behind a small group of people who look like they are dressed for a very special dinner experience. I was worried my second-best posh frock would be a little over the top, but now I'm relieved as it isn't at all out of place. The silky, knee-length lilac dress is simple but it stands out. My hair is twisted up and pinned on top, to complement the open back that falls just above my waistline in a cowl. It's elegant, easy to wear and, thankfully, doesn't crease. The dress might not make the woman, but it certainly gives this woman a much-needed confidence boost.

La Maison Chapelle is indeed very chic and has that old-world sense of romantic elegance about the décor. I wait in the small queue, hoping they will be able to find me a table because I didn't have time to make a reservation.

'We are pretty full tonight, I'm afraid. If you are happy to wait about forty-five minutes then I'm sure I can get a table ready for you, Madam.' The young woman addressing me is wearing a very smart black waistcoat over a crisp, white shirt. With tapered black trousers and a black apron, she looks every inch a Parisian waitress. But her accent indicates she's probably from New York and that makes me smile.

'Thank you, that would be lovely.' I turn on my heels and there, in front of me is Harrison, smiling.

'Actually, I have a reservation for eight o'clock and Ms Castelli is with me. Harrison Buchanan.'

'Ah, Mr Buchanan, of course. Please step this way.'

I flash him a grateful smile and he indicates for me to go ahead of him. We are shown to a corner table for two and Harrison insists that he sit with his back to the room.

'You have to see what's going on if you're going to be making notes.' He grins at me.

'How did you know I would be here?' I ask, rather cautiously awaiting his answer.

'I didn't. I love French food and I booked a table as soon as I arrived. But then I've eaten here before on Vista Blue's maiden voyage. I like the ambience but I will be honest and say that I wasn't relishing the thought of eating alone.'

Now I feel guilty.

'Sorry, I wasn't trying to put you off earlier on. I simply felt that I'm not really going to be good company. Plus, I'm feeling kind of overwhelmed by the size of the ship, if I'm being honest with you. I had no idea of the real scale involved and thought I could aimlessly wander around to discover everything I needed to see.'

It takes us a few minutes to decide on a bottle of wine and peruse the menu. It all looks good and we both go for the terrine of foie gras. I decide upon the coquille Saint Jacques sea scallops and Harrison orders the beef ribs.

'Yes, it can take a while to find your way around,' he remarks.

I'm trying not to stare at him so I let my eyes drift around the restaurant, taking in the lavish decoration. Alongside the entrance there is an intimate and cosy little bar, which leads into the larger dining area. The inlaid marble floor adds to the nostalgic atmosphere, with gold filigree screens and metal accents replicating the ironwork of the Eiffel Tower.

'Timeless, isn't it? This could as easily be a setting for a classic movie. I can just imagine Cary Grant walking through, accompanied by one of those glamorous starlets.'

His comment surprises me.

'I wouldn't have taken you for an old movie buff. Are you a Casablanca fan too?'

He nods. 'My mother's influence, I'm afraid.'

'There's nothing wrong with that,' I respond, truthfully. Harrison is wearing a very smart dark grey suit with a white shirt and a mauve tie. Old-style he'd be described as dashing; a man who feels very comfortable in more formal attire. The hint of grey around his temples suits him and doesn't make him look old, more dependable.

'Should I be worried by that look you're giving me?'

I didn't realise I was studying him that intently.

'Sorry, no, I was just thinking how nice it is to be able to dress up for a change.' *Liar – you hate posh frocks. Saying that simply to try to disguise the fact you were staring at him means you've now given him the wrong impression.* 'Not that I'd want to do that very often, of course, as it's not really my style.'

Suddenly I feel very hot and bothered.

'Really? Well, I didn't like to pass comment but as you've raised the subject that is a rather spectacular dress.'

He arches his eyebrows and quickly raises his wine glass in the air.

'To your first night onboard ship. May there be many more in the future.'

We clink glasses and my first taste of the rich, almost plum-coloured wine fills my mouth with hints of blackberries and, rather pleasantly, apples. Obviously, I'm no wine connoisseur and a smile begins to creep over my face.

'What is it?' Harrison gives me a suspicious look. He thinks I'm laughing at him.

'I lead a very quiet life, usually. This sort of luxurious experience is all very new to me,' I admit. I think it's time to be honest with him.

'What exactly is your job? Are you some sort of test shopper, employed by companies who want to run a check on their customer service status?'

Two waiters arrive at our table, each carrying a plate with a silver dome over the top on an upturned hand. With one deft movement, and perfectly synchronised, the plates are laid before us and the domes removed.

'Wonderful, thank you.' The service really is as good as the food, which scores ten out of ten for presentation.

While we eat I explain what I do in detail and Harrison looks mildly surprised by the number of hours I spend online.

'Doesn't that make home life rather difficult? How do you maintain that work-life balance?'

Do I skirt the issue? I decide there's little point as our paths will never cross again. There's a sense of anonymity in telling a stranger something you'd hesitate to tell a close friend you see on a regular basis.

'My daughter is my life and the focus is on providing for us both. I'm in a happy place now and I've achieved that by deciding I don't need a significant other in my life. It's been liberating, actually, after what I've been through.'

He frowns. 'That sounds bad. You see, I hate being alone as you've probably guessed. I need company. I'm a workaholic, too, but when I'm not working I need to keep busy. I've never been the sort to go and lie on a beach all day. But most things are more fun with someone by your side. My someone just happened to be the biggest mistake of my life.'

It's my turn to frown, sympathetically. 'I'm sorry to hear that. The pain will pass, it always does.' My pain passed, it just took nearly seven years – but the anger still remains fresh.

'It was wrong from the start. I married my boss's daughter and why on earth I thought that was going to work, goodness knows. She was high maintenance and hard to please. A daddy's girl who was spoiled from the moment she was born. My mother did warn me.'

'Mums, eh? Mine worries about me all the time. She thinks being alone is the worst thing in the world. Thankfully my disastrous, all-consuming love gave me Rosie. She is worth every single second of the agony of losing the man I thought I'd love forever. But that was before he showed his true colours, of course.'

It isn't until I finish speaking that I realise Harrison has stopped eating and his jaw is sagging.

'I'm sorry, that was way too heavy. I'm not usually that forthcoming.' I take a large gulp of wine, hoping the alcohol will soon kick in and begin to relax me.

'That's tough. It's hard to trust again, I should imagine. At least in my situation it wasn't really love, even from the start. I sort of knew that, but if you haven't ever experienced it before, then you don't know for sure. She is a very beautiful woman but that instant attraction thing doesn't last long. If you have nothing else in common, life soon becomes a constant string of arguments.'

This time we both raise our glasses to our lips but as we put them back down on the table we're smiling at each other.

'You can rest assured that I'm not looking for a relationship, or a holiday fling, but I do enjoy, and appreciate, good company. Let me show you around, no strings attached. When we part I won't even ask for your number, honestly,' he says openly.

I nod. 'I was thinking the exact same thing. You have no idea how out of my depth I feel on this floating city. Any help you are happy to give is most gratefully received.'

We toast each other and suddenly I feel I'm in safe hands and I can relax.

'Right, get out your notepad and I'll give you a few interesting facts and figures that will be perfect for your article.'

The Morning After the Night Before

Oh, how my head aches this morning. I had two glasses of wine and three cocktails after our extensive tour of decks four and five. Harrison was true to his word; he does know the layout of this ship very well. I discovered two of the other restaurants, the coffee bar and café, the business centre and a massive lounge the other side of the concierge and reception area. We popped our heads into the upper level of the theatre, which is two decks high. Harrison suggested we catch a show there tonight so I can savour the full experience. He told me he can sort the tickets and it wasn't a problem.

Everything is immaculate, of an extraordinary quality and even the lounges are sumptuous and individually designed. Almost like film sets, where a space is transformed into an experience that will transport you into another time and place. We visited a vast library and once inside it could easily have been on land somewhere, wrapped up in an old stone building. Each restaurant is so unique that just the surroundings are an experience in themselves, quite aside from the gourmet cuisine on offer.

And that was only deck five. Down on deck four was where we lingered over cocktails while visiting the casino. I'm not a gambler and I don't usually drink more than a glass or two of wine, but the cocktails seemed like a good idea at the time. Afterwards we visited yet another lounge area where we had several cups of black coffee before saying goodnight. I crawled into bed, my head already beginning to buzz, but feeling content. My notebook is filling up and I managed to get some great photos.

I ease open first one eye and then, very gingerly, the second one. Why on earth I didn't draw the curtains last night, I don't know. Glancing out of the patio doors I can see that we're in port again and, to my horror, there is another ship docked right alongside ours! Not only is it hard to believe we sailed over night and we're in Portovenere this morning, but my room is now on full display to the ship parallel to us. I vault out of bed to find the handset to close the curtains, which is a rather rude awakening given my tender state.

When I told Harrison I was going ashore today as we don't set sail again until 5 p.m. he asked if I'd like some company. I jumped at the offer because I wasn't relishing the thought of wandering around alone. Or worse, other sightseers making polite conversation because that's what good people do when it's obvious someone is a lone traveller. In return, I agreed to have dinner with him this evening before we catch the show. He told me he'd make the necessary arrangements and we agreed to meet this morning in the café.

Reluctantly, I drag myself out of bed to experience the rainforest again, full force. It certainly does the trick and within an hour I'm feeling much better and surprisingly refreshed. I dress quite casually in navy linen trousers with a pale blue top. I manage to find my way down to the café on deck five without getting lost once. But as I'm looking around I can't see Harrison anywhere.

I turn, wandering off with the intention of doing a little window shopping, when I spot him. He waves and I begin walking towards him.

'Sorry, Leah. I overslept. Didn't even hear the alarm going off and that's unusual for me.'

He stands there rather awkwardly and then leans in to give me a quick hug. It's brief enough to be simply a 'good morning' and as he pulls away I give him a big smile.

'Well, my head was very tender first thing this morning,' I admit. 'Now I feel good but I'm in need of coffee, strong coffee. And a croissant.'

We idle away an hour over a simple breakfast. He explains that Portovenere is a medieval fishing village and it isn't an arduous walking tour.

'I took the liberty of booking us a taxi into the city centre rather than catching one of the tours. They set off too early, anyway. Besides, last night I felt that we both needed to have a little fun and lighten up so a gentle start to the day was necessary.' He beams at me, possibly carrying just a little guilt for last night's indulgences. I distinctly remember him saying 'one more won't hurt' – but it totally did.

After several large cups of coffee we leave two half-finished croissants and head off to find our taxi. Large cruise ships are berthed at the new Molo Garibaldi, which is two kilometres away from Portovenere. Sitting on the Ligurian coast it turns out to be a sprawling port and the berths extend way out into the ocean on a series of jetties.

The town itself is a hub of beautiful old stone buildings. The backdrop is one of luscious green vegetation, over land rising up behind the heart of the original fishing village. Distinctive with its waterside row of six-storey buildings painted in an array of colours – from pale yellows and greens, to a soft terracotta – it's picturesque.

'It looks top-heavy,' I can't help remarking. 'Almost as if it could all topple into the water. With so many windows at varying levels, different balconies and an array of shutters, it looks *busy*. I thought the promenade would be wider but it is lovely with all the small boats moored up along the edge.'

'Ah, that's the charm of it,' Harrison agrees.

We stop to watch some fishermen offloading their catch, the smell of the sea surrounding us with a saltiness you can almost taste. That fresh, sharp tang is a reminder that fish dishes don't get any fresher than those served by the local restaurants.

Wandering around the shopping area it's bustling with people: full of restaurants and an assortment of shops. After about an hour we make the gentle climb up to San

Puerto, the church of St Peter. It stands on the edge of a rocky promontory overlooking the deep blue Mediterranean Sea. Standing watch over the entrance to the port, alongside the castle Doria with its sturdy fortress walls, it dominates the scenery. Almost menacingly so.

'It's very *Game of Thrones*, isn't it, with the flinty grey, mottled stone and the way it all seems to rise up out of the rock? There's an overwhelming sense of the medieval about this place. It sends a shiver right through me.'

Harrison nods. 'Yes, it's a wonderful example of the Genovese Gothic style.'

He leads us along the north wall of the castle. We get to peek out of the keyhole-like slits to glimpse a view in miniature of sea, rocky cliffs and sky. I can imagine the soldiers with their crossbows ready to defend the port.

As we look down over the edge of the cliff we see people jumping into the water from various rocky ledges.

'Ooh, that's quite a way they're jumping.' I watch in amazement as one by one a small group line up, waiting their turn.

Harrison raises his arm, pointing to the curving, rocky cliff to our left. 'Do you see that cave? That's La Grotta di Byron, where the poet Byron used to swim. They call this the Gulf of Poets.'

It is stunningly beautiful, especially as today there isn't a cloud in sight and the water is a pure shade of topaz blue. No wonder so many writers, poets and artists found their way here.

It's a fun couple of hours and we take it in turns behind

the camera, trying to capture some perfect shots for my readers.

We leisurely wander back down into town and find a little café to grab a drink and sample the local focaccia. It's about an inch thick and stuffed with cheese and meat. Topped with sea salt and rosemary, it's sliced into wedges and the perfect finger food to accompany a glass of Le Pinete; this local wine carries a very pleasant, slightly sweet scent.

'A good choice.' I raise my glass briefly in the air and look across at Harrison. He's hungrily tucking into the focaccia.

'I've been here before,' he admits.

I watch him eating, curious about why I'm so content to be in Harrison's company when he's little more than a stranger. There's nothing other than a little harmless banter going on between us, which is a fun kind of distraction. He's very attractive, in a huggable way, like a big teddy bear. Or maybe it's more about allowing myself to get to know him because he's a genuinely good person and when you find one, you want to hold onto them.

'I'm sensing you have someone new in your life, am I right? And she might have been in the frame for a while before your ex-wife found out. Although I'm totally sure nothing would have happened before she left you, as that's not your style. You're a gentleman, Harrison.'

Now Harrison is studying my face intently and I can see he's suddenly nervous for some reason.

'Maybe.' He puts a half-eaten slice of bread back onto

his plate, wiping his fingers on a napkin as he looks directly at me.

Why is he being cautious now when he's already told me about his ex and that didn't seem to faze him at all?

'I'm a good listener if there's something you want to share.'

I can feel the turmoil which is now so visible in his eyes as he takes a gulp of his wine. He replaces the glass on the table, twisting the stem idly with his fingers and watching the pale, yellow liquid swirl around inside of it.

'Funnily enough, we met on a cruise, a little over six months ago. Ollie is good looking, intelligent and great company. The attraction was instant and it rocked me to the core.'

Ah. Now I understand. By the look on his face I think that being gay is still something he's grappling with and that saddens me.

'You haven't come out then, I mean, officially?' I'm surprised that a confident person like Harrison should feel the need to hide anything at all from the world at large. It's who he is and that isn't something of which to feel afraid.

'It's about hurting the people you love. Mainly my parents, I suppose. My ex isn't sure about what's going on because you're right, I couldn't have been unfaithful to her. But I couldn't deny my feelings either and I guess I wasn't really sure, myself, until I met Ollie. None of my work colleagues are aware because I keep my private life quiet.'

'But you are going to embrace it, now?'

'It's not just a case of building up the courage to say the words but I will be crossing a line and unable to turn back. Even though I've never been more sure of anything in my life before, I don't know if I have the courage to carry through my convictions. I hate myself for that.'

'Pass me your phone.' Harrison looks at me quizzically but places his phone in my outstretched hand. I add my number to his contact list.

'There you go. If you need to talk then I'm only a phone call away. You must be true to yourself and to Ollie, Harrison, because you are a good man. You deserve a happy life. Don't put this off any longer. When you return I want you to text me and let me know when it's done.'

Harrison nods, placing his phone back down on the table.

'Ollie is a decent guy and he understands that we all have to make the journey in our own way and at our own pace. He knows he's the one for me and we both knew that right from the start. But for me, it's a lot to get my head around, I will admit.'

I sigh. 'That's a beautiful thing to say, Harrison. I'd hoped Antonio was the one for me but unfortunately the man I fell in love with didn't really exist. Good looks and charm were merely a smokescreen. But, I can understand exactly where you are coming from and it's wonderful when it turns out to be the real thing.'

Harrison's eyes crinkle up in a laugh.

'Ollie was jealous, when I told him about our little trip around Monaco but I explained that he had nothing at all to worry about. You're one of the good ones, Leah. He couldn't get time off work and so it's yet another solo trip for me.' Finally, Harrison is looking more relaxed and, I think, relieved. Like he was testing the water and not sure what my reaction might be. I wonder if I'm the first person he's actually told?

'Oh no, poor guy. You were right when you said you're safe with me anyway, because I'm really, really, out of practice at the flirting thing. Even if you had been looking for a little romantic interlude. You have a generous heart, though, Harrison, and I think Ollie is a very lucky guy. You saw that I was struggling a little to find my feet on this trip and your kindness has really been appreciated.' Sometimes the people you decide you want in your life just happen to appear; you instantly know they will make you feel good whenever they are around. Harrison is one of those people.

'And I had no idea someone new was going to come into my life and give me the push I needed. I know that I would never feel complete without Ollie by my side, but it's great to finally admit that to someone other than him. Thank you.'

Our eyes meet and suddenly the waitress is back, looking hesitant to interrupt. We burst out laughing – we are having *a moment*, but it's not the one she's assuming.

Harrison indicates that we've finished and she hurries away with our plates. He immediately lifts his glass in a toast.

'To new friends.' His voice is playful but his look says

something else. He's grateful, I think, to have finally heard himself say it out loud. 'Isn't it funny how you can meet a total stranger and yet immediately feel comfortable with them? Enough to say the things you usually keep hidden away.'

I look directly at him. 'When will you take that big step forward with your parents?'

He shakes his head. 'I'm thinking soon, now. Anyway, I can't put it off for much longer because if I don't commit then Ollie will think my heart isn't really in it. And that couldn't be further from the truth. I simply need to get up the courage to do the deed.'

I can see by the look in his eyes that he cares too much about this guy to risk losing him.

'And for you? Is there no chance at all for you with Antonio?'

Swallowing the last of my wine, I savour the sweet, yet mellow, notes.

'None at all. Antonio deserted Rosie and me; he left us with nothing except a mountain of debt. I can never forgive him for that because it's taken seven years to be rid of the financial worries. But now, at least, I'm free of that.'

He raises his eyebrows. 'But are you free enough of the past to really move on?'

I shrug my shoulders. 'That's the million-dollar question, isn't it?'

I'm not ready to talk more about Antonio yet and Harrison can sense that, so he rather diplomatically changes the subject.

'I don't know about you, Leah, but I'm going to have to take a nap before I'm ready to tackle tonight's agenda. Where would you like to eat this evening? Formal, informal ... before the show, or after the show?'

Harrison has been so kind and accommodating that I feel the dinner choice should be in his hands.

'I'm easy. It's up to you.'

'The Outdoor Grill by the pool it is, then. I'm in the mood for a big steak and plenty of French fries to set us up for the long night ahead.'

'Mm, lovely.'

'Right, let's go find a taxi and maybe rendezvous at seven, at The Grill? That will give us plenty of time before we head off to the theatre for *A Night at the Movies*.'

'Sounds perfect to me. What sort of show is it?'

'An evening of celebration of some of the biggest hit songs associated with movies. It should be quite nostalgic, by the sound of it. Maybe afterwards we could head for the dancefloor.'

I grimace. 'Maybe. Or maybe not.'

~

Rosie is having trouble with a homework assignment and I spend the best part of an hour on the phone to her, trying to help her decide how to approach it. The task is to learn a new skill and then write a detailed account about what was involved in the learning process. After throwing out what felt like a couple of dozen ideas, we seem to be going around and around in circles. It's all 'I don't fancy that,' or 'It will take too long' and I think the problem is more that she's missing me and just doesn't want to finish our conversation.

Eventually she decides that she's going to ask Grandma to teach her how to make bread. It's something my mum has always done and that I took for granted as a child. Rosie seems to perk up once she has a solution with which she's happy and I remind her that I'll be home tomorrow evening. I have a quick chat with Mum and then flop down onto the bed to rest for an hour.

It's a good job that I set my alarm, because I fall into an exceptionally deep sleep. I haven't dreamt about Antonio for a very long time and it's a shock when I awaken with a start – his face still in the forefront of my mind. We always said we'd do a cruise one day. But then we said a lot of things that didn't happen.

Guess it's time for another trip to the rainforest, with the hope the water will wash away the anger that's simmering below the surface. I still struggle with the knowledge that I fell in love with a conman really; I saw only what Antonio wanted to show me and that was charm and charisma. I was young and I let my heart overrule my head. Never again, I vow to myself. Never again.

A Night of Stars

I'm a little late and by the time I reach The Grill, Harrison is already waiting. Service is quick and after we've eaten we find ourselves with half an hour to spare so he suggests we take a stroll along to the Twilight Bar for a cocktail.

The ship set sail again a couple of hours ago and as we walk a light breeze catches my hair. I tentatively glance over the side and realise just how high up we are. The ship seems to be slicing through the water like a knife, sending out a turbulent trail of white–crested waves. I will admit that it is taking a little time for me to adjust. My legs wobble a little, but I think that's more about my fear of heights than it is about finding my sea legs. You can hardly feel the ship moving, but then it is perfectly calm and we don't seem to be travelling very fast at all – it's surprisingly smooth. There is a slight vibration, like a humming that's only slightly perceptible, but this evening I'm feeling it. It is a long way down, though, and now is not the time to have one of my hellish moments where vertigo takes over and I freeze. I suck it up in a determined manner, shaking off the moment.

'That's some dress, by the way and I recognised it instantly. I, um, looked you up online this afternoon,' Harrison says.

'Well, I hope what you read was all good. And you're looking pretty damn smart, yourself. But then you have a great sense of style, Harrison.' He pays attention to detail and I like that about him.

He pulls out a bar stool for me and I slip up onto it as elegantly as I can, given that I'm wearing the long silver-grey dress I bought for the awards ceremony.

The barman appears, a broad smile on his face and a cheery, 'Good evening, what can I get you to drink, guys?'

He places a printed drinks menu in front of us and then fills two sparkling cut-glass tumblers with water. Placing them on coasters bearing the ship's name, he slides them forward on the countertop. Harrison catches my eye.

'Wine or a cocktail, Leah?'

The barman is hovering and I'm feeling playful, and quietly confident with my appearance tonight. Besides, I also have a rather good-looking, trustworthy and fun companion so what's not to enjoy?

'Surprise me.'

Harrison makes eye contact and laughs. 'You trust me to order your drink?' He turns his head to look at the barman. 'Make that two Sex on the Beach cocktails, please.'

A small smile plays around my lips as I hold in a laugh and the guy clearly thinks there's something going on between us. He's trying to act as if he can't hear the banter. We watch in silence as he turns mixing a drink into a piece of theatre. Tom Cruise eat your heart out; the Hippy Hippy Shakes bar scene from *Cocktail* has nothing on this guy.

When he places the highball glasses in front of us they're half-filled with ice and sporting a liquid that is orange on the bottom half and red on the top. With mint leaves, orange segments and a slice of star fruit gracing the edge, it's a work of art. We watch in amusement as he finishes off by adding a straw and a plastic stirrer sporting a cut–out heart to each glass.

We're watched in earnest as we take a sip and in tandem our heads tip back, our eyebrows going up in surprise.

'Hmm, that's good.' I manage to get out before I cough to clear my throat and Harrison nods to endorse it. The guy seems pleased and heads down the bar to another customer who has just arrived.

'What on earth is in this thing? Is it even legal?' Harrison half-whispers.

I can't comment as the vodka in it is still catching in the back of my throat. It turns into a bit of a coughing fit and I have to swallow half a glass of water to quell the spasm.

'Are you okay?' Harrison asks, looking concerned. 'I can taste peach schnapps, for sure.'

'No, it's the vodka that took my breath away as it's pretty strong. Hmm ... I like it, though.'

He raises his glass and I follow suit.

'And a virtual slap, Harrison. Did you see that poor guy's face when you ordered a Sex on the Beach? He didn't know where to look when you began flirting with me. And you kept a straight face! Shame on you. I bet you've never even had one of these before.'

He's chuckling away to himself. 'No, but there's a first time for everything. I'm usually a G&T sort of guy.'

'Truthfully, I am enjoying a little banter because it's been such a long time. I sort of thought I'd lost my touch at being ... frothy and frivolous. Or is that simply single and carefree, rather than in mum and breadwinner mode? You've reminded me that dating can be fun. Not that we're dating, of course ... oh, you know what I mean.'

Nothing could be more unexpected than sitting here with Harrison and the sound of a string quartet on the deck outside playing the haunting 'Radioactive' by Imagine Dragons. We sit in silence throughout the entire song and I know we're both hating the fact that life is full of a stream of seemingly endless complications. Why can't it just be easy?

When the music ends he gives me a sly, sideways glance.

'So are you going to tell me what really happened with Antonio? The bits you've been leaving out?'

I focus on stirring my cocktail, my chin sinking to my chest as I try to stifle a sigh.

'Well, for a start, he wasn't alone when he disappeared. He took my twin sister, Kelly, with him.'

Harrison recoils as if I've just slapped him across the face. 'He *what*?'

Hearing myself say those words and seeing his stunned reaction is like a razor-sharp stab to the heart. My seemingly unbreakable link with Kelly was severed that day and now there's a hole in my heart because it feels like a little piece of me no longer functions.

'I'm sorry, Leah. I had no idea ... I didn't mean to pry but I sensed there was something more to your story. God, how on earth did you get through that time?'

I have to steel myself to continue this conversation but in a strange way it helps to hear Harrison's reaction. It has blighted my life for so long and yet, so few people know the full truth.

'I had to make a pact with myself that the first thing I'd think of every morning when I opened my eyes was Rosie. Knowing I'm a mum keeps me moving forward. But the guilt constantly eats away at me.'

He's watching me closely, the frown he's wearing showing a genuine empathy for my loss that day.

'The guilt? Why would you have any reason to feel guilty for what they did to you?'

'Because I wasn't the only one to lose so much that day. Rosie lost a dad and an aunt: Mum and Dad lost a daughter. I knew something wasn't right with Antonio and, ironically, I was intending to sit down and talk to him that very evening. As for Kelly, well, she'd been avoiding me for a while and it all began after Rosie was born.

'Shortly after I brought Rosie home from the hospital she told me that I had everything she wanted in life. I hugged her and said it would be her turn next, thinking she was talking about settling down, meeting the right man and starting a family. What she actually meant was that she wanted Antonio for herself.'

Harrison's expression changes to anger and he vents his exasperation with a harsh sigh.

'Jealousy is an ugly emotion. You're the victim in all of this, Leah. It's ridiculous that you regard yourself in any way as a part of the problem.'

I shake my head, reaching out to touch his arm to calm his look of agitation.

'I didn't want to face the fact that things weren't right between us, Harrison, and that was a failing on my part. Antonio didn't feel he could be honest with me, so what sort of wife was I?'

He drums his fingers on the countertop. 'Leah, your thought processes are all mixed up here. Seriously, you need to speak to someone about this. A professional. From where I'm sitting it's obvious this has left you with an inability to judge yourself fairly. You think you're lacking in some way because this whole sorry experience has damaged your self-esteem.

'Antonio chose not to talk to you and, as for your sister, well, I'm sorry but she knew the enormity of what she was doing. I know that's hard to hear and probably hard to think about, too. That's why you're still not over it. You never will be until you get it all out and learn to love yourself again, as much as you love Rosie.'

I'm trembling as I sit here listening to his words and he suddenly throws an arm around my shoulders, pulling me into him.

'Hey, it's okay. I'm here for you, lovely lady. We can be a crutch for each other, can't we? You can kick my ass and I'll kick yours when it's needed. Now finish that drink and let's have a fun evening. Life is too short to waste a moment of it and we're both survivors. Watch out world, that's all I can say.'

I look at Harrison with gratitude in my eyes and he smiles at me with a gentleness and understanding that makes me feel blessed. I realise that what I needed most wasn't a romantic interlude but a friend to come into my life and show me the way forward.

'I'll enjoy kicking your ass,' I smile and he tilts his head back and laughs, softly.

~

The entertainment is what you would expect from a West End show in London and is a lavish production. A *Night at the Movies* celebrates some of the biggest blockbuster films and their songs from the Sixties to the Nineties, which instantly transport you back to the storyline.

People are up on their feet dancing along and clapping to songs like Phil Collins' 'Two Hearts' from *Buster* and 'Maniac' from *Flashdance* transports us all back to that infamous, on-stage dance scene. Seal's 'Kiss from a Rose' celebrates the unforgettable *Batman Forever*, while Barbra Streisand's 'Evergreen' recaptures the on-screen magic of *A Star is Born*. I don't think there's one person left sitting when the Bee Gees' 'Stayin' Alive' strikes up and no one can forget a young John Travolta strutting his stuff. But Lulu's 'To Sir with Love' conjures up another era and it's good to hear a classic oldie.

There's a standing ovation at the end and I don't know who enjoyed it more, Harrison or me.

'Well, that was amazing and now I'm buzzing. But I'm going to be shattered in the morning, no doubt,' I admit.

'How about a walk along the deck before bed? There's a beautiful sky tonight.'

As the crowd disperses we make our way up to the sports area on deck twelve. Harrison is right, it's a beautiful, balmy night but there's a lovely cool breeze coming off the water, making it very pleasant indeed. With a surprisingly light sky and no cloud at all, the three-quarter moon is light enough that only the biggest stars are distinguishable and twinkle like pinpricks on a huge canvas.

Harrison stops to lean on the railing, looking out towards the distant horizon.

'Don't mind me if I stand back a little. I have a bit of a fear of heights, I'm afraid. The ship is so huge I can even forget we're afloat, but the moment I look over the side my legs turn to jelly,' I admit apologetically.

Harrison immediately pulls back and we begin strolling along together, doing a circuit of the jogging track which is totally empty.

'It's almost 2 a.m. but onboard the night is still young.'

'Well, that might be the case but I'm flagging. One circuit and I need to climb into bed as tomorrow I have a lot of travelling to do. I'm so grateful for meeting you, Harrison, thank you for understanding.'

'I meant every single word I said earlier on tonight, Leah. I think that we were always destined to be friends and that's why our paths crossed. The universe gives us what we need to move forward but it's up to us to recognise that and act upon it.'

I nod in agreement. 'I feel like I have a constant battle going on inside of me, Harrison and I'm fed up of it.'

He stops in his tracks and I spin around to face him.

'We're both capable of getting through that next step in our lives. We deserve to be loved. You get some therapy and I'll find a way to come out to my parents. Deal? And if we falter we can be there for each other, that listening ear; someone who understands all about living with a nightmare.'

I guess I'd be a real hypocrite if I thought that Harrison's challenge is any easier than my own, but having *therapy* and thinking about loving a new someone? Thankfully I'm now too tired to do more than simply drop into bed, as the ship sails onwards to the port of Civitavecchia.

It's Time to Head Home

I wake just as the ship is docking and I hop out of bed, drawing back the curtains to glance out over the port. There is only one other cruise ship moored up but there's a wide range of smaller ships and boats as far as the eye can see. Civitavecchia is very spread out and it's obviously a popular port, being so close to Rome.

In front of the ship is a jetty with a road leading up to a series of car parks. Parallel with that is a massive, off-white stone building. It's twice as long as the jetty, with an imposing circular tower dominating the centre of it. It's quite a beautiful building and with the sun glinting on the shiny white vessels all around, as ports go it's pretty enough to resemble a luxury marina.

I'm conscious I don't have a lot of time. I did my packing late yesterday afternoon but I still need to put the last-minute things in my case and get myself ready. The shuttle bus will be here at nine-thirty.

It's just gone 8 a.m. when I make my way to the café to

meet Harrison for our last breakfast together. He greets me with a big smile and I really appreciate that he has made this last couple of days an even better experience for me

'Morning, lovely lady. You look good and rested. Did you sleep well?'

He kisses my cheek and pulls out a chair for me.

'I did, surprisingly. How about you?'

He grimaces. 'I spent most of the night having *the* conversation in my head and every time I stumbled. The words just wouldn't flow and I kept imagining the look on people's faces.'

The waitress appears and we order, then settle back in our chairs. I look at him and can feel the battle raging within.

'What's the hardest part of coming out, for you?'

He shakes his head, sadly, looking defeated and shrugging his shoulders.

'Facing up to my own fear, I suppose, that people I love will look at me differently from there on in. What if they don't understand? My parents were, no doubt, expecting me to settle down again, at some point, with a nice young woman, and eventually give them a grandchild, or two. That's the norm for the little village in which they live and now, suddenly, I'm going to turn their lives upside down once more. The divorce was more than enough drama to inflict upon them and this is going to rock their world all over again.'

The coffee arrives and there's a temporary lull in our conversation. I can't help thinking that one glance at

Harrison and the assumption is that here's a man whose life is sorted. And yet, that's so far from the truth.

'I know precisely what it's like to be surrounded by people whose lives seem to fit the mould, because mine doesn't. I hate the fact they feel the need to tread carefully around me. I'm grateful for the help and support I've been given, of course I am, but I don't want people feeling sorry for me. A lot has gone wrong but that only seems to perpetuate the sympathy. I cringe every time someone close to me says it's about time I had some good luck. That makes me sound ungrateful, doesn't it?' I shrug ruefully.

Harrison stirs his coffee, moving his cup so the waitress can lay his breakfast plate on the table in front of him. It's a stack of pancakes with blueberries and I have French toast with crispy bacon. But instead of tucking in, we both play with the food in front of us, our appetites having evaporated into thin air. We sit in silence for what feels like an eternity and then both look up at the same time.

'I'm done. How about you?' The look on Harrison's face makes me wish my stay on board was longer. After a rough night, he needs something to lift his mood.

'Let's get out of here. I feel the need for some fresh air.' I'm already pushing back on my chair.

Harrison offers to walk me back to my cabin but we amble, going slightly out of the way to linger and take in the view out over the port. We stand together by the guard rail, two people united by the baggage they find themselves carrying.

'I wish I could stay just one more day, but I can't. I want

you to promise me that you'll shrug off all those negative thoughts and find someone who is going to cheer you up for the remainder of the cruise.'

He makes a face. 'One of the lonely widows, you mean?'

I smile at him, because there do seem to be a lot of elderly single women on board.

'Yes, that's just what you need! Someone who is out to have a thoroughly good time and would really appreciate a little company.'

He looks at me, studying my face.

'I doubt I'll find another Leah,' he replies, rather soberly.

'I think one Leah is enough for this trip. I'm best tolerated in small doses.'

He laughs out loud and it's good to see his face light up again.

'Well, that works both ways. You managed to drag my secret out of me and that's a first.'

'Friends in need, eh?' My eyes search his face, reaching out to him.

Harrison steps forward to give me a brotherly hug.

'What's the saying? Two heads are better than one? Between us we'll finally knock our lives into shape, you can bet on that.'

He puts a smile on my face, too, but even though I'd love to stay, thoughts of Rosie and home are calling.

'And you need to look into getting some help the moment you get back home.'

I stifle a sigh, but I know he's right and I wonder how often Mum and Dad have longed to say that to me and haven't, for fear of upsetting me? Sally has touched on the subject a few times over the years but always ended up backing off when she saw my less than enthusiastic reaction. I thought I was coping well enough on my own. But maybe I'm not.

~

'Mum, I missed you!' Rosie runs forward, wrapping her arms around me and hugging with all her might.

'How was the journey back?' Mum looks at me over the top of Rosie's head.

'Good. Uneventful. The plane wasn't full and I had a window seat with no one sitting the other side of me.'

Rosie finally releases me so I can hug Mum and Dad. Dad looks a little flushed, but is his usual bright and breezy self. Mum looks drawn and I wonder what's up.

'I'll put the kettle on,' Dad says, heading off to the kitchen. Rosie follows him, probably more interested in grabbing a biscuit than helping with the preparation.

'Are you okay?' I make eye contact with Mum but it only lasts for the briefest of moments before she turns around to sit back down in her chair.

'Everything's fine. You look chirpy considering that must have been quite a tiring little break.'

She's trying to change the subject but I need to know what's gone wrong.

'Mum, I'll only worry if you don't tell me.'

She looks exasperated, glancing at the doorway and then back at me.

'It's probably nothing. Dad's had some blood tests taken because his blood pressure was up. There's nothing to worry about, really, as they're keeping an eye on it.'

It's the little nagging worry that never goes away. Ever since Dad had his heart attack Mum watches him like a hawk, and I know it's a daily worry for her. She's my barometer when it comes to gauging how he's doing and one look at her face is enough to see that she's concerned.

'You will let me know when the results are back, won't you? I thought he looked like he'd been rushing around. Maybe it's just—'

Rosie appears, her mouth full of biscuit as she puts the tin down on the coffee table.

'Grandma and I made biscuits,' she says, a few crumbs escaping, making her put her hand up to her mouth to stem the fallout.

'You know it's rude to talk with your mouth full, Rosie,' I admonish.

'Sorry, Mum. Did Grandma tell you I won the pupil of the week award? I'll find the certificate.'

Dad arrives with a tray of drinks and we soon settle down to allow Rosie to have her little moment in the spotlight. I inspect the certificate, noting that it's in recognition for the excellent work on her project and having the tidiest desk. It seems the island was finished while I was away then, and Dad proudly shows me the photo on his phone. As for the tidiest desk, well that's a welcome surprise.

'Wow – that's amazing! Well done, darling. I'm so proud of you.'

Rosie and Dad exchange conspiratorial smiles. I bet they had a lot of fun finishing off that model. We're so lucky we have Dad; if something awful ever happened it would break our hearts. The fact that his heart attack was caused by the break-up of my marriage is something for which I can never forgive myself. Or Antonio.

Hitting the Ground Running

Even given the amount of online work I managed to fit in while I was away, it was inevitable I would come home to a backlog of emails. In addition to the work generated by the trip itself, I'm going to be very busy indeed. I have a lot of notes and photos to trawl through for what will become a series of articles, as well as the report to compile, and it all takes time.

The hours between dropping Rosie off at school on this murky, grey Friday morning and collecting her speed by but I seem to fly through the work with relative ease. Maybe it's true when they say that a change is as good as a rest. Just as I'm about to switch the laptop onto sleep mode and head out for my second walk before the afternoon school run, a new email pops into my inbox. It's from *Loving Life* magazine and I've long been a fan. I really do have to leave, as I'm already running a few minutes late, so I quickly scan down the email. I'm shocked to see it's an invitation to write for them. I can hardly believe my eyes. I'd dearly love to sit down and savour every single word, but I know I can't. Rosie expects to see me in *the space* and it's become a little ritual. Silly, I know, but it's the small things in life that matter to kids. It's more about the fact that her mum is now at home and the one doing the school runs every day.

When a child only has one parent in their life, it becomes even more important that they feel they have your attention. I hurry off to do my walk, spending the time thinking through the content for the next article for the website, which will be all about Monte Carlo. My mind conjures up a picture of Harrison's face for a brief second and then it's gone.

When I eventually jump in the car, I'm a little breathless. For some reason it was hard going this afternoon, but I have managed to make up a little time. Fortunately, the traffic lights are with me and when I pull up at the school I'm glad I left when I did. I seem to have timed it just right, with only a second or two to spare. One of the other mums is driving the car behind me and as I pull into *the space* she gives me a wave as she drives past. No doubt she's disappointed I beat her to it as she heads off in search of a gap she can squeeze into. There are always cars parked on both sides of the road no matter what time of day it is; it usually entails a long walk back up to the school – even if you get here early.

However, getting here before the main crowd means I have a little time to kill and Harrison is still on my mind. I get out my phone.

Hey, how's it going?

His response is instant so he must have had his phone in his hand.

I was just about to text you! I'm missing your company. However, I've met this awesome lady on board the ship who happens to be a very good opponent at chess. Envious?

I smile to myself.

Chess? You are a man of many surprises.

I can imagine the look on his face.

Well, she's eighty-seven and she's just beaten me twice, hands down. It's not good for the morale. Have you booked that appointment yet?

I roll my eyes.

No, but I will. And good luck with the chess.

I click onto my inbox, desperate to read through the email from *Loving Life* magazine properly, while trying to push thoughts of Harrison out of my head.

Hello Leah,

I've been following your blog for some time with great interest. As one of the leading travel bloggers in the industry right now, the whole team think our readers might be fascinated to find out more about what you do and the places you visit. I was wondering how you felt about submitting something for the magazine?

An article in the style of a series of diary entries would be both lively and informative. Initially we could maybe trial this for three consecutive issues to see how well it's received. Obviously, lots of lovely photos would help to draw the reader in and we'd expect you to provide a selection of high-quality graphics to go along with each article.

If this is something that would be of interest to you, then please get in touch and we can arrange a meeting to talk it through in more detail.

Best regards
Wendy Philips
Editor-in-chief
Loving Life

I look up, letting out a little squeal of excitement. There's no mention of payment but I'm sure they don't expect me to do it for free, even though in truth I would. Just the extra exposure alone is great advertising and what a wonderful thing to be able to add to my bio on the website!

As excited as I am, I haven't forgotten Harrison's text so the next thing I do is to ring the surgery and book an appointment to see Dr Watkins. The mere thought of that is enough to kill my good mood but after the deed is done I do feel a bit lighter. My fingers delight in sharing the news with him.

Appointment with my doctor booked. Watch this space. When you get back home I'll be chasing you by text, so remember that it's your turn next! Enjoy the sun, it's just started raining here. Speak soon.

Suddenly Rosie is there, flinging open the car door and bundling in – all legs, damp coat and backpack.

I realise that Harrison is right; it's time I did something about this chip I have on my shoulder. For Rosie's sake, as well as mine. I study her closely, thinking how perfect that heart-shaped little face is and wondering if maybe she's ready to have another male influence in her life.

I enjoyed being in the company of a man the last few days and yes, my instincts clearly knew I was safe with Harrison, but it felt good. I've gained a new friend and a confidante I feel comfortable with, which was totally unexpected. But he also reminded me how good it feels to interact with a man and enjoy a little harmless, in this case, flirtation. I had no way of knowing that initially, though, so it seems that maybe men aren't totally off my agenda and that comes as a real surprise.

~

It's Saturday morning and Rosie has a practice session for a little event coming up at gym club. She missed her class on Thursday evening because of my return, and I know that won't have gone down very well.

We make it with two minutes to spare and I'm relieved as

Miriam Peterson is a stickler for punctuality. But Rosie and I stayed up a little past her bedtime last night to watch *Shrek*, her all-time favourite movie. We curled up together on the sofa, eating popcorn and munching on a bar of chocolate. That was in between reeling off sections of dialogue that we both know by heart. It was a nice way to end a strange week and I felt it made up a little for my absence.

I give Rosie a kiss and she joins her friends in the changing room while I head off to meet up with Sally for coffee. It's walking distance from the leisure centre and a pleasant stroll, plus my pedometer is clocking up those steps. As soon as I enter the café I see she's already here and I make my way between the crowded tables.

'Hey, girl, I was just about to drink your coffee. You have a bit of a tan going on there, if I'm not mistaken.'

She stands and we hug, then I sink down into the chair opposite her at our regular little bistro table.

'Well, was it amazing?' Sally leans in, eager for my news.

'You'll have to wait until it's up on my blog, but yes, I had an awesome time.'

Sally's eyes open wide. 'Awesome, you say? You met someone!'

I drink half of my coffee in one go, making her wait. It hits the spot and I'm conscious that her eyes are watching my every move as I wipe some chocolate covered froth from my top lip.

'Their coffee is just so good here.'

'Never mind that, tell me all!'

Her eyes are bright and her face is a picture of expectation.

'I met a guy named Harrison. He's taken, but we hit it off from the moment he sat next to me on the shuttle from the airport to the port. So well, in fact, that he's convinced me to talk to my doctor about requesting some form of counselling, or therapy.'

The smile drops from Sally's face and her mouth opens but nothing comes out. I sit, leisurely sipping the remainder of my coffee, giving her a chance to recover.

'He's taken?' she repeats.

'Yes. He has a boyfriend.'

'And you've actually made that appointment?'

'I have.'

She exhales loudly and leans back in her chair.

'He must be one special guy to get you to talk openly about your past. And he's definitely taken? I mean there's no chance at all of a relationship striking up between the two of you? People fall in and out of love all the time and maybe he likes women as well as men. Obviously, you got on very well to talk about ... things. I've never known you to have a friendship with a man before. I mean there was only—'

She stops abruptly and I finish her sentence.

'There was only Antonio. And there is no chance as, although he was married to a woman for a while, Harrison is now deeply in love with a man. But I enjoyed his company and it's making me think that maybe I'm finally ready to move on.'

'At last! Well done, Harrison!'

This time her reaction is very vocal and I raise a finger to my lips to get her to tone it down a little.

'Actually,' she begins, giving me a stern look, 'I'm feeling a bit annoyed. How come you're prepared to listen to this new friend of yours when I've been dropping hints for a long time?'

I can't hold back the little grin that's tinged with guilt because I can understand why she's miffed.

'It was the ambience, I think. New experience, different surroundings and an enigmatic stranger. I guess I stepped outside my life for two days and everything he said made sense. I suppose I was listening properly for the first time, really. And I'm sorry because it wasn't that I was ignoring your subtle hints; it was just a timing thing.'

'Well, I can't be cross because I'm simply glad that time has come, at long last. I mean I know how traumatic it's going to be.'

I put my head down, focusing on my coffee cup. I know that too. There are things I haven't said to anyone and that includes my parents and Antonio's parents.

'Some things happen for a reason and I guess Harrison and I were meant to cross paths. We're going to help one another through what will be a personal worst nightmare for each of us.'

Sally's eyes open a little wider as she realises what I'm saying.

'Poor guy; that's a bit of a bombshell and it sounds like it was a fun, but intense couple of days. I can tell you had a great time, though.'

'Oh, I did. The ship was the most luxurious floating hotel you could ever imagine. It's left me with a yearning to experience a full cruise,' I admit. However, the reality is that at this precise moment that can only be a dream. But one day I'll make it come true.

'Well, maybe you'll get to do that with Rosie and a significant other in tow.'

Now there's an interesting thought.

'Oh, and I have more good news. I've been approached by a magazine about writing three articles for them as a trial. A typical day in the life of a travel blogger. How exciting is that?'

Sally reaches out to place her hand on my arm.

'I'm so proud of you, Leah, and what you've achieved. It's been a hard road to travel.'

I nod in agreement.

'All I owe now is the mortgage. I'm debt-free and for the first time in seven years I no longer lie in bed at night juggling figures in my head. That alone is one huge relief.'

Sally doesn't respond but lets out a sigh instead. It doesn't take much to be transported back to those early days when I first found out the bank was about to repossess our lovely home, thanks to Antonio. He'd been gone less than twenty-four hours when I was informed that Rosie and I were about to become homeless. Realising I could no longer take anything in my life for granted had been terrifying. Surely, even a therapist is going to agree that it isn't humanly possible not to be harbouring at least a residual sense of anger, in addition to the disappointment and hurt?

No Pain, No Gain

If I had realised just how busy I was going to be, then I would have chosen a later date for the trip to Athens. But it wouldn't be fair on Rosie to do another trip without her by my side and now, with school breaking up for half-term today, I'm beginning to panic. We only have two days left before we fly out and I've even had to suspend my walks.

What a week it's been. My head has been in a spin. Dad's blood tests came back on Monday and they've adjusted his tablets, so it's yet another waiting game to see if further tests show an improvement. Mum is on edge but trying her best to put on a brave face.

I had a chat with Dr Watkins on Tuesday and now I have to wait for an appointment with a counsellor he feels might be able to help me.

The agency rang, offering me three photographic jobs. I had to turn down two of them, only agreeing to the third one as I don't want them to take me off their books completely quite yet. I agreed to do it on Monday the fifth of June, two days after we get back from Athens. At least I'll have the weekend to catch up with any backlog on my desk.

On Wednesday, I had a Skype meeting with Wendy Philips and her team at *Loving Life* magazine. We bounced around a lot of ideas and I've promised to deliver the first draft by the middle of June. At £900 per article, I can't afford to mess this up and I'm beginning to realise that I've replaced one pressure for another. I might be out of debt, but now I'm mired in deadlines. But soon I'll have money in the bank for a rainy day and that's something I'd long since given up on dreaming about. Having a safety cushion is a big deal to me. It signals the end of the night-mare situation I've had to live with and the start of a life where financially I'm free.

This morning I finalised my report on the cruise and sent it off to *Sun, Sea and Tide's* marketing director. It was an easy one to write, if rather long-winded. I made a couple of suggestions but they were minor things. I've lined up a series of four blog posts covering my experiences on the cruise and at the various ports. All I need to do now is to sort out the photos, insert them and schedule the posts to go out over the next four weeks. I'm thrilled to have some good quality content and photos that really do bring the experience to life.

Harrison heads home today and I don't know how soon to begin reaching out to him. I figure that he'll need a couple of days to catch up and get back into a routine. Secretly I'm hoping he makes the first move with a text to confirm he has arrived back safely and that will re-start our dialogue.

A Magical Setting

Sunday morning, Mum and Dad call around to help with the packing. Well, it's an excuse because I know they both get a little anxious whenever we go away. Mum and I yank things out of the wardrobes and decide what to put into the suitcases.

'What's the weather like, have you checked?' Mum asks, when Rosie refuses to pack a jumper.

'Thirty-plus degrees. Hotter than we're used to and dry. But you will need to wear something warm you can throw over your T-shirt, Rosie,' I remind her. 'It can be chilly waiting around at the airport and who knows what the weather's going to be like on the return flight. We might come back to rain and it's better to be prepared than to feel miserably cold.'

Her head bobs up. 'I'll wear it then as I'm already running out of space. It's going to be hard to fit everything in.'

Mum looks at me and smiles. If Rosie's case wasn't half-full of things to test on her holiday, then she'd be able to fit in more clothes.

'I'll tell you what, give me some of your things and I'll pop them in with mine.'

I go in search of a few items of jewellery, maybe some nice dangly earrings and a necklace or two, just to brighten up a couple of the flowy dresses I'm packing. They roll up well and don't crease, which is the main thing.

'It's nice to see you paying a little attention to detail again, Leah,' Mum sidles up to me as I gather the items up into a soft pouch.

'I've let myself go a bit, haven't I?'

'No, but I'm glad about your new healthier regime as you've lost that gaunt look you had there for a while. Now your skin has a glow and I suppose it's all that fresh air. And maybe the sea air helped too.'

Rosie has disappeared back into her room to fetch something and I feel that Mum has been waiting for the right opportunity to talk to me.

'The cruise reminded me that socialising can be fun. It was nice to reconnect with the old me. It is still there, somewhere – it just got a little buried for a while.'

Mum wraps her arm around my waist and gives me a comforting squeeze.

'I thought maybe you'd met someone interesting on the ship. You have your whole life ahead of you, Leah and we want you to live it.'

What can I possibly say to stop her worrying about me?

'There is someone I'm keeping in touch with but he's already in a committed relationship. He sat next to me on the trip from the airport and we hung around together. I appreciated having some male company and I have to admit it made me think it's time to start enjoying life again.'

I can't tell her about therapy, or the fact that it's the drama in our lives that initially sparked my friendship with Harrison.

'Well, that's a good sign, at least. I thought a luxurious cruise ship might be a very romantic setting, indeed.'

'Right place, wrong guy, but I experienced a sudden glimmer of hope for the future and what might be. Well, that's if I don't mess it up by making the same mistakes all over again.'

'You've come a long way, honey. Now you simply need to channel all of that energy into bringing some sparkle back into your life.'

'Sparkle, eh? Well, I'm not sure I can promise I'll find that in Athens, but we're still going to enjoy every minute of this trip.'

~

I had to pay for the flights myself, although the stay at the prestigious Plaka Kairos International Hotel is free, as are the transfers to and from the airport. Unfortunately, it was a case of grabbing what was available and we'll lose the first morning of our five-day stay to travelling. The flight lands at just after two-thirty in the afternoon. It's about a fifty-minute run to the hotel, so we're expecting to book in at around a quarter to four. Similarly, with the return journey we head back to the airport at eleven in the morning, so we're going to have to pack a lot into the three full days we have in Athens.

The coach journey up to Heathrow airport is a relaxing start to our trip and Rosie is in high spirits. With her head bent over a tourist guide to Athens, she insists on making a list of things we must see. Suddenly my pocket begins to buzz and I drag out my phone to see it's a text from Harrison. At last!

Hey, lady. I'm back home and I invited the parents round. I'd just told them I was at a crossroads and then the doorbell rang. My neighbours arrived and it turned into an impromptu drinks party. They drank the entire contents of my gin bottle between them all. The words whirling around inside my head would have turned the air blue. My stomach was churning the whole time after I realised the moment was lost.

My heart sinks in my chest.

Poor you! I'm devastated on your behalf. Well done for trying, though. Don't let this put you off.

He responds immediately.

The stomach churning might be down to the three Sex on the Beach cocktails I drank. My measuring skills weren't the most accurate and I was feeling very sorry for myself. I seem to have developed a taste for drinks with a kick and it got me through a tense couple of hours.

I hope he manages to work up the courage to hit this head-on again.

Okay, you might have failed this time, but that wasn't your fault. What's the plan, now?

Rosie is chattering away and I stop briefly to look at her sightseeing list, wondering how on earth it's going to be possible to fit it all in.

I suppose I need to catch my breath and try to psych myself up for round two. It's even harder than I thought it would be. You're the wordsmith, can't you help me out? How do I begin this conversation?

Rosie turns to look at me. 'Are you listening, Mum? Oh, is that work stuff?'

She glances down at the phone in my hand.

'Just a friend who needs some advice, darling, sorry. I won't be a minute and then I'm all yours.'

I type quickly.

Keep it simple. Just say you've found someone and tell them a little bit about Ollie. You're focusing on trying to preempt their reaction and I think that's a big mistake. Just be honest. And don't wait too long until you try again because the stress will screw up your head.

'Right, I'm finished. Let's take a look at this list of yours and see if it's do-able.'

~

The driver holding up the card with my name displayed in large letters is very welcoming. He speaks enough English for us to have a stilted conversation. After escorting us to the car he opens the rear door for me and insists on escorting Rosie around to the other side of the car to hold open the door for her too. As we settle ourselves into the back seat, Christos stows our suitcases inside the boot. Closing the doors and sliding into his own seat, he passes us both a bottle of mineral water and asks if we're ready for him to set off. Rosie looks at me and raises her eyebrows, obviously very impressed.

The drive is very pleasant, although we're glad of the air-conditioning as it's meltingly hot. The lightweight jackets we needed back in the UK are consigned to a heap on the seat between Rosie and myself.

I watch as she stares out the window taking in the scenery that flashes by: intermittent rolling countryside interspersed with built-up areas. The beautifully blue sky seems to shimmer with the heat. The sun shines down quite fiercely on the multitude of plants, climbers, shrubs and trees in the fields and gardens we pass. The vibrant and prolific smattering of colours jump out and delight Rosie. She keeps pointing out things that are gone in the second or two it takes for me to follow her finger. For a small part of the journey we can even catch glimpses of the deep, turquoise blue of the ocean as we follow the coastline before, once again, turning inland.

The journey slows as we hit what I assume is the outskirts of the city centre. For the most part, the traffic flows well until we hit a snarl-up and crawl along for a few minutes before we gather speed once more. The graffiti is a surprise, but then what cosmopolitan city doesn't bear the markings of modern-day culture? Beautiful old buildings sit alongside office blocks that have little character to them, merely a testament to the concrete jungle created in the Eighties; then buildings of the Nineties displaying nothing but glass and steel. An eclectic mix for sure but as we get closer to the heart of the city, there it is on the skyline. With the sun starting to sink lower in the sky, brief glimpses of the Acropolis seem to be almost lit up by its rays.

'Look, Mum, look!' Rosie squeals as she catches her first sighting.

The roads are narrower now and the car turns away from the vista of the Acropolis, into a side street. The gentle incline of a long hill stretches out ahead of us, flanked by hotels and restaurants.

'The hotel, it is here,' Christos confirms as the car slows to a halt.

There's a lot of activity with people walking in both directions and cars parked either side of the street. The hotel sits alongside the pavement and I wonder if road noise is going to be a problem. It isn't until we've climbed the dozen or so marble steps and entered the lobby that I realise how big this hotel is; inside, it's refreshingly cool and tranquil. You can't hear any of the noise from the street and as we walk towards the reception desk a man moves out from behind it to greet us, with his hand outstretched.

'Good afternoon. Welcome to Plaka Kairos International Hotel. How may I be of service to you?'

Rosie is doing a 360-degree turn, taking in the grandeur of the open plan reception area that leads into a conservatory. It's taken up by a large dining room and a bar. There are two massive tree trunks spiralling upwards and out through the glass roof. Everywhere you look there are plants and it has the feel of an indoor garden. All that is missing are the birds.

'Good afternoon. Mrs Leah Castelli and my daughter, Rosie. You have a reservation for us?'

He extends his hand with an ear-to-ear smile on his face.

'Ah, welcome, welcome. We are delighted to have you here, Mrs Castelli and hope that you and your daughter have a most wonderful time sampling the delights of our city. My name is Thanos Fotopoules and I am the general manager of the hotel.'

A porter is already wheeling away our suitcases and heads towards the lift. Mr Fotopoules steers us towards the desk and I fill out a short form while he sorts out our door entry cards.

He's very chatty and insists on giving us a handful of brochures, a walking map of the city and then he runs through some of the facilities available in the hotel itself.

There's a rooftop terrace with a bar, several hot tubs and a sun deck. It has amazing views out over the city, apparently. It's a lot to take in and he doesn't keep us long before personally escorting us across to the lift and up to our room on the sixth floor.

Hotel corridors are the same everywhere and this one is no different. We follow him down a long, narrow passageway. Admittedly it is sumptuously carpeted, but with little by way of decoration. It's well maintained but a little dim with only the inset lights above us imitating daylight. He stops, inserts a key card into a door, swinging it open and standing back so we can enter. Rosie bounds in ahead of me and she stops in the doorway, so I have to encourage her inside but I can see why.

In front of us on the other side of two king-sized beds are wall to wall sliding glass doors looking out onto a balcony. But beyond that, with no obstruction whatsoever to the view, is the Acropolis in all its glory. It's so close it almost doesn't look real.

'There are cranes, Mum. Is it falling down?'

I start laughing and Mr Fotopoules' smile hikes up a centimetre or two.

'No, darling. It's being restored to help preserve it for the future.'

'The bathroom is in here—' Mr Fotopoules pushes open the door to the bathroom which is surprisingly spacious '—and the minibar is inside the wardrobe, as is the safe. If there is anything at all you require please do not hesitate to contact reception by dialling zero. The desk is manned twenty-four hours a day. When you are ready for the tour of the hotel, please to ring reception and a member of staff will show you a variety of rooms and all of the facilities.'

'Thank you so much, Mr Fotopoules. This is a delightful room and that view is one we'll remember forever.'

'Thanos, please, I insist.' His broad and extremely proud smile can't physically expand any further and he seems delighted with our reaction. As he exits and closes the door behind him, Rosie spins on her heels and throws her arms up in the air.

'I love it here, Mum. I'm glad you're so clever and you make me so happy.'

She whizzes over to throw her arms around me and I fight to stop a tear forming in the corner of my eye. I take in a deep breath to calm myself. After all this girl has been through, she can still count her blessings and that touches my heart.

Going Greek

By the time we've had a quick chat with Mum and Dad, freshened up and taken the lift down to the reception area, it's nearly half past five. Walking past the desk I give a nod in the direction of Thanos, who immediately comes across to us with purpose in his footsteps.

'Ah, Mrs Castelli and Rosie, don't you look charming this evening.'

Rosie blushes, feeling rather grown up with her hair pinned neatly into a French twist.

'*Efharisto*,' she says and Thanos nods and smiles, clearly impressed. The truth is that we both only know three Greek words – thank you, good morning and good afternoon. However, I'm proud that Rosie had the confidence to have a go.

'Mrs Castelli, I know you are here to report on the hotel but we also have two villas only a short distance away. We were wondering whether you would be willing to do a special feature on these properties also? They are soon to become available as holiday rental properties, having been let out on a long-term contract which is due to end in

August. I appreciate this will encroach on your time here in the city, though.

'Naturally we would provide a car and a driver for the visit which would take no more than a few hours. In return, we would like to offer you a week's free accommodation in one of the villas at a time convenient to yourself. Please give this some thought and let me know on your return, yes?'

I think a little trip away from the city is an unexpected, and welcomed, bonus.

'That would be delightful, Thanos, thank you. I don't need to think about it at all. We can easily fit that in and I'm sure Rosie's sightseeing plan has a little flexibility, what do you say Rosie?'

She looks up at me and nods. 'Everything is close by, Mum and I know how you like walking. Do the villas have a pool?'

I'm a little shocked by her response but Thanos doesn't seem fazed and looks at her, taking the question most seriously.

'But of course! I also believe that Dr Preston who is currently in residence in one of the villas has his young daughter staying with him. I'll ring him directly to make the arrangements for your visit tomorrow morning, if that is agreeable to you ladies.'

'That will be perfect, we'll look forward to it,' I confirm, thinking this is rather an exciting excursion. We get to wander a little further afield and see what it's like in the countryside.

'Are you off to dinner now? There are plenty of wonderful restaurants in Plaka and lots of shops.'

Rosie's eyes light up.

'We are and thank you, Thanos. Rosie has the route all planned out for us.'

As we head away from the hotel Rosie seems confident reading the map and she announces that we need to turn left, retracing the route the taxi followed a couple of hours ago.

'It's left again, here, Mum, then this should lead us up to the old part of the town. If we went straight on instead, it's only a short walk to the Temple of Zeus.'

'Ah, we passed it in the car but I wasn't entirely sure that was what it was. I'm relieved we can do our sightseeing without having to worry about finding transport.'

I guess the time she spent poring over the guidebook on the coach gave her a real sense of direction. That's quite impressive for a nine-year-old.

Rosie is right and it isn't long before we cross a side road and enter a much wider street that leads up to a square. On the right-hand side it's all restaurants, each fronted by their own individual outdoor dining areas. The tables are covered with brightly coloured tablecloths, matching sunshades and cushioned chairs. The general hubbub of noise grows as we move further along the street and suddenly, to our left is a huge, state-of-the-art building; but it's partly obscured by tall metal gates.

'Rosie, I think this is the new museum but it looks like a rear access point. We must be able to see this from our balcony but we were fixated on the Acropolis up on the hill behind it.'

'We are going to visit the museum, aren't we, Mum?' she looks at me with eager eyes.

'Of course, darling, but for now let's focus on finding something to eat and then we can have a wander around the shops.'

We head in the direction of the main thoroughfare which feeds into a large square with trees and various shrubs. I recognise the heady perfumed scent of jasmine and spot the rich red and pink flowers of spiky-leaved oleanders. Birds dive in and out of the trees in a constant stream as they chase each other off the branches. Around us the air is filled with the sounds of chatter from people sitting outside eating and music from a busker in the square.

'This is Plaka, Rosie, the old part of the town. Isn't it vibrant?'

We stand side by side, watching people pass by and soaking up the atmosphere.

'Greek music is happy music, Mum, isn't it? And everyone is smiling.'

It's true; surrounded by such a wildly contrasting blend of the old and the new, it couldn't be more unique. The museum is a brave and bold statement, an icon of modern times and with a slight turn and tilt of the head a reminder of ancient Greece is a glorious comparison.

'Come on; the other side of the square leads off into side streets packed full of interesting little shops and stalls. I can see the first of them from here.'

There's a steady stream of people moving in both directions and we head away from the pedestrianised square to disappear into a series of narrow, cobbled streets. They are filled with bazaar-style shops selling everything from soap shaped in the style of Greek columns and natural sea sponges, to handmade olive wood carvings.

We're standing in one of the world's oldest cities and it's remarkable. The labyrinth of streets is filled with neoclassical architecture; and then, set back with only a tantalising glimpse to be seen from the road, we discover an ornately-decorated Byzantine church.

I pull out my camera and begin snapping away. What attracts me the most are the fascinating doorways to the houses sandwiched in between the shops. Each front door is different in colour, size and design; most have window shutters painted in the most glorious hues you can imagine. Everything has a sun-kissed and often sun-bleached, Mediterranean feel as we leisurely stroll around.

'Mum, look, an ice cream shop!'

A long queue snakes up to a small kiosk. Several of the people walking towards us have cones piled high with a combination of colours and flavours of delicious looking ice cream.

'Oh, Mum. It looks so good.'

'Rosie, you need to eat some proper food before you think of dessert.' I head in the direction of a small, open-fronted café with about a dozen chairs outside, half of which are full. It looks traditional, with no frills and no menu in English.

We amble up to it and see that most of the diners seem to have a sort of pita bread filled with roasted meat, tomatoes and onions, with fries on the side. There's a sign on the wall with a hand-painted plate of food and the word 'Gyros' printed above it.

'What about we take a seat and order two of those? Then afterwards we can join the queue for that ice cream.'

'You're the best, Mum.'

When in Greece it's time to go Greek and taste a little authentic cuisine.

The Promise of a Beautiful Day

When we eventually make our way, rather wearily, back to the hotel Thanos is nowhere to be seen. Returning to our room there is an envelope lying on the floor just inside the door.

He has arranged for us to be collected at nine-thirty in the morning. Dr Daniel Preston has invited us to spend the whole day at the villa with himself and his daughter, Bella. The car will return us to the hotel in the evening. I'm rather intrigued; is he a medical doctor, I wonder?

'It looks like you're going to need your swimming costume, Rosie. We're off to spend the day at a villa.'

She stifles a yawn but despite her tiredness the thought of a pool makes her eyes shine.

'I wonder how old the little girl is? I hope she's my age, that would be rather cool, wouldn't it?'

'Well, considering it wasn't even on our agenda I think we're very lucky to have this experience. Even if she's a lot younger than you I'm sure you'll have fun splashing around in the pool.'

Rosie looks at me, narrowing her eyes.

'I'm a bit old for splashing, Mum.' With that she heads off in the direction of the bathroom.

I turn up the air conditioning, then wander out onto the balcony to wait for Rosie.

Checking my phone, there are no texts, and now it's time to settle Rosie down for the night. Afterwards, I decide to sit out on the balcony to work for a few hours. This wonderful setting is the perfect place to start writing up my first piece on Athens. I want to do justice to the sights, sounds and smells of a place full of wonders. Sitting here, feeling the heartbeat of the city at night, I'm sure it's going to be easy to recreate that in words.

~

We awaken naturally around 6 a.m. and are happy to lie here chatting for a while. Rosie insisted on sleeping alone in one of the king-sized beds and is lying diagonally like a star fish. I figure she's on holiday and if that makes her happy, then she deserves a little spoiling.

'This is absolute luxury, Mum, isn't it? I mean we have the best view and two of the biggest beds I've ever seen, not just one, but two. And wasn't the ice cream wonderful yesterday?'

I smile to myself, thinking that kids don't need much to turn an average day into an awesome one. If only an ice cream cone was the answer for me. It's fantastic being here but it's a place made for romance, too and I've never felt so alone on that front. That's stupid, I know, as I've been alone for an incredibly long time now but meeting Harrison reminded me that you never know who is going to cross your path. He epitomises the man of my dreams in many ways. Kind, considerate, compassionate and trustworthy. Harrison has all of the attributes I'm looking for in a soul mate, except that one thing – sexual attraction. Now if I could just find a heterosexual version of him the search would be over!

You make your own luck, Leah. You can't find a man if you don't begin to open yourself up to the opportunities around you and no one is going to be perfect. You certainly aren't.

I swing my legs over the edge of the bed, then run a hand through my wayward brown curls. As I pass the mirror I catch a glimpse of myself looking rather crumpled and a little bleary-eyed. Not the best morale booster but when I slide back the patio doors and step out onto the balcony, Athens grabs me and fills me with inspiration. The sky is so blue it doesn't look real and although it's still early, already the heat is beginning to rise up from the street below. A few cars are driving up the gentle incline of the hill as locals head off to work.

Life is good and I've come a long way to be standing here. Every day brings the possibility of a new beginning – the ability to dispense with old habits and take on board some new ones.

Rosie is also out of bed and I can hear her singing in the shower. Mum will be up by now and no doubt making

Dad his first cup of tea. I dial the number and she answers after only three rings.

'Morning, honey. How are my girls today?'

'Great and we slept well. Rosie is in the shower as we're heading out for the day as soon as breakfast is over. How are things?'

There's a slight hesitation and I frown. 'I said, how are things, Mum?'

'Oh dear. Well, it seems your Dad is borderline diabetic. Now don't panic. He's been feeling dizzy and he has that flushing thing going on, so now we know why. The doctor says that with a little adjustment to Dad's diet and if he's willing to do a little more exercise, he's hopeful we can normalise his blood sugar levels without medication. This is about prevention, not cure, thankfully.'

I'm relieved, I think. 'That's positive, then, isn't it?'

'It is; forewarned is forearmed and that means we can avoid Dad having to take yet another lot of pills.' I breathe a sigh of relief and then realise Mum will have heard that.

'We don't always talk our worries through, do we Leah? There are so many things that have been left unsaid and I'm beginning to understand that talking is a form of healing.'

I know what she's trying to tell me but now is not the time. Mum is aware of that fact, because she immediately changes the subject.

'Are you having lots of fun? And did Rosie enjoy her first Greek meal?'

'She did. We had *gyros* – sort of roasted meat and *tzatziki* in a pita wrap. She ate every little bit, including the salad because what she really had her eyes on was the ice cream for dessert. We couldn't finish them as they started melting as we sauntered around the wonderful little streets in Plaka. It was just as well, though, as Rosie was keen to venture inside the bazaar-style shops. Most were rather bijou but bursting with souvenirs, clothes and handbags.'

'We do miss you. Oh, there's the front door, I expect it's the postman. It sounds like you have a busy day planned so maybe we'll speak again tomorrow morning. Same time?'

'Same time. Take care, Mum and love to you both.'

The sound of honking horns draws my attention to the street below where a badly-parked delivery van is blocking the road. There's a little arm waving and a couple more honks before the driver jumps back inside and shoots off up towards the top of the hill.

Well, we're going to have time for a leisurely breakfast before the car arrives and I'm curious about where exactly we're going. I glance across at what I can now identify as the angular glass structure of the Acropolis museum, just one street away. It's hard not to let my eyes wander up to the fascinating cluster of ancient ruins undergoing extensive renovations on the top of the hill. Even from here two large cranes are visible, denoting the scale of the work involved. The draw I'm feeling is powerful and in a way, I wish we were doing that walk today. But hey – an hour or two around a pool has its own appeal.

I notice Rosie is taking longer to get ready these days and I guess that's a sign of her growing up. I rifle through the clothes hung up in the wardrobe and decide on a full-length floral, strappy dress that is cool to wear and colourful. After putting Rosie's hair up last night, I'm going to try to do something with my own hair this morning. Maybe I'm getting used to taking a little more care with my appearance again, too. I remember there was a time when I looked in the mirror and liked what I saw.

Rosie's back looking freshly scrubbed and we swap places. When I return she's looking so cute in her denim shorts and a vibrant blue T-shirt. She's wearing her favourite little bracelet, a simple twist of thin leather with a cluster of wooden beads hanging from it. Dad bought that for her on one of their days out.

My life has caused him a lot of grief and upset, pain too, but Rosie has been a gift to us all. I know his life wouldn't have been the same without her.

'Hurry up, Mum, I'm hungry.'

'I'll be twenty minutes, tops,' I reply, deciding that a little make-up will set off this dress perfectly.

A Day Trip to Paradise

When the car appears, I'm pleased to see it's Christos, again. He takes the small bag I packed from my hand with a nod.

'Good morning, Christos, or should I say *kalimera*?'

He smiles, closing Rosie's door after waiting for her to put on the seat belt.

'*Kalimera*,' he repeats.

Once he's settled in his seat I'm eager to know where we are going.

'I'm curious about our destination. All we know is that we're visiting a villa that belongs to the hotel.'

As he negotiates the car out onto the main road he turns his head slightly, glancing at me in the mirror.

'We're heading for Villa Panorea. Laimos peninsula is about twenty kilometres away. Beautiful views, beautiful beaches. You will like.'

'It sounds wonderful.'

The traffic is quite heavy this morning and it takes a

while before it begins to thin out. When we eventually turn off the main road heading away from the centre of Athens, we immediately start to climb. As the road twists and turns we get to see tantalising glimpses of crystal-clear water and a sand-fringed shoreline.

The rocky drop as we travel along the peninsula, gaining height with every kilometre, makes me a little nervous. Now there are areas of scrub and outcrops of rock, separating large, gated properties that can't even be glimpsed from the road. They nestle, hidden behind high walls, sitting within luscious, Mediterranean gardens.

Eventually, the car slows as it turns into a gateway. Christos lowers his window to press the intercom, which is set back into an impressively high, natural stone wall. The gate swishes open gracefully and we get our first glimpse of the grounds.

Rosie is twisting and turning in her seat, eager not to miss a thing. It's a short drive down to the villa itself. The driveway sweeps around in front of a rather elegant water feature. Made up of a huge rectangular-shaped block of local stone, from which a single jet of water leaps probably fifteen feet in the air, it rains down upon the pebbles surrounding the monolith.

As the car draws to a halt, the tyres crunch on the gravelled drive and suddenly the front door swings open. Christos is already out of the car and opening my door; Rosie doesn't wait for him to go around to her side of the car but scoots across the seat behind me.

'Welcome, Mrs Castelli. And I believe this must be Rosie.'

The guy who steps forward is about six foot one, and has a wiry build with broad shoulders and a very individual look for a doctor. He's very casually dressed in open leather sandals, ripped jeans and a loose white cotton shirt. His smile is instantly engaging, enhanced by his gorgeous tan. His dark brown hair is shoulder length, tucked back behind his ears. He has a close-cropped beard and a pair of sunglasses perched on his head. I take his outstretched hand.

'I'm Daniel Preston and this is my daughter, Bella. Say hello, Bella.'

I try my best to hide the way my heart seems to be jumping around inside my chest as I gaze at the gorgeous guy in front of me. He exudes a genuine warmth that is so tangible it's like a hug.

I ground myself, rather reluctantly, and remember exactly why we're here. Dragging my eyes away from Daniel, I glance across at Bella. She isn't much taller than Rosie, her round little face partly obscured by a long fringe and rather straggly, slightly wet hair that touches her shoulders.

Daniel's handshake is firm and leaves a lingering impression like a tingle on my skin. He offers his hand to Rosie, next, which she takes with a little chuckle. I can see she's delighted to be included and it's a warm gesture. Bella gives a little wave, looking rather subdued but then I'd say she's a year or two older than Rosie. Sometimes kids exude that slightly offhand air when they aren't sure about a situation.

Christos takes his leave, saying he'll return at eight o'clock and Daniel leads us inside.

The stark white of the villa walls is broken up with a series of natural stone panels. The contrast lends a very beach-style air to the overall look. We enter via double glass doors, decorated with intricately patterned wrought ironwork. The hallway is immense and pleasantly cool. A sweeping staircase in the centre leads up to a balconied first floor. The tiles are unusual, consisting of oversized, dark grey marble slabs.

'Welcome to Villa Panorea,' Daniel says, turning to face us. Bella has disappeared.

'This is beautiful and what a stunning location. I'm Leah, by the way. Thank you for the kind invitation, Dr Preston, as I think this was a spur of the moment idea generated by Mr Fotopoules.'

'It's a welcome diversion and please call me Daniel. Wait until you see the views, it's really something. I'll be sorry to leave in many ways.' Daniel makes eye contact and I feel the heat rising up from my chest sending a flush of colour over my face. I swallow hard, wishing I could take my eyes off him but they refuse to budge.

'Um ... have you been here for a while?'

'It will be a year on the twenty-second of August. Here, let me take your bag. Follow me through to the kitchen and I'll make some drinks. Bella, where are you?'

Bella reappears in front of us wearing a bright purple swimsuit.

'I thought Rosie might like to take a swim,' she says good-naturedly.

Daniel looks at me, raising an eyebrow and I nod.

'That would be lovely. She's a very good swimmer and Thanos told us to come prepared to enjoy the pool.'

Daniel carries my bag through to a vast open-plan room at the rear of the villa. As we descend three steps to the lower level the vista in front of us has a shock of blue as the backdrop. From the deep, almost turquoise water of the ocean, to the warm blue of the sky, it's a vision. Wall-to-wall glass doors concertina back and the floor extends out seamlessly, right up to the edge of the pool.

'Bella will show you where to change, Rosie.'

I dive into the bag Daniel has placed on the floor as he turns to walk across to what I assume is the kitchen area. Nothing at all is on view, everything is hidden behind handle-less doors. The shiny white surfaces reflect the dazzlingly blue glow coming from outside, as the sun catches the ripples when the breeze stirs the water.

Rosie seems happy enough to go off with Bella to change and I'm left, facing Daniel's back and thinking that this can't be real. I want to pinch myself and I also badly want to take a photo. Standing here amid the luxury of this unbelievable setting with a guy who doesn't seem to realise the effect he's having on me, is like a scene from a film. If they ever make *The Holiday 2* and Jude Law is otherwise occupied, Daniel could easily stand in for him. Okay, I'm fantasising here, but this tops anything I experienced during my stay on board the cruise ship.

'I make a great cappuccino if I say so myself. Or do you prefer tea?'

I cough, clearing my throat and forcing myself to stop daydreaming.

'Cappuccino would be lovely, thank you. No sugar.'

The coffee machine behind one of the 'press and slow release' doors is worthy of a restaurant. It takes no more than a single touch of a button and mere seconds for the tantalisingly rich smell of roasted beans to reach my nose. He expertly froths milk in a jug and deftly ladles it into the cups, finishing off with a shake of chocolate powder.

Daniel places the two cups on a tray, then pushes the door, which closes as softly as it opened, with a whisper. Everything is shiny, sleek and simple. I find myself wondering where the sink is but Daniel is now walking ahead of me.

'Let's have this out on the terrace so we can keep an eye on the girls. It's great when they're proficient swimmers, isn't it? Kids and water can be a dangerous thing and I think it's important they learn to swim at an early age.'

He's so relaxed and I'm so on edge. I could sit and watch him all day long; something about him is mesmerising. *Come on, Leah, you're here for a reason and this isn't a date.*

'So, you're a travel blogger?'

Daniel sets the tray down on a large glass-topped table, mercifully shaded by a large, cream umbrella. He indicates for me to take a seat as he flops down onto the chair opposite me.

The girls are running towards the pool, laughing and giggling. I see that Rosie has dipped into my bag and retrieved some of her freebies. This time it's a selection of handheld games designed to be used in a pool. Rather cleverly, they are based on being able to navigate items through a maze, which involves a lot of tilting and manual dexterity.

'Yes. I'm here to review the hotel so this is a lovely surprise. I had no idea they owned two villas as well.'

Daniel passes me a cappuccino and I notice there's even a chocolate-covered bean nestling on the saucer, too.

'If you walk over to the other side of the pool and crane your neck a little you can just glimpse the other villa owned by the Fotopoules family. I'm one of a team of four people on secondment here and we're working on a new dig. I opted to stay for the entire year but the others come out every couple of weeks. In between times the other three rooms are let to people working out here on a short-term basis doing field work. Most are lecturers at different universities back in the UK, although we've had a few students working on their PhDs.'

Please don't stop talking; I could sit here listening to you forever. So, he's a doctor of archaeology. He has the palest blue eyes I've ever seen and he's so laid back I envy the sense of being at one with himself that he projects. I'd say he is early to mid-thirties, at a guess.

'Work isn't a chore when it's something you love doing, is it? That's quite a thing, though, to put your life in the UK on hold for a whole year. Obviously, it is a work trip and I'm assuming your daughter is only here for the summer?'

He drains his cup and replaces it on the saucer. I find myself studying his hands; they're large and sturdy. The nails are tidy but he has a few nicks here and there, consistent with digging amongst the ruins, I suppose.

'It hasn't been easy but it's nice to have Bella here for a little visit. It's only for a week, sadly, and then she flies home. Are you happy to leave the girls out here while we do the tour of the villa? Iliana, the housekeeper, is around and I'll ask her to come out just to keep an eye on them.'

'Perfect, thank you.' I savour the last of my coffee while Daniel disappears back inside.

He returns with an older Greek woman, who is wearing a dark grey dress with a white tabard over the top of it. He introduces her but she isn't fluent in English. As I don't have any Greek other than to wish her a good morning, we simply nod and exchange smiles.

As Daniel leads me back inside, Iliana walks towards the edge of the pool. I catch her words, 'You like drinks?' to which she gets an enthusiastic response.

I follow Daniel up the curving staircase, my fingers lightly holding onto the carved wooden bannister. Glancing back down onto the hallway it's grand but in an understated way. It's not overly ornate but crisp, clean lines with no fussiness.

'I love the style,' I comment, worried that Daniel will wonder why I'm so quiet. But it's hard to walk up the stairs behind him and not study his back profile. If Bella is about a year or so older than Rosie, then he probably had her in his mid-twenties.

'If you have any questions, please fire away.'

We step up onto an open, oblong landing with a massive, lantern-style glass skylight above it. He swings open the first door set into the adjacent wall, standing back and indicating for me to enter.

'All four bedrooms are en-suite and have views but only three of them have direct views of the ocean. This is the fourth bedroom and it looks out over the rear garden area. You can get a glimpse of the sea from the far end of the balcony. The en-suite is through there. All of the rooms share the wraparound balcony.'

The décor throughout is very similar. The off-white marble floor tiles run seamlessly from room to room, making the space feel even more luxurious, light and airy. Splashes of colour are limited – a deep grey, lime green and a vibrant, burnt orange. It doesn't overwhelm or distract from the calming ambience. We walk past a separate bathroom and a communal shoe closet, which is a surprise. He apologises before he opens the door to it and explains it's full of dirty boots as that's where all the guys stow their working gear.

Turning the corner, we are faced with another two doors along the back wall which lead into similarly appointed rooms. And the final, master suite is on the far side of the landing. It's large enough to include a sizeable seating area with two comfortable double sofas and a coffee table. The fourth side of the oblong is taken up with the wide galleried landing that looks out over the sweeping staircase and the hallway below.

I notice that only two of the rooms have personal items in them.

'It must feel almost empty with just the two of you here, at the moment.'

Daniel smiles at me with his eyes, rather than with that full-lipped mouth, and I can see he's weighing me up.

'It's quiet, I will admit but I have two other colleagues who come and go. George sleeps here most nights but Aiden is away for a couple of days. There are times when it's been crazy, though and we've had a few people sleeping on inflatable mattresses.' He looks across at me with interest. 'You know, you're not at all what I expected,' he comments without any hint of reservation at all.

'Really? What *were* you expecting?'

'Some hardened hotel inspector, I suppose. I thought you'd maybe strip back the duvets and check that the linen was clean, or wipe a finger around the work surfaces.' He laughs and I realise he isn't serious.

'I don't need to do the finger test, although I have done it a few times in some of the budget places I've stayed in. But at the other end of the market it's more about doing it justice and making it come alive for my readers. How do you describe perfection?'

I'm not necessarily talking about the villa now but Daniel doesn't know that.

'How, indeed?'

The eye contact is like a game of virtual tennis going on between us.

'Let's wander back downstairs as Iliana will be keen to begin preparing lunch,' he suggests. 'We can have a quick wander around the TV room, the laundry, the library and the formal sitting room. Then I think we will have earned a little drink and I don't mean a coffee.'

A guy after my own heart. 'Sounds like a great idea to me. Do you mind if I take a few photos throughout the day? I'll make sure I don't get people in the frame and if I do, then I won't use them on my website.'

'Fine by me. Thanos and his family have very kindly

rented out the villa to us at a massively discounted rate while the project has been ongoing. People don't realise the amount of work still involved in uncovering the yet-to-be-discovered treasures that lie beneath the city. His family are great supporters of the project I've been working on. I'm honoured to be a small part of that and staying here has been a marvellous experience. But all things come to an end and I'll be back home lecturing again in September.'

As we finish the tour, our chatter continues and eventually we end up back where we started. Iliana gives us a nod as she turns to go back into the villa and we stand watching the girls for a moment. They're out of the pool and sitting on a grassy area beneath a gazebo, playing a board game.

'Take a seat. It's nearly twelve and officially almost lunchtime. Red or white wine?'

'I'm easy.'

Fleetingly, I wonder where Daniel's wife is as I watch him walk back up to the house. I sit here, soaking up the vibe of this ocean-side retreat for a moment or two, before getting up and wandering over to the girls.

'Who's winning?' They're engrossed in what they're doing but both look up at me with a smile. The bottle of spray sun protector that Rosie is testing lies discarded on the floor next to them. I'm delighted all the drilling I've done about making sure she doesn't burn is sinking in.

'Yes, we both used the spray, Mum, and Bella thinks it's great, too. This is the deciding game because it's one-all now,' Rosie informs me. 'Bella was ten in April. She lives with her mum, in York.'

Kids can't see anything wrong with asking lots of questions when they meet someone new. And they tend not to hold back on their answers.

'That's nice. York is a lovely place, lots of history there. We visited once, when you were a baby, Rosie. We must go there again sometime.' Why did she say she lives with her mum? Oh, maybe while her dad's away on secondment. Of course.

'You could come and visit.' Bella looks up at me, squinting as the sun is behind me. 'We don't have a pool because we live in a townhouse overlooking the park. Dad doesn't live there now, of course. He lives up near the campus.'

I'm conscious that Daniel could return at any minute and it might sound like I've been quizzing her about him. So, her parents don't live together – hmm, interesting.

'Ah, I see. Are you girls hungry? It will soon be lunchtime.'

'I'll ask Dad if we can have a picnic under the gazebo. It's nice and cool here.'

Well, at least changing the subject worked. I nod, beating a hasty retreat back to my seat. Kids are always hungry so that was a no-brainier. If Bella has been talking about her parents, I wonder what Rosie has told her about us. I hope this doesn't have an unsettling effect on her but there's not a lot I can do now that we're here. At home, everyone knows our situation and it's probably several years since anyone asked her any questions about it. Maybe this wasn't such a good idea, after all.

A Surprising Turn of Events

Daniel steps back out onto the terrace carrying two very large glasses in his hands with a couple of inches of red wine in each.

'Don't let the posh glasses fool you,' he jests as he approaches the table. 'It might look like an expensive wine and it is mellow and fruity, but it was plucked from the local supermarket shelf. Everything looks very different when it's presented in the right way, doesn't it?'

'Absolutely,' I murmur taking the glass from his outstretched hand. I take a sip while Daniel settles himself back down into the seat opposite me. 'Presentation is everything; that's especially true in my line of work. It's the blue skies and the vibrant colours of the flowers that sell a holiday destination. I don't think I've ever posted a photo where it's pouring down with rain because it's all about first impressions.'

We hold up our glasses in a silent toast.

'To that all-important first impression. So, how come

you're here alone with Rosie? Doesn't a working trip like this allow you to bring your husband along? Or is that against the rules?'

I noticed his eyes checking out my left hand just now and probably clocking that I don't wear a ring. A little frisson of excitement stirs in the pit of my stomach. If he doesn't live with Bella's mother then maybe he's divorced.

'My husband and I are separated; it's been seven years now. Rosie and I are used to being on our own.' My voice sounds surprisingly upbeat and I hope he doesn't think I'm being blasé about it.

'I'm sorry to hear that. Bella's mother and I parted ways three years ago. It was always an off-on, fiery relationship from the moment we moved in together. We were both in our early twenties when we first met. If I'm honest, Bella was a wonderful, if unexpected, surprise. Money was tight, though, as I was studying and away a lot on field trips.'

'That must have been difficult. Having a baby turns life upside down,' I admit.

'In fairness, Tricia had to establish a routine where I wasn't a constant factor in it. At first, I thought as time went on having Bella would maybe heal the growing rift between us, but it didn't. Tricia resented the passion I had for my work but I saw it as guaranteeing us a living for the future. I thought I was working for us as a family and that one day we'd get married. I seem to have been the only one labouring under that impression, though.'

The kids are well out of earshot and I nod

sympathetically in Daniel's direction. It's nice to be able to talk candidly with someone in a similar situation.

'Children don't mend a relationship if it's broken; they only add another layer of pressure. Rosie hardly slept until she was about three years of age. If I sat still for more than five minutes my head would droop, literally.'

He laughs, his fingers twirling the stem of his glass as it stands on the table.

'It's a relief to hear someone else acknowledge that. I've always felt a bit ... unfair, thinking that way. Don't get me wrong, life without Bella in it would be lacklustre at best. She reminds me all the time that life shouldn't just be about work, which is why this secondment has hurt a little. But it's an exciting time to be working here and support for the project has never lost momentum.'

Iliana carries a tray down to Rosie and Bella, who are still underneath the gazebo. I hear some excited chatter going on and both Daniel and I turn to watch them.

'Kids are born survivors, aren't they, but that doesn't ease the guilt.' His words have a sad ring to them.

'It's nice that you and Tricia are both still in Bella's life. My husband just disappeared one day and we've had no contact from him ever since. Rosie was nearly two, so she didn't really miss him at first. Then she started school and one day when I picked her up she asked why she didn't have a daddy. That was a tough one.'

Daniel frowns. 'What did you say?'

'I said that some people need time to be alone with their thoughts. That doesn't mean they don't think about us, or that we aren't loved. What was important was that he knew we were happy and that Rosie didn't only have me but she had her grandparents, too.'

He draws in a sharp breath.

'That took a lot of thought on your behalf, I'm sure. And a lot of forgiveness. Are her grandparents a part of her daily life?'

His interest isn't intrusive and I like that he's a man who feels he can speak his mind.

'Yes, and I know I'm very lucky. In a situation like mine you learn to live in fear of the questions your child could ask you at any time. Being caught off-guard the first time makes you understand how important it is to get the answers right. And to be prepared. Especially as there is no right answer other than, in our case, the stark truth that he let us down. I'm still dealing with the fallout from that if I'm being totally honest.

'Thankfully my parents have been there for us, every step of the way. We couldn't have gotten through it without them.'

'And how about Antonio's family?'

'His parents live in Italy. They, too, have had no contact with him. It took a while for Zita and Guido to feel comfortable enough to reach out to me and Rosie. They assumed I'd be bitter and they were embarrassed by his behaviour. But every now and again they send Rosie a parcel and we arrange a chat via Skype. We've been over for a visit on several occasions and it's enough to keep our link alive. They were devastated, though, and they feel they have lost their only son.'

'It's probably as traumatic for them as if he actually died. And have you moved on with your life, or is that a question you'd prefer not to answer? I wondered, because you don't wear a ring.'

Instinctively my right hand reaches out to cover my ring finger, as if searching for the little gold band that I dropped into the rubbish bin the day Antonio left.

'I want to move on. But I'm thirty-one years old and all I know is how to be a mum and a breadwinner. Financially I've had a rough time and I'm only just at the right end of that now. This is my dream job and it's how I pay the bills. Beyond that, well, I'm facing a future that is all new territory.'

Iliana approaches with a tray laden with small plates. We move our glasses as she lays out two linen placemats, napkins and cutlery. The smell of onions, tomatoes and lamb makes my mouth begin to water.

'I hope you like Greek cuisine. We have *dolmadakia*, stuffed vine leaves; this is *tomatokeftedes*, which are fritters; then *souvlaki*, or meat skewers and Iliana's special garlic dip. And a little Greek salad on the side. Please, help yourself, Leah.'

Daniel raises his wine glass to his lips and I watch every single movement. From the way his hand wraps around the glass, to the fact that his eyes close as he savours a mouthful of wine. I notice that the hairs on his forearm are golden brown, in sharp contrast to his deep brown skin. He skewers a *dolmadakia* on his fork and bites it in half.

'Um ... lovely, thank you Iliana.' She bows her head, a little smile wavering about her mouth as I realise she was watching me, watching Daniel.

'Could we have a little more wine please, Iliana?' Daniel asks. 'And maybe a jug of iced water. Thank you. This is delicious and I appreciate you helping out today.'

When she's no longer in sight Daniel leans in a little, lowering his voice.

'Iliana is usually here for a couple of hours each day to look after the villa but when the whole team is around we often pay her to cook dinner for us. It's as good as any restaurant if not better. Thanos kindly arranged for her to be here today to help out. He's keen to impress you.'

My mouth is already savouring the flavourful delights of *dolmadakia*. The rice is delicately flavoured with herbs and together with the yoghurt and garlic dip, my stomach is very happy indeed.

After a leisurely lunch, the girls insist we join them in the pool. It's a bit of an awkward moment but Rosie is aware that I packed a bikini with a chiffon sarong. Eventually I give in and go to change out of my clothes. When I return Daniel is sitting on the edge of the pool in shorts and a T-shirt. I'm rather surprised, assuming he'd want to jump in and swim with Bella, but she doesn't complain.

I'm happy enough to sit alongside him, thankful that I packed my sarong. Rosie insists on spraying us with her sun blocker and we spend a pleasant hour chatting and laughing as the girls do laps up and down the length of the pool.

Mid-afternoon, Daniel suggests we take a little stroll around the garden to discover a shady corner under the trees. The row of sunbeds beckons to me enticingly, perfect for a little snooze now we're all drowsy from eating lunch.

But first he takes me on a stroll past the level below the pool and we stand looking down onto a long, sandy beach that curves away in the distance.

'That's Astir Beach Club. Astir beach is in Vouliagmeni. You can see the long lines of loungers with their rectangular, white parasols stretching out along the swathe of sand. The water here, as you can see, is crystal clear and it's a wonderful place to come for a day out.'

It looks elegantly displayed, rather than the usual haphazard chaos of a beach resort.

'It's a little village,' Daniel adds. 'There are restaurants and various eateries, designer boutiques; you can get a massage or take a walk around a scattering of ancient ruins that are on display to remind you of where you are. If you have time it's well worth a visit.'

'It's something I'll write up in my article but sadly we leave for the UK on Friday morning. Rosie has her heart set on seeing all the local sights which are within walking distance of the hotel. I think it's going to be a rather hectic two days and by Friday we'll be flagging, I suspect and ready for the trip home.'

'So, you'll be sightseeing tomorrow and Thursday?'

I nod my head. He's standing probably no more than a foot away from me and when he turns his head to face me I can feel the warmth of his breath on the side of my cheek. Our eyes meet and suddenly I could be anywhere. Anywhere at all, because all I can register is the intensity with which Daniel is staring back at me.

'Could we join you, perhaps? I've promised Bella we'd

do the tour. I … um, we were going to make a start today but we delayed after getting the phone call, yesterday afternoon, saying you were coming here. When Thanos said you had a young daughter it seemed too good to be true. There's no one here for Bella to hang around with and they do need the company of other kids. Anyway, I know my way around all the ancient sites … and it might be good for the girls to share the experience. You know, save them getting bored when there's only an adult around. What do you think?' he asks.

I feel heady and a little breathless. My heart is pounding and I can only hope my cheeks look sun-kissed and not blushingly red.

'I'd love that … I mean, we'd love that. On the proviso that you allow me to return your hospitality and I foot the bill for the food and drinks.'

His face creases up into a perfect smile. 'You strike a hard bargain, Leah, but if those are your terms then it's a deal. We'll meet you in the hotel reception at nine-thirty in the morning?'

'Nine-thirty it is, then. We'd better break the news to the girls.'

'Prepare for a little squealing and jumping around,' Daniel throws the words over his shoulder as we walk back towards them. They won't be the only ones wanting to do a little happy dance. I'm extremely excited about the next couple of days and suddenly I feel that fate is smiling down on us. Certainly, this is one development I hadn't envisaged.

The Main Attraction

It's a little strange at first, setting off for a day out exploring Athens as if we are a family of four. The girls walk a couple of paces in front of us, chattering away noisily as if they've known each other forever. It's good to see Rosie so relaxed and happy.

'They're getting on well, aren't they?' Daniel's voice breaks my train of thought.

'Yes. Rosie has had a lot of adult company in her young life and I often feel she's older than her years. Does Bella have any siblings?'

I turn to look at Daniel, letting my eyes linger for a few seconds as a little thrill fills my stomach with butterflies.

'No. It's rough on the kids, isn't it? Tricia and I parted quite amicably after selling the house. I guess it's less stressful when you don't have to go through formal divorce proceedings, you simply divide everything up. I bought a place a stone's throw from the university and Tricia bought a town house near Bella's school. It was a tough decision to say *yes* to this secondment and be away from Bella for so long, though.'

'How did Tricia take it? I assume that normally you see Bella on a regular basis?'

'Yes, most weekends up to that point although there were a few months when that plan went awry. But Bella was having behavioural issues at school and for the first time ever Tricia was the one to encourage me to join the project. The first two years after our split were difficult for several reasons and she thought my absence from the day-to-day workings of their lives for a year would allow Bella to finally accept our situation.'

He shrugs his shoulders, like most single parents accepting that you make decisions based on what you think is the right thing to do. Whether that turns out to be the case, is another matter.

I see that Rosie has the map in her hand, but I notice she isn't using it and we retrace our steps from Monday evening as we head towards the Acropolis. As we pass the entrance to the new museum I turn to look at Daniel again.

'It's an amazing building and a huge surprise, isn't it?' I say. 'So modern and yet cleverly tied in with the past with touches that show the thought that has gone into the design.'

He smiles across at me and we stare at each other for a second, or two. He seems pleased I've taken the time to find out a little bit about the museum before our visit.

'It's been contentious, to say the least. Now it's fully up and running I think a lot of people can see it's a fitting tribute to the past, while embracing the future. But opinion will always be divided as feelings run deep and always will.

Personally, I think it reflects what archaeology is all about, though; looking at the past to see how it helps to shape the future. But it takes a visionary to create something this insightful. I can't wait to show you around but we need to head up to the Acropolis first, because it's going to be a scorcher again. By lunchtime we'll be more than ready to find a little shade.'

I nod, turning my eyes back to check out the girls, who are giggling away over some private little joke.

'Kids never fail to surprise and delight you, do they?' I speak out loud the words running through my head.

'That's for sure,' Daniel replies and I wonder if he was thinking the exact same thing.

As we start the long, gentle climb on the wide, pedestrianised street leading up to the entrance to the Acropolis, I pull out my camera and begin snapping away. To the right of us the heady perfume from a cascade of jasmine in flower makes a perfect picture. Then I scan back around taking a few snaps of the girls. To the left-hand side the houses front onto the wide pavement, which is laid with part-marble, part-stone paving. These are grand houses built from local stone, with wide ornate doors and entrances. Some have wonderful wrought ironwork balconies and beautiful detailing such as stone cornices. Many have ornate gates to the side which hint at secret gardens tucked away behind them. Snap, snap, snap. Each door is completely different and adds immense character making every one unique. As I stop to glance up at the balconies looking out over the thoroughfare, I think about the affluent people who have inhabited these houses over the years. What a view and what a place to live.

'You seem to be obsessed with doors,' Daniel comments, and I stop what I'm doing to fall back in line with him.

'They draw my eye, that's all. I love how each of these houses is so different, the finishing touches giving them their own sense of style. Look at that one with the double doors and the raised, pink marble-clad steps leading up to it. What a grand entrance and so fitting for the Acropolis hill, which surely must have been a desirable address stretching way back in time.'

Here, thankfully, there is little graffiti to spoil the sense of grandeur. I turn to my right, pointing to an area peeking out from amongst the greenery and Daniel follows my gaze.

'That's an outdoor theatre; we'll get a great view of that from up on top.'

The girls are slowing their pace a little, as they have wandered away from the grand, marble pathway. They meander in and out of the shrubs and small trees abutting the gentle slopes to our right. The shady pathway runs parallel to the street. I catch a brief glimpse of some stone ruins nestling among the trees, but walk on past, eager to start the real climb we have ahead of us.

The slope of the path beneath our feet is now beginning to bite a little on my calf muscles. Daniel steers us across onto the grass verge and we, too, begin following the smaller path that is now winding its way around the bottom of the hill. It begins to peel away from the main pedestrian area. A large sign indicates that it leads up to a car park.

'Mum, there are some cats wandering around over here. We've seen four already,' Rosie calls out, sounding concerned.

Daniel immediately explains the situation. 'There are a lot of cats in Athens, Rosie. They breed in the wild and don't really belong to any one home, as they do in the UK. The climate is kind to them all year round and they visit their favourite places where they know they will be fed. Sometimes a house will have two or three cats who visit them daily and that's how they prefer to live.'

I keep my voice low. 'I've read about that and was rather hoping Rosie wouldn't really notice it was any different over here. It must be really sad to witness when a cat is sick and doesn't have anyone to take care of it.'

Daniel and I exchange a wary look.

'There are volunteers who get involved and local animal welfare groups. There's no threat of rabies, or anything like that. The cats still mark out their territories and the ones who live up on the hill will each have their own domain. But people are very good about feeding them and most manage to find more than enough to eat. It's not quite as bad as you might think.'

I just hope Rosie doesn't start getting upset about it, as to her they should all have a home and someone to take care of them.

This path is rather pretty, the trees providing some welcome shade from the sun. The lower slopes are quite green in comparison to the stark, pale stone walls and buttresses at the top of the hill, beneath the plateau. As we walk, birds skitter in and out looking for morsels to eat amongst the shrubs.

'The cluster of ancient buildings on top of Acropolis hill have extensive views; very handy for spotting invaders.' Daniel jokes with the girls now we've finally caught up with them. He begins to explain the purpose of this incredible building feat. 'You can see how steep this hill is as we begin the climb just up here. We need to take care on those steps, girls, and watch your footing as the marble can be a little slippery in places. The monuments show the splendour and incredible wealth of Athens during the fifth century. This was a Herculean task and it would have been dangerous work for the people involved.'

Rosie spins around. 'What does Herculean mean?'

Daniel glances across at me and smiles, then rests his gaze upon Rosie.

'Sorry, Rosie. Hercules was a Greek hero and the son of Zeus. Hercules was famous far and wide for his great strength and he was even stronger than many of the Greek gods.'

'They held the first Olympic Games here, didn't they Dad?' Bella chimes in.

Daniel looks pleased. 'Yes, Bella, they did. Hercules' father was known as the Olympian Zeus. In ancient times, this was also regarded as a sacred place, so imagine how many people have travelled this very path.'

Daniel has a way of making historical facts interesting and the girls seem to be lapping it up.

'Before you guys head back to the villa we should all

return to the hotel and go up on the roof terrace. You get an amazing view of the hill from there.'

Daniel nods, flashing me a smile.

'When you see how steep the drop is around the plateau at the top you realise what an achievement it was to build the temples. We are talking about ordinary people without the benefit of Hercules' great strength, who laboured for years and years. For many it must have been their life's work.'

'But the rich people wouldn't have done any work, would they?' Rosie reflects.

'No. But it had to be a team effort. Imagine the people who sat down with a blank piece of paper and it was their job to design temples fit for their gods. When you see the remains up close you'll understand that it took vision and a lot of wealth to make it happen. We are in one of the world's oldest cities and even today, with modern building techniques making the seemingly impossible possible, these remains are still awe-inspiring.'

The real climb has begun and stretching ahead of us now we take the first in a series of flights of marble steps on our ascent. Hand-hewn paths intercept and lead off either side to create little terraces which give us all a break from the constant climb. Daniel and I stop for a moment to enjoy the view before we catch up once again to the girls.

We're now walking in a tight little group as we dovetail in behind the snake of people making their way up to the entrance.

At the top of the steps we reach an open area that has

a gentle slope to it. That too is mostly covered with marble slabs of varying sizes. Several large groups of people from the coaches in the car park below are congregating ready for their tours to begin. But there are lots of families, back-packers and couples all converging on the ticket office. It's less slippery up here but I'm glad we all have rubber-soled footwear.

Once the tickets have been purchased. we head towards the entrance to the site itself. We enter via large, double gates and from here on there's nothing at all to obscure the views. We are, at last, climbing the pinnacle of the sacred rock.

'It's busy already,' I remark as Daniel tells the girls to make sure they stay in front of us at all times.

'I think we timed it just right, as once those coach parties set off that's quite a mass of people.'

The route ahead has the effect of funnelling the stream of visitors as it narrows. The steps are wide enough for people to pass on either side. There is a handrail, but this is a hill which is beginning to feel more like a mountain to me, as we climb. You don't have to look far to see the rocky edge falling away steeply, even if the sheer drop is a very safe distance from the public pathways. The gentle breeze does help, but the sun is already shining mercilessly down upon us. With no shade at all, I can't help but think that Daniel was right and at noon it will be unbearably hot. That's obviously why people head up here early in the morning or, I suspect, towards the tail end of the day.

We climb up onto a rather crowded, flat area before the

next steeper set of steps begin, which are much narrower. With quite a volume of people either stopping to look at the views or chatting, we literally steer the girls carefully through the crowd. Others have stopped to take photos and it is a little harrowing from my perspective, with narrow ledges and some very irregular-sized steps. My legs wobble slightly as my fear of heights begins to take over. Fortunately, I follow Daniel's lead as he grabs Bella's hand. I'm relieved to hold onto Rosie as we climb the steep, almost vertical steps on the next part of our journey.

Rising high above us are the majestic columns of the gateway to the site. I'm trying my best not to show the mounting anxiety I'm feeling. Knowing that the higher we climb, the quicker the drop behind us is increasing, doesn't help matters. I try not to dwell on how I'm going to deal with it when the time comes to retrace our steps. Looking down as we descend isn't going to be quite as easy as the upward climb. Daniel seems to sense my discomfort; when we hit the top step it begins to level out as we walk beneath the towering stone structure. He hangs back so that Rosie and I can go on ahead. I give him a very grateful smile.

'It's huge, Mum,' Rosie sounds awestruck and I agree. The site is much bigger than it looks from ground level.

We are now on the vast open plateau. I feel happier up here, able to forget the steep drop because of the size of the sprawling site in front of us. We all turn to Daniel, expectantly.

'The word *acropolis* is Greek for the highest point. Over there is the temple of Athena Nike and in the centre is the mighty Parthenon. Beyond that is the third main temple, named the Erechtheion. All three were built upon the remains of earlier temples.'

Both girls are listening intently, following Daniel's hand as he points in each direction.

'The Persians destroyed the Acropolis in a great battle. You can see the size of the cranes required as the huge blocks of stone and marble need to be lifted into place. The reconstruction work is nearing completion but it's been a long project.'

Some of the gigantic pillars of the Parthenon look like a jigsaw puzzle of pieces, a mixture of old and new materials.

'When did work here begin?' I ask, marvelling at the time and money that has been spent on the reconstruction.

'In 1975. All of the remaining and very valuable artifacts, the things that were on display inside the temples, are on show in the new museum.' Both girls seem fascinated, although it had crossed my mind that maybe it would be a little too much history for them.

'Will it fall down again?' Rosie looks up at Daniel, awaiting a reply.

'Hopefully not, Rosie. The columns have been rebuilt using titanium dowels, which is one of the strongest metals in the world.'

She looks impressed, turning to follow Bella, who heads off to take a closer look at the Parthenon sitting proudly, slightly off-centre on the plateau.

'Don't wander off too far, girls,' Daniel calls out. 'Make

sure you are always in sight of us as there are a lot of people heading this way.'

'Okay, Dad,' Bella calls out.

'It's breathtaking. Even seeing it with my own eyes, it's like witnessing the impossible. Like the building of the pyramids, feats of engineering that even today would be a challenge. And look at that pillar, I mean so many fragments to piece it back together.'

Daniel nods in agreement.

I stand, head tilted back, and zone out from the people and the chatter going on around me. This was built by people whose gods inspired them to build a lasting testament in their honour. Of gigantic proportions, standing here we are tiny in comparison to the size of even one of the columns. Suddenly I understand what it's like to live in the land of giants; all those mythological tales you learn about at school which fire the imagination.

'It's impossible not to be overwhelmed, isn't it? This is history revealing itself in a very powerful way. It reminds us that what went before was more complex and intriguing than we can often imagine. The words on the page can never do those tales justice, can they?'

Daniel and I stare into each other's eyes for a moment, before I reluctantly look away to check on the girls. They're chatting to a small group of children who have gathered in front of the Parthenon and are looking up at one of the enormous cranes. A guide seems to be explaining how the large pieces of marble are manoeuvred into place.

We continue to stand side by side, watching the girls

and letting the undeniable sense of presence this site has, wash over us. I can see the excitement Daniel feels reflected upon his face. I'm glad his focus is firmly on the majesty of the temples, as it allows me to study his side profile. He's kind, gentle and loving to his daughter Bella. The other passion within him is the sense of connection he feels with history and the desire to bring it alive for generations to come.

It turns out that the Acropolis isn't the main attraction here after all – it's Daniel.

The Magic of Athens

I feel like I've had an epiphany. Are the Greek gods to blame, I wonder? In a place where emotions have always run high – love and hate, ambition and jealousy – is there a mystical power that is reaching down inside of me and forcing me to face up to my feelings?

We are standing on a mountainous rock, with a panoramic view all around us. All you can see is blue sky and a smattering of cotton wool clouds, until you look down on the city below. Is this the nearest to heaven you can get? I wonder if that's why the ancient Greeks chose this place to build their temples, despite the difficulties they had to overcome. Did they feel they had been favoured by the gods to have been given such a wonderful place and that they were, therefore, simply fulfilling their destiny?

Daniel is staring at me; clearly, he's posed a question and is waiting for my response. I pull myself back into the moment, hoping my smile masks a sense of shock as a wave of longing washes over me. Longing to connect with someone and feel loved.

'Um, sorry, what was that you were saying?'

'Shall we head over to the walled area so we can check out the open-air theatre?'

Once again, my foot slips a little on the uneven ground and Daniel catches my arm.

'Hey, steady there. Girls, time to move on. It's getting hot and we need to head back down, shortly.'

Daniel helps me over some of the larger, quite slippery surfaces of marble paving until we're on a swathe of gravel as the path curves around to the rear of the mighty Parthenon.

'Thank you,' I manage to utter, as he lets go of my arm. All I can think about is that my skin is continuing to tingle from his touch.

The girls join us and we make our way to the, thankfully sturdy-looking, wall which has been erected along one side of the plateau. I spin around and begin snapping away while Daniel and the girls look down over the edge.

'This was once a military fortress because you can see out over the land and the sea, which is an advantage when it comes to being invaded. In later times, though, it became a religious centre dedicated to the worship of the goddess Athena.'

'What's that, Dad?' Bella asks and I turn to join them at the wall.

Peering over, I see that it's a sheer drop but because there's a reasonably-sized ledge the other side of the wall my vertigo seems to be in check. We're looking down onto the ruins of an amphitheatre. The sound of a team of men using petrol strimmers to cut back an invasion of grass and wild flowers, carries on the breeze.

'That is the theatre of Dionysus. It's what remains of the outdoor theatre that could originally seat 17,000 people for each performance. Politicians and the rich would sponsor dramas and comedies, commissioning the famous writers of the day. See how the seating is curved in rows facing the stage? There's enough of the stone and marble remaining to see the shape it took. This is an amazing view, isn't it?'

The girls nod. 'So, it was like going to the cinema, but outdoors,' Bella adds.

'Exactly.' Daniel reaches out and touches his daughter's shoulder, giving it an affectionate squeeze.

I look back down towards the town and point.

'Rosie, look! That's our hotel. You can just make out the roof terrace with the hot tubs in the corner. When we get back we'll take Daniel and Bella up there and we can all look back over here to see where we were standing.'

'We should begin making our way down, ladies. There's a restaurant at the museum on the first floor, if you look over there. See that large canopy? It's shady and cool; a pleasant area with wonderful views. Perhaps we can stop for lunch before we tour the museum itself. What do you think?'

The girls are enthusiastic and I nod, clasping Rosie's hand as we follow behind Daniel and Bella.

I wonder what my dear girl would think of my churning emotions? Is it possible to feel so attracted to someone you hardly know? My legs are wobbly but I don't think it's the vertigo this time, it's the endorphins rushing around my body. It's a long time since I felt this alive and it's scary.

~

Having climbed up to the highest of heights, when we reach the museum and descend the two tiers of steps leading us down onto the walkway to the entrance, I immediately know I'm in trouble. Vertigo threatens to steal the floor from beneath my feet as my legs almost give out. From the first step onto the walkway beneath the concrete canopy, which is held up by a series of massive stone columns, the glass floor beneath my feet seems to almost disappear. I'm horrified as it gives me a sensation of being drawn downwards, as if I'm literally in danger of falling through it.

The archaeological dig below ground level is truly wonderful but my stomach is doing involuntary somersaults. It's as if I'm on a rollercoaster and being flipped around at speed. And yet I'm as still as a statue, unable to move. There's no dignified way I can get myself out of this and Daniel flashes me a look, instantly recognising I have a problem. He grabs my arm and almost pushes me sideways onto the adjacent strip of solid paving slabs, leaving the girls standing in the queue.

'Are you okay?' He leans in to whisper into my ear, gently letting go of my arm as my legs begin to firm up beneath me. 'Look, we'll stay in the queue and you walk along here and rejoin the queue once we reach the entrance doors.

The glass finishes there, so you'll be fine. We'll head straight up in the lift to the restaurant.'

I smile, weakly, feeling like a total idiot and worried it will unsettle the girls. Thankfully, looking across at them they haven't even noticed we're not there and are still chattering away to some children standing in front of them.

'Go on, you'll be fine.' He turns to head back and I try to compose myself so I can stroll along looking reasonably calm and collected.

Once inside the great entrance hall, I feel a lot happier and Daniel insists on paying for the tickets, before we walk across to the lift.

'You'll love the outdoor eating area, it's a wonderful place to sit and have lunch. It's located on the overhang that projects out over the entrance walkway. A great area for the girls as well, as there's plenty of space and fabulous views.' He gives me a reassuring smile and a warm sensation begins to rise up within me. I try my hardest to ignore it and drag my eyes away from him.

My phone pings and I yank it out of my pocket. It's a text from Harrison. I pop it back into my pocket without reading it, hoping he's okay but knowing that my head is all over the place and I can't deal with it right now.

The lift doors glide open and there's a significant level of background noise as we approach the restaurant. Daniel steers us across the main seating area and out through double doors onto a large terrace. In the centre there's an oval-shaped canopy supported by modest metal posts all in silver grey, which contrasts nicely with the dark grey marble floor. He's right, it is wonderful up here, the covered seating area providing a welcome relief from the sun's rays. The whole area is enclosed by a wall with a chrome metal safety rail above it. It doesn't obscure the views at all, but makes it a worry-free area for kids to wander and run off a little steam. There are a few children of varying ages chasing each other around as their parents sit and linger over a leisurely lunch. The atmosphere is relaxed, with waiters and waitresses coming and going, while the diners are content to sit back and enjoy the ambience.

Whichever way you look there is a view, whether you are seated, or standing. From this elevation, the Acropolis is directly above us. Like a miniature, so close you almost feel like you could reach out and touch it.

Daniel and I find a table and sit down, letting out a grateful sigh in tandem, which makes us start laughing.

'Tiring, isn't it?' he comments, his eyes following the girls as they look down over the guard rail, watching the activity in the busy streets below.

'Yes. It might take a little while for my feet to recover. It was wonderful though and thank you for making the history come alive a little. Guidebooks are helpful but they're so wordy it can often make it hard going. The girls enjoyed it much more than I thought they would and that's quite something. It's all a little overwhelming when you get that up close and personal with something so mind-blowing.'

He purses his lips, nodding his head. 'You connected with it, that's great.'

I suddenly feel distinctly awkward under his gaze, so I pick up the menu and Daniel follows suit. I connected all right, I just hope he doesn't realise with whom I felt that incredible connection.

We order soft drinks and a selection of dishes so there's a choice for the girls. We end up having to call them back to the table to eat, but they don't sit for very long before asking to be excused.

'Those boys are from Australia, Dad,' Bella informs Daniel. 'That's a long way to come, isn't it?'

'It is,' Daniel agrees, trying to hide the smile that's beginning to play around his lips. The girls race off without a backwards glance.

He chuckles. 'You have no idea how very grateful I am to have your company. Bella and I have been through a tough year in our relationship. It made me doubt that being involved in this project was the right decision to make. Even though it's been an incredible experience to lead a team of extremely enthusiastic and committed volunteers. I've been back to the UK twice to spend a couple of days with her but other than that we've only talked on the phone from time to time. Suddenly, out of nowhere she started to get it into her head that when my work here was done I would be going back to live with her and her mum again. I had to explain that wasn't going to happen and she became very sullen. That all kicked off at Christmas.

'Our relationship since then has been difficult and she seems to think it's my fault her mother now has a new man in her life. They recently announced their engagement and

Bella was shocked, even though Tricia had sat down with her and talked it all through beforehand. So, I had no idea how successful this visit was going to be. I was dreading the thought that Bella would still be blaming me and wouldn't really want to be here. It's a difficult age anyway, as every time I see her something has changed and it reminds me how fast these years fly by.'

He looks sad, as if he feels he's losing her and not simply her childhood as she grows. I sit watching him, happy to be his listening ear. It reminds me of sitting with Harrison, knowing that talking to a stranger had a curiously safe feeling about it.

'I wondered whether she had forgiven me for disappointing her and your unexpected visit came at just the right time. Bella arrived here two days ago. We were cautious around each other at first and communication was a little strained, to say the least. I was worried about doing or saying the wrong thing. But look at her now. Suddenly everything is back to normal as if she understands that life goes on, even when we have no choice but to accept change. Whether we perceive that to be good, or bad.'

His words tug on my heartstrings as a mum. The last thing a parent wants to do is cause an upset in their child's life but the nature of living is that circumstances are seldom perfect.

'It's a little easier for me, I suppose. Rosie has no connection with her father and can't even remember him being around. She's happy with our life and doesn't realise what she's missed out on. But knowing she deserves to have two parents to love her breaks my heart. The pressure on you must have been immense but now, I suppose, knowing that Bella accepts the situation means you can all move on.'

Daniel nods his head, showing no signs of regret – merely relief.

'Bella's mother, Tricia, is in Greece now, with her fiancé, Evan. They're taking a little time alone together after dropping Bella off to spend a week with me. After that I think they're heading to one of the islands for a few days before flying home. I've come to realise that some people are better off on their own. Sadly, I'm one of them and maybe my chosen career hasn't been conducive to a normal lifestyle, anyway. Tricia hated it when I was away on field trips.

'But I'm lucky to have Bella in my life and when she flies home I hope we can get back to talking regularly on Skype. It hurt like hell when she stopped calling me. Still, another two and a half months and I'll be back in York. Hopefully I can agree regular weekend access so that Bella can come and stay over. I have quite a bit of catching up to do before the new academic year begins but I'll have plenty of time to spend with Bella. Besides, it will allow Tricia and Evan to have some alone time together which seems only fair.'

He's free as a bird ... the words pop into my head and I try not to let the little lift it gives my heart show in my reaction. My nerves, however, are jangling like wind chimes.

A Mortal Hero Amongst the Greek Gods

We head up to the third floor in the lift, to view the Parthenon gallery. So far, so good and the pristine floor beneath my feet is at least solid material with no hint of glass.

There's a continuous bench-style seat running along the exterior wall, above which glass panels extend up to the ceiling. I realise this gallery is what we see lit up at night from our hotel balcony.

'Notice how the concrete core of the building makes the perfect surface on which to hang the heavy artifacts. This is the home of the Parthenon marbles, as they are often called. They are *metopes* which simply means a series of marble panels that adorned the outside walls of the Parthenon. Many of the ninety-two scenes depicted were of battles. Some were destroyed, fifteen are on display in the British museum and what you see here has been recovered from the site,' Daniel explains.

We follow Daniel as he moves on.

There's a lot to see and the girls wander around, having the odd giggle over some of the statues, many without arms, some without heads and others merely body parts.

'Do you want to hang around here and I'll whizz the girls around the second and third floors?' Daniel gives me a hesitant look.

'Oh no. There are more glass floors, aren't there?'

I had kept my eyes firmly focused on the short route from the lift to the restaurant and then back to the lift, to come up to the fourth floor. It was bad enough that the entrance to the restaurant was on a mezzanine. It hadn't totally escaped my notice that it seemed to hover in the air, nothing but a wall to wall glass panel making an almost invisible barrier to the huge drop below. I feel extremely foolish. *I can do this*, I tell myself. 'No, I'll be fine.'

'There are wide expanses of glass floor panels so you can see down through the building and there's no way to bypass that completely, I'm afraid.'

His look is apologetically sympathetic.

'I'm sure I can grit my teeth and get through it. After all, this is an exciting experience and one I shouldn't miss.'

I hope that sounds convincing because I have grave doubts, but I can't set a bad example for Rosie. I usually manage to hide my fear by avoiding putting myself in this sort of situation. Ironically, this building is, in a way, my worst nightmare and that was something for which I wasn't prepared. That will teach me to skim when I'm doing a little research. 'Let's do this!' I say, sounding way more confident than I feel.

We bypass the lift and head towards an escalator and while the area at the bottom has a solid floor, the width of the walkway ahead – literally, wall to wall – is made up entirely of glass panels. They seem to be held in place with the very narrowest of supports. I swallow the lump that rises in my throat. *All you need to do is step forward, Leah, and don't get tempted to look down.*

The girls are already way ahead of us, looking at the small displays dotted around. They are obviously enjoying the novelty of yet another glass floor directly below the one we're standing on. At the end of the walkway there's a solid floor and a large display area, but I'm still only a couple of paces in and now my legs have totally frozen. My head begins to swim a little.

Daniel is standing a pace or two ahead of me, unsure about what to do when he turns and sees my distress.

'I can't move,' I appeal to him, wondering if I'm going to faint as I try not to look down at my feet and the deep chasm beneath them. He walks back to me, turning to check on the girls, then grabs my hand.

'What can I do?' he asks, seeing that I'm now beginning to panic. My heart is literally pounding in my ears.

The girls are no longer in sight and he cranes his neck to try to catch a glimpse of them, while supporting me as my body begins to quake.

'Look, lean on me and we'll edge backwards until we're off the glass. Then I want you to trust me. There are opaque glass panels around the sides. If we wait until it's clear of people and we walk quickly, we should be able to avoid stepping off them. You can close your eyes. Once we get to the other side, I'll find the girls and then put you in the lift. You can wait in the lobby; there's a café in the reception area.'

I nod my head and Daniel's support is enough to help me begin inching backwards. People are milling around us, unaware that I'm at screaming point. Even when my feet are on the solid floor the cavernous expanse of glass in front of me seems to have drained my strength completely. My eyes aren't fooled by the fact that the narrow track of obscured glass hides what lies beneath it.

'Right, lean up against the wall for a moment and compose yourself. That's better.'

I take a few deep breaths and this time Daniel slides his arm around my waist. It feels so good and I lean into him, feeling the solidness of his body take my weight.

'Okay. Close your eyes and just keep putting one foot in front of the other. I've got you, Leah. Just think of the girls.'

I nod, unable to speak and let my body sink up against his as he moves us forward. It's a long way and it seems even longer with every pace we take. Suddenly Rosie's voice is there, somewhere in front of us.

'What's wrong?' she calls out and Daniel hastens us forward until we're on the other side.

'Nothing, your mum has a little cramp, that's all. Let's head towards the lift. You don't mind having a coffee while we check out the rest of the museum, do you, Leah?' he asks, as if I'm doing them a favour. The girls seem totally unaware of the reality of my situation.

'No—' A cough catches in my throat, which has gone totally dry. 'Take your time. I just need to sit down and rest my leg for a few minutes.'

As the lift doors close on Daniel's concerned face, I sink back against the wall, my entire body trembling. The other three people who piled in after me are busily chatting away, much to my relief.

If I'd come here on my own with Rosie this could have turned into a total disaster. Daniel has rescued me and I felt so safe in his arms; not just from the gaping glass hole beneath my feet, but I felt protected. He was a true hero in every sense of the word. Just thinking about him makes me feel more alive than I've felt for such a long, long time.

~

I sit with an iced coffee, relief beginning to flood through my body as my equilibrium gradually returns to normal. Vertigo is a paralysing fear that grips you like a vice; you cannot ignore it because it's physical, as well as mental.

My hands are still shaking a little as I retrieve my phone to look at Harrison's texts. There are now three of them.

I tried to talk to my parents again yesterday. Another mega fail. I took them out for a drink this time. I eased myself in by talking about the future and change. Then a guy playing a guitar began singing loudly, making any attempt at conversation impossible. Ironically, they thought it was a great night out.

The second one is an appeal.

Are you there? I've wasted another day and I just can't seem to find the right time and place. This is never going to happen. I need help.

His third one is poignant.

Maybe this is a sign that I'm making a big mistake. Anyway, sorry, I forgot you were away. Hope you're having a good time in Athens.

Oh no! He's weakening already.

We're in the Acropolis museum. I've just had a ghastly attack of vertigo. Don't give up. Repeat. Don't give up. This is not a sign of anything other than it's a hard thing to do. The right time will present itself, so relax.

I press send, hoping he hasn't said anything to Ollie. I'm just savouring the last of my coffee and feeling much more like my usual self, when my phone pings.

Ollie has admitted that he doesn't think I'm going to do it. I've tried to explain but I understand how he feels.

Vertigo in a museum? The Acropolis I can understand but I'm scratching my head over that one.

I smile to myself.

Glass floors. Listen, if you don't want to lose him then you need to be strong. When you love someone, hiding that fact from the people who are close to you is living a lie. Don't be a wimp, it isn't your style. Why assume they won't be pleased for you?

I wonder if that's a little blunt but he comes back with an immediate reply.

Okay. I needed that. You're right. I'll stop engineering it and wait for the right moment to present itself. You are having a good time, then?

Text isn't as chatty as an email and I so want to let Harrison in on what's happening to me. He'll tell me if I'm acting like a crazy woman. I hesitate and there's another ping, this time it's an email. There's no point in talking about this via text, anyway.

A great time. Maybe too great. Speak soon, I promise. I will ring when I get back.

I open the email and it's from Jackie Kimberley, the counsellor Dr Watkins was going to talk to on my behalf.

She's offering me a cancellation appointment next Monday afternoon. I quickly type a response saying I'll be there and wonder how I'm going to fit in the photography job and a session in the same day. I'll worry about the logistics the day after tomorrow and just hope I can accommodate both. One thing is for sure, though, this appointment has come at the right time.

'We're all done.' Daniel and the girls walk up to the table with big smiles on their faces.

'How's the leg, Mum?' Rosie asks, coming up and placing her arms around my shoulders to give me a quick hug.

'It's fine. Totally fine.'

Over the top of her head Daniel and I make eye contact for a little longer than is necessary. Is he blushing, or have the girls been making him rush around after them? I think I have my answer when he reluctantly drags his gaze away. My heart skips a beat and suddenly the horrors of the last hour melt away as if I hadn't felt I was about to die.

As Night Descends

We enter the hotel, the girls still in high spirits and Daniel and I rather wearily bringing up the rear.

Thanos is on duty and looks up from talking to a pretty young Greek girl, who is standing next to him. He says something to her, then immediately walks across the reception area to greet us.

'Thanos, my friend. How are you?' Daniel steps forward, eagerly.

I stand aside while they shake hands. 'I'm good, Daniel, thank you, and you?'

'Good. This is my daughter, Bella.'

Thanos bows his head as he shakes hands, briefly, with Bella. He turns, indicating for the little girl hovering around behind him, to step forward.

'May I introduce my niece, Vana.' She steps forward, smiling rather self-consciously but Bella and Rosie approach her, their curiosity piqued. The girls start giggling as they make their introductions. Thanos turns around.

'Vana is staying at the hotel with us while her parents are away celebrating their wedding anniversary. Anyway, what a lovely surprise this is to see you all here! You look like you've all had a good day. I assume you've been sightseeing?'

'We have,' Daniel confirms, casting a glance my way.

'He's been an excellent tour guide, Thanos,' I add.

'Well, you heard it all from the mouth of an expert. Daniel will be sadly missed when he returns to the UK. Much good work has been done.'

Thanos is very proud of his country, as well as his business, and that's wonderful to see. He's so genuinely warm and seems pleased, as well as a touch surprised, to see us all together today. His face is a picture and as we all look at the girls, chattering away despite the obvious language differences, he's clearly delighted.

'Children teach us so much; it warms the heart to see.'

He's right, of course, their curiosity is innocent and welcoming.

'We're heading up to the roof terrace to enjoy the view out over the heart of the city,' I inform him. 'Would Vana like to join us?'

'I'm sure she will be delighted to accept your gracious offer, thank you.' He lowers his voice a little. 'Vana has been a little bored, I fear, without the company of young friends here. It is indeed magnificent at this time in the evening and I will send up drinks for all with my compliments, so please enjoy. Did you drive, Daniel?'

'No. I came by taxi and it will return later. Can we order something simple to eat – maybe kebabs and fries all round? What do you think, Leah?'

'That sounds perfect. We'll have enough time to watch the sun as it slips below the horizon and see the Acropolis and the museum lit up against the night sky. And before I forget, would it be convenient for someone to give me that tour of the hotel early tomorrow morning?'

'Of course. We have five vacant rooms ready and made up. How about I have the housekeeper show you around after breakfast tomorrow? You can then tour the facilities with my deputy manager and ask as many questions as you like.'

'Ah, that's very kind, thank you.'

All three girls are already standing impatiently by the lift, so after thanking Thanos we make our way over to them. They're talking about the highlights of the day and I'm happy enough to stand back and watch Bella and Rosie tripping over each other's words as they tell Vana what they've seen. My highlight is the entire day – even the scary bit, because if I close my eyes I can still remember the feel of Daniel's arm around me.

'Come on, Mum, or the doors will close.'

I step out over the threshold of the lift quickly, following them all as Rosie leads the way. There's a doorway adjacent to the lift marked, 'Hot tubs and decking area'. We climb two flights of steps and then we're finally on the roof terrace. Despite the amazing views there's no real sense of height up here and a sturdy wall surrounds the entire area.

The light is already beginning to fade and I'm surprised to find there is only one other couple up here. We settle ourselves at a large table alongside the bar area, which isn't open tonight. However, it isn't long before two waiters appear with a tray of drinks and lay our table ready for dinner.

Daniel smiles. 'Ah, Thanos has broken out an exceptionally good bottle of red wine for us. I've had the honour of attending one of his family's barbecues and although it was just a regular gathering it felt like a party. I've never met Vana before, though, and I believe he has two brothers I've yet to meet. The Greeks are very family-orientated and it reminded me of my own childhood a little. Now my family is spread out around the country and a gathering rarely happens these days.'

For a man who said he's better off being alone, he doesn't sound so committed to that theory when he talks. And it's obvious he has enjoyed our day out together.

Daniel pours a little wine into our glasses and we toast each other, both keeping an eagle eye on the girls. But they seem to be having a great time together and Vana appears to be teaching Bella and Rosie some new Greek words.

'Thank you for an informative day.' I glance around, checking the girls are out of earshot. 'I'm really sorry about my little problem but I'm so very grateful to you for coming to my rescue. The girls were taking it all in their stride and I would have been truly mortified if they'd realised what was going on. You were great, really.'

He gives me a sheepish look. 'It was nothing. I didn't realise vertigo could be that bad, if I'm honest. You looked petrified at one point and I thought you were going to faint.'

I laugh. 'Me too. The day was worth it, even the tough bits. But it wouldn't have been anywhere near as enjoyable if it wasn't for the company.'

Oh, why did I say that? Daniel looks across at me intently, and I try to present a nonchalant face. It's not easy as suddenly my stomach is doing a little flip again.

'It has been a lovely day, hasn't it?' He speaks slowly, a slight frown creasing his forehead as if he's deep in thought. 'Are you still up for doing it again tomorrow? I promise to keep your feet firmly planted on solid ground and we can do a circular route that will take us back through the upmarket shopping area.'

The girls appear eager to grab their drinks from the table and must have caught the end of his sentence.

'Are we going shopping tomorrow then, Dad? Can Vana come with us?' Bella asks, her eyes suddenly lighting up.

'Maybe, if Vana would like that and we ask permission. Leah and I are just planning out the day.'

'Yay.' Rosie makes her contribution to the conversation. 'It won't be all history though, will it?' She directs her question at Daniel who gives her a wink.

'Tomorrow morning I go home,' Vana says, rather quietly and both Rosie's and Bella's faces drop.

'Aww ... it would have been such fun!' Bella replies, sincerely. 'I'm sorry, Vana.'

'Me too,' adds Rosie, who then turns to look at Daniel. 'Although my feet did hurt a bit today,' she adds.

'It will be quite a walk again, tomorrow. But there will be lots of shops, plenty of places to sit and grab an ice cream and some magnificent gardens to wander through where we can rest for a while. Just to break up the tour of some rather interesting monuments I think you'll also enjoy seeing.'

I hold my breath, wondering what Rosie is going to say next.

'Your dad is cool, Bella.'

Well, that wasn't what I expected but it's a lovely comment, even if it makes my heart constrict a little. The girls wander off again and I look across at Daniel.

'Moments like this it really hurts that she has no father. My dad has been brilliant with her and they have a lot of fun together but I know she's been robbed of an important relationship. How can Antonio have turned his back on her so cruelly?'

My voice is angry and I force myself to take a deep breath to calm down a little.

'I'm sorry, Daniel. I didn't mean to—'

'An apology isn't necessary, really. I find it hard to understand how a man can walk away from his family like that. He's a fool – look at what he's lost. Have you ever tried to track him down?'

It's an honest question but then he doesn't know the full story.

'No. If he wanted to be found he would have contacted his parents, at the very least, but they don't know where he is either.'

I don't want to go any further with this as I have no desire to spoil the remainder of the evening. Luckily, Thanos arrives escorting three waiters bearing trays of food. Behind him is a very serious-looking Greek woman wearing a very smart black dress and matching cardigan. Daniel immediately jumps to his feet and rushes over to greet her. I watch as her eyes light up.

'Demetra, it's so lovely to see you!' They embrace like old friends and Thanos looks on, smiling.

I notice that Daniel has clasped both of Demetra's hands in his, as he would do to someone for whom he feels a lot of affection. He turns to introduce her to me and I stand, reaching across the table to shake her outstretched hand.

'This is Thanos' wonderful wife who supervises the chefs here when she's not tending to her growing family in their wonderful villa.'

We exchange warm smiles.

'My wife and I have a proposal to make,' Thanos steps in. 'We were wondering if your girls would like to join Vana and spend tonight in our vacant, top-floor suite under Demetra's care? It would be great company for Vana and there's an adjoining door between the two large bedrooms. The three girls can share one room as it has two queen-sized beds. An adventure, yes?'

My heart leaps in my chest but this isn't all about the excited look on the faces of the three girls who are staring open-mouthed in delight. Instead, I'm wonder what Daniel is thinking? It never occurred to me we would be able to grab some time alone together.

'Of course, Bella would love that, Thanos and Demetra. That is really most kind of you, my dear friends.'

I nod in agreement before Rosie jumps in for fear of being left out. 'I'm sure Rosie would enjoy that too, thank you.'

Thanos smiles at Demetra and they both seem delighted. The girls are now hugging each other and it takes a few minutes to calm everything down. Thanos and his wife head off to make the preparations for the sleepover with a difference – I mean, a suite! – and we try our best to get the girls to focus on eating some food.

As we take our seats around the table, laughing and happy, the girls entertain us with their constant chatter.

This is what family life should be all about and for a few hours today we've been living it. The fact that here tonight we represent two broken families and a traditional Greek one, is pushed to the back of our minds. The reality is that all three girls are happy and excited at the prospect of the fun night ahead and that's all that counts.

We end the evening standing in a row staring out at the two marvels that were the focal point of our day's activities. This time next week, this will already be a fading memory and that makes me feel even more desperate to capture this moment forever. Life should be full of high points that make Rosie and myself feel as good as we do tonight. Her little face can't hide what a happy day she's had, or her excitement about joining her two new friends tonight. As for me? Daniel, Bella and Vana are new acquaintances whose paths we are crossing very briefly before we head off in different directions.

We all hug as we say goodnight to the girls when Demetra

comes to collect them. She has a pass key for our room so that Rosie can collect her toothbrush and two nighties; one for her and one for Bella. I can see that Demetra will fuss over them like a mother hen. But when they leave the terrace there's suddenly a strange silence hanging over Daniel and me.

'Don't worry, Demetra will take very good care of them all, I promise. I doubt they will get much sleep until the early hours, though. As some point I'm sure they will run out of steam and fall asleep.' Daniel laughs to himself.

And then there were two.

Just Two Lonely People

Daniel and I sit, idling over the remainder of the bottle of red wine, and I muse over the fact that wine has never tasted quite so good. Every mouthful seems to hit the right spot and then I realise it's not the wine at all.

I'm pretty sure that dawns on me at the exact same time as Daniel is starting to come to the same conclusion. We exchange a glance but neither of us says anything.

If he wanted to, would I? Could I?

In the darkness surrounded only by the lights from the other hotels close by and pinpricks of light from homes dotted here and there on the wide vista in front of us, it is calming. Even our own silence is affirming, as if we are both in accord without having to say a word. But still, neither of us makes a move. I want to reach out and touch Daniel so badly it hurts. Instead, I drain the last of the wine in my glass with regret. The night must end and for fear of saying something out of line, I stand, pushing back on my chair to break the spell.

'Well, it's been a wonderful day, thank you, Daniel.'

He pushes his half-full glass away from him and eases himself up out of his seat to stand merely inches away from me. Our eyes lock and before I know it we're kissing. Who kissed whom first I have no idea because, in the end, it doesn't really matter.

He whispers into my ear, 'Shall I call and cancel my taxi?'

I kick myself for not being cool and making him wait for my quiet 'yes' but the decision was made a while ago. I only needed to know that Daniel wanted this as much as I do.

Fearing only that there would be a sense of awkwardness, that's soon dispelled as he catches up my left hand in his and tugs me closer.

'Let's not waste a moment, then. We're child-free and the night is young.'

I laugh, and it seems to echo around the terrace, with a carefree ring to it. Still hand in hand, Daniel gently leads me down the steps and into the corridor, stopping only to make the call. Then we head to my room. My hands shake a little as I press the keycard up against the pad and it stays red. I turn it over and the green light seems to shine out twice as brightly as before.

'I guess it's a go then.' Daniel's voice is soft and sultry as he follows me inside.

It's not quite pitch-black, as high up on the hill the floodlights around the Acropolis are like little stars, jewels in the white stone crown. Between us and it there is only darkness and we stand, hungrily kissing each other in this surreal setting.

Suddenly Daniel pulls back a little. 'You are sure about this, Leah, are you? I can't deny the chemistry between us but two lonely, single parents having an unexpected night off could get a little wild. It's been a long time for me and I think I won't cause offence if I hazard a guess and say it's the same for you.'

Is he getting cold feet?

'It is but hey, don't we deserve to get a little wild and have some fun? The kids will have a great time so let's stop thinking and start doing.'

I throw myself back onto the bed and kick off my shoes as Daniel does the same. We lie facing each other and I'm wondering if I've forgotten what to do. But then he gently raises his hand to cup my cheek.

'You're a beautiful woman, Leah and I'm sorry you've been hurt. I hope you know that tonight is special but to avoid gossip I'll have to speed away in a taxi at 5 a.m. before Thanos is on duty. I'm guessing the kids will stay up so late they will sleep in a bit.'

I place my index finger against his lips to shush him and with the other hand I begin easing my dress down over my shoulders. Immediately I feel the change in him and then it's all action as his hands are eager to explore my body. I'm laughing and struggling to free myself of my clothes. In the end, we can't wait and it doesn't matter that my dress is around my waist and Daniel is still wearing his shirt and boxers. I slide onto his lap and we move in perfect unison, that moment when there's no room in your head for anything else because you are consumed. Consumed by those wonderful endorphins that take you on a roller-coaster ride of sensation. All you can think of is 'don't stop, just don't stop' until you both collapse back on the bed, laughing and breathless, enjoying the afterglow of release.

We lie in each other's arms for a while, listening to the sounds of cars going up and down the street, sending little flickers of light over the ceiling; people coming home from a late dinner, or visiting friends maybe. This is a reminder that we get into our own little routines believing that's how it will always be, but our kids won't always be young. There will come a point when they are independent and as single parents, we have to plan for that day.

'What are you thinking about?'

Daniel rolls onto his side, to gaze at me in the gloomy light. At least he won't be able to see my smudged mascara, and my messy hair might actually look sexy and not totally unappealing.

'That we owe it to our kids to show them by example that we aren't shutting out the world. That life goes on after relationships break up. I think I've focused too much on keeping afloat financially and it's made me shut off some feelings I felt were redundant.'

Oh. Too heavy. But before I can make it clear I'm not aiming that at Daniel specifically, he responds.

'I'm guilty of that, too. It's just easier keeping things simple. Bringing another person into your life isn't simply one little additional thing to accommodate, it changes the whole balance. I'm still figuring out how to parent on my own when Bella is with me. And I haven't had her in my life as much as I should, so I fill that space with work. When I get back to the UK it will be very different. I can only hope I can rise to the challenge and be the sort of dad she needs. But you already have it sussed, Leah, and I admire you for that.'

'Do I?' It's half-hearted and I know it, because I'm coping but that's it.

Daniel gently drapes one arm across me, curling his fingers around my waist, and sliding the other behind his head as if he's thinking. But within moments his breathing changes and I realise he's asleep. It doesn't take long for me to drop off, too and when I next open my eyes the clock shows that it almost 4 a.m. Our positions have changed and we're both on our sides facing each other. The air is a little balmy even though the air conditioning is chuntering away. I'm naked, having cast off everything at some point and having tugged the sheet over me, no doubt feeling exposed and sensing someone next to me. But Daniel is still half-dressed, his shirt open. I decide to let him sleep for another forty minutes before waking him and lie here, fascinated, unable to take my eyes off him.

Even in the twilight, before dawn breaks, I struggle to make out the detail on his face which is a mass of shadows. Instinctively, I reach out to softly, so softly, place my hand on his chest as it rises and falls, almost to convince myself this is real. His skin is slightly cool from the waft of air directed across the bed but as I slowly move my fingers away, fearing I'll awaken him, I almost cry out. So shocked am I by the raised skin of a scar that I can't quite make out, but which extends right down the centre of his chest. At one end there's a slight depression and while it is obviously well-healed, whatever surgery Daniel has been through is serious.

It sends me into a sudden panic. When he wakes up should I pretend I haven't noticed? Should I ask him outright about it? Why on earth hasn't he said anything? He must have realised that you can't get this up close and personal with someone without them becoming aware of it. And then I wonder if that's why he didn't seem too bothered to strip off as soon as our bodies hit the bed.

Inwardly, I groan. Another man with secrets he doesn't feel the need to share. He hasn't lied to me but he also hasn't been totally honest. But then maybe in his mind this unexpected night together doesn't warrant an explanation. Even in the gloom I find myself shaking my head. I regret nothing but honesty is everything to me. If this was the other way around I would have found a way of dropping it into the conversation. Goodness, if it's a problem with his lungs, what if he'd had breathing difficulties in his sleep? Or if it's his heart – shouldn't a person sharing a bed and engaging in sex with him deserve some sort of heads-up in case there's an issue?

My head is in a spin and I roll over onto my back, shrugging the sheet up under my chin, self-protectively. The next time I glance at the clock I'm shocked because it's ten to five and I reach out to gently shake Daniel's arm.

'It's time to move, your taxi will be here very soon.'

He slowly brings himself out of his deep sleep, making those muffled groaning sounds as he begins to stretch out his body. The moment he realises where he is he grins and the soft light from the window glints on the white of his eyes and his teeth.

'Mm ... good morning, Leah. I didn't snore, did I?'

'No. You're a quiet sleeper.'

'How long have you been awake?'

'Not long. It was a shock when I saw the time but you only have a few minutes. I don't suppose the receptionist will know which room you're in.'

He sits bolt upright. 'Oh. Yes. I'd better get a move on.'

He quickly buttons his shirt before leaning over to kiss my cheek, lingering for a moment despite the lack of time. Jumping out of bed, rather regretfully, Daniel stoops to reclaim his jeans and slip into them.

'This isn't quite the romantic ending I'd envisaged to our amazing night. I guess we were both exhausted, but it seems a waste...' I can sense a real hesitation in his voice. He's not happy to walk away so soon and I wonder if we had more time what exactly he'd say.

'I couldn't help noticing—'

The moment I speak he stops what he's doing for one split second and gives me a horrified look.

'I'm sorry, I must go. I'll be back a bit later. Perhaps give me a call when you know what time the girls will be ready.' His hand is already on the door handle but he turns to glance over in my direction. Daniel is clearly unable to judge my reaction, as I'm unable to judge his, in the greyness of the early morning light. 'That was wonderful, Leah, and I hope you thought so, too.'

~

'Hey, Mum how are you both doing this morning?'

Balancing the phone between my chin and my shoulder, I close the laptop, pleased with this morning's work session. Rosie is out of the shower and I waited to make the call. I knew that she would be eager to share the details of yesterday and last night's unexpected adventure, with Mum and Dad. It suits me fine as I'm feeling a little uncertain, if I'm being honest with myself. Being tempted to jump into bed with someone you hardly know is one thing, carrying that through is quite another. And, yes, what I discovered in the early hours has unsettled me and it was certainly a reality check. It reminded me that Daniel and I are virtually strangers, even though there is this overwhelming attraction between us. And then some.

'We're off to the garden centre this morning. Dad's on a quest for more colour in the borders.' She sounds happier today and content. I'm assuming this means that she feels he's making some progress with his latest health scare. 'How was your first day of sightseeing in Athens?'

Rosie is standing next to me, eager to tell Grandma all about Bella, Vana, and, no doubt, Daniel. I figure it's best to leave her to it.

'Rosie's here waiting to tell you everything. I'm heading off to get ready as day two on the sightseeing agenda promises to be a packed one. But immediately after breakfast I'm doing a tour of the facilities here with the deputy manager, including the two restaurants and the kitchens. Time to fill in the remainder of that questionnaire but this hotel will pass with flying colours from what I've already seen. I'll ring you when we get to Athens airport tomorrow, before we fly out. Enjoy the garden centre. Love to you both.'

Rosie's hand is ready and waiting to take the phone from me. As I finish getting dressed it's hard not to listen to the conversation.

'—big suite on the top floor was awesome! It was such fun and Demetra let us talk until we fell asleep. Vana taught us some new Greek words. Bella said we should go to York to visit her when we're all back home. Her dad is so cool, Grandma. He knows all about the ruins here and Bella says that's what he does. He digs up the ground to find the things that are now buried in the earth. Things people often threw away, he says, or what they had in their homes. Imagine people in the future digging up our rubbish. Plastic plates aren't going to be quite so exciting to dig up, are they, Grandma?'

I smother a laugh and head into the bathroom, as it seems wrong to listen in on their conversation. Besides, today I want to pay a little more attention to my make-up and hair.

Daniel is a strange one, for sure. Yesterday I turned my head a few times and caught him looking at me with interest in those deep, mesmerizing, pale blue eyes of his. He immediately looked away but it was enough to make the hairs on the back of my neck begin to tingle. Last night he alluded to the chemistry between us. Is this what they mean when they use the phrase fatal attraction? Fatal as in destined to failure because even after one night of passion there's no real future in it?

Our lives, and lifestyles, are so very different that we really are at the opposite ends of a spectrum. The only link we share is a broken relationship and the fact that it gave us our beautiful daughters. A textbook case of wrong place, wrong time, but maybe last night was fate making a point and reminding us both there's more to life than simply surviving. But my pulse is racing at the thought of him this morning and that I can't deny.

I place my palms on the vanity counter and lean in closer to the mirror, peering at myself. *What do you really want, Leah?* Am I trying to prove something to myself, and Daniel just happens to be yet another safe option? One that can't go anywhere, but it's enough to make me think I've let go of the past? Or is this sense of overwhelming attraction worth exploring and trying to take further? Or am I kidding myself and it was a moment when anyone could be forgiven for letting down their guard. The fact that he hasn't told me his whole story is a red flag – I know that only too well. If he's capable of keeping quiet about something so important, what else might he choose to hide from me?

I sigh, shaking my head as I stare back at myself. I admit I'm scared of taking the lid off my personal little can of worms when I sit down with Jackie Kimberley. I haven't even been completely honest with Harrison and I'm beginning to feel like a bit of a hypocrite. *You accused him of being a wimp, Leah, but who's really the wimp here?*

I jolt upright, pushing away my thoughts and call out to Rosie.

'We should head down to breakfast, now, darling. Say goodbye to Grandma.'

When I walk back into the room she's blowing a kiss down the phone and it puts an instant smile on my face.

'Gotta go now, speak to you later!' She sounds so bright and confident, it makes my heart soar.

I'm feeling rather cross with myself. *Stop analysing every little thing and start living for the moment*, that little voice inside my head admonishes. *Switch off from everything and have a little fun for a change, Leah. After all, this is your last day in paradise and your last day with Daniel. After last night's turn of events it might turn out to be the start of something: something special. All you need do is, at best, have an open mind, or accept that after today none of this will matter, anyway.*

On the Tourist Trail

Bella, Rosie and I are standing in reception when Daniel's taxi arrives, as I thank Manos, the deputy manager for his very comprehensive tour. Going behind the scenes, everything seems to run like clockwork, with meticulous attention to detail. He tells me that a lot of the staff are related to the Fotopoules family itself. What comes across quite strongly is the pride they have in delivering impeccable service where nothing is too much trouble. We shake hands and I turn, as our visitors are about to step through the doors into the reception area.

Demetra kindly lent Bella one of Vana's dresses and Daniel approaches, scooping her up in his arms and, peering over her shoulder, gives Rosie a warm smile. When his eyes alight on mine his look is a little apprehensive, until he gauges by my reaction that I'm fine.

It is a pity that Thanos has already left to take Vana home, I reflect. But in another way I'm glad in case he picked up on the way Daniel and I are exchanging furtive glances.

I've chosen a knee-length, wraparound dress in deep

purple and with my skin now sporting a subtle sun-kissed glow, I feel good in it. With simple silver leaf-shaped earrings and my curls scooped back in a comb, it's cool as well as rather chic. When Daniel's eyes meet mine, they sparkle a little and I feel the need to briefly look away as, once again, he's making my pulse race. I don't want him to see how unsettled he's making me feel at this moment. When I turn back around he's still looking at me and I laugh, out of embarrassment.

'What?' I ask, wondering if something is out of place.

'Nothing. Nothing at all. I'm just pleased to see you both this morning.' It's not innuendo, though, it sounds genuine enough.

And this is a man who thinks he's destined to be alone? Oh Daniel, who are you kidding? Some lucky women will capture your heart before too much longer and she'll make you see that a relationship can turn your life back around. How I wish that could be me and it was as simple as being attracted to someone and falling in love.

Fleetingly, I wish Daniel could have met the old Leah, the one who believed that anything could happen if you wanted it badly enough. She wouldn't have wasted one second in grabbing his attention, knowing he was a very special man. Now, I weigh up every little thing I do because my daughter comes first. So, he has his secrets – so do I. I can't really hold that against him as that would make me a hypocrite. But hiding my growing attraction to him is hard work, despite my natural hesitancy given the situation. I wonder if Rosie looks at Daniel, thinking about her own dad and what her life would be like with him in it. It's tough, that's for sure, but I can't let what's happened make me throw all caution to the wind. There are two impressionable young girls involved here and neither of us is in a position to talk openly today, even if we wanted to. We can't risk being overhead.

'Can you give me a couple of minutes just to pop this paperwork back up to the room? I'll be really quick, promise!'

I leave them looking at a tourist information stand and when I return the girls already look bored.

'At last, Mum,' Rosie pipes up. She has been very patient as it probably took us a good two hours to do the tour of the hotel before our visitors arrived.

'Right, are we ready for this? Is everyone wearing comfortable footwear?' Daniel asks, brightly.

All three of us nod.

'Follow me, then.'

We make the usual left turn out of the hotel but instead of taking the next left again to lead us back up to Plaka, we carry straight on.

'Okay, ladies. Time to hold hands as we have a couple of busy roads to cross.'

'Look, Mum, I can see part of the Temple of Zeus. I told you it was this way!' Rosie is excited as she grabs my hand. She's keen to push forward but we're standing behind Daniel and Bella, waiting for the lights on the crossing to change.

'You've been studying a map of the city, Rosie. Well done, you.'

Rosie glows at Daniel's praise. He takes a moment to glance directly at her and nod. Positive encouragement is so important at her age; kids generally only want to please until they get to the teen years when everything begins to change.

'We're off. Stay close together guys. You can see where we are heading.'

The traffic is busy and it's a bit of a zig-zag route but at every turn we can look across and see the ruins which aren't too far away. It doesn't take long before we're standing in front of the remains of an arched wall, the first of two archaeological sites.

'This is Hadrian's arch,' Daniel explains. 'Originally it spanned the ancient road which led from the centre of Athens to the eastern side of the city. Not much of it left, is there girls?'

We all stare up at it and he's taken the words out of my mouth. What's left is more of a marker for the site.

'It wasn't a very wide road, was it Dad?' Bella asks, as we head towards our next stop.

'You're right, Bella. The road was single track and most people, including soldiers, would have been on foot. Some would have had small carts, although carts were generally only used to transport goods. The most important military personnel would have travelled on horseback. Wealthy people often travelled lying down on something called a litter, which was like a bed, carried on the shoulders of four slaves. The only other option would have been a sedan chair, again carried by slaves.'

Neither Bella, or Rosie seem impressed by that thought.

'You mean it took four people to save one person from having to go for a walk?' Rosie sounds scandalised.

Daniel nods. 'Yep, that's how it was back in the day.'

'Well, they were lazy and spoiled, then,' she adds, frowning with indignation.

Daniel and I both burst out laughing. Luckily, Rosie doesn't take offence but she lets go of my hand to stroll alongside Bella.

'And this,' Daniel confirms, coming to a halt, 'is the Temple of the Olympian Zeus. It was one of the largest temples in the ancient world. Right, girls, we need to wait for these lights to change and cross over this road. Then we can take a leisurely stroll up to the gardens ahead of us.'

Once we're safely across Daniel falls in alongside me, the wide pavement stretching far enough ahead for the girls to walk and chat.

'I thought today should have a little variety. Maybe keep the history to the minimum as hopefully they'll both want to come back when they are much older. We're approaching the National Gardens; it's pretty and there are some lovely features I'm sure everyone will enjoy. We can stop at the little café there to get a drink. It will take us in the direction of Syntagma square, which is regarded as the heart of Athens. From there we can head towards the shopping area, which will eventually lead us back to Plaka.'

'I think the girls won't be the only ones who will want to come back and spend more time discovering the delights of Athens,' I mutter, thinking out loud.

'It's a lot of walking and we're bypassing some of the other top attractions, but you can only pack so much into a day. It's a pity you have to fly back tomorrow.' His glance is tinged with sadness.

Daniel sounds genuinely disappointed, reflecting my own sentiments. I remind myself that this is a working holiday, so every moment has been a bonus.

'The gates are just up here and we need to steer the girls inside. It's all tree-lined paths, ponds filled with fish and terrapins, and an exotic collection of trees and shrubs from around the world. It's a green oasis in the middle of the city and covers about forty acres in total.'

'It sounds wonderful,' I reply as we hurry on ahead to catch up with Rosie and Bella.

Once inside it's easy to forget the busy network of roads surrounding the gardens and here and there, hidden between the lush greenery, are marble statues. Little pathways run off in all directions and we meander, but Daniel ensures that we are ultimately heading in the right direction, which is parallel with the main road.

We spend almost an hour discovering several ponds, a swathe of orange trees heavy with fruit and hidden relics, half-buried in shrubbery. I'm taking so many pictures that my arms begin to ache holding up the camera, when we come across a little café area.

Daniel orders the drinks while I take the girls off to the find the toilets. When we return the girls take their drinks and go to sit on the grass, while Daniel and I sit watching them.

'This is an unexpected little oasis, and I think I might have bypassed this if we'd been on our own, thinking it was just another park. But it's almost like an arboretum filled with different follies, ponds and fountains. I can't even believe what is on the other side of these trees. Sitting here we could be in a park anywhere. All you can see is greenery all around.'

'One of the benefits of living here this last year is that there isn't an inch of Athens I haven't discovered. I will miss it, but this isn't my home.'

He sounds like he's ready to slip back into his old life once more and I wonder how much of that is down to missing Bella and the time they've spent apart.

'Isn't it weird to think our paths would probably never have crossed back in the UK and yet you come out on a short trip and here we are.' Daniel looks pensive. 'Do we need to clear the air about last night? It wasn't planned, I can assure you, but I'm glad it happened the way it did; it seemed so right and now with your departure imminent it seems wrong somehow.'

I put my drink down on the table. What exactly is he trying to say? Is this a hint about meeting up in the UK at some point? And what is he hiding from me?

'I don't really know what to say, Daniel, because ... well, I'm usually very cautious. I have no regrets at all, if that's what you need to hear,' I reply, trying to sound quite casual.

'Oh, I wasn't ... I, um, guess we both got a little caught up in the moment.'

Suddenly I'm flustered. In the cold light of day this isn't quite as easy as it was under the cover of darkness.

'I think we've been very lucky and Rosie and I are very grateful to you both, Daniel. You've made Athens come alive for us.' There, he has his get out if he's looking for one.

He seems to be studying my face again, as if deep in thought.

'It's been a pleasure. I can't believe this time tomorrow it will be just Bella and me, again.'

And? Is there an *and? Please, say whatever it is that is on your mind, Daniel.* This might be our only chance to talk without the girls within earshot.

Instead he looks down at the table, keeping his thoughts to himself.

I gaze around trying not to feel desperately disappointed. Telling myself that we have the rest of the day for him to get up the courage to say what he's thinking helps a little. Whether another opportunity will arise, I don't know. He doesn't seem to be talking specifically about the girls and a little quiver of excitement runs down my back.

They have quickly formed a bond, it's true, and as a parent that's something to encourage. But Daniel and I have been able to talk quite openly about our respective situations and that, too, forms a bond. Fleetingly, I wonder if my display of anger last night over Antonio has set alarm bells ringing for him? I'm going to get help, though, and then – hopefully – there will be no shadows in my life.

However, last night and being with Daniel has triggered a need deep inside of me whether I'm ready for it or not.

The thrill of being desired and experiencing the act of physical love with someone again is appealing. I think we're both from the same mould; too sensitive for our own good. And therein lies the problem. What if the things you are trying to run away from are too big to share? Even a seemingly temporary fix can be dangerous if you can't control how you feel inside.

Maybe the moment has already passed and it's too late. That would be just my luck and serve me right for being so stubborn. But what if the possibility of an ongoing attraction between us is all in my head and he's simply being polite to pass the time? I could be misreading the signs. Maybe he doesn't feel the same connection that I do at all and that's why he's hesitating. He might feel relieved because I'm the one leaving and walking away. Is he worried about my reaction to the morning after the night before? Or is this about what I discovered and was about to challenge him over this morning?

Suddenly my heart is heavy, despite the brilliant sunshine and the glorious setting around us. And the hope that keeps leaping in my chest.

I watch him as he looks around, studying the trees and looking relaxed. *I'm out of practice*, Daniel, the voice in my head is longing to explain. *I'm ready and I'm waiting, but you need to make the first move if you want to explore whatever it is that is going on between us. You have to convince me that your intentions are good and that you won't hide anything from me.*

It occurs to me that pride is an annoying stumbling

block at times and I wish I had the courage to sweep it aside and ask him for some answers. But I still don't have what it takes to expose my deeper feelings in case I get hurt yet again.

One Blink and They're Gone

As I half-feared, the day has flown by but it has been one full of lots of laughter, some great food and soaking up the vibrancy of a very busy, high-end shopping area. Daniel found us the perfect restaurant where we could sit outside to eat and watch people passing by. We were all grateful to rest our feet for an hour or so, before we continued exploring.

Both girls are happy to do a little shopping and I manage to pick up a couple of souvenirs to take back home as presents.

Eventually we end up back in Plaka, where Rosie steers us towards the ice cream shop. While they wait in the queue I can't resist taking a few more snaps of some of the doorways tucked in between the shopfronts. One property looks abandoned and as I draw closer, zooming the lens in beyond the fancy metalwork insets in the badly decaying door, I glimpse a beautiful staircase. But looking up, there's a hole in the roof where shafts of sunlight cascade down onto the dusty, rubble-laden floor. There is a lot of beauty in this building and I feel sad to see it wasted and neglected. Not all ruins are ancient, I reflect, and this house has a lot of redeeming features.

'Indulging in your door obsession again?'

I switch off the camera and pop it back into my bag, taking the ice cream cornet Daniel is holding out to me.

'I'm sure there's some hidden meaning behind it, because I seem to be the only one taking the least bit of interest. I love this one; imagine the life it's had so far. I hope someone falls in love with the house and decides to restore it to its former glory.'

Daniel stops focusing on the cornet in his hand to look at the building with interest.

'You're right, of course. Even the shabby paintwork has a charm but you're a romantic at heart, Leah. Few would look at this and think about how beautiful it could still be; they'd simply be thinking of the cost involved and the difficultly gaining access through these narrow and crowded streets. Imagine transporting in all the building materials you'd need and then moving in furniture?'

I rather begrudgingly agree he has a point but already the girls are getting ahead of us and it's time to move on. As we approach the square, the hotel is close by now and we've made no plans beyond our sightseeing.

'It's great you were able to take the week off to spend time with Bella. Does that mean the project is going well?'

He nods his head. 'Yes, but it's in its infancy and work

will continue for many years I should imagine. A bit like the dig beneath the new museum where there is layer upon layer of the past just waiting to be discovered. Who knows, I may even get to come back here again sometime in the future.'

There is no long-term plan in Daniel's head by the sound of it.

'I've learnt that you have to be prepared to grab opportunities whenever they come your way,' he adds.

'And fit everything else around it?' I can't help asking the question. If he lives for his work and Bella, maybe that will be enough for him. But, a bit like that old property being allowed to decay, that would be such a waste of an extremely sensitive and passionate man.

'Pretty much. I'm not good with relationships, obviously, and I hate feeling I'm letting people down. I'm never going to be Mr Nine-to-Five, am I? I bet you think I'm a bit of a lost cause.'

Our gazes lock and I can see he really is interested in my response.

'No, not at all. You're naturally cautious and that's a trait I appreciate.'

His smile is warm and engaging; I feel there's something he wants to say to me but as he glances away once more, the girls draw our attention.

'Bella, Rosie, wait for us. Don't get too far in front.' Daniel calls out to the girls, who stop while we catch up. We turn right and I can already see the steps of the hotel further along the street.

'Do you have to head back, now?' I brave the question,

not wanting the day, or our conversation, to end so abruptly and with so many things still left unsaid.

'No, if you aren't tired of our company maybe I could buy us all dinner in the conservatory restaurant at the hotel?' Suddenly his voice is full of enthusiasm. 'If we could get the girls to settle down with a board game afterwards, there's something I need to tell you. It's not easy to explain and I wouldn't want the girls to overhear. But I don't want things between us to end—'

There's a loud yell and when I turn to check that the girls are okay I see that Bella has tripped up on the steps to the hotel. Rosie is bending over her. Daniel and I start running.

'Dad, I've twisted my ankle and it really hurts.' Bella squeezes out the words amidst a flood of tears.

Rosie looks on; her little face has turned quite pale.

Daniel lifts Bella up effortlessly and as we approach the top of the steps Thanos is there, holding the door open. We all hurry across to one of the leather couches in the spacious seating area beyond the reception desk.

Thanos has called one of his staff over and gives him an instruction, his words an unintelligible stream to my ears but the tone conveys his sense of urgency.

As Daniel props Bella up on the sofa, already the staff member is back with some linen napkins and a bucket of ice.

Rosie, too, looks upset and stands, wrapping her arms around my waist as we watch.

'I think we're going to need to get this checked out,

Thanos,' Daniel looks up from his kneeling position with a worried frown on his face. 'Can you call a taxi? We need to get Bella's ankle X-rayed to make sure she hasn't broken a bone.'

He begins packing ice into the centre of one of the napkins and I'm horrified at how swollen Bella's ankle is already. She's no longer crying but the moment he applies the ice she yells out in anguish.

I kneel down next to the couch and Bella grabs my hand.

'It hurts really badly, Leah.' Her tearful little face is ashen.

'The ice will help reduce the swelling and the pain, Bella. You're being very brave and we're so proud of you, aren't we Rosie?'

Daniel, too, is in a state of shock. We exchange glances and I hold out my free hand, offering to swap places. I grab the ice pack and slide across while Daniel straightens, moving around behind me to hold Bella's hand.

'Why don't you take another napkin and dip it in the ice water so you can wipe Bella's face over? It will cool her down a little,' I suggest.

Thanos reappears.

'The taxi is two minutes away.'

Daniel has his arms around Bella's shoulders now and her head is resting against his chest.

'Do you want us to come to the hospital with you?' My voice croaks with the emotion I'm trying my best to contain.

The intensity of the look that passes between us is like

a jolt of electricity. Suddenly everything seems to stand still for a moment and what I see on his face is a mixture of indecision and gut-wrenching sadness. The moment passes and I know what his answer is going to be.

'No. You're leaving early tomorrow and you both need to get a good night's sleep. We'll probably be at the hospital for a few hours. I don't think it's broken, but at the very least it's a bad sprain.'

The look he gives me is full of unspoken emotion and his eyes close for one second as an expression of regret passes over his face. He mouths, 'I'm sorry, Leah,' before bending to scoop Bella up into his arms. We've run out of time.

'Dad, I want my mum.' Bella's voice wavers, as she tries to keep her tears in check.

I glance up to see the driver walking into the reception. In less than a couple of minutes Rosie and I are left standing, arms wrapped around each other as we watch the taxi pull away.

'We didn't get to say a proper goodbye, Mum. I feel really sad. I hope Bella is going to be all right.'

'Me too, Rosie. Poor, poor Bella but I'm sure she'll be fine, and they'll take good care of her.'

It's a horrible thing to happen and my heart goes out to them both. It also feels wrong letting them go off like that. We'll have no idea at all how she's doing, or whether Daniel needs any help. Nothing would make me happier than to be the support that he needs at this moment but it isn't my place. He made the only decision he could, given the circumstances.

'We need to finish our packing, Rosie.' I try my hardest to put a little lift back into my tone. I can't risk letting her see how devastated I'm feeling. Somehow, I need to raise her spirits for our last evening in Athens, when all I really want to do is curl up in a ball and have a good cry.

Home Alone

Rosie hasn't stopped chatting since we arrived at Mum and Dad's house. The travelling yesterday tired us both out and last night we slept like logs so at least today we are both feeling a little refreshed. I'm dropping her off for a sleepover which will allow me to spend some time catching up at home. Rosie is being treated to a trip out to the mall and the new Disney film later this evening. I know how much Mum and Dad miss her these days; it's been an adjustment for us all.

'Are the presents in my bag, Mum?' Rosie quizzes me and I nod.

'Yes. Everything's in there. Have fun and I will see you tomorrow.'

I give everyone a hug and beat a hasty retreat. I woke up with a thumping headache this morning and my thoughts in a turmoil.

The first thing I do when I arrive home is dial Harrison's number.

'Morning, I'm back.'

'Hey, it's good to hear your voice. You sound tired.'

'Tired, jaded, fed up. You name it.'

There's a pause. 'Your text said you were having a good time in Athens. What went wrong?'

Where do I start?

'Everything. I met the most amazing guy and we had one, unexpected, but very passionate night together. On our final night in Athens his daughter tripped on some steps and hurt her ankle, so we didn't even get to say a proper goodbye. He was going to tell me something that might have ... oh, it's hard to explain. They headed off to the hospital and that was it. I'm devastated.'

He tuts, sympathetically.

'Tell me you at least had a frank and meaningful talk?'

A second or two passes and I feel like a complete fool.

'He doesn't even know how you feel, does he?' Harrison asks, incredulously.

'No. I mean, even I'm not sure I could put it into words. The passion was real and that's not something that's easy to fake. I'm sure I wasn't imagining it when I say he felt the same, but we just didn't have a chance to—'

I trail off; without knowing for sure what Daniel was going to tell me I have no idea what my reaction would have been. If he wasn't prepared to be upfront with me then I would have walked away. It's as simple as that but now I'll probably never know for sure.

'It sounds like a long story. How about we meet up halfway between us and do lunch? You can tell me everything. Then you can lecture me because I've made no progress at all at this end. In fact, I'm spooking my parents with so many ad-hoc visits. Dad even asked if I was doing all right for money the other day. It's too embarrassing for words.'

'I'd love to, really I would, but today I have a mountain of washing and some paperwork to attend to. Tomorrow Rosie is being dropped back here just before lunch and we need to spend a few hours together relaxing. Trips abroad are great but they are tiring and we'll probably laze around and watch a few films so she's rested for school on Monday.'

'Hmm.' I can almost hear Harrison's brain ticking away. 'How about a day next week?'

'Monday I'm booked to visit an art studio and do a shoot for a magazine spread. Then I will have to rush home as I have the first session with my counsellor.'

'You did it! Well done, you. How about Tuesday, then? I'll come to you because I know you're governed by the school runs. It sounds like there will be a lot to discuss.'

It's generous of Harrison to make the trip down here, even though a part of me is saying that I should say *no* because I have a lot of work to do.

'Tuesday it is, then. I'll text you my address. We can go for a walk in the forest and then come back here for lunch. If you arrive some time around eleven, then we'll have a good few hours before I collect Rosie. How does that sound?'

'Great. I doubt I'll have any news to share. I'm giving my parents a wide berth for a few days. Ollie and I have dinner plans with friends tonight. At least they're in the know and we can both relax in their company.'

I feel for him as it's a difficult situation.

'Well, have a lovely time. I'm off to clean the house and get as much online work done as I can.'

'I'll be thinking of you at the counsellor's on Monday, lovely lady. It's time to put it all out there once and for all.'

As I lay the phone down on my desk I know he's right and I should have done something about it long ago. There are lots of loose ends that I need to address. I slip off my jacket and walk through to the kitchen. Everything seems back to normal as if Athens never happened and it could easily have been a dream.

I load the washing machine with the first of three piles of clothing lying on the floor and then make a coffee. First, I need to download the photos and I slot the camera's SD card into the reader.

On the screen in front of me a file opens up with a whole raft of thumbnail icons. I highlight them all, then cut and paste them into a folder on the desktop. It takes a little while for them to transfer and I start opening the stack of post in front of me.

Mostly it's junk mail, but there's a credit card statement with a nil balance and beneath that is a smaller envelope that's been written out by hand. I suck in a deep breath as I recognise my ex-mother-in-law Zita's handwriting, although the stamp, too, gives it away.

I open it, wondering why she's writing to us instead of emailing. Usually only birthday and Christmas cards come through the post from Italy.

My dear Leah

I write to tell you some news I cannot share in any other way. I think you will be shocked as we were. I know not how to say this so I tell you what happened.

We had a letter from Antonio. He sent us his postal address, as well as his email address. He is living in Florida in the United States of America.

He begged us to make contact and wanted news of Rosie. He did not ask about you but he said he felt much guilt about the past.

Guido and I do not know what to do. How can we forgive him? And yet he is still our son.

We carry much sadness and it's hard to forgive what cannot be undone. I'm sorry and I know this is hard to hear after all this time. We wait to hear from you when you are ready and will do nothing until such time.

You are both in our hearts, always.

Zita and Guido

I feel like I've been punched in the stomach. I stuff the letter back into the envelope and open the top drawer of the desk, thrusting it inside. I close it with a bang. I don't even know how to feel about that right now and I have too much on my plate to give thought to it.

I drain my coffee cup, glad of the little kick of caffeine and click on the first of the jpeg files. It opens to show a smiley-faced Rosie in the airport terminal with our plane being fuelled in the background.

I relax my shoulders and lean forward, clicking through

the photos one by one. There are a few taken from the balcony of the hotel shortly after we arrived and I continue scrolling through. I sit for quite a while, re-living some of the moments before I eventually sit back in my chair, a frown on my face.

Well, that wasn't quite what I was hoping to see. I probably have forty or fifty shots of front doors and balconies, maybe half a dozen usable shots from the Acropolis but the rest – what was I thinking? Actually, it's clear I wasn't thinking at all. I was taking photos through rose-coloured lenses. Either Daniel, or him with both girls, are in every single frame. I rest my arms on the desk in front of me and lay my head on top. So far, I've never had to resort to using stock photographs that are available online, but I simply don't have what I need to make the articles stand out. Without good quality, unique photographs to mirror the personal account of my travels, the articles on Athens, the hotel and the villa will look contrived, merely an advert.

My head continues to pound and now I'm feeling queasy as well. I go in search of some headache tablets while I sort out what I'm going to do and in what order.

If you can get yourself out from under a mountain of debt, you can unravel this latest dilemma, Leah. Just remain calm and do what you always do – which is to begin working through it. If I focus on getting everything typed up, I can worry about what I'm going to do about the photographs later. Maybe there are a few that can be salvaged with careful use of the crop facility but I know that's a long shot. Daniel seems to be standing in the centre of almost every photo and even just looking at them I'm filled with an intense longing to be back there with him. But I need to pull myself together and decide on my next course of action. Maybe I could use a couple of the fascinating door shots to give a flavour of the labyrinth of streets in Plaka?

I groan out loud. 'How can you have messed up so badly, Leah?'

My words seem to echo around the room and the little voice inside my head is quick to answer.

Fatal attraction.

The Visit

It's funny but when Rosie isn't here I find it harder to focus on what needs to be done. I'm so used to having her around that it feels like something is missing and while I do manage to get quite a bit done, early evening I begin to flag. I don't seem to have any enthusiasm to tackle the outstanding chores, so I have a long soak in the bath. By seven in the evening I'm on the sofa in my PJs. So, when the doorbell rings I groan. I've not been here to order anything online so it must be Sally; I know I should have called her but I'm struggling a little to be upbeat at the moment.

As I swing the door open, sporting the most cheerful smile I can muster, it immediately freezes on my face when I see Daniel standing in front of me. I can't even begin to take this in.

'What on earth are you doing here?' I'm aware it sounds rather unwelcoming but I'm in shock.

'I know I should have called you first, but some things need to be said face to face.'

Daniel makes no move to enter, even though I stand back to let him pass.

'Look, I know it's summer but that's a chilly breeze and I'm freezing here. Can you just come in, please, and tell me what's going on? How on earth did you find me?'

Now he looks miserable, but at least my words galvanise him into action and he moves forward, passing me without so much as a glance my way.

Then I remember I'm wearing my favourite Christmas PJs because the heating isn't on and he's probably embarrassed as it's obvious I wasn't expecting company. And certainly not in the form of Daniel. I close the door and brace myself, before following him into the sitting room. He's standing there looking a little dazed.

'This seemed like a good idea at the time, if an impulsive one. I Googled you and managed to find an address. It's clear we have unfinished business between us. Seeing you standing here, sporting a rather large novelty reindeer on that fetching top, has completely emptied my head of words.' And with that he begins laughing. I glare at him, pretending to take offence and indicate for him to slip off his jacket.

'Look, I'm sorry I didn't think this through properly and I hope you will forgive me, Leah. But it's damned good to see you.'

'How's Bella?'

I place his jacket on a chair and then we both sit down at opposite ends of the sofa. The yawning gap between us signifies the awkwardness we're both feeling.

'Tricia is back in charge and I've been dismissed.' He grimaces. 'So Bella will be fine; she's in excellent hands.'

'And you?'

'Well, it was all such a shock. The accident and then having to leave abruptly when I needed to ... wanted to explain.'

Suddenly my stomach is doing somersaults because I have no idea what he's going to say.

'Explain what, exactly?' I ask, my gaze unwavering.

'Look, Leah, I don't quite know how to tell you this if I'm being honest. I hope you can understand that it's not something I can just throw into a conversation.'

He pauses for a moment and I find myself holding my breath.

'I have a heart problem and what you felt was a scar from the operation I had shortly after Tricia and I split up. That's the real reason why I didn't see Bella for a while; we decided it was best she didn't know. When she's older I'll sit her down and explain it in detail but she'd already been through so much, this seemed like overload at the time.'

When you finally admit to yourself you have feelings for someone and you hear them telling you they have a heart problem, it's like being punched in the stomach. He looks so fit and well, I can hardly take it in even though I've felt his scar with my own fingertips.

'But you're so young, Daniel. Is it a hereditary condition?'

He seems uncomfortable with my question and I can see how hard this is for him as he shakes his head.

'No, nothing like that. But like any illness it leaves more than just a physical scar. It's a reminder that even when the spirit is strong, a body can be weak.'

It's wrong of me to interrogate him and I can see he's shaken by my reaction. But I worry about the people I'm close to and unwittingly I find Daniel has become one of them. I care and yet I don't want to alarm or upset him in any way. So I take the only other option and that's to change the subject.

'How long can you stay?'

He begins to relax, almost collapsing back against the cushions.

'Until tomorrow. I'm on the early evening flight out. I have a coach seat booked for eleven in the morning.'

I'm overwhelmed. Daniel came all this way because he's right, this isn't something he could have dealt with by text, or phone. His body language is telling me as much, if not more than his words. He, too, is devastated by what happened because it's left him feeling vulnerable and that's something he struggles to accept. I want to wrap my arms around him and hug away the bad memories. I want to make him feel whole again.

'When did you last eat?' I probe him gently.

'I can't remember. I'm so tired it's all a bit hazy.'

I slide along the sofa until our bodies are touching and then I half-turn to drape my arms around his shoulders.

'It's going to be fine, Daniel. I'm glad you flew over. Now let's get you something to eat and drink. Then next on the list is a good night's sleep. After that you'll be feeling much better and we can pick this back up in the morning.'

He's too exhausted to argue and less than an hour later I'm propped up in bed watching him sleep and trying to figure out what happens next.

~

'How do you instinctively know what to do and when to do it? I was about to keel over last night and yet this morning I'm bursting with energy.'

'So I gathered. Being woken up at dawn for a little romantic interlude was a bit of a surprise.'

He looks abashed. 'I know, sorry, but I was wide awake and you looked so ... inviting lying there next to me. Your response was instant, though, so I don't feel too guilty about it.'

A sudden flashback of skin on skin and Daniel working his way down my body with his mouth has me swinging my legs over the side of the bed. I'm conscious that he has a coach to catch and we need to be out of the house before Rosie arrives home. The desire beginning to stir inside of me once again is hard to resist, I will admit.

'And there's nothing wrong with being looked after; it's what I do when I care about someone,' I call over my shoulder on my way to the bathroom.

He doesn't answer and as soon as I'm out of the shower we pass in the doorway.

'Don't worry, I'll drive you to the pick-up point. You have forty-five minutes to get ready. I'll throw on some clothes and whip up something for breakfast.'

He stops to plant a quick kiss on my cheek and within minutes he's in the shower, singing some obscure line from a song I've never heard before.

Over scrambled eggs and toast he asks me about the forest and Rosie's school. I realise he's trying to get a feel for our lives here.

'Life is tranquil and true foresters are born and bred here. Those who opt to move to the area come for a reason and that's usually to escape busy city life.'

Daniel nods in between shovelling forkfuls of food, one eye on the clock.

And then, all too soon, it's time for him to leave. We make our way out to the car with some reluctance. I know we have an uphill struggle ahead of us. When our eyes meet and lock, Daniel looks weary, unable to sustain that false sense of light-heartedness. He doesn't speak until we're cruising along on the motorway, trying to avoid the depressing air of inevitability about facing yet another goodbye.

'The trouble with life is that we can't take anything for granted: ever. I had a sharp reminder of that and it has changed the way I look at things, Leah. I'd be lying if I didn't admit that. It's not that I'm overly cautious, it's more that I look at things in a more practical way now. I've said this before; I'm not the easiest of options and when everything I've told you sinks in, I'll understand if you change your mind about me. Even if it's only for Rosie's sake. We have to be careful what we inflict on our girls.'

My face falls, saddened that his thoughts are so troubled and doubting.

'The glass is half-full, even when it's half-empty, Daniel. Life can only be lived one day at a time but it's about making sure each one really matters. That's the only way to live a fulfilling life. Enjoy the moment as best you can and when you look back it amounts to a lifetime of wonderful memories. Even the bad things that happen can lead to good if we learn and grow from the experience. We've both been through a lot of bad things so we're going to enjoy the good times when they finally get here. Surely it's important to show our daughters that you can't live in fear of what might never happen?'

He glances at me, apologetically.

'Ignore me, I'm missing you before I've even stepped on the plane. I'm really looking forward to going back to York now and I'll merely be wishing away the days until I fly back for good. I'm not used to feeling like that. The thought of having someone – you – in my life is something I couldn't ... well, didn't dream would happen.'

Before we know it we're standing in front of the coach and my eyes suddenly fill with tears.

'Please take care of yourself, Daniel. No more skipping meals, that's an order. And text me when you arrive back at the villa.'

His arms cradle around me and he rests his chin on my head.

'Stop worrying,' he whispers. 'I'll be in touch, I promise. Now go and get ready for Rosie's return and act as if nothing has happened. We'll figure out where we go from here. I just couldn't leave things as they were and it was well worth the journey.'

I pull away to look up at him and grab one final, lingering kiss.

'I simply wish you were staying longer. I don't want to let you go so soon, again.'

'Hopefully it won't be like this for ever, Leah. Hold onto that thought. I'll work on getting my head around a future I couldn't even contemplate before you breezed into my life, because I'm not quite there yet.'

I wave until the blue blur of the coach is out of view. My eyes are veiled with tears and somehow I have to pick myself up and get ready to greet Mum, Dad and Rosie. I'm not even sure where I stand, now – it all happened so fast. What did Daniel mean when he said, 'I'm not quite there yet?' Was he referring to his feelings for me, or the fact that his spell in Athens isn't finished? Or maybe his *hangups* because I feel he's almost punishing himself in a way for something that could happen to anyone. When I arrive home and type *heart conditions* into Google there are so many different possibilities that my head starts reeling. Why wasn't he more specific? He flew all this way to put my mind to rest and all he's actually done is made things worse, much worse.

The Aftermath

What a stressful couple of days it's been. Ironically, when life threatens to swamp me, the only way I can cope is to switch off and focus on something else. Something productive, that will at least make me feel like I'm getting somewhere and not drowning in negative thoughts. I managed to get a huge amount of work done and even put in a couple of hours in between watching films with Rosie on Sunday. It should have given me a boost all round after Daniel's visit, but instead, because of that, everything suddenly felt very flat. Rosie was a little tired and subdued; I kept telling myself that it was only to be expected after all the excitement.

Yesterday I had to rush the photoshoot so I could make it back in time for the session with Jackie Kimberley. Today I feel drained but I need to sort out everything that's going around and around inside my head.

When I open the door to see Harrison standing there, I literally throw myself at him.

'Hey, what's all this?'

He gives me a bear hug, almost lifting me off my feet to

help me back inside. I swipe my arm across my eyes, scattering a couple of tears I was trying so bravely to hold back.

'I need some fresh air. Do you mind if we head straight out?'

Harrison is looking very casual in designer jeans and T-shirt. He looks back at me, one eyebrow lifted.

'Guess yesterday was rather heavy then. Come on, let's try and walk some of that stress out of you, lovely lady, before those frown lines get any deeper.'

Raising a half-hearted laugh to try to lighten the mood, I grab my keys and throw a jumper around my shoulders.

'Do we need walking sticks, or anything, to fend off the animals?'

Checking to see whether he's joking or not, I can't tell as his expression is a serious one.

'Aside from the wild boar, who will probably be asleep after their nighttime foraging, it's likely that pretty much everything else will be running away from us.'

'That's a relief,' he says, holding the front door open for me as we head out.

'How was your dinner the other night?' I'm not ready to talk about my problems yet and I do want to get a feel for how Harrison is dealing with his own dilemma.

'It should have been easy, really, just a nice relaxing dinner, but Ollie is rapidly losing confidence in me. It showed and the conversation was a little strained at times. We get on well with Jessica and Paul, who are Ollie's work colleagues as well as friends. But they obviously don't know about the turmoil surrounding my personal situation. We headed home immediately dinner was over on the pretext that I had to get up really early the next day.'

We've reached the end of the cul-de-sac and take the footpath that leads up a gentle slope behind a row of houses. From here on, for miles it's dense forest and I have no idea how long it would take to walk in a straight line before it was possible to catch sight of a house, or a road.

'You really do live in the middle of the forest, don't you? This is quite something to have on your doorstep. We won't get lost, will we – I mean, if you lose your bearings?'

I forget that people who live in a city can't always easily find a large expanse of green space where they can step away from the chaos of life for a short while. It's something I take for granted but I understand Harrison's concern. It might look like we're just wandering around but the ground beneath our feet tells us everything we need to know.

'We're following a well-worn trail; you can see over there the path goes off in two different directions but we're keeping to the left-hand side of the fork. It's a forty-five-minute walk, the way I'm going to take us, but we could wander for hours with only the birds and the occasional hiker crossing our path. Don't worry; I promise we won't get lost. Anyway, how is Ollie coping with the situation?'

We sidestep a large muddy patch in the middle of the well-trodden dirt path and then Harrison falls in alongside me once more.

'He's getting impatient and doubting my intentions. It's just as big a deal for him as it is for me but he seems to take it in his stride. I envy him that. I've asked him to hold back on any announcements until I've told my parents. There are still only a handful of people who know we're together officially. Ollie had wanted to begin making plans to move in together, but he's even stopped talking about that now. In fact, things between us are a little tense, to say the least.'

I shake my head, wondering how Harrison would cope if Ollie suddenly decided to walk away from him. Every passing day probably increases the chances of them reaching that point of no return.

'I know I said you needed to relax a little and the right opportunity would come along, but it's too easy to convince yourself that the right time never seems to present itself. Don't you think your parents would see this as a significant event in your life? One that should be a priority over most of the day to day stuff? If someone interrupts, tell them you're discussing something important and ask them to come back later.'

I look sideways at him and if I'm not mistaken there's a hint of guilt on his face when he turns towards me.

'Ollie has virtually said the exact same thing. It's just that everything will change instantly, and while some of it is predictable, there's a lot that isn't. What if afterwards I end up having regrets about coming out?'

My eyebrows shoot up under my fringe and I can't hide a look of confusion. I thought Harrison was way beyond the point at which having second thoughts was even an option for him. He'd seemed genuinely committed to Ollie and now he's doubting his feelings for him?

'Regrets? I thought Ollie was the person you wanted to spend the rest of your life with?'

Harrison looks uncomfortable, scuffing the toe of his expensive trainers on the small mound of gravelly soil beneath his foot.

'He is and I do. But what if other relationships stop working? I mean, I love my parents too.'

'Harrison, you can't control everyone else's reactions so you have to be true to yourself and carve out the future that will make you the happiest. If people turn their backs on you – yes, even your parents – it will be very hard, but that's their choice. There is nothing at all you can do about that. So why let it stop you from moving forward with your own life? Unless you have doubts you are doing the right thing in being with Ollie in the first place.'

We walk on in total silence while my words sink in.

'I don't have a single doubt about Ollie, Leah, and you were totally right the other day when you said I was being a wimp. I'll sit down with my parents at the weekend and get it done. I'll tell Ollie that, too, so I can't back out this time.'

Our pace is leisurely and we both seem content to saunter along enjoying the peaceful setting. The sound of the overhead canopy of leaves rustling is broken only by birds singing, or fluttering wings as they move amongst the trees. A squirrel darts out, then turns tail and disappears into the dense undergrowth of ferns.

'One down, one to go.' Harrison's words break the stillness and I swallow hard.

'It's my turn to admit that I'm in such a mess right now.'

It takes me a few minutes to think about where to begin and I start by telling him all about Athens, Daniel and Bella.

'Wow, talk about leaving things on a cliffhanger. It sounds like it wasn't purely one-sided to me, though. To spend that much time together you obviously got on extremely well. It wasn't only about the kids, believe me. If he hadn't enjoyed your company equally as much he would have found other things to do with his daughter. And you say he lectures at the University of York? That's quite a trek from here.'

I hadn't even given that any serious thought. It was sort of eclipsed by everything else.

'When I said we didn't even get to say goodbye that was true at the time but it's not true now.'

Harrison's jaw drops when I tell him about my concerns after sleeping with Daniel; and my fears for what he chose not to tell me. He looks a little shocked. But when I then go on to talk about Daniel's impromptu visit on Saturday night it stops him in his tracks.

Thankfully, we're on the last leg of the walk and home is in sight.

'Why on earth did you feel you had to wait for him to tackle the subject of that scar, first? You should have asked him outright the night you slept together. And now it sounds like you're still no better off, Leah. After everything you've been through, it's bound to be difficult for you to find the courage to put your emotions on the line again.'

I unlock the door, unable to come up with an excuse that doesn't sound lame for either my less than proactive part in this, or Daniel's less than open behaviour.

'This shouldn't be solely about being afraid of getting hurt again, but about understanding what you are getting yourself into. From what you've told me the two of you certainly had no problem letting down your guard in front of each other; and getting physical on both occasions. So why isn't he being honest with you about whatever's wrong with him? Unless he doesn't have long to live.' His gaze doesn't falter and I nod, my bottom lip wavering slightly as I fight off tears.

Harrison steers me by the shoulders into the kitchen and sits me down at the small table.

'I think you're in shock, lady. Tea, or coffee?'

'Coffee, please.' My voice is reduced to a mere whisper.

'This session you had yesterday with your counsellor. Are you going to share anything about that with me and did you talk to her about this new development?'

He clatters around while we wait for the kettle to boil and makes so much noise that I'm unable to answer his question. When he takes the seat opposite me I stare down at the coffee mugs between us for a moment or two while I gather my thoughts.

'I told her a part of it, but not everything. When I downloaded the photographs which I took while we were in Athens, I was horrified. I have half a dozen usable ones at most. I have maybe fifty of front doors of all shapes, sizes, styles, age and in various states from pristine, to rotten and falling apart. The other hundred plus seem to have Rosie, Bella and Daniel, or just Daniel, in all of them and they are virtually unusable. They look like holiday snaps and not photos taken by a professional.'

Harrison has been stirring his coffee the entire time and he looks at me with his mouth open.

'What are you going to do? That's a disaster for you, isn't it?'

'I discussed it with Jackie, after telling her my whole story pre-Daniel and I mean everything. She specialises in bereavement counselling, but also handles post-traumatic stress and surviving life-changing traumas. I was there for an hour and a half. She suggested that the doors were symbolic and maybe it was about this inner yearning to start all over again. Reassurance that it's never too late, no matter what's gone before. And as for the other photos, well, she pointed out that they all looked like normal family photos. But we weren't one unit, we were simply two parents trying to ensure our kids had a good time. It was a sort of false normality, really. How sad is that? I didn't mention that Daniel and I had jumped into bed together. I didn't want her to think I was a bad mother, or anything. And as for Saturday night, well, I'm still trying to get my head around that. Daniel texted me when he arrived home because I asked him to and it simply said "I'm here and it's not the same without you" – nothing more.'

Harrison extends his hand across the table to pat my arm.

'Hey, you're a wonderful mum and you didn't palm Rosie

off on someone just so you could sleep with him. The two of you found yourselves alone together; two lonely people with a heck of a lot of chemistry going on; it happens. Anyway, the sessions will help you work through all of this *if* you're honest with her and it could significantly alter the way you look at things. But you said you told Jackie *everything*, so what exactly did you mean by that if you skirted over the Daniel issue?'

My eyes are beginning to glisten but I refuse to cry. I swallow hard, forcing back the lump which now seems firmly lodged in my throat.

'There's one more thing I haven't told you yet about what happened seven years ago.'

His expression changes as he hangs on my every word.

'The day I lost my sister I felt that a part of me had been ripped out. I was so full of my own pain that I wasn't much use to anyone. I didn't stop to think about how my parents were dealing with it.

'Suddenly one daughter disappears, the other one falls apart and there's a toddler to be looked after. Three days later, shortly after I'd found out the bank was about to repossess the house, my dad had a massive heart attack. He spent nearly a month in hospital. Six months later he was still off work and the moment he'd been dreading had arrived. The HR department contacted him with an offer of taking early retirement. Dad loved his job, it was important to him but his recovery was so slow and he couldn't drive; he really had no choice in the matter.

'He's a lot better now but his life still hasn't returned to normal. He potters around trying not to get under Mum's feet and is a taxi service for Rosie when I'm not around. I feel that what happened stole his life out from under him in more ways than one. And poor Mum, we haven't even mentioned Kelly's name since that fateful day. But she didn't die; she's still out there, living her life somewhere, without us.'

We sit in silence sipping our coffee.

'What a complete nightmare this is for you. Does Daniel know about what you've been through with your dad? I don't know quite what to say, Leah. Antonio and Kelly should have faced up to the situation and admitted what was happening between them rather than run away like they did. You were in shock at the time, who wouldn't have been? Your parents obviously don't blame you in any way for what occurred, so why would you blame yourself? And don't even think about saying "if only" because you'd immediately go down in my estimation. That sort of logic works both ways.' Harrison's tone is firm.

'I admit that there was a time when I ventured down that road but I soon realised it wasn't going to change anything. I have something to show you.' I walk into the other room and grab Zita's letter from the desk drawer. When I return I hand it to Harrison before I sit back down.

He reads the letter more than once, I think, because it's so short and he seems to be taking his time. He holds it up, shaking it back and forth in his hand with a smile on his face.

'This is great news. With an actual address, it's going to

be a lot easier filing for divorce and finally begin cutting all ties with your ex. Then you can focus on getting to the bottom of Daniel's problem, which might not be as bad as you fear.'

When he sees I'm unable to raise a smile of my own, he slides the letter back inside the envelope and places it between us on the table.

'Argh. It's all so complicated and it's all swirling around inside my head. But I can't get past wanting to know whether Kelly is still there with Antonio. And what does he want? Why has he suddenly decided to reach out to his parents now?'

Harrison's smile fades as I continue.

'It's like the worst possible storyline for a soap opera, isn't it? The things you watch and don't believe can possibly happen in real life. What if he wants contact with Rosie again?' I express my worst fear and see from his expression that I'm not being paranoid here.

'You need to talk to a solicitor and I know exactly the man for you. There's no point in dwelling on this alone, you need professional advice. Then, I'm on a quest to find out a little more about Daniel. I have your back and if you are serious about him, what's that saying?'

I cast around, trying to think of sayings I've heard repeated ad nauseum over the years.

'*Hell hath no fury like a woman scorned*?' I can't see how that fits in relation to Daniel. But it might for Antonio, although I ceased having any feelings for him years ago.

'Nooo! I think it's one of the quotes that aren't credited

to anyone but have always been around. It goes something like this: *it takes a minute to like someone, an hour to love someone but a lifetime to forget them.*'

I repeat it over to myself a few times. It is going to take me a very long time to forget Daniel if I walk away without getting to the bottom of what's going on. That's one thing about which I'm very sure.

'There's absolutely nowhere to go with the Daniel thing for the time being, Harrison, until he's ready to talk about what happened to him. But thank you for listening. And who is this solicitor you know? I'm not sure I have the energy to take on anything else right now, even if I want to be rid of Antonio legally, as well as emotionally.'

'Oliver Parker-Smith isn't only a solicitor, he also specialises in family law. And he's good at what he does.'

I lean forward, my eyes wide with surprise.

'Your Ollie is a solicitor?'

'I'll get him to give you a call and you can take it from there. As for the other matter, I love solving puzzles and I've learnt that the best approach is one step at a time. We need to know a little more about this guy who has caught your attention.'

I don't like the sound of either suggestion, if I'm honest, but Harrison means well. What harm can it do, I wonder? I ought to find out where I stand in case Antonio tries to re-establish communication and as for Daniel, well I can only wait and see what happens next. Unless Harrison is planning a quick trip to Athens.

He wouldn't do that, would he?

Life is a Rollercoaster

As I head towards the school this morning, I can tell there is something on Rosie's mind. It isn't until we're parked up, twenty minutes before the school bell, that she begins talking to me.

'I miss Bella and Daniel, Mum. I wonder how Bella's ankle is doing?'

I hate lying to anyone, least of all my lovely daughter but I can't mention Daniel's visit.

'She probably had to rest her foot for a few days, Rosie, that's all. Bella will be feeling a lot better by now.'

I put up my hand to brush back a lock of hair that has fallen over her forehead, obscuring a part of her face. She looks sad.

'Are you looking forward to our next trip away? The summer holidays will soon be here and it's only two months until we visit Le Crotoy, in France. Imagine a brand-new apartment block literally on the beach and we're going to be staying in one of the penthouses. Unfortunately, not all the holiday apartments will be finished but a few of them will, and there are bound to be other families with children there. It will be a nice chance to make some new friends.'

There's a pout going on, which is unusual for Rosie.

'That's great, Mum, really it is but I thought we'd be seeing Bella again. She thought so, too.'

This is so awkward.

'York is quite a journey from here, darling. Besides, Daniel is in Athens still. Maybe when he's back home he'll get in touch, although I suspect he will be very busy at first. He's been away for a long time.'

At least my response seems to have brightened her up a little even though I feel the need to prepare her to be disappointed.

'Bella is lucky, isn't she, Mum? She still has both her mum and her dad, even though they don't live together.'

A little knot begins to form in the pit of my stomach as her conversation switches from one major headache, to another. I can't think of anything at all I can say in return. If Antonio intends to reach out to Rosie, could I refuse? Should I refuse? Rosie is watching me, intently, totally unaware that the timing of this conversation is so unfortunate.

'She is lucky, darling. We're happy though, aren't we?'

She nods, then opens the door of the glove compartment to look for a CD. I switch on the engine, grateful for the distraction of a little music. I try not to think about Antonio and Kelly, pushing away thoughts about whether Rosie has a stepbrother, or sister by now. Wouldn't that be a sound reason for making contact? Bringing a child into the world makes you look at everything very differently indeed. The knot is quickly turning into a sensation of nausea and I force myself to stop thinking before I get dragged down any further.

'Mum, I can't find my jumper and everyone is going in.'

Rosie's voice shakes me back into consciousness and I have no idea how long I've been in this reverie. Her school bag is open on her lap and she's rooting through it, beginning to panic.

'It's on the back seat, darling, with your waterproof jacket. Why don't you take both, as those clouds look threatening?'

I reach back while Rosie closes her bag and checks her hair in the vanity mirror – that's a first.

'Sorry, Mum, I didn't mean to make you feel sad.' She throws her arms around me and her words touch a chord. 'I'm not the only kid in school who doesn't have a dad but I know I have the best mum. See you later; love you loads.'

She grabs the jumper and jacket I'm holding out and stuffs them under her arm, one leg already out of the car. I clear my throat before I can answer her, my emotions getting the better of me.

'Love you too, darling. Have a great day.'

~

As soon as I arrive home I phone Harrison.

'Morning. I forgot to thank you for giving my number to Ollie and I wondered if you knew when he was going to call me?'

'He said it would be in the next day or two, but I know

he has back-to-back meetings this morning. You won't do anything until you hear from him, will you? You don't need to respond to Zita's letter straight away.'

It's not the only reason I'm calling him.

'Okay, I promise. I also had an idea about Daniel, and I wanted to run it past you. It will take me way beyond my comfort zone and involve me telling a lie. That doesn't sit well for me but I'm in an impossible situation and I can't think of another way around it.'

My palms are feeling sweaty and I can hardly believe I'm seriously considering this option.

'I'm at my desk looking him up as we speak! I don't know if you've checked but his bio is on the university website. If you do a general search on his name, page after page of items come up. He's been involved in a lot of projects over the years and he has so many mentions it's hard to find any personal information about him. He has written a lot of articles and published quite a few academic papers. I'm feeling better about him, the more I read. So, what's this idea of yours?'

This would be a bold and risky step for me to take, so I need someone else's opinion before I do anything at all.

'Thanos offered me the use of the villa for a week after asking me to do a special feature on it. I think he meant once the current lease is up and before it goes back for hire as a luxury holiday villa. I'm sure Daniel mentioned he's only there until midway through August. I do have a photo crisis, though, and I know that it's highly likely some of the rooms in the villa are free, at the moment. It's a legitimate excuse for me to go and stay and one that wouldn't put any pressure on Daniel.'

I've been talking fast and I stop to draw breath, wishing I could see Harrison's reaction.

'You're prepared to fly back over?' It sounds like he doesn't necessarily think it's a good idea. 'Why not wait a bit and see what his next contact with you brings?'

It makes sense, I know, but I'm already too caught up in this because I think I'm in love with Daniel. Regardless of whether or not that turns out to be a terrible idea or the best thing that's ever happened to me, it's the truth. Love isn't something you can switch on and off, no matter what problems arise.

'Rosie is going through a bit of a rough patch, having enjoyed Daniel and Bella's company. Suddenly we're alone again. And now with all this worry about Antonio ... I have yet to gain a real understanding about Daniel's situation. If it's bad news then I have to think about protecting Rosie, above all else. How could I bring someone new into her life if she was going to end up having to let him go before too long? Even if my actions end up breaking my heart and Daniel's, I can't possibly put her through any more than she already has to handle. This could potentially be an impossible situation. Although it would also be hell knowing what Daniel was going through because I can't help how I feel inside. I simply have to go back for my own sanity.'

He doesn't hesitate but jumps straight in.

'No, it's tough but perfectly understandable, Leah. You

are a wonderful mum and you know that. You have had a photo crisis of sorts, so it isn't a lie as such. And even if you can only get over there for a couple of days it will allow you to grab those snaps and, hopefully, discover why Daniel is being so cagey. The timing of this is an absolute nightmare for you, isn't it?'

I sigh, acknowledging Harrison has a good grasp of my dilemma. A part of me wishes I'd never crossed paths with Daniel, but my heart is desperately trying to hang on to any small vestige of hope.

'By the sound of it he has another, what, nine or ten weeks there? Have you looked into flight availability, given that we're heading towards the middle of June? I don't think it's going to be cheap, either. And what about your work?'

I nod, then realise he can't see me.

'I know. I'm going to start looking for flights this morning, after I call Thanos. Daniel managed to get a flight somehow and I'm equally as determined. I feel it's an imposition having to ask Mum and Dad to look after Rosie at such short notice, but if it all works out I'll take the earliest flights available and work around that. I need to get to the truth, Harrison, so I can decide whether it's best to walk away from it all now. Daniel said he would understand if I changed my mind but ultimately gave me nothing much on which to base a decision.

This new development with Antonio is going to test me to the full and I can't rise to that challenge when I feel like I'm falling apart inside. It could end up sending me spiralling into a depression and that simply isn't an option. Just when I thought the future could only be bright and I was excited about it, now everything seems up in the air again. Instead of one dire problem, I now have two. Maybe in life you only get what you're prepared to fight for and naturally I'm going to fight for Rosie. But I also believe in my heart that it would be wrong to ignore the way Daniel makes me feel, or what I believe he feels for me. I have to do something, Harrison, or I know I'll always be wondering *what if?*'

There, I've said it.

'Good for you, lady! I guess we're both learning the valuable lesson that if it's worth having then it doesn't usually come easily. Ring or text when you know what's happening. I'm killing time before I head in to do a big presentation, so I might not get back to you immediately. But you know that I'll be thinking of you and keeping everything crossed.'

It's not sympathy in his voice but genuine empathy.

'And your little plan for the weekend's revelation is still in place? No threat of it being thrown off course?' I enquire.

'None at all. And Ollie and I have agreed to start thinking about where we want to live.'

Hearing his words give me hope: Harrison is going to make it happen and this time he won't let himself down. Now I have to do the exact same thing before I get myself into an even bigger mess.

The Action Plan

By the time I pick up Rosie and she settles down in her bedroom to tackle some homework, I'm feeling frazzled. It's been a day of nonstop telephone calls and surfing the net. Thanos was very understanding and I did have to ignore the uncomfortable feeling I had knowing my motive was only partly about the photo disaster. He commiserated, probably assuming the SD card had failed as I wasn't too specific. He even offered to have someone take a few shots for me if I told him exactly what I needed. At that point, I had to think fast and after thanking him, managed to reinforce the urgency by saying it was going to be easier to write up the feature for the villas while I was there. I also pointed out I hadn't viewed the other one and that it would be well worth featuring both. It was enough to make it sound plausible.

Booking flights was a total nightmare and in the middle of it Sally dropped by for a quick cup of coffee to catch up. I didn't have the energy to tell her about Daniel, so I skated over the trip and said I was returning briefly to cover a separate feature.

Instead I voiced my concerns about Zita's letter, as she was once friends with Kelly, too. Sally was shocked and, like Harrison, said that I shouldn't do anything at all until I'd spoken to a solicitor.

As soon as she left I was back online, watching the clock ready for the school run. In the end, the cheapest flights I could book were flying from Heathrow to Frankfurt, then onwards to Athens on Friday the sixteenth of June, returning via the same route on Sunday the eighteenth. I'd have two evenings, one whole day and part of Sunday to sort everything out.

Talking to Mum and Dad wasn't easy as I didn't want to lie to them about the trip. Besides, from what Rosie had said I knew they were curious about Daniel and Bella. I simply said that I'd been invited back, which was true, and it was a chance to get to know Daniel a little better. They were so pleased that I had to make it clear they should be very careful about what they said to Rosie. And that's next on my action list. What do I tell her?

I'm in the kitchen stirring the homemade spaghetti bolognaise sauce and trying to come up with something suitable to say when my phone rings. I don't recognise the number and when I answer it's a man's voice.

'Hello, is that Leah?'

'Yes, it is.'

'Harrison asked me to give you a call, I'm Oliver Parker-Smith. I wondered if you'd be free to Skype sometime this evening? I gather you have a young daughter and I didn't want to ring at an inopportune moment. I will need to run through some personal information with you to begin with.'

'Of course, thank you. We're just about to have dinner and by the time I settle her down it's probably going to be around eight o'clock before I'm free. Is that too late, Oliver?'

'Please, call me Ollie. No, that's fine. I'll have Harrison text you my Skype ID. If you can send a request, I'll add you to my contacts ready for the call. Hopefully we'll speak later.'

'I appreciate it, Ollie. Many thanks.'

Rosie appears for the tail end of the conversation, probably hungry and wanting to know when it's going to be time to eat.

'Five minutes, darling, and this will be ready. Why don't you grab a drink and lay the table for me?'

'Okay, Mum.'

She was bright enough when I picked her up from school and she's much more like her usual self again, I'm glad to see.

'How do you fancy a long weekend at Grandma and Granddad's a week from Friday? I'm going back to Athens to photograph the other villa and the flight times are awful. And the journey is via Frankfurt, so it's going to involve a lot of time hanging around in airports and not much actual time in Athens.'

Her head pops up and her interest is piqued.

'I don't suppose Bella will still be there, Mum, will she?' I can follow her thinking.

'No, darling. She'll be back home in York by then, I'm afraid.'

'It's boring at the airports, isn't it? Will Daniel still be there?'

Her back is now towards me as she lays out the table mats and the coasters for the drinks.

'Yes, I'm annoyed I couldn't get direct flights and Thanos has confirmed that Daniel is still there. He isn't returning home until after the school holidays have begun.'

'I bet Bella will be getting excited.'

'Grandma and Granddad said something about a trip to the beach, what do you think about that? And they wondered if you might like Callie to go, too? I could talk to Naomi and check whether she's free.'

Rosie spins around, her eyes bright.

'Ooh, that would be great, Mum. You're the best.'

I'm just relieved she doesn't feel I'm leaving her out; once again, Mum and Dad have come to the rescue.

'Later this evening I have an important phone call to take so I thought we'd eat, sit and watch something on TV together and then I'll settle you down about seven-thirty. If we start watching a film down here and don't finish it, then you can watch the end of it in bed, maybe.'

'Okay. Sounds good. Mum, why don't you go out on dates?'

I freeze, looking at her innocent little face asking what she obviously feels is a reasonable enough question. The seconds begin to tick by.

'Well ... because life is rather busy and I don't really have the time.'

She seems to be mulling that over.

'You're always busy, Mum. What if there's never time? And what if Dad never comes back?'

I had no idea she even thought that was a possibility. But then we rarely talk about it and when we had the first conversation she was very young indeed.

'Sometimes people aren't right for each other, Rosie, and they grow apart. Meeting a special someone is something that just happens and you don't always have to go out on a date for that to happen. A bit like when you make new friends. Your paths just happen to cross. Maybe one day, who knows? As for Dad, well, he'll get in touch when he's ready but we need to be prepared for the fact that it might not happen, darling.'

She's still too young to face the facts and it's hard talking about it whilst trying not to say anything that will colour her judgement. Either giving her false hope, or worse – communicating my anger and what amounts to disgust at the situation Antonio left us in.

'I was wondering, that's all. Someone's mum has just got remarried and she has a new surname now. That must be really weird.'

I jumped to conclusions there and I am a little relieved to hear what triggered this line of questioning. I'm not looking forward to that phone call with Ollie, but I need to know where I stand before I respond to Zita.

~

When I press the answer icon on my laptop the face looking back at me is very personable. Not instantly attractive, like Harrison's, but friendly and the sort of person you feel you can trust. Ollie is sitting in a study; behind him is a glass-fronted case filled with books.

'Before we begin, and on a very personal note, thank you for being so supportive to Harrison. There aren't many people he can confide in and if I was the jealous type I'd be concerned as he mentions your name daily.'

I let out a little chuckle.

'I hope you've read our texts as that should reassure you. He's like the big brother I always longed to have, but don't tell him I said that.'

It's Ollie's turn to laugh and his voice is deep, and warm.

'This weekend will be a landmark and I can't wait until it's over. Anyway, let me tell you a little about my background. I'm a divorce solicitor specialising in assisting families to work through the issues which follow on as a natural consequence. I am a member of a family law organisation which is committed to the constructive resolution of divorce. This means taking a non-confrontational approach, which I believe is the only way to get through a very difficult time. How many years have you been separated?'

'Seven. There has been no contact at all between us. Rosie was almost two years old when Antonio disappeared.'

Ollie's head bends slightly and it's obvious he's taking notes.

'It would help me considerably if you could talk me through what happened in detail. When Harrison gave me your contact details he did mention that your husband had recently contacted his parents. They sent you a letter, I believe – could you let me have a copy of that? Once I have the full picture we can look at what sort of outcome you are looking for and what steps need to be taken.

'It's unfortunate that you didn't start divorce proceedings while you still had no idea of his whereabouts. Harrison mentioned he lives in Florida now and that could slow down proceedings. Much depends upon you both agreeing on the best possible resolution when it comes down to taking care of Rosie. Also, whether or not he is looking for access or shared custody and the arrangements for financial support throughout her childhood.'

I know this is all matter of fact stuff to a solicitor but I'm horrified.

'I want nothing from Antonio. I'm hoping he expects nothing from us in return. He hasn't seen his daughter for nearly seven years and I doubt he would even be able to recognise her. She certainly wouldn't know him. I don't want to rob Rosie of anything but my fear is that he'll come back into her life and then let her down again. I couldn't bear that, Ollie.'

He looks up at me from the screen and nods his head in acknowledgement.

'Let's begin by gathering the facts together. I'll be better placed, then, to talk you through the process and the options open to your husband so you have a better understanding of how it all works.'

My heart sinks a little when I hear his words. Naively I had assumed Antonio would have no rights to Rosie at all.

It's a long call and Ollie obviously knows exactly what

to ask to elicit the information he requires. I'm sure he hears similar stories all the time. However, it's still hard for me to talk about it, so soon after having to relive it all by telling Jackie Kimberley my complete history.

Afterwards, Ollie says he'd be surprised if Antonio intended to make any financial claims against me. My draw drops at that point, as I hadn't even considered that possibility, but I let him continue. I had explained that the equity of the house was eaten up by the arrears on the mortgage payments. The fact that I then had to pay off, out of my own pocket, the money owing on the credit cards and other debts, he felt was significant enough bargaining power. He asks me to think about whether I really didn't want to make a claim against Antonio, even for child support. My head is aching with it all but I tell him straight that I don't intend on taking a penny from Antonio out of principle, even if it was offered.

Ollie goes on to explain that the big unknown is whether Antonio was going to make any demands regarding access, or custody of Rosie in the future. My blood runs cold at the thought, even though common sense tells me I might have no choice. I ask him what happens when two parties can't agree and he says simply that a judge would make the ultimate decision, but only after a series of steps had been taken.

'If you were both in the UK it would be easier as you could sit down, with or without the help of a dispute-resolution service, and agree a parenting plan. If you failed to reach an agreement then there is a service known as

CAFCASS who get involved. It stands for Children and Family Court Advisory and Support Services. Social workers assess the home environment and most certainly a child of Rosie's age would be interviewed to find out what she would like the outcome to be. The judge would make his decision based upon those reports.

'You will need to obtain his address and if you like I can draft you a suitable reply to his parents' letter. As he has chosen to have no direct contact with you at this stage, the less you say, the better. He's only enquiring after Rosie's wellbeing, for the moment. Although it seems that his parents are asking for your views on what they should do next, my advice is that you do not get involved in any way at all.'

I'm feeling overwhelmed and fearful. Ollie can see my distress as it's not something I can hide.

'Leah, nothing is going to happen overnight. Rosie is settled and has been for the last seven years; no judge would undermine the way you have cared and provided for her. All of that bodes well. Let's concentrate on getting that address so we can begin the process. You can rest assured that I'll do my very best to keep costs to a minimum, especially given your circumstances. The aim is to make this as smooth and painless as possible on all fronts. He would have to be a very unreasonable man to start making demands after such a long period of total silence. Let's not preempt a worst-case scenario, but hope for a satisfactory outcome for you and Rosie.'

We disconnect and I reach for my phone to text Harrison.

Just finished Skyping with Ollie. He's one lovely guy. If anyone can help me, it's him. I'm afraid but I won't dwell on it because at least I don't feel I'm alone in this battle. Ollie says I should hope for the best. Life, eh?

When I climb into bed it's hard not to keep replaying some of the things Ollie said over and over in my mind. However, experience has now taught me that worry solves nothing, so I must focus on the things I can control, instead. Simply because I have no other option.

My phone pings and it's a reply from Harrison.

My other useful contact is a martial arts expert; let me know if you need his services. James Bond eat your heart out … this guy is a lethal weapon.

It's enough to put a little smile on my face as I lay my head down on the pillow. What would I do without Harrison's friendship? At the moment he's keeping me sane.

Working All Hours

By the time Saturday comes around I need a break from work. I'm back to doing all the hours I can and it is good news in one respect, because my bank balance is growing fast. *Loving Life* were very enthusiastic when they read the first article I submitted and things are looking great on that front. My website hits grow daily and the changes I made accommodate a lot more general advertising. But with unknown solicitor's fees looming on the horizon I have no choice but to take on every advertiser who comes my way.

Rosie has another practice session this morning at the gym and, as usual, I drop her off then head to the café to meet Sally.

'You look tired,' she says, hugging me. 'Sorry, that was tactless of me. Of course you're tired, you never stand still for a moment.'

I see her cup is empty and I flag down a passing waitress to order two cappuccinos.

'I'm drained more than tired. Still, no point moaning about it. I'm just getting as much done as I can before I leave for Athens again next Friday.'

Sally gives me an excited grin. 'Footloose for three days, eh? I hope there will be something more than just those stunning views for you to admire.'

I wonder if I should tell her about Daniel, but my phone pings and it's an email from Harrison.

'Sorry, I've been waiting for this and I will need to do a quick response.' I forage around for my purse, then hand Sally a twenty-pound note. 'I think we deserve cake, as well, don't you?'

She smiles, humouring me and makes her way to the counter.

Hi Leah

Well, it's done. I feel like a deflated balloon, sinking to the ground and with nothing to hold me up. It's going to take me a while to recover, after living on my nerves for weeks on end, now. The upside is that the reaction from my folks wasn't quite the one I was expecting. I sat them down and began pacing, then I thought of you and I just blurted it out. I said that I'd found my life partner and his name is Oliver.

Mum immediately burst into tears and threw herself on Dad. I stood there looking at them both, frozen to the spot. Then Dad looked up and said, 'Thank God. We were convinced you had some awful illness you'd been hiding from us this last couple of months. That's good news, son. All we want is for you to be happy and for a long time we feared you'd never find that.'

I asked them how they felt about it being common knowledge at some point and they didn't seem bothered at all. Mum was more concerned about when they would get to meet Ollie and asked whether his parents knew. I explained that he'd come out a couple of years ago but hadn't been in a long-term relationship until now.

I'm on my way over to see Ollie and we're going to visit his parents, next. My parents have invited us both around for dinner next Saturday. And that's it. The sky didn't cave in and the ground is still beneath my feet. You were right. It's never quite as bad as we fear, is it? Our own imaginations can conjure up greater demons than often exist in real life.

I couldn't have done it without your support, Leah, so know that I'm here for you always.

H

I type a quick response.

Your future starts here. Enjoy it and give Ollie my best regards. Lx

When I look up Sally is back with two huge slices of Victoria sandwich.

'I do hope that's a man you're emailing.'

'It's Harrison, you know, the great guy I told you about. He's just told his parents about Ollie and it was a big deal for him. No more hiding from now on. Ironically, they were convinced the secret he was hiding was some sort of serious illness. His mother burst into tears of relief!'

'Honesty is always the best policy. You have to be really clever to live a lie.'

I nod, shovelling in a fork full of cake, aware of the irony in her statement and trying not to let it turn the mouthful of delicious sponge in my mouth to ashes.

'Speaking of liars, Harrison put me in touch with Ollie, who is a divorce solicitor dealing mainly with family issues. He drafted a reply for me to send to Zita. It didn't say much, mainly explaining that while I did require Antonio's address because I was going to be serving him divorce papers, I couldn't advise them on how to respond to him. After seven years of being apart I hoped they would understand why it was necessary for me to move on. He said it was best not to be drawn into a conversation and to keep it simple.'

Sally gives me a sympathetic look.

'You must surely be coming to the end of the misery all this has created in your life. Hang in there a while longer, Leah. How's your dad doing?'

'Better. He's lost a little weight on the new diet he's on and his blood pressure and sugar levels are now back within the normal range. Mum has no intention of letting him become diabetic and they, too, now do two walks a day. Ironically, I've missed a few lately.'

'Well, you're busy and all these things suck up time. Five days and you'll be flying off again, though.'

Daniel's face pops into my mind and it's hard not to groan about the uncertainty of what lies ahead. Sally is looking at me curiously, no doubt wondering what I'm thinking, so it's definitely time to change the subject.

'Anyway, how's life in your household? Are they all behaving themselves?' She has three dogs and a husband, all of whom seem to test her patience to the limit at times but she loves them all to death nonetheless.

She sniggers. 'Do they ever? Tyler has decided to lay some new flooring in the sitting room. He spends more time swearing at the boards because they won't click together, than he does laying them. It's going to take him forever. Gruffalo has a poorly paw and isn't sleeping well, so that means no one in our house is getting an undisturbed night's sleep. He had me up three times last night with his whining. I tried my best to console him so we didn't all have to lose the entire night's sleep. The vet thinks it will take another four or five days for the infection to clear and the cut to heal.'

'Ah, poor little thing. I don't envy you the disturbed nights, though, it's like having a baby all over again.'

The moment I finish speaking I look up to see that she's gone bright red in the face.

'Um ... that's another little bit of news. Seems I can get pregnant, after all!'

I throw down my fork with a clatter and jump up, leaning across to throw my arms around her.

'That's brilliant! How long have you known? I had no idea!'

I slide back into my seat and we're both beaming from ear to ear.

'I saw my doctor yesterday after work. He did the test and says I'm six weeks along, so early days. We aren't going to tell anyone, well, just you until I'm past the three-month stage.' She leans closer, lowering her voice. 'To be honest I thought I had a water infection.'

'Ha! Ha! I love it. Congratulations, Sally, I'm thrilled for you both.'

I think back to when I first found out I was expecting Rosie. Life looked so wonderful then, stretching out ahead of me with nothing but good things on the horizon. But look at how far I've come. Sally is right, I simply need to hang in there for a little while longer. Good things are coming my way, something deep down inside of me is telling me that loud and clear. How exactly everything is going to fall miraculously into place, I don't know, but I don't think that gut instincts can lie or mislead.

I'm trying not to fret over the fact that I've heard nothing at all from Daniel. Contrary to Harrison's advice I decided I'm going to spring this visit on him and I hinted to Thanos that I thought it would be a nice surprise for Daniel to have some unexpected company. I sensed a little amusement in his voice so I hope Daniel's reaction is a positive one, because if it isn't it's going to be a hellish few days. Maybe all I need to do is start believing and stop fearing the worst. But it wouldn't be the first time in my life I misjudged something quite badly and ended up getting burnt, would it?

When I collect Rosie after class she's quiet, and I make several attempts at conversation on the drive home. Silence reigns until I open the front door. Discarding her gym bag and coat in a heap on the floor she lets out a sigh.

'Mum, I'm getting tired of going to classes. It's okay, but I think I'm growing out of it. After this exhibition is over can I give up gym? Would you mind?'

I look at her serious little face, wondering what has sparked this.

'You don't have to go if you don't want to, Rosie. But are you sure?'

She chews on her lip, screwing up her face for a moment.

'Yep, I'm sure. It was fun but now it's a bit ... boring. Don't tell Mrs Peterson I said that though, as it will hurt her feelings.'

I keep a straight face. 'No, of course not.'

'It's time for a change and I'd quite like to try a Taekwondo class, instead.'

My little girl is growing up and beginning to make her own decisions. I'm rather pleased about this development, as the art of self-defence is a great skill to begin acquiring at a young age.

'We'll sort something out, then.'

'Thanks, Mum. Besides, only two boys go to gym club and Callie said there are lots at her class.'

Boys. Oh, dear me! I'm so blinkered these days, what else have I missed? She comes across to give me a hug.

'Life should be fun, Mum, shouldn't it? Or, that's what Grandma says, anyway.'

'And she's right, Rosie. We must never forget that.'

Suddenly any work I have planned for this weekend is shelved.

'How about tomorrow we go for a swim in the morning and ten pin bowling in the afternoon?'

Her eyes shine like the lights on a Christmas tree; she sparkles.

'Awesome!! You're the best!'

Filled with Both Dread and Excitement in Equal Measure

I watch Rosie chasing around the back garden at Mum and Dad's. She has managed to entice Scruffy through the hole in the fence, even though it's only eight in the morning. She's all legs and arms, growing upwards and not outwards. My beautiful little girl hasn't just hit another growth spurt but she's changing in so many other ways too. I think she's going to be much more adventurous than I am and that thought makes me happy.

It's time for me to leave for the airport and when I call out she comes over to give me a lingering hug. I'm proud of the fact that she's confident enough not to feel that I need to be there every minute of every day. Rosie is so excited about the weekend ahead and the fact that she's having an extra day off when everyone else is at school. I know my parents dote on her but she's well-balanced and doesn't every child deserve a little spoiling occasionally?

'Travel safely,' Mum says as she wraps her arms around me. 'I'll be thinking of you and hoping Athens doesn't disappoint the second time around.'

Me too, Mum. Me too.

She steps back and scans my face for a moment. I've said little but Rosie has mentioned Daniel and Bella's names numerous times since we arrived back. I know she can see the nervous excitement that's rising up within me, which is barely containable.

Dad is next and he whispers in my ear, 'Have some fun, Leah. And we'll take good care of our girl.'

As I set off I wonder if this trip is going to feel different, knowing it could end up breaking my heart. Or making me the happiest woman alive. But it doesn't and I feel no guilt whatsoever at surprising Daniel, as I need to see his initial reaction. I know Rosie is going to be fine and the thought of seeing Daniel again is exhilarating because no matter what reservations I have, hope is something I'm tenuously holding onto like a lifeline. But it will be a long day, that's for sure, and with a two-hour wait at Frankfurt I probably won't arrive at the villa until sometime after 6 p.m.

Thanos said that if Daniel isn't there, to give him a call and Iliana is only minutes away. The thought of having to sit around waiting for Daniel to return if he's out for the evening is agony, but that might be the price I have to pay.

~

My taxi is late but the driver is very apologetic indeed, explaining that an accident caused a lot of congestion on the way to the airport. His English is extremely good but he doesn't say a lot on the journey and I'm too nervous to make polite conversation for the sake of it.

It's so good to be back. Watching the scenery whizzing past the car window transports me back to that day when Rosie and I had our first glimpses of Athens. I had no idea it would cast a spell over us, for that's what it did. Even working holidays are very enjoyable but Athens was extra special and that's not something you can engineer.

The air conditioner is blasting out in the car and already I'm glad of it. I long to step under a cool shower and wash away the dust and grime of the day. At long last the car draws up in front of the gated access to the villa and the driver presses the buzzer. My stomach begins to perform little somersaults, which is ridiculous as I can't even be sure that Daniel is going to be there to greet me. But as I step out from the car and the front door opens, there he is – staring at me, as if he can't believe what he's seeing. But it's swiftly followed by a smile that rings true. He's clearly delighted to see me and I utter a silent prayer of thanks.

'Welcome back stranger. I had no idea you were coming.' he says, stepping forward to give me a hearty, welcoming hug. It's so good to be in his arms again that my legs almost buckle beneath me. The smell and feel of him is comforting and my heart is pounding in my chest.

It leaves me speechless, so I ease myself away from him to turn back around and hand the driver his tip.

The driver gives me a nod and deposits my suitcase on the doorstep, which Daniel immediately picks up as he ushers me inside. It gives me enough time to compose myself, take a few discreet deep breaths and think of an appropriate opener.

'It seems unreal to be back here again so soon but I have to re-take the photos. I've had to drop everything to get this sorted as I don't want to let Thanos down.' It sounds convincing, even to my own ears but that's the difference between something that's based on the truth and a total lie.

'Well, I haven't seen him since I arrived back after my little trip. The dig has unearthed a very rare find indeed and it's put me behind on the preparation for my handover.' Daniel throws the words over his shoulder as he leads me up the sweeping staircase. 'You have no idea how wonderful it is to see you, Leah.' There is excitement in his voice but also a hint of shocked disbelief. All I can think about it why he couldn't have found a few minutes to text me? And if the discovery is that big a deal then I'm rather disappointed he didn't want to share his good news with me.

'George Emmet is here still but I can't remember if you bumped into him on your first trip. He's an old friend of mine and we've done quite a few digs together. Are you too tired to eat? Iliana was here this morning and has prepared a large dish of moussaka. If that's too heavy for you I can put together a quick salad.'

Daniel must be nervous because he hasn't stopped

chatting. He pauses at last, placing my suitcase inside the door to the master suite. I know I look crumpled and hot, and I'm so nervous I'm finding it hard to know what to say. Daniel is looking at me expectantly.

'How's Bella's ankle?'

'Much better, thank you. It was a pretty bad sprain, though. Tricia said it was painful for about a week after she was able to put her full weight on it, but you know what kids are like, nothing stops them for long.'

'Good. Right. Um ... maybe a shower and a change of clothes would make me feel a little less travel-weary. Give me half an hour?'

'Absolutely,' he says but doesn't move.

After a few seconds he grins. 'Right. See you out on the terrace whenever you are ready. Red or white wine?'

'Surprise me,' I reply, hoping that this is going to be a night of surprises. If that is indeed the case, it's already off to a flying start.

As he exits, closing the door behind him, I grab my phone to text Harrison.

OMG – I'm with Daniel and he's nervous!!! He's been busy with the dig, some big find apparently. I can't believe I'm actually back at the villa, or that I'm doing this. Off to shower. Wish me luck!

By the time I'm slipping into one of my strappy little dresses and about to turn my attention to putting up my hair, Harrison has responded.

Tell him you missed him. That's an order. If you don't have the courage to say anything else at all you MUST, repeat MUST say those words. No regrets on this trip, whatever happens.

I close my eyes and exhale sharply, feeling like a nervous teenager all over again. I'm conscious Daniel is waiting downstairs and I quickly twist my curls up off my neck and fasten them in place with a large clip. A little touch of mascara and a swipe with a lip gloss wand will have to do tonight. A pair of crystal, pearl drop earrings adds a little something and I finish off with a spray of perfume; I'm not too dissatisfied. This is about as good as it gets and I want Daniel to see I've made an effort for him.

As I descend the stairs the house is quiet and I assume Daniel is in the garden. However, when I walk into the open plan area, the state of the usually clear, pristine work surfaces and uniform doors hiding probably every appliance you could ever wish for, gives me a shock. Daniel looks hot and bothered and there's stuff absolutely everywhere.

'What on earth are you doing?' I can't help asking. Is he preparing for a party?

'Making a bit of a mistake and I'm afraid Iliana is going to be most upset. I thought I'd do a starter to impress you. *Saganaki* is deep fried cheese drizzled with honey and a salad on the side. It's not difficult so I have no idea how I've managed to make so much mess.'

He looks around in dismay. Every single item he's used is out on the counter top and instead of putting things back, he keeps adding to the chaos. Half of the unit doors are open and it's in total disarray.

'The moussaka is in the oven, though,' he offers hopefully.

'Okay. You finish off what you're doing and I'll start tidying up. Good idea?'

He grins at me sheepishly. 'If you don't mind.'

I gather up an armful of salad items, returning them to the larder fridge. Then I hunt around to find the right home for an assortment of things he seems to have used in his cheese dish. There are several different types of dried herb, some flour and an open packet of crisps. I raise an eyebrow. Did he use those as well?

'Oh, um … that was my snack. I haven't eaten all day.'

I try to keep my face composed as I turn, looking for the sink. I don't want him to think I'm mocking his efforts. His rumpled frustration is just adorable and it's hard to keep my hands to myself.

'I need to wash this top down. Point me in the right direction.'

Daniel spins around to look at me as I stand, poised with some kitchen towel clutched in my wayward hands to keep them occupied.

'Press the button on the floor with your foot.'

As I do, part of the countertop swings up to form a backsplash and reveals an inset, double sink.

'Clever. I like it.'

By the time Daniel has finished with the deep fryer, I place the individual salads and the pot of honey on a tray he has ready and waiting. He scoops the slices of cooked cheese onto the two plates, satisfying himself it looks presentable.

'It looks a lot tidier now, thanks to you. I'm not very competent in the kitchen and I'm afraid it shows.'

'I'll buff up the worktops once dinner is over. Iliana won't suspect a thing.'

Daniel carries the tray out and I follow with a bottle of wine and two glasses.

'When is George due back?' I ask, wondering if he'll be joining us for the main course.

'Not until late, if at all tonight. He's at a birthday party for one of our colleagues.'

'And you missed the celebrations?' I look at him quizzically.

'I wasn't in the mood to party. Too much going on inside my head at the moment, I'm afraid.'

Daniel places the tray on the table and I take a seat, buzzing with happiness.

As he drizzles the honey over the hot cheese I take a moment to look around, remembering the last time I was here. Tonight, it's much cooler, but pleasantly so and the air isn't quite so stifling as it had been.

'There's a lovely little breeze going tonight,' I comment, inhaling deeply to savour the smell of the sweet jasmine in the air around us.

At last he's ready to sit down.

'Please, don't wait. This is a dish best eaten when it's still warm.'

I've never had fried cheese before and I'm curious. I'm not sure I like the idea of it, if I'm honest, but after the lengths he's gone to, I should at least give it a try.

It's a total revelation. 'Hmm ... that's wonderful with the honey. It doesn't taste fried, does it? It could be baked. And it's called *saganaki*? That sounds Japanese.'

Daniel is busy pouring wine and hasn't touched his plate yet. I pop another piece of delicious cheese into my mouth and lay down my fork, putting my elbows on the table and resting my chin on my upturned hands.

He's gone from chatting nonstop, to suddenly clamming up.

'I'm glad to be back.' I throw out the words to see his reaction.

Daniel doesn't respond but hands me a glass, his eyes not wavering from mine. I lower my arms, wondering if I'd been trying to create a little barrier between us. Self-preservation, maybe.

'And I'm glad you're here. I meant what I said when we parted last time.'

I sit back, cradling the glass in my hands, recalling his comment that 'it wouldn't be like this forever but he wasn't quite there yet?' Suddenly, the words that are going around and around inside my head slip softly from my lips. 'I missed you.'

Daniel sets his own glass down, running a hand through his shoulder-length hair to scoop it back from his face.

'After I arrived back at the villa it took me a while to settle into my routine. You kept creeping into my thoughts and I had to keep pushing you away. I have a job to finish off here and loose ends to tie up. I knew you'd understand that.'

It's worrying that he feels he has to explain. The devil on my shoulder wonders if he's simply making excuses. Thirteen days with no contact at all after a solitary text isn't exactly reassuring.

'Of course.' Reluctantly I lower my eyes, feeling a nuance of tension growing between us.

He picks up his fork and begins eating. 'It's not bad, even if I do say so myself.'

I am hungry and even though my nerves are on edge, it doesn't dull my appetite. Sitting here, alone together, sharing a meal is like living in a dream.

When the plates are empty Daniel loads up the tray to take the dishes inside. When he returns he has a large candle in a glass holder. He places it to the side of the table and lights the wick.

'Twenty more minutes for the moussaka. Time for you to tell me your plans. How long are you here for? I bet Rosie wanted to accompany you. This must have really upset your workload.'

'Hey, Daniel. I'm back early. It was tiny party food and I'm still starving. What's cooking? Oh, you didn't say you were expecting company.'

I assume this is George but he seems to have appeared out of nowhere. A moment of something akin to resignation flashes over Daniel's face before he recovers enough to introduce us. I shake hands with George and he leans in to kiss my cheek, leaving Daniel to look on with a hint of annoyance. Is he cross because George has walked in on our dinner, or because he's acting so friendly towards me?

'I'm not interrupting anything, am I?' George asks, looking from one to the other of us.

We both shake our heads, plastering on awkward smiles. Daniel heads off to the kitchen to grab an extra glass while George engages me in conversation about the awful music people play at parties.

'It doesn't matter what country you're in, or who you are with. It's like re-runs of the Eurovision Song Contest. Man, there's plenty of good music out there and they choose the stuff they play in elevators.'

I think it's going to be a long evening.

A Goodnight Kiss

George is quite a character and we have been laughing all evening as he regales us with tales of some of his riskier pursuits. He's a bit of an adrenalin junkie by the sound of it and he is totally oblivious to the candid looks passing between Daniel and me.

Ironically, instead of retracting into his shell it's making Daniel even bolder. On several occasions, he purposely engineers a reason to walk around to my side of the table. He seems to be constantly topping up my drink, even though I'm merely taking the odd sip, and each time he lingers by me. I'm flattered by the way he takes every opportunity to either place a hand on my shoulder or brush his fingers against my arm. In the end, we are openly giggling about it, but it doesn't seem to stem George's flow at all.

It's well after midnight when George eventually stands, quite abruptly, having drunk most of the contents of the two empty wine bottles on the table and says goodnight.

He isn't even totally out of earshot before Daniel leans in to say, 'I thought he'd never run out of steam.'

I burst out laughing, nervous energy now coursing around my body. I've never felt more awake or more alive than I do right now.

'I'm sorry. There's so much we need to discuss now we have the chance and I had no idea he even intended coming back here tonight. George is great company but he's a party animal at heart and he doesn't do quiet dinners. I know you are here for a specific reason and you have a lot to do tomorrow, but can I help in any way? If you need to retrace your steps I can be your guide and we can maybe claw back a little time to...'

He hesitates and even in the moonlight I can see he's buzzing just as much as I am.

'... pick up where we left off?' I suggest.

He nods. It's obvious that neither of us is referring to the sex – this is about all the things that were left unsaid.

'My biggest fear is being lied to because of what Antonio put me through. I realise with hindsight that I never really knew him at all and that's a scary thought. I have to be sure you understand that I won't settle for less than total honesty, even if it's painful.' I know Harrison would be proud of me for saying out loud the words that are going through my mind.

'I understand that and yes, I've been busy but I've also been wrestling with my conscience. I was reluctant to contact you because ... well, life is complicated, isn't it? I'm not really in a position where I'm able to commit long-term to anything right now. I hope that changes in the future, but I can't be sure and it would be wrong of me to pretend that isn't the case.

'I could see you were horrified by the thought that I'd had problems with my health and so I walked away knowing I'd only added to your worries. With hindsight it was unfair of me to start something with you and yet, here I am with yet another chance and I can't help myself, Leah. I was captivated from the moment I first saw you.'

We lean in towards each other and Daniel takes my hand, drawing me to my feet. He wraps his arms around me, snuggling me close to his body and I love the heat of him radiating out. He's solid, like one of the pillars from the Acropolis, and I feel wanted, safe and strangely at peace, all at the same time. I hold my breath, unwilling to break the spell. Standing completely still, tantalising seconds turn into minutes.

Then he finally lowers his head, his mouth brushing against my ear before he moves away to begin speaking again.

'We take so much for granted in blissful ignorance and then when things go wrong it shakes your belief that life can ever be wonderful again. I felt your pain and anger when you were telling me what had happened to you and Rosie. No wonder I sensed the cautiousness around you and I could see that my own troubles compounded that. But neither of us could deny the attraction we felt for one another, could we? And that's why I flew over to see you. But having stepped into your world briefly, I began to realise how hard you've worked to put your life back together again. You deserve someone who doesn't come with a multitude of problems.'

His words are tense with emotion but still he's skirting the main issue here and I think he's very aware of that. Sadness and frustration begin to gnaw away deep inside of me but I don't want to preempt where this could lead. He pulls me close to allay my anxiety and I rest my head against the solid muscle of his chest. I can hear his heart beating so loudly and I can feel the passion within him, as his arms travel down to encircle my waist.

'I need to know for sure if there really can be an *us*. I can't rush into anything either, so that's not a concern to me. I've started seeing a counsellor and she told me that before I can put the past behind me, I first need to grieve over what happened.

'You see, I didn't just lose my husband that day because he also took my twin sister, Kelly, with him. As I started to piece things together I found out that Antonio's business had folded weeks beforehand. The bank was already preparing to repossess the house and there was over twenty-five thousand pounds of debt on credit cards that were in our joint names. He'd been living a lie for a long time and doing whatever was necessary to make everything appear as normal.'

Daniel's arm flexes and tightens around me.

'Unbelievable!' His tone is one of shock and disgust but it demonstrates the level of honesty I'm expecting in return. He pauses for a moment, resting his head against mine and then begins speaking again, softly. 'So he didn't just rip your marriage apart, he ripped your whole family apart, too. What sort of man does that and can walk away knowing the devastation he's leaving behind him? It's not just selfishness, it shows a total lack of conscience. Jeez, Leah, you're one strong woman simply to survive in the aftermath of that.'

'I needed you to understand, Daniel, that I took the biggest risk of my entire life in flying back here to see you. I don't know what I have to offer if I'm honest, but being around you made me feel something I haven't felt in a long time. I wasn't simply Rosie's mum for a while there. I was a woman finding herself drawn to a man, even though I'm scared to love again. But the choices I make going forward affect Rosie, too. I can't risk making a monumental mistake again.'

He gives me a comforting squeeze.

'Sort of sums up both of our lives at the moment, by the sound of it. Nothing ever seems to slot into place easily and there's always someone else to consider first and foremost. But that's no reason to give up on something even if it takes us down a difficult road to begin with.'

I draw my head away from him, tilting it back to look up into his eyes.

'I need to tread so carefully, Daniel, and I know it would take a very special person to understand that; someone in a similar sort of position who appreciates that responsibilities can't simply be waved aside, no matter how much that hurts. Whatever it is that you are holding back needs to be said if we are to have a chance of taking our relationship forward. It took me a while to think about what I need to share with you and, to be honest, tonight I just want to sink into bed and sleep. But I'm here, waiting to listen when you are finally ready to open up to me. If you can't do that, then I have to walk away no matter how much it hurts. Or how much I'm beginning to care for you. I leave on Sunday morning and I need to fly home knowing where I stand.'

We peel away from each other and Daniel grasps my hand in his, drawing me to the steps leading away from the terrace. We walk, hand in hand down towards the path below the swimming pool and gaze out over the rippling waves of the ocean. The moonlight is dispersed on the water by the soft breeze. It scatters shards of silver like erratic glitter, circling outwards until it dissipates and the next breath of wind recreates the scene again and again.

'I understand, Leah. You deserve no less than that. Just give me a little time to face my own demons first and find the right words.'

I nod in tacit agreement, and he swings his body around to stand facing me, grabbing my other hand, too.

'What's the plan of action to sort out your problem with the photos?' he asks.

'I need to retrace my steps. A few in the National Gardens maybe and the Temple of Zeus, again. One of the Parliament building and then back here I need to take lots of photos of both villas. Thanos was going to arrange for access to the other villa, too?'

Daniel raises my fingertips to his lips, not taking his eyes away from my face.

'The painters are currently working on it and we can view it at your leisure. They work Saturdays so we won't need a key. All of that is easily do-able. Shall we get the boring stuff out of the way first thing in the morning? And I'd like to take you somewhere special tomorrow night. I'm not willing to risk another night with George, as amusing as he is.'

We exchange meaningful smiles.

There's nothing more I would love than to fall into bed next to Daniel tonight, but I know that would be a big mistake. I need to reinforce what amounts to the ultimatum I've given him and he's as good as admitted it isn't going to be easy for him. That fills me with dread but I have to be patient and wait until he's ready.

As we part company at the door to the master suite, Daniel and I share a lingering kiss. His lips are gentle and seek mine out eagerly, while his beard tickles against my skin. We both want more but know that surrendering to the act of physical love requires letting go of much more than just your body. When your emotions are in turmoil you feel vulnerable and the decision he has to make might end up finishing everything between us. That sort of level of respect is the only way I can move forward with, or without him. The fact that I've now made it very clear to Daniel is a dilemma he needs to think long and hard about.

I fall asleep with the imprint of his kiss still lingering on my lips in a very real way. Can dreams come true when the right person comes along? Is this our destiny and not just a little detour on the rocky path of life? But what if he can't face up to his fears and put them into words so that I can understand what's going on? I know how hard it was for me to share my own personal humiliation. My eyelids close, exhaustion claims me and, thankfully, drags me down into a deep and dreamless sleep.

Retracing Our Steps

I awake abruptly and open my eyes with a jolt, the sunlight instantly reminding me where I am. Grabbing my phone I see that it's almost 6 a.m. There's a text from Harrison sent fifteen minutes ago.

I hope you are waking up to the start of a great day after a wonderful night.

He has even attached an emoji of a blushing face. My fingers tap away.

It was wonderful but not in that way. I'm fragile, remember? I'm excited about today, though.

He's online, too, and the response is instant.

Wish I was there, it's raining here.

I smile to myself.

Glad you aren't. Three's a crowd!

Seconds later there's another ping.

Sounds promising, then – enjoy! Dinner with my parents tonight so they can finally meet Ollie. Wish me luck. Text me when you can and let down that guard of yours.

I send him back a smiley face emoji and open up my inbox. There's an email from Zita and Guido. They say they understand about the divorce and enclose the address Antonio gave them. They go on to say they will reply to him but will say nothing at all about me. They will tell him only that Rosie is doing well. They end with: *our son has broken many hearts and he has now to live with that.*

Now is not the time for me to deal with this so I simply forward the email to Ollie. I add a brief note to say that I will respond simply thanking them and leave it at that. I hate the fact that this seems to have created a bit of a barrier between his parents and me, once again. However, I have no choice but to wait until Antonio's intentions become clear in case he tries to use them. They mean well and will never get over what he has done. Zita and Guido are proud people who would never, knowingly, hurt anyone but I have no idea if Antonio respects that fact.

Next, I text Mum to say I'll ring later in the day, hoping to catch them at the beach.

There's a light tap on the door and as it opens a rather dishevelled-looking Daniel comes into view.

'I thought you'd be an early bird. I have coffee, or is it too early? Are you working?'

I sit up in bed, smiling at Daniel as the door swings open a little wider and he stoops to pick up two, not one, mugs of coffee.

'Do you mind if I invite myself in?'

I run my hands through my curls, wondering what my bed hair looks like this morning. But Daniel is beaming at me so it can't be that bad. He looks like he's just leapt out of bed himself. There's something rather endearing about that.

'You're a sight for sore eyes. I slept like a log, even though my mind was churning after last night. How did you sleep?' He hands me a mug and I pat the bed next to me; Daniel sits on the edge, turning to face me.

'Great, thanks. I wasn't working. Just checking my emails and texts. My estranged husband has finally made contact with his parents for the first time since he left. They are warm people, devastated by what he did and they didn't know how to respond. I have a solicitor now who is going to start divorce proceedings. Late yesterday afternoon they sent me Antonio's address and I've just forwarded it to my solicitor, Ollie, so the papers can be served. Antonio is living in Florida but beyond that I have no idea why he's reaching out to them now. Apparently, he asked about Rosie.'

Daniel frowns, looking pensive.

'You sense that trouble is brewing?'

I nod. 'I should have sorted this out through the courts long ago when his whereabouts were unknown. It would have been much simpler as he obviously didn't want to be found then. Now, when he receives the papers I have no idea what his reaction will be. I don't want anything from him but what if he wants access to Rosie? I can't trust him and I struggle to accept he has any right to be an influence in her life after what he's done.

'I know my sister is equally to blame and they conspired together. Bridges have been burnt and there is no coming back from that. As I told my counsellor Jackie, they are both lost to me now. But this final hurdle is a huge one and I can't trust him to do the right thing.'

He reaches out with his free hand to lay it over my own, which is outstretched on top of the duvet cover.

'And in the middle of all this mess, our paths cross and that's another situation that isn't straightforward,' he adds, quietly.

Reluctantly withdrawing his hand, we sit looking at each other as we sip our coffees. It's certainly a statement with which I can't disagree.

'I understand, Leah, and you must be feeling sick with anxiety. It's hard to think of anything else with a worry like that hanging over your head. I know only too well how that feels. Bella is about to face the upheaval of Tricia and Evan's wedding. She's adamant she will never call him Dad, but he's still going to be a significant part of her life. Tricia is upset about it, but I told her that Bella needs time to adjust. The truth is that it hurts me too, in here.' He taps his hand against his chest. 'I don't want some other guy being a father to her and the guilt trip over that is immense.

'Oh, I'm careful not to influence her in any way, or endorse the moments when she's angry with them both. Accepting him means accepting that her mother and I will never get back together again. That's hard for a child to battle with and it's tough to be the one trying to guide her through it. I have to encourage her to accept him because this isn't about how I feel, but about making her life as smooth and happy as it can be.'

It takes a real man to be able to acknowledge that and own the vulnerability he'll probably never lose.

'You're a good man, Daniel and a wonderful father. I don't think I'm capable of being as selfless if my worst fears are realised.'

He places his empty mug on the bedside table and takes mine from my hand. Turning around he draws me into him and I savour the warmth of his embrace until he releases me and stands up.

'You're strong and resourceful, Leah and you will get through this. Shall we get ready for an early start and meet downstairs for breakfast on the terrace before we head out? Let's get those photos out of the way as quickly as we can. What do you say?'

'Sounds perfect to me.'

I throw back the lightweight duvet and jump out of bed to stand in front of him, wrapping my arms around his neck.

'Taking it slowly is hard, isn't it?' I murmur as I let my lips lightly touch his cheek.

He groans and pulls away from me, turning on his heels as he heads for the door.

'You'll never know how hard.' He throws the words over his shoulder and I stand there smirking to myself.

~

When I walk into the kitchen breakfast is ready on a tray: two small bowls of Greek yoghurt surrounded by a variety of sliced fruits and berries. The coffee is brewed and the cups await, sitting ready on the counter top. Daniel is standing on the other side of the island with his back to me, dispensing tablets from a foil strip into a pill box divided into daily compartments. When he realises I'm here he immediately shovels everything back into the basket and stows it away in a cupboard below the island.

'Vitamins and supplements,' he explains. 'My daily ritual. I'll just pour the coffee if you want to head on out.'

I take the tray and notice that an empty foil strip lies discarded, next to it. Funny, but that doesn't look like a vitamin or supplement packet. Then again, I don't take anything myself so I wouldn't know. Maybe I should and the benefits would improve my spirits and energy levels. I do give Rosie a special children's multivitamin. She loves it because it tastes like one of her favourite jelly sweets.

We don't linger too long over breakfast as we're both keen to head out. This isn't sightseeing as such and will feel like the ultimate déjà vu. But more importantly I think we both want to factor in some time to sit and relax somewhere together later today. Hopefully, no third party will be involved this time, amusing though George was.

Daniel manages to find a parking space in one of the side streets close to Hadrian's Arch. It's a bit of a squeeze but he expertly manoeuvres the car into it in three simple shunts. Parallel to us is a little gift shop and I'm drawn to step inside, Daniel rather reluctantly trailing behind me.

We wander around and I stop in front of a display case with some small trinket boxes and shaped pebbles in white marble. Carved into the top of each of the boxes is a different flower design.

'Oh, I must buy one of those for Rosie. She'll love it. White marble will always remind us of Athens.' Daniel pretends to browse while the nice man wraps up the present for me. He makes polite conversation, assuming we're a couple and I struggle to keep a straight face.

When we step back outside Daniel looks at me, pointedly.

'Right. Camera primed and working?' he checks, grinning across at me.

'Don't knock it: it's because of my photographic faux pas that I'm here. I was too busy having fun to check what I was capturing and that, I'm afraid, was entirely down to you.'

'Is that a confession? Let's hope second time around you get the perfect shots you need and I'll try my best not to get in the way.'

We walk quickly, Daniel catching my hand and it's wonderful walking along with him by my side. We approach the remains of Hadrian's Arch and saunter past it without stopping, heading straight for the Temple of Zeus. I can't help thinking about the first time we were here. How I longed, then, for Daniel to grab my hand and show me that the connection I felt with him wasn't one-sided. And now, here we are, the two of us alone together. It's hard to believe and I almost want to pinch myself in case this is simply a figment of my imagination.

'Okay, lady, do your thing.'

Daniel stands back while I snap away, this time stopping to check and deleting the photos which fail to show off the remains to their best effect. 'It's hard not to marvel at it all over again but time isn't on our side. Forgive me, Zeus, but I'm a woman on a mission today. This one's done, so now it's on to the park.'

He raises his eyebrows. 'You're really focused when you're wearing your work hat. I'm already feeling the pressure and I only hope I can keep up the pace.'

I smile at his teasing and he catches my hand, turning as he leads us in the direction of the crossing which will take us over to the path that runs parallel with the gardens.

'I hate rushing but something tells me I will come here again and next time I won't miss a thing.' I have no idea why that thought pops into my head, but it does.

'I'll forgive you then, but you could spend a week just touring the museums alone. I'm sure the Greek gods will understand. Everything has a time and a place, that's why they were never put off when it took hundreds of years to complete a build. Emperors and kings came and went, as did political turmoil and enemy attack. Patience, perseverance and sheer determination was how a mighty empire grew.

'I'll follow your lead once we're inside. So long as we keep heading in that direction, then we'll eventually come out at Syntagma and the Parliament building. That was on your hit list, wasn't it?' He points diagonally and I nod.

'Yes. I can't possibly do a feature on Athens without it. I'll also grab a shot of the tomb of the unknown soldier.'

We step through one of the gated entrances to the gardens and I hover just inside. Angling my camera lens upwards, I capture a perfect row of palm trees that soar high above us. Then we meander; some paths are familiar but it's fun to discover other trails which lead to an unexpected vista with a statue and often a bench.

Daniel seems happy to follow me around and I can feel his eyes constantly watching me.

'You know this vertigo thing you suffer from, well ... I've booked somewhere very special for dinner tonight. I need you to trust me that I wouldn't take you anywhere that isn't completely safe. But it might involve you having to keep your eyes closed for a couple of minutes at one point.'

I spin around, taking a few shots of him as he grins back at me.

'Now I'm worried. Why will I need to close my eyes?'

Click, click, click. He rubs his hand down the sides of his beard, rather absentmindedly and peers across at me.

'It's on a hill but we can take a little ride up to it so there's no climbing involved. There are just a few steps that might make you nervous, so I'll need you to close your eyes and let me guide you. I'll be by your side the whole time. Promise.'

We stand gazing at each other, the chemistry between us almost tangible.

'You'll be disappointed if I don't agree, won't you?'

He's still running his fingers down either side of his chin which is a telltale sign he's a bit nervous.

'The food is amazing and I think it's an experience you shouldn't miss. It's nothing at all like the glass floor incident and once we're up there you'll feel safe, really. If I didn't think you'd absolutely love it, then I wouldn't be pressing you.'

How can I resist, when I gaze into those wonderful eyes? I was given a second chance for a reason and I'm not going to let a little fear get in the way of Daniel's surprise.

'As you were good enough to rescue me a couple of times on my last trip it would be ungrateful of me to spoil your plans. I guess the answer is *yes*; I'll put myself in your capable hands once again.'

He walks towards me, placing his arms around my waist and drawing me into him.

'If Athens hasn't already captured your heart, it will tonight, I promise you,' he whispers into my hair.

And how about you, Daniel? Can I capture your heart? The decision to let me in is all yours.

One Enchanted Evening

After a long chat with an excited Rosie, who wants to tell me all about her day at the beach, I look at my watch and see it's time I started to get ready. I dress with care, paying attention to every little detail. I keep my make-up light, but use a dark grey eyeshadow to make my eyelids smoky and extra mascara to make my eyes stand out. Tonight, I've decided to scrunch up my curls and let my hair hang loose to frame my face. A pair of crystal pearl drop earrings add a touch of sparkle as I turn my head.

Fortunately, I brought a pair of silver pumps with me, thinking heels might be a mistake given Daniel's warning. And instead of wearing the long dress I packed, I opt for a slinky, knee-length midnight blue little number. It has a plunging V-neck and the fabric twists in a knot at the waist. A series of small silver chains hold the top together, backed by a sheer blue voile panel to stop it being too revealing. It looks elegant and rather Greek, to my eyes.

I have no idea where we are going but I'm excited at the thought of the evening ahead and nothing is going to spoil it. Rather unexpectedly, there's a tap on the door.

'Come in, I'm almost ready.'

But when the door swings open it isn't Daniel I see, but George standing before me.

'Oh, hi George.'

He's staring at me and I do believe his jaw has just dropped a little.

'Oh ... um. I just came to say goodbye as I'm staying in town tonight and you'll probably be gone before I get back tomorrow. That's quite some dress, Leah, if you don't mind me saying.'

I can't help smiling as George is harmless enough.

'Thank you. And it's been lovely getting to know you a little, George.'

He steps forward to kiss my cheek and then stands back looking a little sheepish.

'I ... um ... haven't seen Daniel this lively since, well, ever, I suppose. He's a good mate and a great guy who has been through a lot. I've known him for a long time and we go way back. What I'm trying to say is that I'm glad you two are getting along so well and you're managing to get him to talk. That means something and it's the lease of life that he needs.'

With that he turns and exits, leaving me with a warm feeling. For all the banter going on last night it was clear the two of them are great friends and George was happy to see Daniel so relaxed.

The door stands ajar and moments later there's another tap. This time it's Daniel who appears.

'Did you see George?' he asks. 'He wanted to say goodbye to you. It seems it's going to be just us here at the villa tonight but the taxi has arrived, so I don't see any point in changing our plans now.'

Daniel hasn't taken his eyes off me and I feel the heat rising in my cheeks knowing that when we get back there will be no interruptions. He's looking so cool in a white linen shirt, the cuffs folded back exposing his tanned forearms. Wearing navy jeans and a pair of brown brogues, he's made a real effort and we're coordinated, which makes me smile.

'What's funny?' he asks curiously.

'Your jeans match my dress.'

'So they do; you look amazing, Leah – that dress is beautiful. Are you ready?'

'Lead the way.' I grab my bag and a navyshawl, then follow Daniel downstairs. My stomach is tied up in knots as I try my best to appear calm. But when he looks so good that's not easy to do.

It's about a twenty-minute drive across town and we pass the National Gardens and the Parliament building, entering an area Daniel informs me is known as Kolonaki. We didn't manage to walk up this far with the girls the day we were here. Apparently, it is regarded as the most fashionable district in Athens. Well-to-do ladies walk by with their dogs and as we drive around Kolonaki square it's surrounded by designer stores, cafés and smart gift shops. I manage to take a few snaps while the car is stationary, enough to give a feel for the ambience of this area. Then we start to climb a little as we enter a maze of smaller streets which seem to be mostly residential. In between there are a few cafés, bars and smaller, boutique-style shops here and there. Some look like little art galleries. Still we're climbing and as we wait at a small junction I look to my left to see a very steep street. There must be a dozen individual but very long runs of marble steps. Separating each level is a wide flat area and most seem to have a bench or two, so people can stop to catch their breath and enjoy the view. Either side of the wide steps is a narrow pavement, but the gradient looks perilous from this viewpoint.

'That's one serious climb,' I turn to look at Daniel.

'That's the second easiest route, after taking a taxi, of course.'

'Is there a third option?'

He looks at me and shakes his head. 'You don't want to know, trust me. Right, this is it.'

The taxi pulls up and Daniel thrusts a note at the driver, saying something in Greek. The driver gives him a smile and a salute, as we both exit the car.

When I join Daniel on the pavement I look up to see a sign marked 'Funicular'. I gulp. I can't really see the 'fun' bit in this, at all! *Don't spoil it, Leah*, I tell myself. Trust Daniel.

'Okay. All you will see are some steps up to the carriage. We'll travel up backwards and when we get to the top there are a few steps to climb. But I'm going to be there holding onto you. It isn't far to the restaurant and you won't be near any sheer drops whatsoever. Are you ready?'

Daniel takes my arm and squeezes it, reassuringly.

'I'm good to go.'

We step through the entrance and as we queue to buy tickets I can see the very steep track leading up into a shaft at the rear. However, less than a minute later an enclosed, bright yellow carriage slowly descends and it doesn't look scary at all. It looks robust and state-of-the-art.

'Most of the people in the queue already will head for the front-facing seats, hoping to get a glimpse of the view as we ascend. But we'll make for the backward-facing ones. It's a really smooth ride and it doesn't take long.'

As the passengers decant and the queue begins to shuffle forward, we wait for the last couple to disembark before we're on the move and it's too late to back out.

Daniel encourages me along confidently as we mount some rather steep concrete steps and negotiate our way into the second carriage. He's right and we find a block of two seats facing four people on a bench seat in front of us. There's a little jerking movement as we set off but aside from that it's relatively smooth; enough not to worry me unduly, although the shaft seems to extend above us a long way. There is staged lighting, so it isn't pitch black and that's a comfort.

Several times I can feel Daniel glancing my way. He squeezes my hand, checking I'm not freaking out, I suspect. But I'm calm. As we draw near to the top and natural light begins to filter into the shaft, he leans into me.

'Hold back and let everyone else get off first.'

It's a couple of minutes before he stands, extending both of his hands to pull me to my feet.

'Now, I want you to keep focusing on my face. Don't look anywhere else because I've got you, Leah. Deep breath.'

I follow him to the door of the carriage and inhale deeply, as Daniel steps out and grasps my arm the moment my feet hit the first step. He glues himself to my side so I can't see what's behind us and the few steps in front don't seem so bad. We reach a small landing area and now the steps are inside a building and we're away from the shaft.

He's close behind me as I focus on not tripping up and suddenly we're on another level and to my right is what looks like a bar. It has a panoramic view out over Athens. Daniel steers me across another small landing and out into the open, where we climb one more flight of steps. There are people on a large terrace, eating and drinking. Around us at every turn you catch a glimpse of a stunning view that goes on for miles and miles.

We follow a rather uneven stone path and take the first turning through a wooden archway into a restaurant. Daniel turns to face me. 'I'm so proud of you,' he whispers.

A waiter approaches and Daniel says something in Greek. The young man indicates for us to follow him and we walk through a bar area with bistro tables, out onto a terrace. Now I feel that we really are on top of a mountain. However, when I see how beautifully laid out the tables are with their perfectly white linen tablecloths, crystal glassware and silver cutlery, with that backdrop – it takes my breath away. The waiter pulls out a chair and I sit down gratefully, my legs perhaps a tad more unstable than I'd realised.

'Wine?' Daniel enquires, and I nod, unable to take my eyes off the view. 'This is Lycabettus Hill, isn't it? The one we see from the centre of Athens. I saw it in the guidebooks and ruled it out as an option. This isn't a hill, this is a mountain. Look how high up we are. This must be on a par with the Acropolis.'

'It's just over 900 feet high. The Acropolis hill rises only 490 feet above the city. Originally Athens would have been a small cluster of houses around the Acropolis but now you can see for yourself how far it extends.'

In front of us is a vast sea of twinkling lights and many of those are coming from people's homes. It's like being a voyeur seeing this aerial view which maps so many lives.

'And the other side of this wall?' Alongside me is a low stone wall and out of the corner of my eye I can see what appears to be a flat area that gently slopes away. I took great pains to focus on being seated, rather than catching a glimpse of what lies beyond it.

Daniel reaches out across the table.

'Grasp my hand and lean to look over the side. I won't let go.'

I was expecting a sheer drop, given that it feels we are perched way up in the sky but I'm surprised. There are a couple of levels that seem to wrap around the hill and it forms a wide, stepped path. People are coming and going, but in places there is a sheer drop down to the next level of the curving path below. For most people, it wouldn't present a problem and they are passing with ease. The slopes are covered in a mixture of lightly wooded areas and dense shrubbery. I can smell the scent of pine trees even from here. Some of the exotic plants have sent up flower shoots five feet in the air and there are cacti and succulents everywhere.

The waiter is back and pours out two glasses of wine, handing us a menu.

The light is now beginning to fade quite quickly and another waiter appears to light the candles on each table. Together with the soft exterior lighting, it seems to enclose the space a little, making it feel less exposed. I can't concentrate on the menu because my pulse is racing. I feel both elated and exhilarated at the same time.

'I think my endorphins are getting me a little high,' I admit as we raise our glasses to toast. 'My head is spinning a little.' But I know it's not just the fact that I'm over 900 feet in the air.

'To a perfect night with the perfect companion,' Daniel murmurs, leaning in towards me.

'I was thinking the exact same thing. To you, Daniel, and thank you. Why don't you order for us both so that I can calm myself down a little and adjust to this view.'

That raises a cheeky grin.

Settling back in my seat I watch Daniel as he peruses the menu, taking his time before he indicates to the waiter he's ready. Instinctively I pull out my camera and start snapping away. A lot of them are of Daniel, I know that, but I also scan around getting some background shots.

As the sun sinks even lower on the horizon, darkness

begins to settle around us like a cloak. Behind us, on the peak, is a wonderful old church built out of the local creamy-white stone. Suddenly it's bathed in low level lighting, adding to the magic of this unbelievable setting. The darkening sky is filled with stars and a crescent moon looks down on us. Even through the viewfinder on my camera it's breathtakingly beautiful.

'Daniel, this is stunning.' I can't hold back the emotion in my voice.

'No regrets? I did the right thing?'

'I'm feeling on top of the world,' I declare. It's followed by my nervous laughter. 'And my legs are still shaking just the teensiest bit.'

'Don't worry – I'm not proposing we take the path down. It's not for the faint-hearted, or people with a nervous disposition. But it is safe and the views just keep on getting better and better. There are a lot of butterflies and you often see wild tortoises. But I think you can save that for daylight hours on your next trip.'

Two waiters appear with *fassolada*, which Daniel tells me is a cold soup made with white beans, carrots, onions, tomatoes and oregano topped with a little extra-virgin olive oil. It's absolutely delicious and a perfect starter.

The next course is marinated vegetables with feta crumbs and aged balsamic vinaigrette. After that it's a dish of mushrooms, zucchini and tomatoes cooked in a saffron bouillon. Each course is beautifully presented and the portions are a perfect size, not too filling.

The main course is picture-perfect; chicken breast

cooked with artichokes and peas in a lemon dill sauce. I take several photos because the plate looks so stunning. Daniel is laughing at me.

'What? This is exactly the type of photo that will make an article zing. My readers are interested in the food they're likely to eat while in Greece.'

He nods, humouring me and leans across to pour out a little more wine.

'I like that you are passionate about what you do. I understand that.'

'Did you always want to be an archaeologist?'

'From an early age, pretty much.'

'How did you even know it was an occupation?'

He sits back, one hand twisting the stem of his wine glass.

'I didn't. I was playing in the garden one day and I was digging around like kids tend to do. I found a stone with an interesting pattern on it and it turned out to be a fossil. My parents bought me a book about it and then another, and another. By the time I was seven years old I was hooked. By then I'd nagged them to take me to all sorts of places on holiday where I could root around. My fossil collection began to grow but after a trip to the museum in York I discovered Roman mosaics and artefacts. I was fascinated to think that lying beneath our feet and beneath other buildings were the remains of earlier civilisations. To a young boy's mind that represented discovery and adventure. Who wouldn't want to dig and be the one to find a relic from the Roman Empire?'

I chuckle. 'Not you, that's for sure.'

Daniel smiles back at me, the candlelight making his eyes shine.

'I can be very boring at times,' he concedes but I shake my head, firmly.

'No, not at all. While I doubt I'll ever be inspired to dig, it is fascinating not least because they were so clever. Plumbing, drainage, Roman baths, mosaic floors, road building ... you have to applaud their skills.'

'It's unusual to be able to talk work to anyone outside of the university. You're a surprise, Leah, but then you were from the moment I met you.'

I think back to that morning less than three weeks ago. It feels like Daniel has been in my thoughts for a lifetime. And yet, on the other hand, it also feels like it all happened only yesterday.

'I was surprised that day I first saw you; I expected someone much older. Dr Daniel Preston has a very mature ring to it.'

My words are met with a smile and a tilt of an eyebrow.

'I'm thirty-five. I'm supposed to be in the prime of my life but it doesn't feel like that.' He gives a very dismissive laugh which sounds jaded and tired. Is he referring to his health problems, I wonder?

'Life has a habit of throwing a curve ball when you least expect it. Look at me, thirty-one and in need of a counsellor to sort myself out. It's not something I'm proud of because it makes me feel lacking in some way.' I'm trying to make it easier for him by demonstrating that everyone has problems. The clock is ticking and he's running out of time to convince me he can honour a commitment to total honesty between us.

His eyes search my face. 'Why now? I mean, why wait so long?'

I look away, a sigh seeming to empty my lungs of all air for a second or two before I can inhale once more. 'Because I'm scared of moving on and what that means, but I know it's time. Letting someone into my life – our lives – means everything will change. Jackie says that *the familiar* has become like a prison for me, inside of which I feel safe. That's a horrible analogy and I think she knew how I'd react. I'm the only one holding me back now. It's time to move on but that means taking a brave step forward and embracing a life where nothing is guaranteed.'

'But was there are particular catalyst that made you reach out to a counsellor after all this time? he presses gently.

'A promise I made to someone. We were on the same cruise and struck up a friendship. You know how we all tend to be drawn towards like-minded people? Well, Harrison and I connected because we were both travelling alone and in need of a listening ear. When everyone else around you is having fun and really all you want is a little break away from your daily worries, I think we rather stood out from the crowd.'

I see his brows knit together in concern and then one eyebrow raises slightly.

'And you're sure he's just a friend?'

'Yes. He's divorced and his parents probably thought at

some point he'd find another woman to settle down with. He has found his soul mate but tonight is the night he introduces Oliver to his parents for the first time. Even in this day and age it's about expectations that we feel are placed upon us. He had no idea how his family were going to react to the news and very few people knew his secret. I understood how he felt.

'A lot of people know my husband isn't around anymore, but only my parents and my best friend knew what Kelly did, until I told Harrison and you. People lie or omit things because it's easier and less painful than telling the truth. I told Harrison he had to do the deed sooner rather than later or he'd lose Ollie. In return he told me I needed to talk to a professional or I'd never learn to trust anyone again. I'm glad he did.'

Daniel's frown begins to melt away as he visibly relaxes his shoulders. He thought I was going to say there was another man in my life and seeing his relief sends a flutter through me.

'I'm glad, too. You should be proud you finally took that step.'

A small smile begins to make my lips twitch.

'I wish I'd done it before now. I didn't know I was going to meet someone so ... interesting, so soon.'

He laughs. 'Phew! I thought for one moment there—' He breaks off suddenly, looking rather embarrassed.

'The only person standing in the way of *us* now is me, isn't it?' he declares quietly.

I stare directly at him. 'Yes.'

'The words are in my head but they're not quite in the right order yet. I'm working on it.'

I take a sip from my wine glass, peering at him over the top of it, my eyes smiling playfully. The chemistry between us is both tantalizing and scary at the same time.

We've finished eating our main course and they clear the table. Daniel reads aloud the dessert menu and we decide that crushed mille-feuille with vanilla cream, ice cream and passion fruit liqueur sounds like a good idea.

With traditional Greek music playing softly in the background we end the evening sitting with our hands touching across the table. Daniel was right; this was an experience I would not have wanted to miss. I will always remember and treasure this memory. I feel I've been plucked out from my own little world and deposited somewhere else; a new and exciting opportunity to dream of a fresh start. A place where anything is possible, even if it is just for one night.

The darkness is now so encompassing that when we make our way to the funicular I don't feel at all anxious. I negotiate the steps on firm legs, happy to be able to lean against Daniel and know he's there for me. For no reason other than it makes me feel good. But only for tonight because tomorrow I go home and back to my real life. I still have no idea whether Daniel will end up disappointing me. But the sparks are like fireworks going off in all directions at once and they're too spectacular to ignore.

How Do You End Such a Perfect Night?

It's almost midnight by the time the taxi drops us back at the villa. It feels late but it's obvious we're both loath to bring the night to a close.

'How about a glass of wine by the pool?' Daniel suggests, as he closes the door behind us.

'Perfect. It's a big place when you're on your own here, isn't it?'

As he turns on the lights and we cross the hallway, our footsteps have a hollow ring to them.

'It's rarely this quiet. The team of additional volunteers from the university who are coming out for the holidays will be the last bunch to stay here. Thanos and his family have been very generous and aside from allowing us to have this place at a very reasonable rate, they are great benefactors. A dig is a very costly and time-consuming thing. This particular project is privately funded and there are many smaller sponsors involved, the Fotopoules family being only one of them.'

Daniel talks as he grabs glasses and a bottle of wine. We head outside and he stops to turn on the garden lighting.

The pool looks so inviting as we wander down to the edge. I slip off my shoes and take the glasses and bottle from Daniel, waiting while he rolls up the legs of his jeans. It seems a shame not to change into our swimsuits but he doesn't suggest that and I guess it is a little late for a dip.

We settle ourselves down, letting our feet dangle in the deliciously warm water.

Around us the night is full of little sounds reminding us that an army of insects and animals continue their nighttime pursuits.

'Is that constant background sound the grasshoppers chirping? Or is it another sort of insect?'

Daniel passes me a glass and shifts alongside me, closing the gap between us.

'It's usually cicadas – they rub their forewings against their hind legs. They aren't as large as the grasshoppers but they sure do make a lot of noise.'

The air is still warm, pleasantly so, and the scent carried on the gentle breeze seems to be a mix of different perfumes.

'I can smell jasmine but there's something else heavy in the air tonight. Can you smell it, too?'

Daniel tips his head back, taking a deep breath and looking up at the sky as he concentrates.

'Ah, that's the yellow margaritas. They grow like weeds down on the lower level and extend over the cliff edge. It's more noticeable at night and when the breeze is coming off the sea.'

The water in the pool shimmers, the garden lights bouncing off it and fragmenting as we move our feet gently back and forth.

'This doesn't feel real, does it?' I reflect, thinking out loud.

Daniel's foot comes to rest alongside my own.

'You're real,' he confirms, letting his foot linger for a few seconds before drawing it away.

'After I fly home to York it's going to take a while to sort myself out again and I wish that wasn't the case. Adjusting to the new routine when I'm back at work and beginning a regular relationship with Bella all over again won't leave much time for other things.'

Even as he's talking his hand comes to rest over mine, curled around the edge of the pool. If this is it, his big exposé, then he's misjudged me and I'm not falling for it. Time to call his bluff.

'Maybe all we were ever meant to share was the short time we've had together. Perhaps neither of us will ever be ready.'

'Are you saying right place, wrong time? Do you really believe that or are you angry because I'm not quite—' He sounds horrified, but I don't turn to look at him.

'Perhaps we fell under the spell of Athens and that air of invincibility it seems to have hovering over it. Like the Greek gods are still in control, looking down upon us and steering what happens, so for a brief moment we believe anything is possible when that isn't the case, at all.'

'And what would you say to those Greek gods, Leah?'

This time I turn to face him as I speak.

'That I'm just a woman looking for the love of a good and honest man.'

He lets out a long, slow breath but it isn't a sigh.

'And you deserve to be loved by someone who can be everything for you and Rosie. I don't know if I have what it takes to fill that role because of the life I lead. The distance between us geographically in the UK is the least of the problems, in a way.'

A dull sensation akin to pain seems to settle in my chest. Is this his designated moment to clear the air and despite my repeated warnings he's failed us both? We sit in silence for a while before reluctantly glancing at each other to signal that it's time to make a move.

Heading back inside, Daniel turns off the lights and we end up outside the door to the master suite. Standing here looking at each other, neither of us is sure about what to say next. The seconds pass and Daniel draws close, looking down into my eyes.

'Thank you for a wonderful day. One I'll treasure forever,' he whispers as I look up at him and my heart sinks. Is that it?

He lowers his face towards mine, kissing me softly on the lips before drawing away. I watch as he turns and crosses the landing without looking back.

I open the door and go inside my room, reluctantly shutting it behind me. But even as I'm taking off my make-up and getting ready for bed, I can't settle. It's not long before my feet are padding across the tiled landing and I knock softly on Daniel's door, before twisting the handle to open it. I didn't fly all this way to give up so easily.

Inside it's dark, only the soft glow from the moon outside giving the tiniest glow to break the darkness. I stand there in my over-sized T-shirt, shifting from foot to foot.

'I don't want to be alone tonight even though you've disappointed me more than you can ever know.' A slight shiver courses up through my body as I await his response.

I see Daniel's form as he sits upright, holding out his arms to me.

'I'm glad you're here. It was so hard to walk away from you, Leah. I did try but the right words didn't come.'

Climbing onto the bed he pulls me down to snuggle up against him.

'I just need to be held for a while.' My voice is so low it's hardly audible, as I fight back tears which reflect the emotional turmoil I'm feeling. How many chances can you give someone before you give up on them?

Lying here wrapped in Daniel's arms in the velvet darkness, it feels so right and I want him to know that. I begin slowly by trailing my hand up and down his arm and he shifts position, turning into me. My hand snakes up and over his top and suddenly, after a few frantic moments of tugging and yanking, we're both naked. Nothing else matters anymore except for the fire that is consuming us as we explore each other, driven by a desire that blots everything else out. Every little touch thrills me to the core and feeling Daniel's urgent response it's obvious our bodies are in tune, even if our minds are not.

I gently push him back onto the bed and slide one leg over his, easing myself up into a sitting position. His hands wind around me and slide down over my curves, his grasp tightening and his breathing heavy. As I look down at him in the moonlight I can see the scar quite clearly and my heart misses a beat. Then two.

'Daniel ... please tell me what happened.' My fingers lightly dance over his chest and follow the imprint of the rope-like scar which tracks down his torso. Suddenly the fire in my veins turns to ice and I realise I'm holding my breath.

His hands suddenly fall away and reluctantly I slide into a lying position so I can drape my arms around his shoulders. 'Clearly you've been through a terrible experience and psychologically it's still very traumatic to face up to. I get that, really I do. But you can trust me, I promise.'

He clears his throat then rolls towards me but his face is half in shadow. I can only see a little glint from the moonlight catching his eyes.

'If I admit my fears to you then it makes them real. If they remain unsaid then—'

'Then they aren't any less real, Daniel, but maybe together we can face up to them. Find a way to live with it and the consequences.' He can hear the sincerity in my voice as compassion takes over and suddenly this isn't about him telling lies or holding back. It's about looking into the face of raw fear.

'Those weren't vitamin supplements you were taking before, were they? I thought it was a bit strange on the first day here with the girls when you didn't get into the pool and kept your T-shirt on. And tonight, when the water looked so inviting ... you still couldn't bear to let me see your scar.'

I can't keep the note of disappointment out of my voice.

'God, that tears me up hearing that tone in your voice, Leah. Please just listen to me as I want you to understand why I didn't tell you.' He pauses, assembling his thoughts. The seconds tick by.

'Sometimes, still, I find it hard to believe what happened. And yet the memories never leave me. I contracted a simple flu-like virus. Lots of people had it and were fine. I wasn't. I got sicker and sicker, until eventually I was rushed into hospital with a very high fever. I had developed pneumonia and was put on a strong course of antibiotics. It wasn't long before it was clear something else was wrong and a severe reaction to the drugs sent my immune system into over-drive.'

I raise myself up onto my elbow so I can see Daniel's face more clearly. He's wearing a pained expression and avoiding my gaze. I discreetly swipe away with the back of my hand a tear that has spilt down over my right cheek, hoping he hasn't noticed. His anguish is almost tangible.

'It was a tough couple of days but the resulting damage to the heart muscle was irreversible. I knew it was serious but it wasn't until I was informed that I was going to be assessed for the heart transplant list that I realised my life was in imminent danger.'

I place my hand gently over the centre of Daniel's chest,

desperate to feel the reassuring pound of his heartbeat. He's well now; he's fit and strong, that's all that matters, I tell myself.

'I have the heart of a nineteen-year-old man who died when his motorbike crashed into a car. You don't get to meet the donor's family but we exchanged letters through a third party. They said they wept when they heard that the person receiving their son's heart had a daughter and that even in death his life had purpose.'

I can't hide my tears any longer and Daniel hauls himself upright to draw me into his arms. We sit holding each other for a long while.

'Tricia must have been frantic with worry and I can understand why you chose not to tell Bella.' I can't quite keep an even keel to my voice and it wavers a little.

'It all happened about three months after Tricia and I split up. She was involved but it was difficult and I made her promise she wouldn't tell Bella. It was the transition period for us anyway and Bella simply assumed I was busy sorting out the new house. I rang her as often as I could, well, on my good days. That's why I always keep covered up because I don't intend to have that conversation until I feel she's ready and it won't send her into a panic about my health.'

It's so hard to process this information but the fact that Bella doesn't know seems wrong. But then isn't Daniel merely trying to protect her? Maybe I'd do the exact same thing for Rosie and he's right, but at any age it would be a worrying revelation.

'It's rather shocking, isn't it? It's taken a while to get the meds right but the regime I've been on for the last fourteen months is working well. I only need regular echocardiograms, which I have done at a local hospital. In the first year after surgery I had several biopsies to check for any signs of rejection but aside from adjusting the mountain of pills I take, it was all good. This year again, I passed all the tests with flying colours. But there are no guarantees.'

'I can't even begin to imagine what you've been through, Daniel.' There's a question burning on my lips but I don't think it's one I can voice. As if he's reading my mind Daniel answers it for me.

'You're wondering what the prognosis is for the long-term. My consultant tells me it's good, as long as I get my check-ups and keep taking the tablets. It's a case of everything in moderation and leading as healthy a lifestyle as I possibly can. The majority of the problems occur at the beginning, shortly after surgery and I sailed through that phase. But every infection and virus I catch poses a real threat.'

No wonder he prefers not to think about it. It was a simple virus that did the damage in the first place.

'So you choose not to tell people about what you've been through because you're scared they'll look at you differently, or because you're always waiting for something to go terribly wrong?'

He turns to face me. 'Since splitting with Tricia I haven't been close to anyone and in a way that has made my life a lot easier. The only person I worry about is Bella.'

'So starting over again with someone new in your life is a responsibility you can't handle?'

He nods. 'Look at your reaction, Leah. You just put your hand over my heart as if you were checking it was still beating. Now I've told you, will it make you treat me any differently?'

I know my face is probably as bathed in shadows as Daniel's is to me, but even so I keep my expression calm and relaxed. 'Of course not. I'm just sad to think of what you've been through but I would never have guessed.'

'Ha! Good attempt, Leah, but your body language is definitely saying something else. This conversation has not only killed the passion but now you're considering every little word before you say it. I'm not made of glass and I won't break. The heart I have is strong but I'm not sure it's fair to inflict this future on someone else. Particularly someone who has already been given such a rough ride in life. And that's what my conscience has been wrestling with this past two and a half weeks.'

Now it's Daniel's body language that is giving him away, because despite what his mouth is saying, his arms don't loosen their hold. We're each gripping the other as if we never want to let go. Whether I like it or not, what I feel is a wide range of conflicting emotions but that's not a bad thing. It helps to understand why he's been so incredibly hesitant to get into another relationship; but I can't pretend it isn't a shock or the last thing I could possibly have expected him to say.

I decide that there's only one way to show him that he's wrong and that's to reignite the passion. It's a risk but one worth taking. He responds instantly when I press my lips to his and tease them open with the tip of my tongue. I swing myself around to sit facing him, desperate to prove I refuse to let this change anything between us. But any thinking is brought to an immediate halt as Daniel leaves me in no doubt whatsoever that he's fit and strong. And willing.

Afterwards, we lie together, drifting in and out of sleep and the conversation we had seems like something out of a surreal dream. Just the closeness of him and the way he wraps his arms around me makes me feel at peace. Daniel isn't a taker and he isn't a user. That endears him to me even more so and yet I realise that is the battle to be fought and might be what will ultimately threaten to keep us apart.

You can't escape from the realities of life, can you? There's no point in pretending that Rosie, Mum and Dad won't factor in every decision I make in the future. Responsibilities and relationships often seem to conflict with our hopes and dreams and yet people like Antonio will always serve their own interests first. I'm not like that and neither is Daniel. It's rarely as simple as being able to grab what you want from life, or even what you believe will make you truly happy. But tonight, my mission was to make Daniel feel wanted and appreciated; he makes me feel special and I hope I've made him feel special, too.

Some Goodbyes Are Harder Than Others

It's early when I steal out quietly, so as not to disturb Daniel. I hardly slept, so many things were whirling around inside my head. I shower and change, then pack my suitcase, switching into auto pilot mode. Heading downstairs with my camera, it's time to gather my thoughts and grab a quiet cup of coffee out on the terrace.

It's another stunning day, the line where the blue of the sky meets the azure blue of the water is almost impossible to distinguish. It's time to ground myself and I go through a mental checklist of the photos I've taken. Villas done, tick. Temple of Zeus, the National park, Syntagma and Kolonaki done, tick. The wonderful views taken from Lycabettus Hill are a real bonus, although for me they represent a memory to cherish forever. I stand, then wander around and grab some shots of the ocean and the picturesque garden. Even looking down onto the sandy shoreline of the Astir Beach Club in nearby Vouliagmeni, there's hardly a soul to be seen this morning.

Why am I here if my feelings for Daniel are going to come to nothing because I'm asking too much of him? Before I can even contemplate the answer to my own question, his voice comes out of nowhere. I turn to see him standing next to me.

'I wish you had another day here and we could spend it lazing down there on the beach like tourists.' He sounds wistful, leaning in to kiss my cheek and add a cheerful, 'Good morning.'

'You were sleeping peacefully when I slipped out. I didn't want to spoil your chance for a lie-in.'

He grabs my free hand, wrapping his own around it. Just the feel of his skin sends a little shiver down my spine and when I look up into his eyes it's a curiously intimate moment.

'I seldom sleep like that, in fact I can't remember the last time I had a dreamless sleep that was so restful.'

Reluctantly, I withdraw my hand to replace the lens cap on my camera so we can head inside. There's a glass of water and Daniel's pill box on the counter top, next to two mugs of coffee and a plate of fruit.

'I'll grab the yoghurt while you get the dishes,' I offer.

Moving around each other in the kitchen, it's like some weird dance in slow motion. Every single movement seems to mean something, as if we're disturbing the air around us and the other person can feel the effect rippling outwards. It serves only to increase the awareness of our proximity.

'What time will your taxi get here?'

We exchange glances then peer up at the clock on the wall in tandem, which shows that it's just after 9 a.m.

'An hour. I'm all packed and ready to go.'

'Good. We can linger a while over breakfast then.'

As we head back outside I wish I could stop time, conscious that each second that passes is one less we have together.

Daniel is making a huge effort to be bright and breezy, so I follow his lead. We lay everything out on the table and take our seats next to each other. Simple things like reaching out and touching his arm, or when he passes me something and our fingers touch, seem even more meaningful. Sensual and pleasurable, given that we are both aware that inside the house the hands continue to move around the clock: counting down until it's time to say goodbye, yet again. There's still so much to say but it's hard to know where to start and we're running out of time. It's Daniel who finally gets up the courage to begin the conversation.

'You were right and I owe you an apology. I should have told you the whole truth from the very start and it was unfair of me not to do so. Even worse, I blew it the second time around when I flew out to see you with the express purpose of telling you what had happened and then bottled out. But you gave me yet another chance and came back here again, and that was clearly a big deal for you. Especially as you didn't really know what you were walking into.' He looks at me with anguish written all over his face.

I smile and he does a double-take, a questioning frown creasing his brow.

'I came back because I hoped you'd trust me enough to tell me everything, Daniel. Last night proved to me that your feelings for me are strong enough for you to overcome a huge hurdle. We both have baggage we can't ignore. I have an anxious time ahead with a divorce looming and your daughter is going to need you even more as that wedding of Tricia's approaches. As for the other matter ... it's a part of your life journey, as tough as it's been to go through it. From what I can see you are thriving, and you've been given all the assurances from the doctors, but you act as if you expect your life to be cut short at any moment. What if Bella picks up on your anxiety?'

It's tough love, I know that and I'm not trying to judge him or his reaction to something that is so emotive, as well as physically challenging. Walking around with someone else's heart inside of you means you have life because they lost theirs. How can that thought not be a part of your every waking moment?

'You make it sound simple but we both know there's more to it than that.'

I nod in agreement, my core full of compassion. 'Of course there's more to it, there always is, Daniel! But you're fit and well now and as for the other problems, we just need to work out how we're going to get around them. When it comes to future health issues, well, any one of us could get sick at any time. You can't let it hang over you like a sentence that can't be avoided.'

His look is one of reluctant scepticism.

'So you think we can do this, we really can make it happen and have our happily-ever-after?'

'Why not? As you said, we'll take it one step at a time.

I wish I had a magic wand to solve all of the issues but what I do have is determination and patience. If you want this as much as I do, then together we'll make it work somehow.'

'But there are no guarantees—'

'—for anyone, about anything in life. So what do you think?'

His eyes search mine and I can imagine the range of emotions flashing through his mind right now. I lean in to him and kiss him gently on the lips. He pulls away, briefly, smiling across at me.

'I want to be there with you on the end of the line whenever you need me, until we can be together again. If you have a problem with Antonio, then I want to know about it and if you need me urgently there I'll fly back from Athens early. Is that understood?'

Reaching out to touch his cheek a part of me longs to stay here, even though I know that isn't possible. 'Understood. We'll find a way through this, Daniel. I know we will.'

My voice sounds more hopeful than I feel at this particular moment. Tick tock; tick tock – our time together is running out. My mind tries not to focus on the fact that I need to savour every last moment we have together. Once again, I don't want to leave him and this time, knowing what I know now, it's even harder.

I push the plate in front of me away, unable to find any hint of an appetite with all of this swirling around inside my head.

'Focus on getting this divorce sorted and once that worry

is behind you we'll decide on our next step. Our time apart will either make us or break us.'

Daniel reaches across to grab my hand as he speaks, entwining our fingers. I know we're both thinking about last night and drawing strength from it. Here and now, this feels very real and my heart actually aches. It's the same pain I can see reflected on Daniel's face and I know we're each struggling to maintain our composure with varying degrees of success. It's as though we're being slowly ripped apart with each passing second and, once again, it's agony.

'Falling in love with someone is ecstasy,' Daniel's voice is husky, 'but it's also painful in other ways.' I nod my head in agreement because it's as if he's reading my mind.

~

We stand, hugging each other, the sound of an idling engine setting my nerves on edge. As we let go we exchange a faltering smile and I can see how emotional Daniel is, too. I begin walking towards the car, then turn around to wave as he stands in the doorway of the villa. I want to imprint his image on my mind so I have it there for comfort until we meet again. My heart feels heavy and I'm struggling to breathe, as if I'm having a panic attack. What if things don't come together once he flies home and this turns out to be the last time I see him? Could fate be that cruel?

When he flew over to the UK he said he would understand if I changed my mind because it's complicated. But the love between a man and a woman can be as powerful and all-consuming as the love between a parent and a child. We would both fight to our last breath for our kids and I don't intend letting anything get in the way of our own happy ever after if it's avoidable or fixable.

Huh! I've done exactly what I promised myself I wouldn't do again and that's to let my heart rule my head. But this time, it doesn't matter, I reassure myself firmly, because this man is a keeper and together we have to find a way to make it work.

~

I'm back in the UK. Feeling lonely and missing you like crazy and we've only been apart a few hours! What have you done to me, Dr Preston?

I press send and then wish I could recall my text. It sounds way too needy. A few seconds go by before there's a ping.

Missing you more! I've been sitting here waiting for your text, not wanting to believe how far away you are right now.

Daniel's visit feels more like a dream than something that actually happened. But I can't stop my heart from leaping at the thought that he might feel the same way. Now I simply have to begin working through the steps to sort out my divorce so that Rosie and I can finally move out from under the shadow Antonio created in our lives. Knowing it might be one step closer to the prospect of our being a part of Daniel and Bella's lives only increases my determination. Could we eventually be together, as a blended family unit? Or will Daniel himself have second thoughts and decide it's too much responsibility welcoming Rosie and me into his already fragmented life? What I have to accept is that the future is still very uncertain.

Picking Up the Pieces

I arrive back home feeling quietly optimistic one moment and fearful, the next. The result is that a very strange mood has settled over me. I make a monumental effort to appear light-hearted and upbeat but Mum and Dad aren't fooled. Thankfully, Rosie is slightly distracted when she opens her present. But only a few minutes later she's asking about Athens and Daniel.

'How is Bella's ankle now, Mum, and are we going to meet up with them when Daniel flies back to England?'

Three pairs of eyes watch me, awaiting my response with a sense of hopeful anticipation.

'Maybe, darling. Bella is fine now; it was only a bad sprain. Daniel is going to be very busy when he first arrives home but he will be in touch when he can.'

I can read the expression on Mum's face. She wants to know what happened but all I can give her at the moment is a reassuring smile.

Rosie chats almost nonstop in the car, clearly having had a good time and lots of fun on her day out with Callie and her grandparents. Whenever she seems to be running out of steam I ask a simple question and she's off again.

Once she's safely tucked up in bed I tackle my emails. Lots of new advertisers wanting space, several offers from hotels wanting to be featured and Wendy from *Loving Life* magazine confirming the publication date of my first article. I also have the deadline now for the second one.

I whip through it all relatively quickly, then download the Athens photos from the SD card without even looking at them. I feel like a robot going through the motions efficiently but without any emotional attachment whatsoever. I can't even get excited about the potential new business coming my way.

I'm conscious that I have had no contact at all with Harrison since his last text on Saturday morning. I have no idea how his meal with the parents went and I feel mean. But he's going to ask about Athens and I know only a phone call will do to discuss that, so I dial his number.

'Hey, it's me. I'm back.'

'Leah, about time! Is no news, good news?'

I bet he's sitting there with his fingers crossed for me, as he's that sort of a guy. But suddenly I feel awkward as it would be wrong of me to share Daniel's secret. Even though I trust Harrison implicitly and value his opinion, it's not mine to divulge.

'First of all, how was the meal with Ollie and your parents?' I feel bad that I didn't text him Sunday morning but I know he'll understand once I explain.

'There was a pretty rocky start but it soon improved.

Ollie was nervous and Dad sort of put him through his paces, almost vetting him; wanting to know about his background, why he decided to specialise in family law and divorce, and it took a while for everyone to begin feeling comfortable with one another. I think it was only nerves all round, but the tension was awful for a little while there.

'Ollie is very close to his family and once we moved on to that topic the mood lightened. He has three sisters and he trotted out a few anecdotal stories that were rather endearing. Actually, I felt a little sorry for him as being the youngest it seems he was bossed around an awful lot.'

This is a two-way conversation and I need to focus, even though my head is still all over the place.

'Did you discuss the future?' I ask, tentatively.

Harrison seems remarkably relaxed about everything, which is in sharp contrast to his previous levels of anxiety that had almost bordered on paranoia.

'We thought it was best to tackle everything up front. Ollie and I are in the process of putting our houses on the market and once we have offers we'll begin looking for our future home together.

'My parents are throwing a party for my dad's birthday in August and they were both in agreement that it would be a good time to introduce Ollie to the entire family. I am a little nervous about that as there are a lot of them. I have three uncles and two aunts and a horde of cousins. Plus, various friends who attend all our family parties. Of course, Ollie accepted the invite there and then out of politeness. I only hope he's up to it on the night, as even I struggle to cope with them all. My family certainly know how to party.'

'I'm so happy for you, Harrison. That's one enormous hurdle you've jumped.'

He doesn't reply instantly and I begin to feel uncomfortable.

'Well, I'm waiting. How did it go with Daniel? I've been worried about the lack of contact but Ollie told me to stay calm and wait until you were ready to talk.'

I let out the long, deep sigh I've been holding in. It's a mixture of joy, frustration and excitement. Plus, I don't really know where to begin.

'It was certainly a rollercoaster ride,' is what I eventually manage to say.

Harrison lets out an expletive.

'You went all that way to have your heart stamped upon?' He sounds angry on my behalf.

'Not in that way, Harrison. I mean emotionally. It was an unbelievable few days and Daniel didn't disappoint on any level, at all.'

'Well, that's good news, isn't it? You sound all loved-up, lady!'

I laugh; Harrison just seems to understand and I can hear how happy he is for me.

'I am but my head is still all over the place and I have to ground myself. First of all I need to get the divorce sorted and then when Daniel finally gets back he'll bring Bella to visit us so that the girls can spend some time together.'

Harrison lets out a loud exclamation. 'What? That's the extent of the plan so far and you're happy with it?'

'There's no point in getting ahead of ourselves, Harrison. And in the meantime we'll both be going through quite a major upheaval and we can support each other through it. It's a great way of cementing our relationship.'

'Ha! You sound more like a builder's mate than a woman on the brink of falling headlong in love. If you haven't already,' he declares, clearly puzzling over the fact that I'm suddenly downplaying everything. Somehow I know he'll figure out that if I'm not sharing something with him, it's for a very good reason.

'We had a frank talk and I can see now that I have trust issues. The best way around that is to take it slowly. If I'm going to worry about anything now it's what that rat of a husband of mine might do when he receives the divorce papers. I need to focus on becoming a free woman and how I'm going to pay for it. When Daniel returns to the UK in August, we'll have a much better idea about how things are panning out.'

Harrison makes a sound along the lines of a protracted 'Hmm' but he's too much of a gentleman to pursue it.

'I think I need to meet this guy who seems to have allayed all of your fears and put you at ease so readily. Perhaps we could all go out for a meal together when he gets back. I want to satisfy myself that he really is as good as he sounds.'

I can't help chuckling to myself. Poor Daniel will have to face Harrison as well as my dad.

'He was a little jealous when your name came up. He asked why I suddenly decided to talk to a counsellor and, of course, that was down to you. I explained you were already taken.'

Harrison laughs. 'I bet that was some conversation. Well, everything I've read about him and his work so far sounds genuine enough. So I guess you're in safe hands.'

It's touching that Harrison has spent time checking Daniel out on my behalf. 'When you meet him you'll understand that isn't necessary. He's kind and caring and genuine.'

'Okay, I get the message and I'm thrilled for you, lovely lady. I'm just a bit anxious about the upheaval to come, I suppose.'

I'm pushing all of that to the back of my mind for now because there's only so much I can cope with at any given time. Besides, there's no point in speculating about what might, or might not happen. I know that Harrison would be frowning if he knew that the only person I can talk to about it all is now Daniel himself. And we text constantly; my phone is rarely out of my hands at the moment.

I realise that what I'm doing is precisely what I accused Harrison of doing with his situation. I'm avoiding the real issue here. Is it irresponsible of me to gloss over some hard truths in order to grab the happiness I long to have? Have I the right to expect my family to cope with the fallout if something goes wrong, when they have absolutely no idea there's even an issue? Daniel's secret will have to be shared eventually and I'm not even sure I can fully understand the implications. All I know is that I want to be there for him whatever happens. But what impact will this have on Rosie and my parents for the future? I bitterly regret it's a question I can't ask Harrison because his endorsement would be reassuring.

I Am Woman, Hear Me Roar

I turn to meditation and for the very reasonable price of £7.99, a CD takes me on a daily journey to a calmer place. My working days are filled with routine. School run, walk, meditation session, work, walk, school run. Dinner, quality time with Rosie, bedtime story and a final meditation session.

Then I tackle one of the two elephants in the room. I jump online to read up as much as I can about child custody and parental access rights, until I'm so tired I simply drop into bed. Most of it is anecdotal, as Ollie has given me chapter and verse on the law. But judging by what I've read when it comes down to it, there's often a lot of heartache following bitter and drawn-out battles. It's not at all unusual for estranged husbands to step back in to claim right of access, or apply for shared custody.

Even worse is the complication when the parents are in different countries. I try not to read the stories about cases where a child is handed over in good faith for a visit but then never returned. I shed tears as I read how a parent suddenly loses all access to the child they once took care of; sometimes years pass while everything is tangled up in litigation. Forewarned is forearmed, but it's depressing. Exhaustion means I'm too tired to dream, or at least remember what goes through my head in the dark hours of night.

Daniel and I now talk on the phone more than we text and just to hear his voice is like a welcoming hug. We are committed to keeping up each other's spirits but time just seems to be stretching out endlessly with little happening to move either of us forward.

At weekends Rosie and I plan something different each day so that our hours are filled and happy. Now she no longer has gym club there are no restrictions until she decides what she wants to try next. Taekwondo is still high on the list, although she's adding to it on a daily basis and the latest one is a sewing class.

I'm now being sent all manner of things to test and review including backpacks, suitcases, a fashion range of crease-resistant clothing – you name it, I get it. Which is great, but it means I'm really busy.

My second appointment with Jackie was what sparked the purchase of the meditation CD. She felt it was something that would help me to learn to detach myself from my worries. Even if it is only for two half-hour sessions each day. With my stress levels at an all-time high that is bound to affect Rosie, so I have to at least try to do something about it.

When I started seeing Jackie I thought she would come up with answers, but really all she does is ask a question to start me talking. And then she'll ask another question and when I think about it, what she is doing is getting me to look inwardly and challenge myself. Why do I blame myself for the fact that Kelly is lost to us all? Why should I have been left with large debts about which I had no prior knowledge?

I'm beginning to accept that I can only control my own actions. What other people do, or don't do, is not my fault even though it might have an impact on my life. It doesn't change anything but it finally lessens the guilt. I felt I should have been able to see through Antonio; but if I had then maybe he wouldn't have been in my life long enough for us to have had Rosie. That was a sobering thought, as she is everything to me. My concern focuses now on Antonio's intentions and future actions.

Another thing I've learnt is that it's okay to admit when I'm feeling down and vulnerable. But I also need to acknowledge that I'm a strong person who has survived a real ordeal and nothing should rob me of that satisfaction.

We have talked a little about Daniel but I haven't told her how close we have become. Daniel and I chat every night for about an hour before going to sleep. The new rule is to give the highlight and the lowlight of the day to remind us that life is about achieving a balance; and not simply focusing on the negative. We keep each other moving forward with positivity and purpose and that's all I need to stay strong.

My phone buzzes and the caller ID tells me it's Ollie.

'Hi Ollie, how can I help?'

I save the file I'm working on and stand up, needing to stretch my legs.

'We've had a response from your husband. Before he signs and returns the paperwork he wants to talk to you.'

I suck in a deep breath and my heart starts to pound in my chest as anxiety begins to take hold. My fears were real, not imagined and now he's making his first move.

'Has he made any other demands?'

'Nothing at all, as yet.'

I take a few deep breaths, trying to slow everything down so I can stay in control and focus on the conversation.

'What do you advise?'

'With no indication at all of what he wants to talk to you about and given that he has no legal representation, I would advise exerting caution here. Especially given the circumstances. That first contact may well be an emotionally driven one, on both sides. The last thing we want is for a heated exchange so early in the process.'

I knew this was coming; Antonio is going to start making demands because from bitter experience I've learnt there's always a reason behind everything he does.

'Can we force his hand and say a call is unacceptable?'

'Of course. Although it might be that what he wants to talk about doesn't involve custody or financial issues relating to the divorce itself.'

'An explanation of his actions, you mean?'

'It's possible. Either way, I would advise that if any such

conversation does take place it should involve either myself, or an independent third party as a witness. It could avoid potential fallout further down the road. People's memories can play tricks because they hear what they want to hear. As a trained mediator, though, I should emphasise that it's important to keep the lines of communication open if at all possible.

'In this case it's a starting point. If he lived in the UK, we would arrange a face to face meeting to begin with. That isn't an option so I'm going to suggest you come up to our offices in Leeds and we can book a conference call. That way I can sit in on it with you. If I feel either of you are straying into areas which are best dealt with in other ways, I can then intercede on your behalf. How does that sound?'

It may well be easier if I'm on neutral ground and maybe add some weight to the seriousness of the situation from Antonio's perspective. He'll no doubt think it's acceptable to have my phone number and that would be a mistake.

'Okay. Let's get this over and done with as soon as possible. Just arrange a time and a date and I'll be there. I can't have this question mark about what he wants hanging over my head for much longer. If there's going to be a battle then I want to know exactly what he's after. Thanks, Ollie. I couldn't face this on my own, it would be too much.'

'I'll respond immediately and email you the details, including directions to our offices. I know you are concerned but a frank discussion at this stage could be very helpful to the process.'

I was praying that Antonio would simply sign the papers

and return them, taking away any thoughts of a potential custody battle. If this was simply about him wanting to catch up on how Rosie is doing, he would have written to me via his parents. No, this is Antonio sending a clear signal that he feels he has the upper hand before we even begin.

'I'll be in touch as soon as the date has been confirmed. Take care, Leah, and try not to worry unduly.'

~

Having settled Rosie down for the night, it isn't long before Sally arrives in answer to my panicky phone call to her earlier on.

'Thanks for popping around. I need to talk to someone. But first, I'll put the kettle on. How are you feeling?'

Sally closes the door behind her and follows me through into the kitchen, flopping down onto one of the dining chairs.

'Ghastly every morning until about half past ten, then I perk up for the rest of the day. Aside from that I'm hungry all the time but that's it. The website is growing busier by the day and it's hard not to be constantly snacking. My diet is now officially on hold although I am trying to make sure what I'm reaching for are the healthier options these days. Crisps, biscuits and chocolate bars have been banned from the house.'

I raise my eyebrows in surprise at the sheer determination in her voice.

'Good for you. I can offer some nuts or dried fruit if you're in the mood.'

She laughs. 'No, I'm good, I've just eaten, thank you. So, what's this worrying new development with Antonio?'

I carry our drinks across to the table and sit next to her. It's all still sinking in and fear is wrapping itself around me like an invisible net, drawing me down to a place I don't want to go.

'Ollie rang the day before yesterday to say Antonio wants to talk to me. I'm heading up to the solicitor's offices tomorrow for a conference call. Ollie is going to sit in, in an advisory capacity.'

'Is Antonio aware of that? I mean, there's no way he could insist on talking to you alone? What if he starts making threats?'

'Yes, he's aware. Ollie says if he tries that we'll simply terminate the call and insist that any communication from that point onwards should be in writing. Ollie has warned that things can deteriorate really quickly, though, so his advice is to take a very cautious, but receptive approach. Antonio hasn't appointed a solicitor but I'm scared, Sally.'

She looks at me, pulling a long face.

'He shouldn't have any rights at all, Leah. He doesn't deserve any consideration, if you ask me.'

I nod. 'I feel the same way, especially as he has literally torn this family apart. But that's an emotional reaction and the law is clear about his rights. Obviously, the debts he left behind and which I have now cleared, will be taken into account if he tries to demand any money from me. But mostly I'm worried about a custody fight over Rosie, given that he lives in Florida now.'

Sally looks aghast.

'I had no idea he could exert any rights at all after such a long period with no contact. Even ignoring the fact that this situation is of his own making.'

I stare down into my coffee mug. 'Ollie did explain at the start that the court will only take into consideration what is in Rosie's best interests. And I agree with that in principle. But if a man can tear a family apart with his selfishness, then abandon his wife and daughter for seven years knowing the situation he left them in, how can he ever be trusted?

'However, if Antonio decides he's going to begin making an effort, then it appears that I have no legal right to refuse him contact unless I can prove neglect, or abuse. And if I could it would be after the fact, which I find totally horrifying. If we can't agree on an appropriate level of access to Rosie it will be for the court to decide. Ollie said that Antonio's lack of consistency will be taken into account, but the court will still opt to give him a chance. He told me that it would be a grave mistake to adopt a rigid position as there are no provable concerns over safety issues. The reason the court won't attach much weight to what happened in the past is because it's possible for someone to see the error of their ways and change.'

Sally shakes her head.

'You've always provided a safe, nurturing environment for her, but what if Antonio says he can now offer the same?'

I shrug my shoulders. 'I sincerely hope that doesn't

happen because I could never place my trust in him again after what he did.'

Sally's frown deepens. 'So, the only other option is to reach a mutual agreement?' Her tone is one of disgust.

'Yes. If we can't agree, then we go through a dispute-resolution service and thrash out something called a Parenting Plan. Ollie is also a trained resolution practitioner but Antonio could insist someone else is appointed.'

We look at each other with something akin to frustrated disbelief plastered all over our faces. It's beyond a joke.

'This is appalling, Leah. Morally it seems so very wrong and I don't care what the law has to say on the matter.'

I nod in agreement, still grappling with the real fear that I might have no choice but to hand Rosie over to Antonio at some point. What if he disappears again, this time taking her with him? A cold chill begins to settle in the pit of my stomach.

'The reason I wanted to talk to you is that it's easy for me to see this solely from my own perspective. Ollie can only advise me on the technical detail of the law, obviously, and a lot of this is worst-case scenario stuff. But I need you to step back a little and think about it from Rosie's perspective. You've known her all her life. She knows nothing at all about what's happening and I'm not even sure he wants to come back into her life until I've spoken to him.

'Maybe he's after money, having convinced himself there would have been spare equity in the house – which there wasn't. But he was always good at fooling himself and you only need to look at the way a once lucrative business fell through his hands and ended up amassing large debts. Most of the items on the credit card bills were business-related expenses; it allowed him to ignore the truth of the situation for months and when things were about to fall apart he just ran away.

'If the worst happens and he's adamant he wants to begin a relationship with his daughter, morally have I the right to fight against that? Would I be robbing Rosie of the chance to get to know her real father? Should I be the one to ask for her opinion before all of this kicks off?'

Sally sits back in her chair looking at me in a state of bewilderment.

'That's a tough one. I think you should wait until you've spoken to him before you talk to Rosie. This will come as quite a shock and if it's hard to handle as an adult, how difficult will it be for a nine-year-old child? My advice is that you get all the facts first.'

My head is aching with it all.

'Every child obviously wants to believe their parents are both loving people who put them first and that's the example I've set.' I never thought to question how wise that decision was at the time.

'Rosie has no real idea of what her father did, or the type of person he is – or the state he left you in, does she? Maybe you're been too protective, Leah.' Sally is, ironically, reflecting my own thoughts now.

'I have never uttered a single negative word about him in front of her. He wasn't in her life and the least I could do was not to spoil the illusion that he was essentially a good man. She would simply see this as a chance, at long last, to begin a relationship with her estranged father because he was reaching out to her. And who could blame her for thinking that? But on the reverse side of that, what if he has changed? Then maybe I'm not putting her interests first. Would I be in danger of acting out of a sense of revenge for what he did if I fight him every step of the way? The initial problem might not have been my fault but the way I handled it is firmly down to me.'

I can see the empathy in Sally's eyes and the acknowledgement that it's an impossible dilemma.

'It's a horrible situation, Leah. You must be sick with worry as there are so many unknowns. If your worst fears are confirmed, then reaching an agreement would at least give you a voice in this. However, you have to show him you have a loud voice and you aren't going to be afraid to use it. I'm here for you, Leah, I only wish there was something I could do to help. Do you want me to drive you up there tomorrow? Ollie's office is in Leeds, isn't it? That's a long drive and some company might be a good idea. I don't think you should be up there on your own for this meeting.'

'That's a very kind offer, Sally, and appreciated. But I'm taking the train and Harrison is going to ferry me to and from Ollie's offices. I couldn't face the drive and Harrison is aware this could be a horror story in the making, so I'll be in good hands.'

I sit with my shoulders hunched, everything I'd been bottling up has been expelled and now I'm left with only gut-wrenching fear. The timing of this is horrible and my hopes for making Daniel and Bella a part of our lives seem to be an impossible dream right at this moment. It's all such a mess, my heart is breaking. But that's not something I can talk about with Sally, not least because I can't even contemplate having my hopes and dreams shattered, leaving only a big gaping hole.

Sally's arm wraps around my shoulders and we hug, both in tears.

'Let's hope it is only a quick divorce or money that he's after. If we all chip in what we can to help then maybe you can simply pay him off. But promise me that everything you do will go through Ollie.'

I wipe my eyes and then blow my nose. 'It will be tempting to ask him how much he wants to walk away but I couldn't take anyone's money. At least I don't owe anything so I could probably get a loan. I don't want my daughter's well-being to be put at risk, Sally, that's my only concern.'

Her arm tightens around me.

'Time to say a few prayers, I think. I'll be sending positive thoughts your way tomorrow. Obviously, Rosie will be with your parents but you haven't spelt this out to them yet, have you?'

It's a real effort to pull myself together.

'No, they think it's a routine meeting to talk through the process. Dad's doing well and I don't want him worrying about this until I know what's happening. You have no idea how much it's helped being able to voice all my thoughts out loud to you. Everything inside was a jumble, because ever since the divorce papers were served I've had to contain my thoughts to stop myself from going mad with worry. It's time to replace emotion with cold, hard determination. Tomorrow I need to show Antonio that where Rosie is concerned I intend to fight for what I believe is right. I'm not going to accept anything at face value.'

I refuse to let this get in the way of a chance to grab some happiness for the future. When the time is right I hope that Rosie can cope with the outcome of the divorce. I don't want her to feel conflicted as Daniel and I try to find a way through the problems. Hopefully we will be able to turn the idea of becoming a blended family into a reality. Although, just coping with that would have been a big ask of any nine-year-old. But with her biological father coming back into her life, that could threaten to pull her in two different directions at the same time. Oh, why did this have to happen *now*? Why not in six months' time?

I'm Nobody's Fool

The train journey allows me to determine my plan of attack. Okay, so I could have been the evil wife who made Antonio's life unbearable and drove him into someone else's arms – but I wasn't. And none of that has any bearing on what is right for Rosie, after the divorce anyway. I need to get real because this was never going to be a clean fight. It has to be tactical.

My phone pings and it's Daniel.

Good luck and stay strong.

I stop for a second to respond.

I'll call you afterwards. You are my rock! Thank you for the pep talk last night. I've come out wearing my boxing gloves!

A smile creeps over my face as I press send, conjuring up an image of him in my mind. Getting today out of the way will be like lifting a huge weight off my shoulders. I can't wait to shed the gnawing worry that has been constantly eating away at me, keeping me tossing and turning at night. Daniel has been there to listen to my angst and keep me positive. I freely admit that I don't know how I would have kept going without cracking up over the past couple of weeks if he hadn't been on the other end of the phone.

When I walk out through the main exit to the station and see a friendly face, it immediately gives me a boost.

'Harrison, it's so good to see you. Thank you for being here for me today.'

He knows every little detail of what's going on. Even my very worst fears and the things I haven't been able to voice to Ollie, because I've shared everything with him. But I also know that Ollie won't divulge anything and on the reverse side of that Harrison won't pass on a single word I say. In a way, he has become my sounding board, although I know he's firmly in my corner so his views aren't exactly impartial. However, he is very honest with me and I appreciate that.

'You look different somehow. Are you okay?' he asks.

My face is set and I'm ready to do battle.

'I've made a few tactical changes to the plan. I couldn't live with myself if this divorce ends up turning Rosie's little world upside down, only to end in disappointment. Ollie is in for a bit of a shock. I can either act like a hapless victim in all of this and that could put Rosie at risk, or I can use the law to my full advantage. So that's what I'm going to do.'

Harrison and I link arms as he steers me towards his car.

'Thank goodness! I've been feeling anxious on your behalf, lovely lady. There are times when assuming everyone plays fair is a distinct disadvantage and I'm relieved to see you have arrived in a fiery mood. Watch out Antonio, you might be in for a real surprise.'

For the first time since all this began I'm able to laugh with some level of sincerity attached to it. The transition from being powerless to feeling powerful hinges on one thing only: and that's having something with which to bargain. And the law is very clear about that.

~

'Ollie, there's a change of plan. I want to talk to Antonio in private to begin with.'

Ollie's expression changes instantly from a warm welcoming smile, to a grave look accompanied by a deep frown.

'I'm not sure that's a good idea, Leah. Can I ask the reason why you've suddenly changed your mind?'

'There are a few things that need to be said off the record. After that, I think it will be helpful if we outline to you what we've agreed and maybe you can then tell us how we move that forward legally.'

He looks apprehensive. 'You're taking quite a big risk here, Leah. My advice is that you don't commit to anything without a great deal of thought and without the benefit of professional advice. However, you are the client and I am required to take my instructions from you.'

We're facing each other across his desk and Harrison is outside in the reception area. The inner sanctum of a solicitor's office isn't as formidable as I'd expected it to be. They could be dealing with anything here, but the truth is that a lot of emotional and financial turmoil is handled within these four walls.

'My mind is made up and I'm convinced this is the right thing to do.'

'As you wish. But if you feel you are being bullied in any way, or manipulated, then I'll be waiting on the other side of that door and all you have to do is call me back in. Are you ready?'

I nod. As ready as I'll ever be.

Ollie grabs a folder and a pile of papers, then escorts me from his office back through reception. Harrison gives me a firm nod of encouragement as we walk past him. Ollie simply looks directly ahead. We turn into a short corridor and he stops in front of a door which opens into quite a large, conference-style room.

I settle myself down and after a few minutes a light on a console in the centre of the table starts blinking and Ollie leans across to press a button. There are a couple of clicks and suddenly, for the first time in over seven years, I hear Antonio's voice saying 'hello'.

'Good day, Mr Castelli. My name is Oliver Parker-Smith and you are through to the offices of the Chambers and Royal Legal Practice. Mrs Castelli is here waiting to take the call and has asked that I vacate the room for the first part of this meeting. Are you happy to agree to that change in format for today's discussion?'

Antonio coughs, clearing his throat and then replies with just the one word to confirm his agreement.

'I'm now leaving the room and will await my client's instruction to return.'

Ollie gives me one last look, checking whether my mind is made up; I give him a brief nod and the vestiges of a nervous smile. Waiting until the door closes behind him, I take a few deep breaths and begin. This is a conversation over which I need to demonstrate control so that it's clear I'm taking a firm stance. I want Antonio to understand that my solicitor has an important role in this but I'm driving it every inch of the way.

'We're alone, Antonio. What is it you wanted to say to me?'

A few seconds pass and I wonder if we've been disconnected, but suddenly his voice begins to fill the room.

'This isn't easy, Leah. It's been a long time. My life is different now and I'm sorry for what happened before. I have someone new in my life and I also have a two-year-old son. I want to remarry and it's time to put a few things right, first.'

I keep taking those slow, deep breaths.

'And that was why you contacted your parents and gave them your address? You knew that I would start divorce proceedings. But what about my sister?'

He clears his throat once again, a bothersome little cough

that reveals how nervous he is and that could give me an edge.

'This is harder than I thought it would be ... Kelly and I went our separate ways only a few months after we ... left. I haven't heard from her since then so I don't know where she is. Look, I'm a different person now, really I am. I'm settled and my partner and I have a nice house; I have a good job and I want to get to know Rosie again. She has a stepbrother and Annie says it's the right thing to do.'

Oh, now it's Annie who has fallen for his charm and is convinced she can make him a better person. Same old Antonio. It saddens me that it's Annie's influence and not his own conscience that has made him regret the error of his ways and the hurt he's inflicted on me and Rosie. No doubt he hated having to tell her anything at all about his past. Without a divorce he can't marry her, though and I bet the picture he painted of me wasn't a pretty one.

'I hope you have plenty of money then, because divorce can be a costly process.'

There's a sound of something hitting the floor, maybe a notebook or a pen and I think my words have startled him.

'What do you mean?'

'You left behind a lot of debt, Antonio, and there are maintenance arrears with regard to Rosie for the last seven plus years. Then, obviously, there will be your share of her upkeep until she's old enough to be independent.'

'I don't have any spare money, Leah, so don't think you're going to get a huge lump sum out of this. I mean, I know

I should be contributing to her upkeep, but the debt wasn't my fault and surely that's in the past now.'

Nothing is ever Antonio's fault; that's the way he leads his life. Will there ever come a point in the future when he walks away from Annie and his young son, too, I wonder?

'That isn't how the law looks at it, Antonio. But I'm willing to waive any financial claim against you if you agree to the terms I'm proposing. My solicitor will then put it in writing for us both to sign. Under the circumstances I'm merely putting Rosie's interests first and foremost. By law you have a right to have access to your estranged daughter and I'm not disputing that. However, if we are unable to come to an amicable agreement on both a financial and parental access basis, then this could turn into a very costly battle. I don't think that's something with which you are going to be happy, either, but I intend to stand firm to achieve what I feel is right for Rosie's future.'

He gives a bitter laugh.

'So, this is payback time? You're going to make this as difficult as you possibly can for me. You hate the fact that I'm happy now and that I wasn't happy with you.'

He hasn't changed at all. Does he feel no guilt at all about running away with Kelly and how that affected our lives here? Or the impact on Rosie as she faced the future without a father figure in her life?

'When Rosie was old enough to ask the question, there was no way I could tell her why you suddenly disappeared from our lives. I gave her vague reassurances that your absence didn't mean you didn't love her. None of us have ever spoken to her about the aunt she wouldn't even remember; the sister who betrayed me in the worst possible way. It's as if Kelly never existed but something will always be missing now she's no longer in our lives. And Antonio, you are equally to blame for that.

'So, my answer is that this isn't payback time, at all. I think it's a very generous offer given the dire financial situation you left me in. My proposal is that I waive any claim against you for your half of those debts and any form of maintenance payment: whether historical, or in the future. In return for that considerable concession I will agree to you establishing regular contact with Rosie via Skype. If you succeed in building a meaningful relationship with her, then I'm prepared to bring her over for an accompanied visit at some point by mutual agreement. I will expect you to foot the bill for all of her travel arrangements and as a demonstration of goodwill I will cover my own costs for that, and any subsequent visits. But that will be the full extent of the access arrangements until she is no longer dependent upon me.'

The silence is hard to bear but I know this wasn't at all what he was expecting to hear. Instead of having the upper hand, suddenly I'm making it clear how much he stands to lose financially. If he ends up having to agree to a payment plan he'll have no choice but to tell Annie about the debts he left behind. That isn't going to impress her very much, is it? Maybe he was naïve enough to think that financially this wasn't going to be a drain on him. Forcing my hand to instigate the divorce served his purpose and he thought that meant there would be no cost to himself.

That's the way he always breezed through life when I knew him; ignoring anything he didn't want to accept, or which didn't fall in with his plans. Now he's focusing on keeping his new partner happy with thoughts of a wedding.

I wonder if he regrets having had no contact at all with Rosie, because having a two-year-old around must remind him of what he has missed. But if he was motivated by a genuine desire to make up for the past, get to know her and be a part of her future, then you would think that he'd want to help provide for her, too. Out of principle, if nothing else. Why would he support one child of his quite happily and not the other? Unless he thinks he can take me for granted and continue calling the shots to achieve whatever is on his personal agenda.

'I think you're exaggerating. I can't be expected to keep two families at the same time and no judge can demand what I don't have to give.'

I'm so calm I surprise myself. He expects me to take sole care and responsibility for Rosie, while wanting to exert his rights to have unlimited access to her. This is first and foremost about being free to get married again. It has never crossed his mind to wonder how I was managing to keep a roof over Rosie's head, pay the bills or put food on the table. He still has no sense of responsibility whatsoever. Unbelievable.

'This is a one-time offer, Antonio. Take it or leave it. But those are my terms. If you aren't prepared to agree to this then you'd better appoint a solicitor and the discussions can be conducted via our representatives.'

'And waste money I don't have? This could ruin me and the life I've built over here.'

I say nothing. I've had seven years of living in a financial nightmare and I have nothing on my conscience.

'This is blackmail, Leah.'

'On the contrary, it's the law by which everyone has to abide. Including you, Antonio.'

'It doesn't cost me anything and we get this divorce through as quickly as possible?'

I can almost hear his thought processes. Annie will get her wedding and his life goes on as normal. Of course, Annie will assume that being married means something to Antonio and that it guarantees a rosy future for her and her son. All I feel is a sense of pity and empathy, from one woman to another.

'Agreed. This is your chance to get to know Rosie, Antonio, so don't let her down. All she knows about you is that you needed some time away and her expectation was that at some point you would come back into her life. You are starting with a clean slate, so make this about her and not about you. It's your chance to prove yourself as a father. I'll ask Ollie to join us and we can spell out the details of our arrangement.'

As I walk towards the door I don't feel like I've won, but I do feel that I've safeguarded Rosie from potential harm in the only way I possibly can. There are no winners in a situation like this, but from the little he's already said, it's patently obvious that Antonio hasn't changed at all. It's sad that Rosie will have to discover his shortcomings for herself but there's nothing I can do about that. If she decides she doesn't want him in her life at some point in the future, then at least I won't have influenced that in any way.

'Ollie, we've reached an agreement in regard to future contact with Rosie and the financial implications arising from our divorce. Can you come back in and we'll run through the terms? Antonio and I would like to get this signed off as soon as possible.'

Only a Fool Would Get in my Way

Harrison quizzes me as he drives me back, wanting to know every little detail and is clearly delighted that I'm walking away with the result I wanted.

'I feel ... elated! And strong.'

He's laughing as I'm having a hard time containing my jubilation. I feel victorious. I gave nothing except for what I was prepared to give in fairness to Rosie.

'I need a drink – and make it a large one!' I exclaim.

'Yes, ma'am. Will the bar in the station do?' Harrison pulls into the car park and points to a sign advertising The Whistle & Flag.

I glance at my watch. I have just over an hour until the train departs.

'Perfect. And when you see Ollie, later, can you thank him for me? I'm not the easiest client and I've been so driven by my emotions that I haven't always listened to his advice. He did an amazing job talking to Antonio, though.'

'Did Antonio say anything at all about your sister?'

'Only that they split up not long after the disappearance and he doesn't know where she is. A part of me longs to have news of her. Knowing what I do about Antonio, now, perhaps it is within my heart to forgive her. But maybe her whereabouts will always remain a mystery because she can't forgive herself. Kelly knew perfectly well that after what she did my world would fall apart and that Rosie's life would change forever. I feel like I never really knew the person she was, because you have to be cold-blooded indeed to do that to anyone, let alone your twin sister. I used to be able to feel her presence, in here.' I tap my chest. 'But now there's nothing; any link has been severed and that's why I feel Kelly will never return to us. I can only hope that wherever she is, she's safe and happy.'

'Maybe she fell under his spell and if he fooled you, he could also have fooled her. But I guess you'll never really know that for sure.'

I shrug off any thoughts of Kelly. That's now a thing of the past for me and the only one who can change that is Kelly herself. If she ever does come back, I know I'll deal with it.

Harrison pulls into a parking space.

'This is the thirty-minute parking pick-up zone; will that be long enough to enjoy that celebratory drink?'

I nod and open the door; Harrison locks the car as we head off towards the bar.

I have to walk quickly to keep up with his long strides. He turns his head slightly to look at me as I trot along half a step behind him.

'How's Daniel?' His lips curve upwards in a teasing smile.

'He's good. Fifty-three days until he flies home.' I smile up at him but I can still see his concern. 'Daniel has been a tower of strength. He understood that today was crucial for me but now it's sorted, I can finally think about moving on. I will admit that so much hangs on Rosie's reaction and he has similar concerns about Bella. She, too, has to adjust to a new father figure coming into her life when her mother remarries, in addition to Daniel stepping back into a more hands-on role again. We have a mountain to climb to make it all work and so much could still go wrong. The decision isn't ours alone.'

Harrison is already perched on a bar stool and as I hoist myself up next to him we exchange a look of reluctant acceptance.

'What can I get for you tonight, guys?'

'Red?' Harrison looks at me and I nod. 'Two glasses of a Shiraz, please.'

The bartender walks away and Harrison begins to drum his fingertips on the bar counter.

'Come on, say whatever it is that's on your mind,' I urge.

Now Harrison isn't even looking at me.

He reaches inside his pocket and pulls out his phone. After tapping away for a few moments he hands it to me.

'You need to read this article. It appeared in the *York Daily Recorder* over two and a half years ago.'

The headline makes my stomach lurch.

Dr Terry Carpenter takes over as dig coordinator at Upper Reach after colleague falls ill

It has been confirmed that Dr Carpenter will take over supervision of the dig, after complications following a viral infection hospitalised fellow lecturer and archaeologist, Dr Daniel Preston.

The site has been run by the university for several years and accounts for an important part of the field work experience which attracts budding archaeologists to York.

A representative confirmed that Dr Preston's condition continues to worsen after the virus caused irreparable damage to his heart. He is currently on the waiting list for a heart transplant. A group of colleagues are planning a charity walk to raise funds in support of the hospital where he's being treated.

The university has set up a page on their website where people can register an interest in taking part or can make a donation to the fund.

Harrison is studying my carefully blank face.

'You knew all along?' He levels the accusation at me.

'Daniel told me on that last night we were together.'

He lets out a huge sigh of relief. 'Thank God he told you. I've been dreading breaking the news to you. Why didn't you tell me?'

I pass the phone back to him.

'Because I still have to get my own head around it and I also felt it was his secret to tell. It happened a few months after he split from his wife and even Bella doesn't know. He's strong and fit, but when I felt his scar...'

I look across at Harrison and give him a sorrowful look. 'The last couple of weeks have felt like overload. I'm not ignoring anything, just side-lining a few things on a temporary basis until I have the energy to deal with them properly.'

'I'm not trying to give you a hard time, Leah. I just wanted to check that you know what you're getting yourself into.' He means well and I know I haven't been straight with him but I also know Daniel wouldn't be happy if he overhead our conversation. The problem is that I need to talk to someone about this and Harrison is so great at listening and understanding what really matters.

'I have no idea what the life expectancy is for someone who has had a heart transplant, but I believe there's always a chance of rejection.' My words have a hollow ring to them and I can see how worried Harrison is, loath to address such a sensitive issue.

I raise the wine glass in front of me to my lips and take a huge gulp.

'Daniel takes a lot of medication twice daily and that will continue for the rest of his life. He has regular check-ups, though, and everything is fine according to his doctor. I did some online research and the days and weeks following the procedure are when the patient is most at risk. His prognosis is good, and many transplant patients go on to lead a very full life. I just wish he'd told me sooner because my reaction to his scar was one of total shock as it was so unexpected. He initially mistook that for hesitancy, as if it changed how I felt about him and that wasn't true at all.'

We sit together looking across at our reflections in the mirror on the back wall of the bar.

'How do you start a conversation like that when you're only just getting to know someone? It can't be easy, Leah.'

Harrison's face reflects sympathy, tinged with sadness and I put my hand on his arm to give it a squeeze. It means a lot to me to know that he can see it from Daniel's perspective.

'He thought I wouldn't be able to cope when I found out, but now he understands he was wrong. It simply put everything else into perspective for me. Antonio was the last unknown in the whole thing. Now that's finally resolved I can focus on the future.

'The rollercoaster ride that is my life isn't quite over yet, but the end really is in sight. All of the right components are there for a happily-ever-after ending, but like everything in life, it's all about timing. We have two young girls to consider who have both been through so much already. It never was going to be simple, was it?'

'No, but I doubt it could get any more complicated,' Harrison mutters.

'Daniel is a fighter and I'm a fighter, too. We can make this happen, Harrison, I really do believe that but I need to convince Daniel it can work, too. I know he has moments when it overwhelms him. He so badly wants to do what is right for Bella, Rosie and me. What worries me is that in the end he'll decide we are better off without him in our lives.'

Harrison looks puzzled. 'Why would he think that way?'

'Because he genuinely cares about us and he can't guarantee what his future will hold. Which is totally crazy as no one can do that, anyway. But it's a nagging doubt in his head that won't go away and I don't know if he will give into it.'

Harrison extends his hand to cover my own and presses it gently. Sometimes there are no words to offer comfort and this is one of those moments.

The Heart Instinctively Knows When You've Found The One – Doesn't It?

I didn't make plans for this weekend because in all honesty I'm running on empty and it shows. The weeks of stress have taken a toll and what my mind and body needs now is a little rest.

Rosie seems to understand that I'm not quite my usual self and suggests I put my feet up, while she reads a book. Instead, I phone my neighbour, Naomi, to ask if she'll do me a huge favour and take Rosie to Callie's martial arts class this morning. When I break the news to Rosie she's jubilant.

'Aww, thanks Mum! What should I wear as I don't have a uniform like Callie's?'

Bless her, always practical.

'It's white, isn't it?'

'Yes.'

'How about your white leggings and a plain white t-shirt? That way you'll blend in. If you like it then we'll get that uniform ordered ASAP.'

Rosie walks over to give me a hug and my heart constricts.

I need to tell her about Antonio but I'm anxious about how she will take the news. After that, I'm hoping that I will be able to talk to her about Daniel in a meaningful way.

'I really think I'm going to love doing this, Mum. Will you come with me next time?'

'Of course, I will. I'm just a little tired today from the long trip yesterday, that's all and I have a few boring things I have to do. I was thinking about ten pin bowling tomorrow, what do you think?'

'Oh, that would be great, Mum!

Rosie charges off to change. When she reappears, she does a few kicks and arm movements reminiscent of the ninja turtles in action. They used to keep her glued to Nickelodeon and it makes me smile. But change is coming and somehow I have to start sowing the seed so that Rosie begins to think of life outside of her tight little circle.

'Rosie, I know you love it here but what if we had a chance to make a fresh start somewhere new? Maybe closer to a town where there is more going on? There will be classes like this one and lots of other clubs to choose from. What do you think?'

She stops throwing herself around to stare at me with a pinched look.

'We'd leave the forest and Grandma and Granddad?'

Before I can answer her the sound of a car horn announces the arrival of Naomi and Callie. Rosie is out the door in mere seconds, after giving me the briefest of kisses as she's so excited.

Naomi opens the car window to call out.

'Thought I'd take the girls out for lunch afterwards and back to mine for a film?'

'Great, thank you. Is Callie up for ten pin bowling tomorrow and we'll stop for lunch at the complex?'

'Sounds good. Are you okay?'

I smile, shrugging my shoulders at the same time. 'Ticking over. You know how it is.' I feel jaded and wish I hadn't tried to begin that conversation with Rosie just before she left. It was a stupid thing to do as I need to have her undivided attention.

The girls are fidgeting in their seats, eager to get off and I wave to them, pretty sure they're too busy chatting to notice. At least Rosie doesn't appear to be dwelling on what I said, so I breathe a sigh of relief.

Closing the door, the quiet almost hurts my ears. I've had a headache now for the best part of twenty-four hours and the first thing I need to do is to take some painkillers. It was a late one again last night, as I was online desperate to find out as much as I could about heart transplant surgery. Daniel must have been through hell and I so wish I'd been in his life then to help him through it all.

As with everything you read on the internet there are some conflicting views and statistics. I tried to keep to either medical websites, or accounts written by transplant recipients themselves. It helped to reassure me that the prognosis for a long and happy life is down to having regular checks, taking those tablets and leading a healthy lifestyle, just like Daniel told me. It's a huge relief and made for interesting reading. It rammed home how important it is that people sign up to the NHS Organ Donation register. When a death results in one or more people's lives being saved or made better, it's a truly wonderful legacy to leave behind. I signed up immediately and berated myself for not having done it before. Because of one kind donor I now have the chance of spending the rest of my life with Daniel and for that I will be eternally grateful.

Armed with a page of notes from my online research, I go into the kitchen and pop the kettle on, then grab my phone and call Mum.

'Hey, it's only me. Rosie is out with Callie for most of the day and I wondered if you wanted to call round later. I can tell you all about the appointment with the solicitor yesterday. I'm sorry I couldn't really say anything when I collected her last night but I was too tired to go into it, even if Rosie hadn't been there.'

Mum tuts.

'My poor, dear girl. I knew there was more to it than you were letting on. What time works best for you?'

'I'm about to make an important phone call so give me an hour, maybe an hour and a half. That's another thing I want to tell you about. I'm confident everything is going to be okay, so don't go worrying about it but it will be a bit of a saga.'

'At least you sound optimistic this morning, so I'll take that as a very good sign. We'll see you later then, honey.'

I add an extra half a spoonful of coffee granules, savouring the rich, almost bitter aroma as the hot water hits the mug. I'm going to need this, I reflect, as I sit at the table and dial Daniel's number. It rings an agonising five times before he picks up.

'Hi Leah, it's good to hear your voice.'

A tingling sensation starts to rush around my body, increasing my rate of breathing. I have to focus on remaining calm and sounding bright and breezy. I can't deny that I still feel a little tearful after what I read last night but it would be a big mistake to share that thought.

'I'm missing you like crazy. It would all be so different if you were here. All of a sudden my body seems to be rebelling and I have a pounding headache.'

'You've been under tremendous pressure, Leah. It's time to relax a little now the worst is over.' His voice is upbeat and I wish I could see his face.

'I'm home alone as Rosie is out for a few hours. Have you talked to Bella yet, today?'

'First thing. She's okay. I can tell from your voice you aren't your usual self. Is it just that headache or is it something in particular that's worrying you?'

'Sometime very soon I'm going to have to sit Rosie down and tell her that Antonio will be coming back into her life. I don't know whether to tell her about *us* first.'

There's a brief pause.

'I feel bad it's yet another thing you have to contend with but can't it wait until I'm back and we can tell Rosie and Bella together?' His voice reflects the anxiety he's feeling and I know he longs to be here to support me.

I keep getting flashbacks; watching Daniel laugh as I

re-took the photos in the National Gardens and feeling his arms around me as we lay together on the bed.

'I really hope and pray our girls will love the family unit we will become together, Daniel. But in order to attain that, one of us will have to be uprooted. As you already have an established job and I work from home, it makes sense for me to sell the cottage. The next part isn't going to be easy for Rosie, or me, I will admit, but if I sit her down and start the conversation I can gauge her reaction and talk through any concerns she might have. Kids are pretty resilient and what we will be able to give them is a loving family environment. I just wanted to hear your voice before I start the dialogue. I also need to talk to my parents because I've rather kept them in the dark, too. I think they all know something major is happening and it feels wrong to pretend otherwise.'

I have no idea how many seconds slip by, but it feels like forever before his voice breaks the silence.

'Look, are you sure this is the best solution, Leah? Leaving the forest is only one of the options we've discussed and I don't want you rushing into this and then regretting your decision.'

Is he having second thoughts as I've feared all along? Is that why he wants me to put off sitting down with Rosie?

'But it's the only one that really works and we both know that.' My heart is heavy as I acknowledge what my gut instincts are telling me. It's going to take time for this to sink in and for all of us to grow accustomed to the idea. With just over seven weeks until Daniel flies back I need to get that initial conversation out of the way, before we next meet up. I want our future to kick off on a high with everyone signed up and looking forward to welcoming Daniel and Bella into our lives.

'You're one strong lady, Leah, but I think it's wrong to rush this. I feel useless being over here when I should be by your side but it's not for much longer.'

I put down my empty mug, the caffeine shot was a nice little perk to the system and is already helping to dull the throbbing in my head. But as my thoughts focus, so my senses sharpen and I'm now hearing warning bells – loud and clear.

'People who love Rosie and me simply want us to be happy. They will understand and York isn't a million miles away, just a car journey. Rosie will flourish, I have no doubt of that. It's the transition period that concerns me but after that life could be so wonderful for us all. You think Bella won't take the news well?'

I'm pushing him, I know that, but I need him to reassure me he's ready to commit.

'Yes, obviously I'm concerned about having the talk with her but come on, I already know you better than that. You're worried sick about Rosie's reaction and how your parents and friends will take the news. That's why we need to be … cautious.'

Cautious? That doesn't sound like a man convinced he's doing the right thing.

'Daniel, I'm about to put everything on the line for you, for our future together, and it sounds to me like you're wavering. Of course we want our daughters to be happy and that's why we need to start talking to them now.'

There's a heavy silence between us for a few moments and my heart sinks in my chest.

'Is there anything else you want to mention? I don't feel we're done yet.'

I gasp because now he sounds angry with me.

'Seriously?' I throw the word at him, unable to understand why this conversation is going so badly wrong.

'Seriously.' He repeats the word as if it's an accusation.

Well, maybe there's a little anger and frustration building up inside of me, too and I see red. 'Okay. I've signed up to the NHS Organ Donor register.'

I hear him draw in a long, slow breath.

'I knew it would be too much to expect anyone to handle.' His voice is full of regret and he ends the call without warning. A tear rolls down my cheek. I glance down at the list of questions I wanted to discuss with him after doing my research last night. I thought this call was going to be a turning point, when we put the last hurdle to bed and shared our plans with the girls. What should I do now?

The Letter

They say you should never react in anger and I take a while to calm myself before pressing re-dial. However, the moment I hear Daniel's voice the tension is back there between us in an instant.

'Leah, I can't talk to you about this right now. I need to think.'

'You need to think ... well, I need to know where this is going, Daniel, if it's going anywhere at all, that is.'

His laugh is tinged with bitterness and I'm at a loss to understand that.

'What aren't you telling me?' I know my tone is one of accusation but I'm exasperated. I've been patient but there is a limit.

'I ... literally two minutes before you called I'd just finished talking to Tricia. I knew something was up because she kept questioning me about Bella's stay at the villa. Then she tore into me. It seems Bella has been talking about you and Rosie – a lot. Tricia was really angry. She said that my behaviour had been inappropriate and that Bella was at an impressionable age.'

I gasp. 'But nothing happened between us when the girls were around. I don't understand why anything Bella could have said would upset Tricia.'

Daniel sighs. 'She wasn't specific but you and I know the girls never so much as saw us holding hands. So I can only assume that Tricia has been questioning her and has jumped to the wrong conclusion. I can sort of see how it might look and why she was concerned. I mean, when Bella hurt her ankle I wasn't at her side, I was talking to you. Tricia threw that at me and said I needed to take better care when I'm *supposed* to be in charge of my daughter. Can you imagine how that made me feel?'

No wonder he was upset.

'But that's not fair, Daniel. It could so easily have happened when Bella was with her. It was an accident. Didn't you explain that?'

'Leah, I'm not a fool. Of course I did. But Tricia said that Bella hasn't been sleeping well recently and when she asked her why, Bella told her she didn't even want to go to the wedding. She made it clear that Evan would never be her dad. Bella then said that she wanted to live with me because soon she was going to be a part of a real family. Tricia said that our relationship is undermining Evan's efforts to get close to Bella and accused me of purposely trying to upset their wedding plans.'

Now I'm confused.

'I don't understand. I thought you said you hadn't talked to Bella about us, at all?'

'I haven't and I have no idea what's really going on in

her head, but clearly I have to tread warily. I can't upset Tricia or have her thinking that I can't be trusted to put Bella first when she's with me.'

Now I'm really angry.

'This wouldn't have happened if you had already talked to Bella about us, Daniel. Children can sense things even if they don't know what's actually going on. As for Tricia, well, it sounds to me like she's upset because things aren't going as smoothly as she planned with Evan, and she's taking it out on you. You have to stand up for yourself and explain what's really going on.'

Silence.

'You aren't going to do that, are you?' My tone wavers as it begins to sink in.

'I can't right now, it's a difficult time.'

'Then there's nothing more to say.'

I hesitate before pressing the end call button, but as the seconds pass and he doesn't speak I know there's absolutely no point in waiting for a response. Reluctantly, my finger performs the task and I throw the phone down in a state of utter despair.

Several hours later I sit in front of the computer screen and begin typing.

My darling Daniel,

Your hesitancy isn't only about the tension between Tricia and Bella, is it? You've known for a while about Bella's natural anxiety over the forthcoming changes in the run up to the wedding. And that it will all settle down very quickly afterwards because she'll have you home, too. We've talked that through and I thought you were at peace with it. Tricia is trying to lay the blame at your door and I think you are turning that into an excuse for backing away from me. You, too, are fearful about change and what it represents. So now I'm going to be honest with you and tell you what I'm thinking.

I believe that we're all damaged in one way, or another. If not by the hurt inflicted upon us by other people, then from experiences that change us, and not always for the better. Some end up becoming bitter, resentful maybe because they failed at something and their pride is dented. Others feel they have never been given a lucky break, labouring under the illusion that's all it takes, when the truth is that it's down to relentless determination. We are each responsible for making the decisions that take us forward and map out the future. Even when we keep getting knocked down, we have to bounce back every time with a stronger resolve. Sometimes that means letting go of one dream and chasing another. That's the inevitability of life.

I also believe that even in our darkest hours we are all dreamers, no matter what life throws at us. Ill health, I realise, is one of the worst battles to fight. I cannot even begin to imagine what you went through and I won't pretend that isn't the case. You were staring at death and it must have been hell thinking about leaving Bella behind and the memories you would never have together. That will have been torture for any parent, especially when the best years are yet to come.

But – and it's a small word that changes everything – you were given another chance. Maybe the damage the virus inflicted wasn't a part of life's plan for you and fate was putting right an error. Or maybe you were experiencing it so that it could shape your future in some way. What I want you to think long and hard about is whether you are in danger of limiting yourself and wasting the precious opportunity you have been given.

I understand your reservations given all that you've been through. Being scared to live your life to the full in case something happens isn't living, though. It's faking it and what sort of message does that send to Bella? It's tantamount to giving up when you have the prospect of a wonderful future ahead of you.

My fear is that you will end up looking back on your life – however long it is – with needless regret. Your transplant was a blessing and not a curse. I know from witnessing my dad's heart attack that it does colour the way you will look at everything after glimpsing how fragile life can be. I also know that each day is precious and that's what quality of life is all about. It isn't about the number of days we have, but about what we choose to fill those days with – and that should be love and happiness.

As much as I love you, Daniel, I have to accept that you aren't ready. Whether that's to face your unspoken fears, or the fact that you feel your illness took something away from you. My heart is telling me you haven't accepted what happened and in some way you feel it has changed you. All I can say is that the Daniel I met is a loving, wonderful and vibrant man who made me instantly fall in love with him. It's time you started to believe in yourself again.

But – and as I said, it's a small word which often carries enormous weight – I can't let you back into my life unless you are ready to commit. Not just for my sake, but for Rosie's and Bella's sakes, too.

There will always be problems to face and you and I have to be strong enough in our relationship to overcome anything that happens in the future. To do that I need to know you can defeat those demons and finally let go to step into a new future as one family, together. This is about all or nothing, I'm afraid, because I love you too much to settle for less.

It's time for you to make a decision and there's no point whatsoever in pretending otherwise. You're pushing me away and it's breaking my heart. I'm here and I'm waiting but now it's up to you.

Leah x

I don't even re-read the words I've typed; I save the document and attach it to a blank email and with one press of a key it's gone. Somehow, I have to pick myself back up because tomorrow is another day and I have problems of my own to face. If Daniel can't face his, then the dream stops here.

Facing Facts

When Mum and Dad arrive, they are both subdued and I can see how heavily my problems are still weighing upon them. I feel like the worst daughter in the world and I am. And now for the next round of assault on their emotions. It makes me feel sick to my stomach but then I'm still reeling over the argument with Daniel and the ultimatum I had to give him.

We hug and then they sit together on the sofa. I notice Dad immediately grasps Mum's hand as I tell them all about the agreement with Antonio. Mum's face is pained and Dad looks angry.

'He shouldn't have any rights. I don't want that man having anything to do with our granddaughter.' Dad's eyes blaze and Mum turns towards him, placing her hand lovingly on his shoulder.

'Roger, the law is the law. I feared this would happen but we have to consider it from Rosie's point of view. She's curious about her father and that's only natural. Maybe he won't let her down and the damage he's inflicted upon us all has taught him something. If he makes Rosie feel loved, as opposed to being abandoned without thought, that would be a wonderful thing.'

Dad scowls. 'He's a liar and a cheat, Maggie, and I don't trust him. Think of the damage he could do if he comes into her life and then leaves again!'

Mum shakes her head sorrowfully and I watch as they speak the words that have been going around in my own head, relentlessly. I want that miracle for my daughter but I fear Antonio won't be able to deliver.

'We don't have a choice, Dad. Antonio has rights and this was the least damaging option. I had to forego any financial claim on him as that was the only bargaining tool I had. My worst fear was that he'd apply for shared custody. At least this way I can keep an eye on the contact between them.'

I feel apologetic, not only about the agreement but that I've brought all of this heartbreak and controversy into their lives for a second time.

Mum looks across at me.

'You did well, Leah, please don't think we underestimate the toll this has taken on you. And Roger, we can't wrap our girl up in cotton wool. The world is a harsh place at times and a part of growing up is learning to judge right from wrong. If Antonio doesn't meet Rosie's expectations then she may well turn her back on him, anyway. But if he isn't quite the monster we fear him to be perhaps there is some love within him for his daughter. To Rosie that would mean the world and it's a gift only he can give her.'

Dad looks humbled, taking Mum's hand in both of his and giving it a squeeze.

'It hurts, Maggie, even though I know Rosie longs to hear her father say he loves her and he's sorry. But is Antonio capable of that? He tore our family apart and I'll never get over it.'

I know they're both thinking about Kelly.

'She isn't with him anymore. He told me they broke up only a couple of months later. He's with someone else now and he has a two-year-old son.' I wasn't intending to share this information. I'm not sure whether it makes it worse, or better for them to know that. They both stare at me with blank faces, then turn to look at each other.

'Perhaps, one day, she'll return,' I offer, my voice wavering a little.

Dad's shoulders are slumped as he looks directly at me. 'Some things can't ever be forgiven, Leah.'

Mum's eyes are glistening and I don't know what to say because it's true.

'We'll get through it and I'll be watching Rosie closely. I'm going to sit down with her tonight and explain what's going to happen.'

'It is a lot for such a young little head to cope with; so many changes to come and no guarantees they will bond. But then that's life and we can't remain stuck in this limbo we've been in for such a long time. Either way, Rosie has to find out what her real father is like and I can only hope he has changed.' Mum eases herself up off the sofa and Dad stands next to her.

I walk across to them and we hug. The seconds stretch out and my life seems to flash before my eyes.

'Ring me later to let me know how it goes with Rosie, darling. We'll be thinking of you both.' She shoots Dad a meaningful glance.

'We'd rather hoped you'd be talking to us about Daniel, too. Mum said you mentioned you had other news? We never question Rosie about anything, you know that, but she often refers back to the Athens trip. And she's excited about meeting up with Daniel and Bella once he's back in York.'

I don't quite know what to say to them. 'It's complicated, I'm afraid. Just like everything else going on in my life at the moment. That's another conversation I need to have with her when the time is right.'

The look that passes between them makes my heart sinks into my stomach. I've done it again. It's one worry after another. But all I could say to them now, hand on heart, is that I can't foresee any further changes on the horizon. It looks like it's going to continue to be just Rosie and me.

~

I'm alone and the house is so quiet I can't settle to anything. I feel that my plans for the future are unravelling faster than a ball of string rolling downhill.

The slam of a car door sees me heading downstairs and I swing open the front door to be greeted by two giggly girls. I hitch up the corners of my mouth to stop my bottom lip from trembling.

'Well, you two look like you had a good time,' I smile at Rosie and Callie as they high five each other and wave out to Naomi. I daren't approach the car for fear she will see that something is up.

'Thank you!' I call out instead, and Naomi puts up her thumb in acknowledgement as Callie runs back to the car.

'Bye, Leah, bye Rosie. See you tomorrow!'

As I usher Rosie through the door and remind her to hang up her jacket, my anxiety is growing by the second.

'Let's head into the kitchen. I've made your favourite strawberry milkshake with an obscene amount of ice cream. I thought we could sit and have a little chat while we drink them.'

'Have I done something wrong?' her voice questions, as she wrinkles up her nose.

'Not at all. Come and settle yourself down at the table and I'll explain.'

I grab the shakes from the fridge and carry them across to the table, watching that eager little face. Those bright, shining eyes and the long dark hair which is so badly in need of a trim make my heart melt.

'A lot has happened in a short space of time, Rosie. Your dad is coming back into our lives but—' Her face starts to glow with a smile that comes from deep within and my heart sinks. 'Okay, you need to listen carefully to what I have to say, Rosie. He misses you and very soon we're going to arrange for him to Skype so you can chat together. Dad lives in another country now and he has a new life. Because he's happy, he wants to get to know you again and that's wonderful news, isn't it?'

She nods, a little too enthusiastically. 'Why can't we be with him? Why does he have to have a new life somewhere else?'

'Because you can't help who you fall in love with, Rosie and your dad has fallen in love with someone else. They make each other happy and that makes me happy for him.'

I'm skirting the issue, I know, but I want to let her down gently.

'But I don't know him, Mum. And he doesn't know me.' The corners of her mouth are beginning to turn downwards.

'And that's why he wants to talk to you. You can tell him about school and the things you enjoy doing. He misses you, Rosie, and he's never forgotten you.'

A frown creases her brow as she considers my words. 'You're getting divorced, aren't you? Is this because of Daniel?'

I look at her unable to mask my shocked expression. I'm floored before I even begin. I had no idea her mind would go off on this tangent. What do I say now, given that I'm not sure Daniel will ever be ready to move on? I stall by lifting the glass in front of me to my lips, nodding my head to indicate for her to do the same. She doesn't move a muscle and I can feel her eyes weighing up my every move.

'No, Rosie. Dad and I are getting a divorce because he's been gone a long time now. Sometimes people don't make each other happy. It's sad, but it's true and it's no one's fault.

It's taken him a while to sort out his life, that's all and I'm excited for the two of you to spend time getting to know each other at last.'

I plaster on a smile that's as fake as snow in the UK in August. Rosie studies my face, a look of suspicion directed at me.

'If you didn't like Daniel would Dad come back here, to us?'

I shake my head, and this time the gentle look I give her is a heartfelt one.

'No, honey, I'm afraid not. Dad has a little boy and he's going to remarry.' Damn it – why did I say that? Too much, too soon! I wish I could take it back, rewind the moment but I'm desperate here. There is no way to smooth over this but she's only nine, for goodness' sake. I shouldn't even be having a conversation like this with her.

'He loves someone else more than he loves us? Is that why he's never sent me a birthday, or a Christmas card?'

I sigh, as exasperation at my inept attempts to explain the impossible begin to overwhelm me. Do I blunder on or give her a hug and stop here?

'Mum, I'm not a little kid anymore. I want to know the truth.'

My head snaps upwards as I look at her in surprise.

'I realise that this is hard to understand, Rosie and it will make more sense when you are older. It's because your dad is finally happy that he now misses you more than ever. When you talk to him you can ask him whatever you want and I'm sure he'll explain it as best he can. Life isn't always simple for adults, either. I can't answer for him, my love because I simply don't know.'

Now she looks cross. 'I'm not sure I can forgive him for leaving us, Mum. Can you?'

I'm reeling, not even sure how to answer her but she's waiting for my response.

'It's time to move on, Rosie, for all of us.'

She looks confused and I watch as she intertwines her fingers resting in her lap, a sure sign that she's anxious. 'I overheard you talking to Daniel on the phone the other night and it sounded like you were making plans for the future. I didn't say anything because I was kind of pleased about it. I don't want you to be lonely anymore, Mum. Doesn't Daniel want us?'

A sob catches in my throat. Does she feel this is a second rejection for us both, I wonder, and my heart constricts at the thought.

'When I met Daniel, I knew he was a very special man indeed, Rosie. However, when you bring a child into this world it means they are always the first priority in your life because you want their happiness over your own. Daniel has to put Bella first, too, and sometimes it's not easy to make everything work even though you desperately want it to. Is that something you can understand?'

I can't read her expression but her eyes are searching mine.

'So I wasn't a priority for my own dad?'

I feel like we're going around and around in circles. It's too much for her to take in and I need to draw this to a close.

'Adults don't always get it right, Rosie. And then we're sorry. Let's see what happens, shall we? I'll find out when that first chat with your dad is going to be and we'll take it from there. Any time you want to talk to me, I'm here to listen. What I can't promise, honey, is that I'll always have the answers to your questions. That makes me feel bad but it's the truth. And as for Daniel, we've become friends but that has nothing to do with the divorce, Rosie, and I hope you can understand that. I am sorry, though, because I know this leaves you with a lot of mixed feelings. We'll work it out, I promise.'

Rosie slides off her chair and comes around to give me a hug.

'I never want you to feel bad, Mum, because you're the best. I simply want you to be happy.'

A New Day and the Sky is Blue, Not a Cloud in Sight

It's two weeks until Rosie is back at school and the first four weeks of the summer holidays have literally flown by. We've been to Le Crotoy, in France; headed up north to have our first experience of glamping – in the poshest tents you could ever imagine; and we were invited to sample the delights of a circus-themed, long weekend at a holiday camp near Brighton.

'Mum, do you want me to get the door?' Rosie shouts down the stairs, but I'm already out of my seat and heading in that direction.

'No, it's fine, darling, thank you. I'll bring lunch up in half an hour.'

'Okay, ta.' Even before I reach the door I can hear both Callie and Rosie shrieking with laughter in the background. What kid doesn't love the Minion movies?

Opening the door, it makes me smile to see Sally standing there.

'Well, this is a lovely surprise. Ignore the noise from upstairs, it's Minion fever. Come on through.' We hug and she follows me inside.

'I've just had a scan and I wanted to show you the photos. I'm so excited, it's beginning to feel real at last!'

I glance down at her tummy and she smiles to herself, giving it a rub.

'It's not a jelly belly now, it's all baby. Really. I've been super good on the eating front.'

'You are positively glowing, so you must be doing something right. What would you like to drink? I have herbal teas: peppermint, chamomile or ginger.'

'Ooh, ginger sounds good, thank you. Look at this – it's a miracle, isn't it? And I thought it wasn't ever going to happen for me.'

I take the print and look down at the tiny little thing, so cosy in its environment.

'Ahh ... I can't wait to meet him, or her?'

'We've decided we don't want to know so it will be a surprise. Although we were both watching the screen without blinking, our eyes looking for little clues!' She starts laughing.

'It takes me back. Savour every little thing, Sally, because time flies by and you only have to look at Rosie now to see that. Can you remember when we sat looking at the scan of her?'

'I do. And you're so right. You're looking a bit better than the last time I saw you.'

I busy myself making the drinks and avoiding eye contact.

'Life is starting to even out and I'm holding it all together somehow,' I reply. 'The new arrangement with Antonio is going well enough and, so far, he hasn't let Rosie down once. They speak twice a week and it's enough for the time being, as the first couple of calls were difficult. I don't get involved but I will admit I stay in the kitchen, well within earshot. To ease some of the silences I suggested Rosie make a little list of things to talk about and that has really helped. Antonio is also getting better at asking the right questions. She hasn't "met" little Bradley, yet, but we've both heard him occasionally in the background. I know she's curious but it's still early days.'

Sally is watching me intently and as I turn to walk across to put the mugs on the table our eyes meet.

'How are your mum and dad with the Antonio situation?'

'Good. Happier now they are a bit more relaxed about the phone calls. It was the right thing to do but Rosie's reaction has surprised us all. We assumed it would be a big deal, but in fact she doesn't really talk about it afterwards. But the main thing is that she isn't upset in any way by it.'

'And Daniel?'

I had ended up confiding in Sally shortly after I'd emailed Daniel the letter. It was obvious to everyone around me that something had gone very badly wrong. I was unable to mask how heartbroken I was to walk away from Daniel. She admitted she'd had an inkling something life-changing had happened to me in Athens. Being the friend she is, she also realised it wasn't straightforward. Her fear was that I'd met someone who was already married and she knew that would have been an impossible situation for me.

'I've heard nothing at all.'

The doorbell rings yet again. I can hear the sound of feet clattering down the stairs, so I know it's the postman. Rosie is expecting a special package. She's been asked to test out some new underwater goggles and this afternoon Naomi is taking them swimming. Rosie would have been so disappointed if the parcel hadn't arrived in time. I can hear some very excited chatter going on.

'Mum, they've arrived and there are three pairs in different colours. Which colour would you like, Callie? Oh, there's a parcel for you here, too, Mum.'

Rosie hands me a small box and returns to investigate the contents of her package, spilling polystyrene beans everywhere.

'Steady, Rosie. Those things are a nightmare to pick up.'

'Can I have the purple ones?' Callie asks and Rosie hands over a pair of very stylish-looking goggles. Then she holds up a pink pair in one hand and a blue pair in the other.

'Which colour do you like best, Mum?'

I'm unwrapping my little box, wondering what on earth it can be as I wasn't expecting anything at all.

'Blue. Definitely,' I reply.

Inside the outer wrapping is a box with a lid, a bit like a jewellery box. I prise off the lid and inside is a small card bearing a handwritten message.

From Athens with love. Daniel x

I gulp. Beneath the card is a small white marble pebble in the shape of a heart.

Callie, Rosie and Sally are all staring at me.

'I wondered when this would get here,' I offer as an explanation, as I hold the perfect marble heart in the centre of my palm and curl my fingers around it. I pull myself together and discreetly pop the card back in the box so I can focus on Callie and Rosie. They are both now wearing swimming goggles and Sally is laughing.

But all I can think about is the heart I'm holding within my hand. He's finally coming home but what does this mean? Is it a parting gift, a way of saying that final goodbye before he picks his old life back up again?

~

It's eight-thirty and Rosie is in bed. I'm lazing back on the sofa, a glass of wine in my hands and the white marble heart on the coffee table in front of me.

I don't know if talking to an inanimate object is something about which I should worry but it's meaningful. I saw this heart in the shop that day I bought Rosie's trinket box. There was only one, the others were oval, or round. Marble is a hard material to work with and so getting the perfect heart shape is quite something.

I rest my head back against the sofa and look up at the ceiling as if it's transparent. I think about the darkening sky above me.

'Was there a master plan or was it merely wishful thinking on my part?' I imagine Zeus, surrounded by the other Greek gods, looking down on me. Daniel will be flying back tomorrow and I can't pretend I haven't been counting down the days. But with no contact at all for weeks, it's clear he's not ready to commit and I have no choice but to accept his decision.

In the films based on Ancient Greek mythology the gods were always plotting and scheming, demonstrating their control over the unfortunate mortals. But maybe there were times when their efforts were to good intent and it was as much about love, as it was the power struggles. Isn't the power of love supposed to overcome everything? Obviously not in my case.

There's a rap on the front door. It's probably a parcel from Amazon, although our local delivery guy usually rings the bell. I bet he doesn't have kids because he often delivers quite late and it never occurs to him he could wake someone up.

I put down my wine glass and walk to the door, swinging it open about a foot as I'm always a little cautious at night. When I peer around the edge of the door, Daniel is standing there.

'Hello, Leah. I'm back.'

It takes a few moments for me to engage my brain. I turn and walk back into the sitting room in a daze, leaving Daniel to close the front door and follow me inside. When he reappears in front of me we face each other, awkwardly avoiding eye contact. I watch as his gaze is drawn towards the white marble heart lying on the coffee table.

'I thought that was a romantic touch.' He grins at me and I hesitate for a second.

'Oh. I thought it was a rather poignant parting gift.'

Daniel stares back at me, clearly shocked by my reaction. He coughs, clearing his throat and I can see how nervous he is as he begins talking.

'It's so good to be back at long last; I've been dreaming of this moment ever since I read your letter,' he declares, his voice demonstrating the effect it had on him. 'I'm here because I'm ready to commit to you, Leah, but that wasn't something I could say until we were face to face once more. I've been on my own for too long and I allowed Tricia to get inside my head. I need you to believe me when I say I've finally got my act together, because I can't risk losing you. I love you way too much to let anything get in the way of our future and I'm sorry it took me a while to sort myself out.'

I close my eyes for a brief second, my head in a whirl, and when I open them again they fill with tears of sheer relief.

'That's all I needed to hear, Daniel. I didn't know if I was asking too much of you and it was unfair of me.'

He steps forward to draw me into his arms and I know that at last he really is mine. The smell and feel of him brings back achingly beautiful memories of the nights we've spent together, unable to fight the overwhelming attraction that exists between us.

'It really is beautiful,' I add, as we both turn to stare down at my little piece of Athens.

'I went back to the shop the day you flew home that second time, to buy it for you.'

I stare up at Daniel's face wanting to take in every little detail and I can see that he's tired but happy. But there's also a real sense of relief and determination in his body language.

'You didn't bring Bella with you?'

Daniel shakes his head.

'No. I drove straight here because I was so scared it was going to be too late to convince you to give me one last chance. I've been frantically trying to get a flight for over a week and all I managed to save was one day. I hoped that would be enough. I knew everything would hinge upon this moment and I've been a nervous wreck thinking about it.'

As his lips hungrily seek out mine, any worries we were harbouring silently slip away; I knew from the very start he was *the one* and that feeling has continued to grow, even after I sent him the letter. The truth is, I simply couldn't imagine my future without him in it.

'You have no idea how elated I'm feeling to know that this is really happening.' He's slightly breathless as he whispers into my ear the words I feared I'd never hear.

His lips are on mine once more and I know they are exactly where they belong. Daniel will be the perfect stepfather and Bella will become the sibling Rosie has always longed to have, because this is destined to be. And I'm going to love my stepdaughter as if she were my own.

'Do you think your parents will ever forgive me for stealing you and Rosie away?'

'I think they will forgive you anything when they see how happy we are going to be. The future starts here, Daniel and it's going to be a wonderful adventure.'

It wasn't just a little piece of Athens in the shape of a white marble heart that arrived in the post today; with it came all the love within Daniel's heart and that was indeed a miracle worthy of the might of the Ancient Greek gods.

Right time, right place and the right man – at last!

THE END

Epilogue

Standing here and watching the party in full swing I'm counting my blessings. Mum has baby Alyx on her lap and Dad is next to her, fussing over him as he once did with Rosie when she was tiny.

Our little boy, our blessing: whose Greek-inspired name means protector of humanity and whom we hope, like the girls, will grow up to be compassionate, considerate and generous of spirit. It's our nod to the young man whose heart has made all this possible.

As for the girls, well, they are up and dancing. This morning's squabble, when they discovered they both wanted to wear similar outfits, is already forgotten. Until the next time, of course and it makes me laugh. Only a year ago they wanted to dress like twins. That thought does send a little stab to my heart as I think of Kelly. My life feels just about as perfect as it can get without the ability to turn back the clock and change the past.

Harrison approaches, smiling, and gives me a hug.

'It's a great christening party, Leah. Ollie is questioning Daniel over the trials of having a six-month-old baby in the house.'

My eyes light up. 'You're seriously thinking about it, then?'

He nods.

'You both have a lot of love to give, Harrison and that's all any child needs.'

I can see the hope and optimism in his eyes and whatever happens I'll be there to support him.

'It's been a long journey for you, hasn't it?' he says, changing the subject. 'I know you're happily settled in York now but do you miss the forest?'

'A little; we have popped back to see Mum and Dad several times, although at the moment it's easier for them to come to us. They seem to thrive on the chaos in our household and to be honest, I'm glad of the help. They immediately take over baby duties and it gives Daniel and me a breather.'

Harrison smiles and I know that having seen how he is with Alyx, it isn't just Ollie whose dearest wish is to become a dad.

'And how's Daniel doing?'

'Amazingly. It's been nonstop since our wedding and then he took the arrival of our little surprise in his stride. Even though it coincided with his promotion at work. But his whole outlook on life now is so different. He's involved in a support group for patients in those first few months after transplant surgery. Daniel shares his experiences and answers the questions they often find difficult to ask the medical staff. It's been cathartic for him.'

'That's good to hear and everyone certainly looks happy. I was sorry to hear that Antonio let Rosie down in the end.

I think you weren't surprised, though. How did she take it when he just stopped calling her?'

I shrug my shoulders because in the general scheme of things it wasn't a big deal.

'I think Rosie was relieved, if I'm being honest. Oh, she desperately wanted him to love her as a biological father should – but a child can tell whether someone really cares about them, or not. In comparison to the way Daniel is there for her, it was clear Antonio had no real interest in building a lasting relationship.'

Harrison tuts.

'Unbelievable. That man has no conscience whatsoever. And how about you? Aside from the tiredness of having a baby who still doesn't sleep through the night and keeping everyone and everything in your household running smoothly. I can't believe you still manage to find time to run your website.'

I laugh; he's right about the tiredness but this phase won't last forever.

'I'm fine. Alyx has brought us all together in a way that's hard to explain. He's a blessing and makes our family feel complete. I just feel so lucky, Harrison, that I have to keep reminding myself that this isn't simply a dream. It's the life I've always dreamt of having – full and surrounded by the people I love – and it's real.'

He leans closer, placing an arm around my shoulders and giving me a squeeze.

'You survived some very tough years bringing up Rosie on your own, Leah, and the happiness you have now is because you're a very giving and loving person. You deserve this, make no mistake about that.'

He looks me directly in the eye and I can see this gentle man means every single word of it and he couldn't be happier for me. I have to take a deep breath before I begin to speak.

'I couldn't allow myself to believe I would ever find a man I could let into my heart again. It wasn't simply my trust issues, but feelings of vulnerability. I didn't think I was lovable, Harrison, so I pushed all thoughts of love away and became this warrior woman instead. But inside the hurt never went away. Then Daniel came along.'

And he does. At that precise moment.

'Um ... shouldn't I be the one with my arm around my ever so lovely wife?' Daniel teases Harrison.

I get one last, gentle squeeze and Harrison pulls away so the guys can do a manshake.

'Make way, I have champagne!' Ollie appears cradling two champagne flutes in each hand. 'I thought a toast was in order. Well, really, I looked across and I was feeling a little left out.'

Harrison and Ollie exchange intimate smiles, then Ollie raises his glass in the air.

'To Alyx, one great little guy who has brought change, happiness and a reminder that the future is full of wonderful surprises!'

Daniel and I burst out laughing. Next week he's having the snip. It's not that we don't love surprises, of course, but maybe the next one could be a little less expensive and demanding ... a family holiday maybe. And I have the perfect destination in mind. I've had an invitation to sample a family holiday at the Astir Beach Club in Vouliagmeni. Athens, here we come!

Acknowledgements

We visited Athens in May of 2017 and I was so inspired by the ambience and the overwhelming sense of timeless history that it had to be the setting for my next novel. We had a wonderful time; met some truly lovely Greek people who took us to their hearts and came away vowing we'd go again, quite soon.

As someone who has always suffered from vertigo I thought sharing what is a very real fear that can literally immobilise a person, might help others who suffer in similar vein. And yes, I did freeze when it came to the glass floors and the funicular (cliff railway), but that didn't stop me from enjoying both experiences. With a little support from my lovely other half, Lawrence, and closing my eyes at particularly difficult moments, we did it!

But a storyline often finds an author having to research an area in which they have no knowledge whatsoever. The subject of organ transplant was new to me. What I learnt only scratched the surface because of the nature of this story. If you want to know more, then simply visit:

www.organdonation.nhs.uk/register-to-donate/register-your-details

where you will find lots of useful information. Every single person on the donor waiting list is a loved one to a wide circle of people whose lives they touch. The thought of death giving life is wonderful, isn't it? And often it doesn't just affect one life, but many. And it's just a click away.

It's time to give a shout out to my amazing editor, Charlotte Ledger, who is a real pleasure to work with and continues to support, encourage and challenge me – constantly – on my writing journey. You rock, lady! And to the awesome Ceri, for helping to make this story the best it could possibly be.

There are so many friends who are there for me through thick and thin. They suffer periods of silence when I'm head down, writing. I hide myself away to spend my days with characters who become very real to me and I'm sad when a story draws to a close. But when I pop my head back up it's like I've never been away and no-one refers to the fact that I'm such an erratic friend! Special mentions to Kate, Shona, Sue, Claire, Janice, Noemie, Suze, Anniek, Kaisha, Anne, Grace, Barbara, Katie and Michele ... and my very supportive blogger friends!

As usual, no book is ever written without there being an even longer list of people to thank in getting the book out there, publicising it and, of course, the kindness of readers and reviewers. You continue to delight, amaze and astound me with your generosity and support; it's truly humbling. Without your kindness and those reviews and book sales I wouldn't be able to indulge myself in my guilty pleasure ... writing.

Feeling blessed and sending much love to you all for your constant support and friendship, Linn x

HELP US SHARE THE LOVE!

If you love this wonderful book as much as we do then please share your reviews online.

Leaving reviews makes a huge difference and helps our books reach even more readers.

So get reviewing and sharing,
we want to hear what you think!

Love, HarperImpulse x

Please leave your reviews online!

amazon.co.uk kobo goodreads Lovereading 

And on social!

/HarperImpulse @harperimpulse
@HarperImpulse

LOVE BOOKS?

So do we! And we love nothing more than chatting about our books with you lovely readers.

If you'd like to find out about our latest titles, as well as exclusive competitions, author interviews, offers and lots more, join us on our Facebook page! Why not leave a note on our wall to tell us what you thought of this book or what you'd like to see us publish more of?

/HarperImpulse

You can also tweet us @harperimpulse and see exclusively behind the scenes on our Instagram page www.instagram.com/harperimpulse

To be the first to know about upcoming books and events, sign up to our newsletter at: http://www.harperimpulseromance.com/